£3

Also by Aaron Pogue

The World of the FirstKing
Taming Fire
The Dragonswarm
The Dragonprince's Heir *(coming in 2012)*

The World of Hathor
Gods Tomorrow
Ghost Targets: Expectation
Ghost Targets: Restraint
Ghost Targets: Camouflage *(coming in 2012)*

The Dragonswarm

A novel by Aaron Pogue

Published by Consortium Books, 2011.

This is a work of fiction. Similarities to real people, places, or
events are entirely coincidental.

THE DRAGONSWARM

First edition. December 20, 2011.
Copyright © 2011 Aaron Pogue.

ISBN: 978-1468103410

10 9 8 7 6 5 4 3 2 1

My name is Daven Carrickson, savior of the town of Teelevon. I've been called a beggar and a murderer, an assassin and a traitor. I've been called Sir Daven in glory, and Daven Dragonprince by men and monsters.

In the autumn of my eighteenth year, when I was still hiding from the memory of my terrible adventures, new adventures found me.

1. Knight of the People

My feet itched to flee, and my fingers itched for a sword. Sweat slicked my palms despite the chill in the air. My eyes flicked around the little stone-walled garden, taking in every detail of the terrain. My heart pounded, and my limbs tingled.

But my adversary held no fear. This certainly wasn't an enemy I could conquer, and I wasn't willing to run. I took a slow, calming breath and turned to face my fate.

Isabelle smiled.

She was lovely. She wore a light cotton dress with a white knit shawl that hid her shoulders and showed off her sun-dark skin. She kicked a foot idly, at her ease on the white marble bench surrounded by winter blossoms. Her eyes followed a falcon soaring in the middle distance, and my eyes followed hers.

Without looking my way, she swallowed once. "We need to talk, Daven."

"Of course." My right hand twitched toward hers and then twitched back. She wasn't holding my hand today. She clasped hers together in her lap.

She didn't seem to catch my motion, but she turned to meet my gaze at last. There was more fear in her eyes than I had thought. But she was a brave girl. She set her shoulders and gave me a weak smile. "It's about us."

I nodded. I licked my lips. "I have loved every moment we spent together." I wasn't sure if I meant the words to stall her or to help her out. They were the truth, though. I'd known her for six short weeks, but it had been a lifetime. It was the best life I'd ever known. I opened my mouth to put that in words, but she dropped her gaze and stopped me.

"You..." she started, and then glanced up and trailed off. A hint of red touched her cheek. "You are nothing I ever expected. You're like no one I've ever met. Certainly like no commoner." She hesitated, heard her own words, and her blush deepened.

I found no offense in it. I was as common as they came. I touched her shoulder to reassure her. "You're like no nobleman's daughter I've ever met."

The corner of her mouth turned up in the hint of a smile. "You've met a lot of them, have you?"

I couldn't find an answer to that. She glanced up at my silence, saw my face, and the delight that danced in her eyes almost eased my heart.

But she dropped her gaze to her hands again. "I just...I don't know how to say this."

"I understand, Isabelle. I do. We're so different, it's hard to believe—"

Her head snapped up and she nodded. "Precisely! That's just it. It's hard to believe any of this happened at all." She took a deep breath, shook her head so her long hair danced around her face, and put on a smile.

I waited for what had to come.

She took my hands, then, both of them in her silk-soft fingertips. Her smile flickered again. "I never imagined this would be so hard." She squeezed my hands and caught my eyes, and I saw terror in hers. "Daven Carrickson...." She trembled, but she did not break our gaze. "Daven, dear," she said.

Her eyes shone. I cleared my throat, and she blushed. She blinked. She smiled. "Daven, will you marry me?"

My jaw dropped. For a moment the world spun around me. Something like a laugh escaped me, and I saw a little frown stab at the corners of her eyes. I shook my head. "Isabelle...what?"

She straightened her back and looked down her nose at me. "I am *trying* to propose."

"I thought...I didn't...." I squeezed her fingertips. "I would *love* to marry you." I caught a cold breath and let it out. "But we can't."

"We can," Isabelle said, confident now. "I can make it happen. All I need to know—"

"No," I cut her off as softly as I could. "We can't, Isabelle. I have no name. I have no land. Your father is a baron." And a friend of the king's. I didn't say the words, but that relationship was the largest obstacle.

Isabelle waved my objections away. "No, I've thought about it. He could adopt you as his heir." She made it sound a simple matter.

"He has heir enough in Themmichus," I said. I thought of my young friend, the good-hearted boy I'd known too briefly during my stay at the Academy of Wizardry. I would have given much to see him again.

Isabelle frowned at me. "Themm's a little boy. You are our hero. Our savior. If not for you, my whole family would be dead now or prisoners in the rebels' camp." She shuddered at the memory, and I closed my eyes in sympathy.

After a heartbeat she pressed on. "Regardless. Father sees as much in Themmichus as you seem to. But you needn't be a baron's heir. For one, there is no law—"

I shook my head, and she cut off again. There was a law. The children of Ardain lords had long been allowed to choose their own spouses, but none of them would be allowed to wed a fugitive from the king's justice. I was wanted for murdering a soldier of the King's Guard.

She should have known it too. Themmichus knew, and he had written of me often. Isabelle and I had never discussed it, though. And now, staring into her blue-gray eyes, I couldn't bring myself to give it voice. Instead I hung my head. "Do we need to hurry? I would love to marry you but it will be...complicated."

Her shoulders rose and fell in a sigh. Tears shone in her eyes. She nodded short and sharp. "I know. Of course it will be complicated. I just...I'm ready to get started. I don't want to wait."

I did. Complicated was too kind a word. We could not make arrangements without drawing a judgment from the crown. And I knew already what that judgment would be.

My time with Isabelle was doomed. It always had been, and I had always known. My heart's desire was only to delay the inevitable, to be with her as long as possible.

And again I could not put it into words. I held her gaze, and she leaned forward to kiss me on the lips. "You are my future, Daven." Her face blossomed into a smile. "I want to get it started. Right now."

There was fear. There was caution and regret, all born of the reality I knew too well. They faded into the farthest corner of my mind when I saw her smile. "And I, too," I said, a little breathless. "I love you, Isabelle. Only—"

I didn't get to voice my objection. She popped to her feet, and summer sunlight glowed in her eyes. "I love you, too. I'm so delighted. And now I have a surprise for you!"

She bounced on her toes, and she couldn't contain her smile. Within my mind, caution and fear struggled free again. I rose slowly, eyes fixed on her, and asked, "What?"

"You *will* have a name." She laughed and caught my hand. Before I could say a word she dragged me down the white gravel path toward the baron's house.

"I have told Father my intentions," she said. A whole new terror gripped my heart, but she dispelled it an instant later. "He is thrilled. As I said, he wasn't willing to adopt you, but he found another option. He's elected to name you a Knight of the People."

I stopped cold at that. She couldn't drag me a step farther. Her grip on my hand spun her in a little circle, and she met my eyes with a startled curiosity.

"A knight?" I asked.

She nodded, and the smile that crept across her face echoed in my spirit.

"A Knight of the People." I breathed the words with a reverence. It meant honor. It meant true power. It meant a name of my own, free of my father's disgrace.

"For what you've done," she said, stepping close. Her eyes were wide, and they did not quite meet mine. "You are a hero, to all the people of this barony. No one has ever deserved the honor more." She twined her fingers in mine and pressed closer against me. "And who would object to my marrying our own Knight of the People? You're better than a prince."

My breath caught in my throat. My heart pounded. I felt her warmth against me, felt it pour into me. Sir Daven of Teelevon, Knight of the People....

"Father has already set things in motion," Isabelle murmured against my chest. "He has tested the waters among the people, and they love you. He's commissioned your papers. And of course he has written the king."

My blood went cold as a Northlands winter. Fear and sadness came crashing back. "The king?"

"Of course," she said lightly. "And we're in luck. He's in Tirah, still, so the messenger should have arrived in a matter of days. We could have an answer as soon as tomorrow."

Her words struck me like blows. She must have felt the tension that stretched my body like copper wire, because she unwrapped herself from me and withdrew a pace. She looked up at me, cautious and uncertain. "What's the matter?"

"The king," I said, and the words tasted bitter. It was time we discussed these things. "Take me to your father. We need to talk."

We found Baron Eliade in his study, where a fire blazed on the stone hearth, and heavy curtains hung over glass-paned windows. The baron himself seemed untouched by the winter chill. He wore thin cotton shirt-sleeves, his silken coat thrown carelessly across the back of an empty couch.

He was bent forward over a mess of papers on his desk, reading reports from the pages in one pile and scribbling his own notes on a fresh page under his right hand. His brow was knit in concentration and more than a little worry. His jaw clenched so hard the muscles stood out like heavy cords, and sweat gleamed on his forehead.

I understood his concern. Winter came kindly this far south, but still it emptied the fields. And this year had been a hard one on the barony's harvest. An army of rebels had set up in siege outside the town, stealing food and disrupting any attempts to work the land.

I had freed the town from that siege. Six weeks ago I'd dispersed the rebel horde with the help of a bloodthirsty beast that owed me a debt. I had made myself a hero, but here before me was a man with a harder task than mine had been. He had a thousand mouths to feed and insufficient resources to do it. I understood the troubles that creased his brows, and I had worse problems to offer him.

He didn't look up when I entered the room. He did when Isabelle followed me one step later, and in a heartbeat the fear and frustration vanished from his face. He gave Isabelle a broad smile and pushed the pages away. I saw the trouble still hiding in the corners of his eyes, in the tension across his chest, but he hid it well.

That smile darted over me and back to his precious daughter. "Ah, you're here!" he cried. He pushed himself to his feet. "Did you tell him? You must have told him."

"She did." My voice sounded grim to my own ears. "She told me everything, my lord."

"Your lord. Hah! We can't have such formality," he said, but I saw his smile slipping. "Soon enough—"

"I'm sorry, my lord, but we have trouble." I thought I would see anger in his eyes at the interruption, but I only saw confusion. Isabelle stepped to my side and laced her fingers with mine.

Pain stabbed at my heart. I didn't want to admit what I had done. I didn't want to see the shock and disappointment in their eyes. I didn't want to feel her cool fingers pull away.

But I could not escape it. Not now. I set my shoulders and met the baron's gaze. "I killed a man" He opened his mouth to object—he was a man of war himself—but I pressed on. "It was a soldier in the King's Guard."

The baron's face went pale at that, and Isabelle made a tiny sound. She didn't drop my hand.

I nodded to the baron. "It was an accident, a mistake brought on by a wizard's reckless actions. But it is a mistake for which I have not paid." I held his gaze for a long moment, then dropped my head. "I will have to pay for it now."

Eliade said nothing. After a moment Isabelle cleared her throat. "I...I don't understand."

The baron spoke before I could answer. "They know your name?" Without looking I could feel his gaze against me.

I nodded. "He knows everything about me."

The baron's breath escaped him in a great, weary sigh. I glanced up. He seemed suddenly smaller, more frail than I ever could have imagined the big man.

He shook his head. "And I sent him a letter. I told him just where to find you. I'm sorry, Daven. Isabelle."

My jaw fell open. "Sorry? No, my lord. How could you have known? I'm sorry I brought this trouble to your house. I'm sorry I hid it from you."

He should have been furious. Any lord I'd ever heard of would have been. But this was the man who had raised kind-hearted Themmichus and brave, beautiful Isabelle. This was the man who had taken me in. In six short weeks he'd become more a father to me than any I'd ever known.

And he did not fail me now. "There is still time," he said, eyes flashing with strategies and plans. "We may find a place to hide you. I can bring the king to reason."

My heart pounded with gratitude and hope as much as fear. I turned to Isabelle and found her nodding enthusiastically.

"The people love him," she said. "He can live with any of them. The Smiths would keep him in style. Or Thomas Wheelwright. He has space enough—"

The baron shook his head. "No. It would be asking them to defy the crown. That is a grave offense. We cannot place this burden on them."

He didn't mean it as an accusation, but the words struck me like a blow.

Isabelle wasn't fazed. "Then we can keep him here. There are rooms enough in this house to lose one man."

Eliade dismissed that idea as well. "No, Isabelle. The king's trackers are careful men. Even given his love for us, we will not easily thwart his search."

Isabelle almost answered again, but I stopped her with a touch on the wrist. I met the baron's gaze.

"Don't," I said.

"Young man, you'd be hard-pressed to stop me."

"And yet I must." Regret burned sour in my throat, but I swallowed it along with the memory of a kind old wizard half-dead from a wound he took while trying to hide me from the king. I could not do that to this man, and certainly not to the woman at my side.

So I dropped her hand and held his gaze. "Don't risk these things for me. You've already done more than I ever could have asked. I'll face the king—"

"You won't," the baron said, and his word was law. "Not without some intercession. These are hard and hasty times, and too much tragedy could catch fire in his wrath."

I met his gaze for a moment, then dropped my eyes. I had no wish to die, and that was all I could expect from the king's justice now.

I licked my lips and nodded. "Very well, but I will not endanger you and yours. I'll run. I can survive the wilderness—"

The baron smiled, though it was grim. "We grow our wilderness much harder here than the one you know."

"No harder than a headsman's blade," I said, and he grunted in agreement.

Then silence fell, resignation and regret heavy in the air between us. My hands flexed and relaxed a dozen times, and my mind raced on ahead. The earth was hard and dry out here, the mountains high and harsh. But I had never lived an easy life before I came into this house. I'd find a way.

Isabelle interrupted my thoughts with a tiny sound. She took a half-step forward and raised her hands toward the two of us. Our eyes fixed on her, and she hesitated. But then I saw her set her jaw. I saw a fire in her eyes. She meant to argue once again, and I steeled myself to tell her no.

But she said just one word. "Palmagnes."

I knew the name. It was a place from legend. An enchanted fortress. A temple to power and wisdom and authority. A stronghold impervious to every power, magical or mortal.

I cocked my head, confused. It was an old, mostly-forgotten piece of the legends of the FirstKing. It had to be a myth.

But then behind me the baron let out his breath with an interested sound. "Hmm. Now that could work."

"The FirstKing's fortress? The Tower of Days?" My eyes snapped back and forth between them. "It's just a story."

"It's not," the baron said.

"It's a pile of ruins," Isabelle said in patient explanation. "It is little more than rubble."

The baron nodded. "Yes but there would be some shelter there. And no one enters those lands. No one would find you."

I took a step back. "You really mean it?"

The baron nodded solemnly.

Isabelle gave me an excited smile. "It's half a day's ride, I understand." She threw her father an acid look, but he ignored her.

She went on, sliding closer to me again. "We should go scout it out. Make sure you know the way, in case you have to go in a hurry."

The baron's eyes snapped to Isabelle, and I saw them narrow. After a moment he sighed. "That *is* a good idea. And if I were to go—or worse, send an escort—it would draw too much notice. But the two of you going out for a ride...."

He trailed off, and Isabelle beamed. She caught my hand again and bounced a shoulder against my arm. When I looked down she grinned. "We're going to Palmagnes."

Despite everything hanging over us, I smiled. I couldn't help it. I leaned closer to her. "That's exciting, is it?"

She bobbed her head and answered in a whisper. "Father has never let me go."

He cut through our quiet conference with the heavy boom of his voice. "That's right. Because it is dangerous."

Isabelle rolled her eyes. "They say restless spirits and soulless ghouls wander among the ruins."

The baron grunted. "I'm far more concerned with biting asps and feral dogs." He leveled a threatening finger at me. "You watch out for her, wizard. Return her to me whole."

"Of course," I said. "With all my care."

He nodded. "Well enough. Go. Send for the horses and some food. Might as well take some gear now too, so you can travel light when the time comes."

I nodded. "Will there be water?"

"Last I checked the well still ran clean, but that's been most of a decade now. You'll have to check on that while you're there."

I tried to think what else to take, what other preparations I could make, but there were too many unknowns. Still, if there was clean water, I could get by.

Isabelle was anxious to go. She darted out to arm's length and tugged on my arm, but I lingered to consider the plan one more time, trying to think of anything else I need-ed to ask of the baron. I found nothing. But I saw him frowning, clearly calculating, and he looked up to see his daughter trying to drag me from the room.

He opened his mouth. A moment later he said, "Go. Make your preparations. But before you leave, come find me again. We have another matter of business yet to settle."

Then he dismissed me with a wave, and I followed Isabelle into the wide stone corridors of the sprawling house. We went a dozen paces before she led me around a corner and down another long hall. I had to hurry to keep on her heels, and I felt my smile creeping back. "You really can't wait to see these ruins."

She stopped, startling me, and turned on me with more anger than joy in her eyes. "How could you keep this from me?"

Her voice was a hiss, and she stepped very close to me. It was not a tender gesture.

I licked my lips. "I was afraid. I did not want you to know that part of my past."

"I could have done so much to protect you, Daven. I could have made this go away. And now instead we must run and hide."

"I'm sorry, Isabelle."

"You should be!" she snapped, but then her face softened. "Come on." She nodded down the hall, then started walking again. "Palmagnes is not a friendly place, and we must make our preparations. It will not be easy to convince my father to let me stay there with you."

My heart faltered. "Stay with me? No. Resolving this mess will take some time—"

"And I would not be without you for so long." She never turned, never slowed. "But Father will not understand. We'll save that fight for later."

I followed after her in a daze. She wanted to be with me. She was prepared to face the discomfort and dangers of a harsh wilderness with me. She was prepared to fight her father, and with her father to fight the king for me. She was prepared to marry me. She'd asked, hadn't she?

While I was thinking, she was searching for a steward she could trust. Now she found him and rattled off her orders with a brisk authority. I watched him nodding quickly, trying to memorize all the many things she wanted. Then she sent him scurrying off and dragged me down another hall.

It was too soon to talk of marriage. Of course it was. But I wasn't at all surprised by her initiative. She was the bravest soul I'd ever met. Injured but unscarred, informed but unafraid. I wanted that. I wanted her, and far more for the spirit, for the perspective, than for the comfort and the kindness she could offer.

She led me to the stables and requested two riding horses and two pack animals to lead. The stable master sent boys scurrying to fetch the horses even as servants began arriving in ones and twos with gear for our journey. Isabelle watched it all with an air of satisfaction, and I just stood watching her. A man could build a life around a woman like that.

But first there was the king. And then the dragons, too. Six weeks in Teelevon, and we must have heard sixty new rumors from the north. Mighty serpents swarmed the quiet seas, they said, and ships weren't safe to sail. Dragons flew the skies at night, they said, and whole cities were burned to ash by dawn. We heard a hundred different versions of Tirah's burning or the capitol's. Of the King's Guard defeated or the wizards at the Academy. Of the world overwhelmed by dragon hordes.

They sounded nothing like truth, but I knew there was some core to it. I'd met a dragon firsthand, and I'd seen half a dozen more with my own eyes. Tirah *had* been attacked, and the King's Guard with it. And those who knew of such things had assured me worse was coming. The dragons were waking.

I swallowed hard and kept my eyes fixed on the woman before me. It would be no easy task to build a life we two could share. But she turned to say, "That should do quite well. We'll be on the road within the hour." When she caught me staring, she gave me a curious little smile, and I knew I had to try. I would find a way.

It started with keeping her safe. If the baron was right, that meant keeping her away from the ruins of Palmagnes. As she led me back to her father's study, I fought not to think how much gentler my exile would be with her at my side.

We stepped into the study, and it all fled my mind at the sight of the sword in her father's hands. Cold steel, burnished with age but carrying an edge that shone from constant care. The baron stood in the center of the room, sword's tip grounded between him and us, hands crossed easily on its pommel. His stance was relaxed, but I recognized danger in it. Readiness. His expression was grave.

Three men stood behind him, all just as serious. One was the chief steward of the baron's household. Another was Thomas Wheelwright, a friend of the Eliades and an esteemed name in the community. And there on the end was the barony's Kind Father, dressed in the rich formal robes of the Benevolent Priests. All among them met my gaze with level, measuring looks. None among them gave me any confidence.

For one long, dreadful moment I stood staring at the blade and remembering my every crime. Then Isabelle squeezed my hand and whispered in my ear, "Step forward, Sir Knight."

2. Fort Palmagnes

I knelt before the baron. The three witnesses shifted closer behind him, but I fixed my eyes on the point of the sword where it scarred the polished wood of the study's floor. The edge looked flawless.

"Daven of Terrailles, son of Carrick," the baron began in ceremonious tones, "do you come here with greed or malice in your heart?"

My mouth was dry, my throat tight, but I managed to find my voice enough to ask, "Here, my lord?"

"To the Eliade Barony," he said. "To the land and people under my care." He maintained the formal tone. "Do you mean them any harm?"

My answer came clear and easy at that. "No, my lord. Never."

He gave a grunt in response, then asked, "Daven of Terrailles, son of Carrick, do you come here under loyalty to any man save the king or his appointments?"

I swallowed hard at that. I thought of the rebels, and of their wizard leader who had offered me a place of power among his ranks. He'd asked only that I kill the king.

And I'd had the power to do it. The king struck me as capricious and some of his most faithful enforcers little better than rabid dogs. But he was king. I blinked once and answered honestly again, "I do not. I have remained loyal to the king."

"Daven of Terrailles, son of Carrick, do you come before us the master of any lands or peoples within His Majesty's realms?"

The question caught me off guard. I forgot myself, and looked up into the baron's eyes. "What?"

A frown touched the corner of his mouth, and I dropped my eyes again. He asked, "Have you any titles? Any properties? Any people of your own?"

I couldn't guess at the significance of the question, but I shook my head. "No, my lord. I have nothing."

"Very well," the baron said, pronouncing his judgment. "By the law of this land and of its people, and by the law of God set forth by the king, I pronounce you here and now a Knight of the People." My eyes followed the blade of the sword as he raised it to touch me lightly on each shoulder. "You knelt Daven of Terrailles, son of Carrick, but I command you to rise, Sir Daven of Teelevon, Knight of the People."

I almost disobeyed his order. I knelt still, eyes wide in disbelief as I stared up into his. Then the three men behind him stepped forward with smiles. Thomas gestured me to my feet and I rose in time for him to shake my hand heartily.

And then Isabelle was at my side. I saw tears in her eyes and a smile on her face, and turned back to the baron to find him smiling now, too. It was restrained, but I saw again the kindness he had shown me before. I bowed my head to him. "Thank you, my lord."

He shook his head. "For the service you have done my people, you deserve no less." Thomas and the Kind Father both chimed agreement to that, but the baron ignored them.

His gaze was still solemn. "This ceremony would have better been done before a crowd at the first day of a public festival, but we do not have such luxuries. Great trouble comes with the winter, and we all have dire work to do if we are to survive at all. You have given us a chance."

I nodded. He had given me a chance, too. It wasn't an answer—the title of Knight would not shield me from the king's justice—but if I could weather that storm, the title would make an engagement to Isabelle far less complicated. I held his gaze for a moment, then bowed my head once more. "I thank you again. I am honored and humbled by the appointment."

The baron glanced over his shoulder toward the witnesses, then said to me, "There are rights and responsibilities to go with the title. Among them, you are due a plot of land within my personal holdings. You have not had time enough to see much of them yet—"

Isabelle spoke up right on cue. "I will take him, Father. You have pressing matters. I can be his guide."

Thomas frowned and the Kind Father's eyes opened wide in shock, but both looked to the baron for a response. He sighed and shrugged and nodded with a show of frustrated reluctance. "Very well. I trust him to your hands." He turned to me. "And her to yours. These are dangerous times."

"Then it is well that I have a knight to protect me," Isabelle said. A footfall drew her attention to the corridor behind us, and I turned to spot a stableboy waiting with hat in hand. Our horses were ready.

Isabelle met my eyes, then turned back to the men. "Please excuse us." She dipped her head, turned away, and left. I cast an apologetic glance behind and followed her from the room.

At the stables I found a tall chestnut waiting for me. Isabelle climbed ably into the saddle of her roan and took the leads for both the laden packhorses. Then she caught my eye as I tried to find a comfortable position in my own saddle. When I finally turned her way she gave a little laugh.

"Is everything well with you, Sir Knight?"

I couldn't manage more than an injured grunt. Her laughter died and concern showed in her eyes. "You *can* ride?"

"I can ride," I said. "Not well, but I can ride."

She nodded slowly, then turned and clucked to her horse. She started across the courtyard at an easy walk, and I managed to fall in beside her.

"We'll take it slow," she said. She glanced around, then reached across to squeeze my hand where it gripped the reins too tightly. "We'll make a pleasant ride of it. You'll do fine."

I smiled back, lips pressed tight, then held my tongue while we picked our way out of the little town. It was a laborious journey, my horse dancing erratically to the tension that thrummed through my arms and legs. Isabelle divided her attention between answering cheerful greetings from the townsfolk and whispering advice to me.

When we finally slipped past the last line of houses and out into the wide, empty land outside the town, I took an easier breath. Three paces later I was riding more easily in the saddle, and my horse was keeping a more natural gait. I felt Isabelle's eyes on me and turned to her.

"I never noticed before," she said. "Do city streets really trouble you so much?"

I glanced back over my shoulder toward the town, then shook my head. "Not at all. I grew up in the City. But the little riding I've done has all been in open land."

I turned forward again and looked down the long road at the wide, flat plains stretching all the way to the horizon. "It's easier out here," I said. "There's nobody to hurt with a moment of carelessness."

"Nobody but yourself," she said. "Or me."

Her voice turned soft toward the end, and when I looked I saw her biting her lip and watching me. I couldn't hold her gaze. We rode in silence for a while after that, putting the town far behind us.

I remembered what she had said in the halls of her father's house. I remembered what she'd asked me in the garden, too. Three times I opened my mouth to break the silence. Three times I shut it again without saying a word.

At last she moved her horse half a pace closer to mine. "I didn't know you'd lived in the City."

I looked her way. I shrugged. "I mentioned it the first time we met. At the palace."

She thought for a moment, then gave a slow nod. "You said you were a beggar."

"I was a beggar," I said. "And a carriage driver. And then I left the City to become a shepherd."

She sighed. Her eyes were unfocused, and I saw the hint of tears in them. I reached across to squeeze her hand, as she had done earlier.

"I know so little about you," she said. Her voice shook. "Six weeks we've been together, and I barely know anything." She caught her breath, and a blush touched her cheek. "I asked you to marry me. You must have thought me so stupid."

I shook my head. "I think you're courageous. And impulsive. And I admire you for both. I think you've found a lot of success by deciding what you want or need and pursuing it aggressively. "

She didn't answer that. This time I broke the silence. "I'm sorry I've kept secrets. I didn't want—"

"I know," she said. Her voice was a little raw. "You already said you didn't want me to see you for what you were. I'm just realizing now...."

She trailed off. I gave her time, but she didn't complete the thought. At last I asked her, "What?"

"I'm just now realizing how much you kept hidden."

"I didn't," I tried, then had to swallow hard and start again. "I wasn't trying to hide anything. I just saw no opportunity to bring it up."

"I thought you were joking," she said. "About being a beggar in the City. About being a shepherd, too, no matter how you insisted."

"But—"

"No." She shook her head. "That's not all my fault. You act nothing like a beggar. You act nothing like a shepherd or a fugitive. You may dress the part of a stable hand, but you walk like a soldier and speak like a wizard."

I looked down at the shirt I wore. It was not the finery Isabelle had given me as a gift, but it was far nicer than anything I'd worn for most of my life. The rest...I shook my head. "I never meant to deceive you."

"The worst part," she said, not hearing me, "is how much I loved you."

"Loved?" I asked, hearing too clearly the past tense.

"I fell in love with you the day we met at the palace," she said. "Did you know that? I told Father that very evening that I had met the man I would marry."

She looked over as though she expected an answer, but I had none. "That was foolish," she said. "But sometimes little girls are foolish. Father told me how much you had angered the king. He told me how you left in a burst of fire and smoke, defiant of the crown. It all seemed terribly romantic."

"The king hated me already then," I said. "That was the first step toward my crime. It was on the road from there to the Academy that I killed a man."

She nodded. "I understand that now." She cast a long gaze out over the parched land before us. "I didn't know it then. I knew someone mysteriously turned up on the Academy's doorstep about a week later, bloodied and bruised by the King's Guard, and this dashing hero quickly befriended my scrawny little brother."

I dropped my eyes. "It really worked the other way around."

"Father never made the connection. But I knew it had to be you. I read every letter. I told myself stories about you. I fell more and more in love with this fantasy...."

I couldn't bring myself to look, but I could hear the tears in her voice. I said, "I'm sorry I disappointed you."

"That's just the problem," she said. "I had all these fantasies about you, but I never *truly* loved you until the day you showed up here. My town was doomed, and my family with it. I was captured. All hope was lost. And then you stepped into my tent, every bit the hero I'd imagined you to be."

She caught her breath. I risked a glance, and she was looking right at me. Her smile was bent in kindness; her eyes were drawn in sadness. "And then you stayed. You stayed, and you were real. I made a fantasy out of you, Daven, and then I loved you for making that fantasy real."

She dropped her eyes. She knotted the reins of the pack horses in her hands. "That's all I wanted from you," she said. "That's all I want from you now. I don't want any more apologies. I don't want any more fantasies. I want what's real."

I licked my lips. "And if it's not as good?"

She met my eyes and smiled through tears. "Something real is always better than a fantasy. Always. Have faith in me. Please."

I nodded. Then I said, "Of course. I will." She gave me another smile, and we both took a hundred paces to catch our breath. Then I reached over to squeeze her hand again, and I asked gently, "Where would you have me start?"

"Start in the City," she said. "I have never properly met a beggar before."

I told her my story. I told her of my father who had run afoul of the king's justice and spent the last years of his life rotting in a public prison. I told her of the work I'd done to keep us fed. I told her of the grief that followed after his death, and then the liberty.

We stopped for lunch and I told her how I'd fled to the luxurious Terrailles province outside the City and found a job as a shepherd. I told her of the other boys there I'd trained to fight with the sword, and of the night a Green Eagle from the King's Guard came to interrupt our duels. I told her of the wizard Claighan who had taken me to meet the king, and of his strange and foolish plan to teach me the value of magic.

I told her of the soldier I killed by my own hand.

She kissed me then, while tears burned in my eyes, and sometime later we returned to our horses and continued on to the south. I did not resume my story after that, and she did not ask me to. I would in time, and she knew that. I would keep no secrets from her, but this secret had cost me much in the telling.

So instead she talked for a while. She told me stories about the lands we were passing. She seemed to know every family. She told me about the Carters who had lost seven baby daughters in seven years. She told me about the Dales whose grandfather had been the fifth son of a royal house but who moved to Teelevon for love of a farmer's daughter. She pointed out the broken road that used to lead to Cara, and the hills so rich with iron that the soil here burned red.

And so we passed an afternoon moving farther and farther from civilization. The farms grew further apart as we went, and smaller and smaller. The river Teel still trickled in and out along the rocky earth, but no crops would grow far from its shore. Farms dotted its shallow banks, but everywhere else was red cracked earth.

As we went the horizon grew closer. Ugly, jagged mountains tore at the sky, and even the foothills were hard and sheer. The whole of the continent funneled down to a single point this far south, and the mountains that blocked the coast wedged in on either side of us until our whole vista could not have been more than a dozen miles from left to right.

She finally drew rein at a bit of desert much like all the rest, and as I climbed down I couldn't see why we'd stopped this time. There were trees here—a full pace taller than most of the shrubs we'd passed by—and a bit of a stream, but not much to recommend the place. I took the opportunity to stretch my legs, then finally turned to Isabelle to ask, but she only met my eyes with the spark of excitement in hers.

She motioned me to silence and led her horse over to one of the thorny little trees. I followed her example, scanning the ground around me for some indication that we'd arrived, but there was no path and no structure in sight. Still, we tied the horses up, and then she turned without a word and started across the cracked earth.

As we walked, a jagged shape on the horizon slowly separated itself in my vision from the black mountain range beyond. It seemed to drift into the foreground, all harsh angles and shadows in the red light of afternoon. Even in the heart of winter, heat hung in the air without a breeze to stir it, and the only sound was the crunching of dirt beneath our boots.

And then we topped a small rise, gained a new perspective, and the pieces fell into place. In an instant I recognized the shape of ruins within the jumble—ancient walls of stone that must have stretched for a mile in each direction, and a great crumbled mountain back behind them must have been a tower once. I stared in awe, trying to reconstruct the tower in my imagination. Trying to see how tall it must have been, to leave so much rubble two thousand years later.

Beside me, Isabelle breathed, "It's beautiful."

I looked over at her. "Beautiful? You mean that?"

She met my eyes and frowned. "How could I not? They say this fortress protected fragile humanity from the mindless monsters that once swarmed through the pass beyond. They say one man stood against the darkness and fought it to a standstill until others could come take up the cause."

I stared at her until she began to blush. Then I shrugged. "They also say he learned the depths of suffering and pain here. That he came to this place to escape humanity. That he passed through hatred and found the love that eventually united all the lands of man."

She smiled at me. "Of course. But if he hadn't waged his war here, there would have been nothing left to love beyond." She took a slow step toward the ruins, then turned and held out a hand for me. "Come fight the monsters for me, Daven. I want to see it more closely."

As we went closer, we discovered it would be more difficult than either of us had expected. The walls were crumbled but still more than three paces high in most places, and their old shape made even the rubble a sheer climb.

We found at last where the northern gate had once been, its span long since fallen into a pile we could scale, and beyond that we found the courtyard.

Within, the shape of the ruins became clearer. The walls had made a triangle, its point stabbing toward the southern pass, and at its center had stood the tower. We pressed through thorny scrub and picked our way carefully across treacherous stone, climbing down the far side of the gateway's rubble and into a lower clearing.

In the clearing I saw some signs of humanity—a pit carved out for a campfire, a discarded bit of harness—but even those signs were scant and marked with age. Mostly the place was still, serene, and buried in the black shadow of the ruined tower.

Isabelle never took her eyes from it. She stared, and I could see a hunger in her expression. I wanted to stare, too, but I could not forget the warnings her father had given. So I stayed close at her side and picked a careful path for her. I scanned the ground for any sign of a biting snake, listened closely for the soft footfalls of wild dogs.

And still I did not see the dragon until it moved.

A boulder three paces ahead of us uncurled. It had looked like nothing more than a jagged bit of gray rock, dappled here and there with spots of rust red, but in the space of a breath it stretched out into a dangerous drake.

It had a body the size of a large hunting cat, with underdeveloped wings folded tight and tucked close around its ribs. Its short legs sported razor-sharp talons, but I spent far more concern on the spike-tipped tail three paces long and the sinuous neck supporting a head full of cruel teeth.

I had no idea if this beast could breathe fire like its larger cousins, but even without that threat it boasted a half dozen different ways of killing a man.

Or woman.

I reacted the moment it moved. Old habits threw me into motion while my mind still reeled in surprise. I fell into a fighting stance, turning my body to expose as little of it as possible to my enemy. I took a breath and let it go, and that quickly I was relaxed, poised on the balls of my feet, one arm extended toward the monster, the other stretched out behind me as I pushed Isabelle out of harm's way.

I faintly heard her cry of surprise and pain as she stumbled and fell back, but I could spare no attention for that. Even as I'd fallen into my old dueling stance, I'd played out a new trick as well. I looked on the world with a wizard's sight, sensing the flow of energies and powers that lay beneath the fragile appearance of reality.

There was little to see here. The sun glowed with a distant fire, far too distant to reach, and there was no wind to speak of. I sensed the dance of cold, dark waters in the far depths of an ancient well, but it offered me nothing of value in this fight.

I had all that I needed in the earth, though. The earth here—the old worked stones, the hard-packed ground beneath the shadow of the tower—it thrummed with untapped power. I wore no sword on my belt, but with a thought I reached out to the ground beneath my hand and summoned forth a weapon.

The raw energy of earth poured up in grains too small to see, a vaporous cloud of black particles that coalesced around my hand, forming into a hilt tailored to my grip. Above that I formed a cross piece—its design stolen from a masterwork weapon I'd once won off a king's tracker—and then a blade stabbed out from nothing, a pace long and with an edge sharper than any blacksmith could have made.

I built the blade in the time it took to think of it, and before it was fully formed I sprang forward to meet the deadly drake. But the beast moved fast as lightning, slithering aside and snapping its long neck away from my vicious strike.

Before I could adjust, a voice exploded in my mind. *Aha! It is you,* it said. *I have found you at last!* The voice rang with a vicious malevolence that nearly drove me to my knees.

Nearly. I stumbled, but a cold black strength deep in the back of my mind rose up against the intrusion. I drew on that strength and forced the echoes of the dragon's voice away. I hesitated only long enough to reach out with my mind, to gather great handfuls of the rocky earth in my mental grasp, and then I sprang at the drake with another lunge.

Once again it tried to dance aside, but this time I threw the earth up against it. A wall of stone sprang up from nothing, not a pace long but shoulder-high on the drake and close enough to trip it up. I sensed surprise and the beginnings of an exclamation in the back of my mind, but I dove forward in a perfect lunge and buried my blade in the drake's side.

I left it there. I darted back before the snapping neck could catch me with its vicious fangs. I dodged a wild lash of the deadly tail. Then I extended my hand and my will once more, and the ebon sword melted from the dragon's side and flowed into my hand. Blood and ichor gushed from the wound it left, and three heartbeats later the little drake fell still.

I turned to Isabelle. She sat on the rocky ground almost within arm's reach, staring at me with wide eyes. Her knees were pulled up close, and she cradled her right hand against her chest. I could see the shock and fear clear in her eyes but no serious harm. I took a moment to scan the terrain behind and above, but there was no other movement.

I fell back into my wizard's sight and used that, too, searching for the telltale empty stain of a dragon's Chaos shadow among the vibrant energies. I turned in both directions, but I saw no other blackness than the dead beast at my feet.

I let the vision fade and stood panting for a moment, staring at the thing. Then I stepped to its side, pressed its neck beneath the heel of my boot, and removed its head with one swing. Isabelle made a tiny sound like a whimper. My conjured blade buried itself three inches deep in the hard earth from which it had been made. I took one more long, slow breath, then let the blade dissolve again to dust.

Then I went to Isabelle. I fell to my knees at her side. Her eyes were locked on the gory remains of the slain monster, so I reached out gently to turn her face to me. When her gaze met mine she shuddered.

"Isabelle," I said, loudly and clearly, "are you injured."

She shook her head, eyes still unfocused. "I never knew it looked like that."

I frowned. She still cradled her right hand against her chest, and I saw the bright red smear of blood staining the fine cloth of her shirt. When I reached for her hand she shied away.

"You're hurt," I said. "What happened?"

She shook her head. It was a frantic little gesture. "I have never seen a monster before. I have never seen a hero slay a dragon." Her gaze drifted back up to my eyes, and at last she focused on them. There was fear and understanding in her expression.

She licked her lips. "It is uglier than I thought."

I nodded once, slowly, then reached carefully toward her hand again. "What happened?"

She looked down, then extended her arm. I took it with extreme care, but still she gasped as soon as I touched her skin.

The blood came from a dozen scratches where she had caught herself on the rough stone of the earth. The pain, I suspected, came from a sprained wrist. I shifted my grip, and she winced again.

I met her eyes once more, and they were crinkled in pain.

"It hurts," she said. She sucked in a deep breath, then pushed it out slowly. She held herself still for a moment, then her expression twisted in pain again. "I'm sorry, Daven. It just hurts so much."

"It's not broken," I said. "But it's a vicious sprain. Those always hurt, but you will be fine once you're home." She nodded, lips pressed tight while tears touched her cheeks. I fought down pain of my own to see her hurting like that and breathed in admiration, "You are always so strong when you need to be."

She laughed at me, if weakly, and I said, "You'll be fine, but we should get you home. Let's head back to the horses."

She didn't make it four steps before crumpling to her knees. I rushed to her side, falling into my wizard's sight, but there was a delicacy to healing magic that I could not begin to attempt. And all my power over Chaos offered me almost nothing to help her here.

She leaned against me and whimpered, and I could not do nothing. So I took her arm again, as gently as possible, and stretched it out before her. She groaned. No matter how careful I was, every tiny jostling motion was stabbing at her.

I closed my eyes for a moment, thinking. Then I reached out with my will just as I had done before and drew impossibly fine grains of power from the earth beneath us. I bound it with my will, shaped it with my hands, stretching it into a gauntlet around her hand and wrist. I made it paper-thin and iron strong and bound it in place.

It made a splint she couldn't have broken with anything short of a blacksmith's hammer. I took her bound-up hand in mine and tugged it lightly toward me. She winced, but I could tell it was more from expectation than from real pain. I knew it in the way her arm moved, the way her elbow jutted out to follow her hand without any movement in the wrist.

We sat for a moment in silence, and she caught her breath. Then I said, "That should help."

"My private wizard," she said. She didn't manage to put any levity behind the words. I didn't blame her.

"We should get you back to town," I said. "The Kind Father can do far more for you than I've done."

She nodded. I pushed up, then helped her to her feet. We made our way more slowly now, back up on the gateway's fallen stones, then out onto the cracked plains outside the ruins. We could see the horses, still tethered to scrub some short way off, but our steps dragged.

And I realized with some surprise that it was as much my fault as hers. My feet dragged across the ground. I felt a bone-deep weariness. I tried to force myself to move faster, to hurry Isabelle closer to safety, but I couldn't find the strength.

Isabelle startled me from that puzzle with another. "Why did the dragon not attack you?" she asked. She surprised me when she spoke. "Even after your first swing, it only seemed to watch. But they are said to be bloodthirsty things."

I missed a step and nearly fell. I started to stammer an answer, then caught myself. I shook my head. "I surprised it," I said at last, but it sounded like a thin excuse.

How could I tell her the truth? The monster hadn't only watched. It had spoken to me. How could I describe the depths of that one idea? I felt a cold chill at the thought.

I had heard a dragon's voice before, but this one had sounded nothing like the creature that helped me clear the siege around Teelevon. Vechernyvetr had been a mature black dragon, ten times the size of this little drake, and we shared some kind of spiritual bond. But even Vechernyvetr had not spoken into my head with the crushing force I'd felt from this creature. It seemed absurd, coming from the tiny beast.

And yet it had nearly overwhelmed me. Perhaps it should have. Perhaps the drake had expected it to do just that. I suspected that was precisely why it had made no other move to attack me. But I had gained more than a voice in my head when I bonded with Vechernyvetr. I had gained the timeless, bottomless strength of their kind. It was a foreign thing, an unreliable thing, but more than once my life had been saved by that dark fortitude deep in my mind.

But with the danger gone, the strength had left me, too. It left my body aching. My shoulders and arms felt weak, my lower back and the balls of my feet. It was a familiar pain—so familiar that it had taken me this long to register it and still a moment more to recognize it.

It was the honest pain of hard work. I stopped where I was, halfway to the horses, and threw a thoughtful look back toward the place where the drake had fallen. I remembered the little wall I'd made of earth, paces of hard-packed dirt heaved up and rearranged.

My arms hurt, too. My wrists and fingers throbbed, and I had a suspicion that had more to do with the delicate work of shaping my sword and Isabelle's splint. I had shaped Chaos magic before, and perhaps it had left me weary before, but it had never worn me out this thoroughly.

Isabelle squeezed my hand in her uninjured one. "Daven? Are you well?"

I shook my head, and then again more violently. I raised my eyes to hers and nodded once. "I will be well," I said. "I spent more of myself than I realized fighting that beast."

She hesitated for a heartbeat, biting her bottom lip, but then she nodded back at me. "You did heroic work."

"Come on," I said. "To the horses."

The pack horses whinnied as we approached, and all four animals stepped nervously away from me. Isabelle soothed them, and with a firm hand she finally brought mine to me and held its bridle until I was in the saddle. I reached across to offer her the same favor, but she swung herself easily up even in spite of her injured hand.

She spent a moment considering the pack horses' leads, and I smiled ruefully. "We did not accomplish much."

"I have seen the fortress," she said, thoughtful. I found her gaze fixed on me, and after a moment she smiled. "And I have seen you in battle. That was worth a day's ride."

I shook my head. "That was not worth your injury." I took a deep breath and let it out. "Bring the horses closer." She did, despite their protests, while I mustered my strength. Then I took on my wizard's sight and reached to the earth beneath the scrawny tree. I carved out a block of it with my mind, about the size of a grave, and turned it into a cloud of dust.

My shoulders screamed in protest, but I leaned across to grab the saddlebags draped across the pack horses' backs, and I heaved them hurriedly into the hole I'd made. I got the last one in, then released the earth energy and buried a good tent and a week's worth of rations two paces beneath the ground. I stretched out with the last of my energy and pulled the extra mound of earth into a needle point another pace tall, a tiny obelisk in the shade of the scrub tree.

Then I collapsed forward against my horse's neck. Isabelle said nothing. I could feel her eyes upon me, but she only reached across for my reins and led me along with the pack horses back toward town.

3. Wizard, Warrior, and King

Between Isabelle's aching wrist and my exhaustion, we made slow going on the journey home. The sun was already set when we left our horses in the courtyard, and I had to rap loud and long to rouse the stable master to tend to them.

When he saw the state we were in, he yelled for a stable boy to carry word to the baron and fetch us some aid. "And I'll send word to my lord and his son," he added, bowing his head to Isabelle.

Isabelle stepped sharply forward at that. "His son? Themmichus is here?"

"He arrived not half an hour gone," the stable master said. "All at a rush. His poor horse was in quite a state."

In an instant, Isabelle forgot the stable master and the boy. She caught at my sleeve with her uninjured hand, tugging, but didn't even wait long enough to pull me after her. She darted from the stables, and I had to hurry to catch up.

Across the courtyard and through the great front doors. Down the broad corridor and into the baron's study. She crashed into me in the doorway, already rushing back out while I tried to follow her in.

But she just growled in irritation. "It's Themm. I should have known he wouldn't be here."

"Isabelle," I said, trying to catch her. "It's late and you're hurt. I am anxious to see your brother as well, but it can wait until morning."

She opened her mouth and I saw a dozen arguments flash behind her eyes. But she only said, "He'll be in the larders." Then she was off again.

So we hurried through dark corridors until we spotted the warm, flickering light in the distant kitchens. We heard voices too.

"We know the danger, and we have our plans in motion." The baron's booming voice came calm and clear.

And then another answered. "Plans? You call these plans? You'll bring a doom upon us all!"

Even knowing he was there, it took me some time to recognize Themmichus's voice. It had gained a deeper baritone since I had known the boy at the Academy of Wizardry, but the greater change was the anger. I had never heard him speak with such ferocity.

We entered the room before the baron could answer. Given the expressions both men wore, that was a fortunate turn. The baron's face was a thundercloud, and he towered over his son.

Although...he did not tower as much as I'd expected. Themmichus had grown much in the last year. He was still thin as a blade, in sharp contrast to his father, but he was only a hair shorter than me now. He wore a wizard's black robes as well, instead of the apprentice's garb I'd seen him in last. They lent him an air of authority, and he wore it well.

So caught up in their fury, neither of them had noticed our entrance. Isabelle hesitated for less than a heartbeat, then she darted between them. She cried, "Themm, you're home!" and threw herself into his arms. I saw her wince of pain, I saw Themm's astonishment at the greeting, and then I saw Isabelle's calculating expression, quite at odds with the enthusiasm in her cry.

It worked, though. It drew the attention of both men to Isabelle, even if neither was fooled by her show of emotion.

Themmichus pushed his sister out to arm's length. "Hello, Isabelle," he said. His voice was cold. Without turning my way, he said, "Hello, Daven."

"Themmichus," I said. "Last time we spoke, we were friends."

He threw me a glance over his shoulder. He made it cold, hard, but I saw the compassion and fear he was fighting to conceal.

He grunted. "It has been a dark year since then. You do too much honor to my loyalty if you think—"

I snorted and moved closer. "And you do a lousy impression of the spoiled prats who shared that school with you."

He rounded on me, and I saw the same ferocity I'd heard in his voice before. I saw his fear, too. He made no effort to hide it now. It was the fuel to all his rage.

"This is no joke!" he shouted. "This is my home, Daven. This is my family. You cannot guess what that is worth, but you are a doom over us all."

I fell back a step. Isabelle grabbed his arm. "That isn't fair! Without him we would not be here at all. He has been our protector—"

"A fine one indeed," Themmichus snapped. "I see you come home from a quiet ride in the country with a splint upon your arm."

The baron gasped, likely seeing it for the first time. Before he could exclaim, Isabelle spat back, "He saved me from a dragon! A sore arm can barely compare—"

"And you would have faced this dragon if not for him?" Themmichus asked. Isabelle's face flushed, and I saw frustration burning in her eyes, but she could find no reply.

Themmichus nodded. He turned back to his father, dismissing Isabelle and me both. "You see?" he said. "From a

Windsday ride. He is too great a threat. You must send him away."

"Themm—" I said.

He raised a hand without turning, but it was enough to cut me short. "I'm sorry, Daven. I am. I admire you, but we cannot take this risk."

I could hear the hitch in his voice, the sound of regret. He did nothing to hide it. But despite that regret, there was perfect certainty in his accusation.

I stepped up behind him before I answered. I placed a hand on his shoulder and he tensed at my touch, but he didn't pull away. "Themm, you're right," I said.

He turned slowly and met my eyes. I nodded. "You're right. I have to go. Your father knows it. Isabelle knows it. We only delay long enough to make some hasty preparations."

Themmichus shook his head furiously. "No, there is no time for preparations. You tarried here six weeks too long."

"That's enough, Themm," the baron said, his voice heavy as a hammer. "Danger though he might be, Daven has earned our protection."

"No," Themm said, turning back to him. "I'm sorry, Daven. But, Father, there's something you need to know."

"He knows," I said, and I saw surprise flash on Themm's face. I nodded. "I told him everything. Themm...I'm sorry I left the Academy. I'm sorry I had to leave you, especially like that. But I will bring no suffering on this house."

"You do not understand," he said.

I felt a flash of anger, but I fought it down. "I do understand," I said. "I have not had a family to love. Not before."

"Daven—"

"No. You were right about that. But I love this family almost as strongly as you do." I had not noticed Isabelle moving to my side, but she placed her fingers in my free hand.

I smiled. "I will leave before the king comes," I promised. "I will bring no doom on this house."

He turned back to me yet again. He wore a sad smile while he shook his head. "You have misunderstood me" He sighed. "You have already doomed them."

In the far distance, a heavy hand banged loudly on the outer doors. Themmichus nodded in resignation. "The king is already here."

Isabelle gasped. The baron grunted. The thunderous knocking came again, and servants began moving noisily throughout the house.

The baron stepped forward. "Someone will be coming to stoke the fires. We must leave. I should meet the king in my study anyway. Isabelle, take Daven through dark corridors and get him from this house. Themm—"

"I will come with you," he said. "The king knows I am here, and I may be of some assistance."

The baron held his son's gaze for a moment, then nodded and left the room at a trot. Themmichus started after him, but he stopped in the doorway and turned back to me.

He met my eyes. He swallowed. "I did not know you as a wizard," he said, choosing his words with care. "But there are rumors. You should know the king has brought more wizards than just me to Teelevon. If you try a working in this town, you will light a beacon for them all."

I felt a bitter twist at my lips. These wizards knew nothing of my magic. But, then, I knew little more of theirs. I held Themm's gaze, and I nodded. "I understand."

"Take care," he said. "I would see you again someday."

I gave him a smile. "You will. Now go and buy me some time."

He left the room, and a heartbeat later Isabelle and I were stealing down dark halls as well.

I expected her to lead me toward the back of the house and the servants' exits there, but we'd barely gone a dozen paces before she pulled me off the servants' hall and up a narrow spiral stair to the house's second floor.

Six weeks here, and some parts of the house were still a maze to me. I didn't know where we were going until Isabelle pushed the door open and rushed me in. I found myself in a small but comfortable sitting room, and I only recognized it when I saw the light blue riding cloak thrown across a couch. I had been here once before, but one sitting room looks much like the next.

I had certainly never been in the adjoining room, but Isabelle hurried me straight to the bedroom door and shoved me on through.

"Isabelle!" I hissed, but she just shook her head and shoved harder.

"This is no time for modesty," she said, chiding.

"This is no time to scandalize your father," I said, though I relented and went on into the room. "Not when he could send me to the headsman with a moment's thought."

She cocked her head, considering me for a moment. I frowned. "What?"

"He could always do that, Daven." She said it lightly, amused. "He doesn't need the king's hounds for that."

"All the more reason—"

She hushed me with a finger on my lips. She stepped up close against me so she could shut the doors of the bedchamber behind her, and I felt a sudden heat surge in my face and neck. She smelled delicious, and I could feel her warmth. I was suddenly very aware of the massive bed less than a pace behind me. I licked dry lips.

For a long moment she stared up into my eyes, and hers shone with knowing. And laughter. "Something on your mind?" she asked.

"Yes," I said. I had to clear my throat, and I tore my eyes from hers. "Yes. The king and his soldiers. Your father. They are here searching for me—"

"And they would never believe I would hide you in my own bedchamber," she said. "They wouldn't believe you'd dare. They wouldn't believe Father would allow it."

I raised my hands and caught her shoulders. I took a slow breath and then a slow step back. "We already discussed this," I said. "If I stay here, they will find me. And the toll upon your family will be worse than you can imagine."

Her eyes and lips both tightened in an instant's stubbornness, but then she gave a little sigh and smoothed them out again. She turned to slip past me and stood tugging at the covers on the bed, needlessly straightening them. "Then what is your plan?"

I closed my eyes and thought through my options. After a moment I nodded. "I'll hide here," I said. "For all the reasons you said. It was a good idea."

She said nothing. I turned back to her, and found her waiting patiently. She tilted her head. "And then?"

"I'll go to the fort as we intended. The king's men have probably traveled far and fast. They'll need rest. But I do too, so I'll hide here for a few hours and get some sleep, then slip away before dawn while the king's hunters are sleeping off their late-night search."

She measured me with her eyes for some time. Then she said, "Are you sure you mean to sleep?"

I almost laughed. She prowled one step toward me, and I was searching desperately for the willpower to object, but she froze in place. Her eyes narrowed, her head turned, and a heartbeat later I heard it, too: footsteps in the hall, and coming fast.

I spun back to the room, eyes searching frantically, but Isabelle was calm. She stepped up behind me and planted a hand between my shoulder blades. She shoved me toward an open wardrobe. I stumbled one pace then ducked inside, slipping among her soft hanging clothes. She pressed the doors shut behind me while I squirmed to turn back to the doors, to find a position comfortable enough I could hold it.

"Hush!" she hissed, and her voice was at once stern and apologetic. "Daven, be still!"

Those words struck me. A cruel master had used them often during my days at the Academy. He had locked me in a dark closet and commanded me to work his magic.

But now it was Isabelle. "Please," she whispered, and I could barely hear her through the door.

I raised a hand and touched the door's polished grain. I took one long, slow breath, then let it out. I heard her sigh, and an instant later an insistent *bang* on the outer door.

Another followed the first, and then a deep voice I knew too well called, "Isabelle Eliade, are you there?"

I heard her father farther down the hall. "She might be anywhere," he said.

"This late at night?" the soldier asked. "I think not." He knocked again. "Isabelle Eliade! You may be in grave danger. Come to the door."

It was the voice of Othin, an officer of the King's Guard and a truly terrible man. I wanted to stop Isabelle, to keep her from him, but I dared not make a noise. I heard her cross the chamber, heard her pull the bedroom doors almost closed, and heard her open the hall door just as a new clamor began.

I leaned against the wardrobe doors. I longed to push them open, if just a crack, but I didn't dare. Othin had a fearsome reputation as a tracker and thief-catcher, and he had a personal grudge against me.

I was no mere mortal, though. Trapped in the darkness, I found the stillness I could never summon for Master Seriphenes. I took on the same wizard's sight that had allowed me to move the earth by sheer will, but now I used it just to look.

To the wizard's sight, the wardrobe's walls were as nothing. Instead of the paper-thin fabric of reality, I saw the underlying energies and powers—true reality. I saw the shape of earth and water and willpower that had been made into the cabinet around me, but it was a tiny, insubstantial thing. Beyond I saw the frilly carpets and frail tapestries, and beneath both was heavy, hard-hewn stone half a step away from raw elemental earth.

And blazing bright within the room beyond was the life-blood of four figures. I saw Isabelle and Othin, the baron and the king, all clustered in her sitting room. I couldn't read the flare of vibrant power to distinguish one form from the other, but I knew Isabelle. She stood closest to me, but I think I would have known her shine anywhere.

"Father," she said, a little breathless. "Your Highness! What can I—"

Before she could say more, one of the other figures brushed roughly past her and into her private rooms. That one had to be Othin. My fists clenched at my sides and my jaw ground painfully. He had dared to lay a hand on her. I wanted to lash out at him.

Instead I held my place and cowered in the darkness. I expected her father to object, but he stayed as meekly silent as I. The king spoke as though nothing had happened.

"My dear Isabelle, look how you've grown!" he said. There was brittleness to the cheer in his tone.

"Hard years have passed since last we met," she answered, and her voice was cold. "In fact, I'm surprised you could find the time to visit us with such pressing business on your hands."

I kept an ear turned to their conversation, but most of my attention was fixed on Othin. I watched him move through the room, searching. He started at the wall opposite me, peeking behind a folding screen then checking the window latches.

"Hard years indeed," the king was saying. "The rebellion hardly broken before the dragons came upon us."

"The City's under siege," the baron said, his voice grave. "And Tirah has been attacked as well. Timmon tells me his wizards have the power to hold them off, but not enough to turn them away."

"Not near enough," the king said. "And so far we have only faced attacks in threes or fours. We have news from distant corners where flights of twenty or more dragons attacked as one. The news grows darker every day."

"Then why have you come here?" Isabelle asked. She hurried on, more diffidently, "Surely these threats outrank even your generous love for this family."

The king gave a great weary sigh. "Alas, they do," he said. "But there's another threat among them: an assassin who stole boldly into my palace at Tirah, and perhaps even summoned the first of the dragons that attacked me."

My lips peeled back at the king's accusation, and I watched Othin move on through Isabelle's room. He checked the bed, the reading nook, and the fine mahogany chest.

The king went on without pause. "The boy is a fugitive. Expelled from the Academy and hunted by the Guard. He's dangerous and bloodthirsty. He speaks clever lies and leaves a trail of death wherever he goes."

Othin moved methodically around the room, and I could see him coming toward me. Of course he had suspected the wardrobe from the first. It was the only suitable hiding place in the room. But as long as I was hidden here, he had been safe to check the rest of the room. He came now toward the last refuge in the room.

And I could see all three of the others shifting, watching his progress. The air was heavy with expectation and nervous fear. The king's voice fell into that atmosphere like hissing venom, "And I fear he has found favor in this house."

I stretched the fingers of my right hand, aching for the feel of a sword's grip, and forced a slow, calming breath. Othin stopped just outside the wardrobe. I reached out my will to the energies around me, and time seemed to slow.

I could have formed a sword from the stones of the wall, or from the attenuated earth energy in the wardrobe's walls. My arms still throbbed with the pain of the effort I'd expended, but there was strength enough left for one more strike. I was sure of it.

A fire burned in the hearth, too. It seemed tame on its bed of stone, but there was more than enough heat there to consume the soldier—and his master as well, if it came to it. For one slow beat of my heart I focused on the dancing flame and felt Othin's dismal presence on the other side of the doors.

But I'd had my chance to turn these men to ash, and far more to gain then than I had now. I shook my head, one swift motion, and felt a sharp tension ease between my shoulders. My breath came more easily, too. I pulled my attention closer, spread the fingers of my hand, and focused my will on the seeds of earth in the wardrobe's doors.

The gap between the doors stood straight and clear as the edge of a blade. I focused on a spot near waist height, where the door's handles would be, and pulled the substance from both sides across the gap, binding them together. It worked, and as I saw Othin's arm extend toward the door I stretched the seam, up and down, until the substance of the two doors merged into one unbroken piece.

He jerked on the handles. Both doors rattled on their hinges, but they did not give at all. He spat an angry curse and pulled again, heaving so hard the whole wardrobe shifted on the stone floor, but the doors held. He cursed again, more vicious than the first.

"Here, now!" the baron snapped. "There is a lady present."

"Indeed," the king said, not at all chastising. "What have you found?"

"The room is clear but for this cabinet," Othin said. "I see no lock, but the doors will not budge. Perhaps some magic—"

"No magic," Isabelle said hastily. "It is an old piece, and warped."

"It must be checked," the soldier said. Then added, "For your safety, of course."

"Of course," the king said. "Try again."

He did and heaved the wardrobe half a pace across the floor. I'd have feared him toppling it, but given the sheer weight of the thing it was remarkable he could move it at all.

I could hear the strain in his voice when he said, "It is no good. The doors are stuck fast."

"I see," the king said. "Well, we can send some guards in case he's there, but I doubt the boy would be lurking in these chambers. Even a scoundrel would not stoop to shame this girl's honor. Is that not so?"

Othin snorted. "Send for a sharp ax, and let me open these doors."

"Father!" Isabelle cried, genuinely afraid, and I had to stop myself reaching for the burning coals of the fire. I saw the baron move closer to her, soothing, and I felt some of the anger ease in my chest.

"I assure you again, Timmon, we have seen nothing of the boy since he returned from the day's ride. He certainly would not trespass in my daughter's private chambers."

"Far more likely he's drinking at Duncan's common room," Isabelle said. "Have you looked there yet? Or in his *own* rooms?"

"We have guards there, yes," the king replied. "And some can be sent to scour the tavern as well. Othin."

"Your Highness?" Othin asked. Just two words, but they tread close to rebellion, so rich with defiance. "I believe—"

"We will post guards for the girl," Timmon said. Then he added, "For her safety. Consider, Isabelle. Where else might he be?"

"He might be in this chest," Othin growled. He slammed a fist against the wooden panel an inch from my face. "Get me an ax."

"An ax will be got," the king said, treating the soldier to the same chill tone he'd offered Isabelle before. "And guards will be stationed. But here and now, you have your orders."

I saw Othin still as a tracery of living fire, the heat of his anger and passion, and it flared brighter for four heavy heartbeats. My whole body tensed as I watched to see what he would do. I stretched my will toward the fire, I clenched my hands in ready fists. I poised myself, ready to strike if he chose to break down the doors by the sheer force of his fury.

But then his anger cooled. I saw him fall back a pace, and then he turned back toward the other three. He said softly, "Yes, Your Highness," and left the room.

"Do send four men to guard the room," the king ordered as Othin slipped past. "And...send one to find an ax. Just in case."

From the corridor beyond, I heard Othin say again, "Yes, Your Highness." And then he was gone.

The three left in her sitting room stood some time in awkward silence. Then at last the king said, "You must understand what a threat this boy represents."

"I have seen it demonstrated," the baron replied. "He is a master of no small power."

"Precisely!" the king said. "And reckless. And defiant of authority."

"He sounds a great nuisance," Isabelle said, sounding bored. "If it please you, I have found this day's events quite tiring."

The king hesitated again. At last he said, "For your safety—"

The baron hurried to say, "I'm sure your guards are quite sufficient to the task."

I saw the flash of fury before I heard the outraged bellow. "You dare to interrupt your king?"

"Not in the least." The baron laughed. It sounded fragile to my ears, but his voice was still steady. "I only hasten to reassure your majesty. You seem greatly troubled—on my humble family's behalf—and I regret that mightily."

"I shall see to my own concerns, Burton." But the flash of anger was gone. "We shall speak of this more."

"Of course," the baron said. "And of the hunt for the murderer as well. I'll place all my household staff at your disposal."

The king *hmph*ed lightly, but he seemed mollified. The baron took some confidence from that. "Let us go and speak with my steward. He should have some word for us by now."

They turned to go. I raised my hand toward the wardrobe doors and began undoing the bonds I'd made. The baron and the king both headed to the outer door...and stopped when four new shapes arrived. The guards. They started to move into the sitting room, but the baron objected. "Oh, my lord, please." His tone wheedled in a way utterly at odds with the man's personal power. "For my daughter's honor, do not place them *in* her chambers."

"You seem too little worried, Burton," the king said. "Far too little for the safety of your daughter and your house." The words were an accusation, the tone sharp as a skinning knife.

It took the baron a moment to find his answer. I held my breath, straining to catch every last word.

"My lord," he said at last, "through all these many years, you've never let me down. You've offered such protection to my house, I *cannot* fear so long as you are here."

I felt my lips peel back in an angry snarl. The king and all his army had left this town to die, besieged by the rebel army. If not for my intervention, they would all be starved or murdered by now. Yet the baron was forced to pretend gratitude—

And the king saw nothing wrong. He sighed, long and loud, and clapped the baron companionably on the back. "Oh, good Burton. Oh, at last I understand. And of course that stands to reason. You've never known the dangers I've so often kept away."

The king chuckled, then barked to the guards. "The corridor will do. But watch this door for your life, and remember your instructions."

They withdrew. The king and baron left as well, and Isabelle closed her outer door. She stood for a moment, leaning close and likely listening, but I could see no subterfuge in the corridor. The guards stood at attention, and the other two faded down the hall.

I let the bonds on the wardrobe doors dissolve and pushed back out into her room a breath before she came in. She closed the inner doors with great care, then turned to me. My wizard's sight failed me then, my concentration shattered by the expression on her face. Her eyes were wide with fear, her breathing hard and hot. She threw herself against my chest, and I wrapped my arms tight around her. She shook with little tremors. I hated the king.

"Hush," I said soothingly, smoothing her soft hair. I whispered near her ear. "You were so brave and clever and strong. You saved my life."

"He never," she started, too loud and gasping. She choked it off, then caught her breath and said through clacking teeth, "He has never spoken to my father like that. He has never looked at me—" She shuddered, head to toe, and I squeezed her close again.

"It will be well," I said. "But this is what we spoke of in your father's study. This is *why* I must be gone."

She nodded, a frantic little motion, and sniffed lightly. "I understand," she said. "I'll come for you."

"Isabelle—"

"No," she hissed, suddenly fierce, and her fingers gripped too tightly on my arms. "I will come to you." I tried to argue, but she gave me no time. "I'll wait until it's safe. But I will come to you." Her voice shook with silent sobs, but she spoke with certainty. "I'll meet you beneath the twisted tree."

I pushed the hair back from her face. Tears in my eyes now, I smiled at her. So strong. So brave. "I love you, Isabelle."

"I love you, too."

"Be safe," I said. "Wait until he's gone. And take special care with Othin. He is not a man of reason."

She jerked her head in another nod, and her fingers closed more tightly still.

"I need to leave," I said, but the last word was not out before she shut my mouth with a kiss. She threw herself up on her toes and knotted her fingers in my shirt. She kissed me with all the heat and passion I had seen in the glow of her lifeblood. She kissed me breathless.

It seemed to last a very long time. Still, it was done too soon. She stepped away from me, eyes wide, lips slightly parted. My heartbeat hammered in my ears. It hammered louder. Then I recognized the furious pounding on the outer door. Othin bellowed from the hall, "Isabelle, open the door. By order of the king."

"He's found his ax," she said. I saw terror in her eyes.

"Stall him if you can," I said. I reached out my will, and the wardrobe's doors fell closed. I bound them together again to give him something to do. "But do not provoke him. He is a dangerous man."

"Be safe," she said. "I'll come for you soon."

I flew to the window and flung it wide. It took three breaths before I could catch my wizard's sight again. When I did, I saw the fire of life outside, motion in the night, but none was close enough to see my escape. Aching muscles screamed their protest, but fear gave me strength enough to slither through the deep stone window. I hung for a heartbeat by my fingertips, Isabelle's face framed in the window above me.

She touched my hand, and I felt her warmth. Then there came a great crash as the outer door slammed open. I dropped into the darkness.

4. The Monster

I fell into a roll when I hit the hard cobblestones of the stable's courtyard. I made the move less gracefully than I'd have liked, but I did it without breaking bones. I heard the *snick* of Isabelle closing the window above me as I stumbled to my feet, and I dared not delay. I passed the stable at a lurch, wishing there was time to steal a horse.

I knew Othin would not have left this escape entirely unguarded. There was no one directly outside the window, but the reason was clear enough: the high-walled stableyard offered only two escapes—an arched gate onto the town square, and a door back into the master's house. I flew toward the gate, flitting through deepest shadows, then stopped beneath the great stone wall to stretch my awareness on ahead.

Twelve men were gathered there, ten of them shining with the silver lines of worked steel. Ten soldiers, silent and still. Waiting there for me. The other two surprised me. They shone with a different power—a backlight of perfect white, a halo behind their lifeblood—with a shine that reached out to light the darkness around them. I stared at them, bewildered. My heart pounded more loudly than any other sound in the night.

Then I heard a frustrated groan, and Themmichus's voice. "I told you, this is a waste of time. If he were hiding in the house, my father would have found him by now."

Themmichus. And then I understood. That was the glow of authority. Power over reality. Those two were wizards, capable of the same sight that showed them so clearly to me. Sweat stood cold on my skin, and I trembled. Then the other wizard answered Themm, "Be still!" harsh and vicious, and the strength went out of my legs.

I caught myself on one knee. It was Master Seriphenes, the man who had tormented me in my brief stay at the Academy. "You have your instructions," he went on, bored and condescending. "Now watch the yard. Or shall I inform Lhorus you are *still* unable to do as you are told?"

"That won't be necessary," Themmichus said, with none of the sniveling apology his father had stooped to. I saw the shift in his energies as he turned. I saw a flare in the sharp white light behind him as his attention passed over me. "But I assure you—" he was saying, but he cut short. I knew exactly what had stopped him. He had seen me hiding here.

Seriphenes must have known it, too, because I saw the same flash of his attention. "What—" he started to ask.

I did not wait to hear his exclamation. I threw myself into a sprint. Two paces brought me to the gate, and I saw them arrayed there just as I had expected. Three on the right, three on the left, with four more spread in a half-circle between to block the way completely.

I heard shouts of surprise. Seriphenes cried his orders, warning, but the words were lost in the alarm from the soldiers. I heard Themm shouting as well, apparently in panic, but it seemed he was deliberately confusing the Master Wizard's commands.

The two wizards stood together off to the left, so I angled right. I aimed for the gap between two of the soldiers in the half-circle, but it was not room enough to slip through. I was all too aware of the glowing lines of the swords in their hands—solid steel fashioned with a power my strange magic could not touch. But I remembered a trick I'd used before. I reached out to the earth before me, even as I sprinted forward, and whipped it with my will so it roiled beneath the feet of those two guards.

It was enough to throw them from their feet. It felled me, too. Weakness stabbed into my legs, and I faltered. I scraped my hands on hard cobblestones and struck with a shoulder to save my jaw. I kept my legs moving, kicking, and found strength to heave with my arms. I made it to my feet again as I scraped through the gap I'd made, and then I was pelting down the silent street away from them.

I stretched back with my awareness and nearly fell again when I clipped a cobblestone with my left foot. I kept moving, though, and turned my attention to Seriphenes. Even as I did, I saw the noonday blaze of his focus, and it flashed toward me. He shouted to the soldiers, "I have him!" In the same instant I felt bonds of air clamp tight around me. I slammed to a hard stop within their grasp. I grunted and looked down at bonds I knew too well. The wizard's apprentice Archus had used them against me once before to march me to my death.

I was no longer the boy I'd been then. Though they were crafted of invisible air, I could see the bonds around me clearly in the wizard's sight. I could see the way he had bent wind to serve his will. How he had convinced this bit of air to pretend it were hard as steel. He had told reality a lie and enforced it by his will.

Another wizard might have challenged his construct, might have forced reality back into its proper shape, pitting his own will against that of Seriphenes. But I was no wizard. I was something else. Instead of changing the false air around me, I caught at its true heart—at the fragile threads of contorted energy—and waved the air aside as though I were lifting back a curtain.

And that easily the bonds dissolved. It cost me less than the trick with the earth, too, for air was easier to move. In all, Seriphenes's spell might have brought me short for ten seconds, and then I was moving again. I heard him curse behind me, heard the bafflement and the first trace of fear in his voice as he screamed, "After him! You fools!"

But I was already far ahead. I heard them pounding after me, and without turning I cast my wizard's sight back. Seriphenes was among them, ahead of them even. Old and spindly though he was, the dark-eyed villain sprinted just as hard as I did, and already I could see the gathering glow of his next spell.

I slowed just enough to gather my focus. I touched the earth beneath me, borrowed enough from the cobblestones at my feet to shape a ball of stone the size of my fist. Then I turned in place, between one pace and the next, and threw the stone in his direction. I hadn't the strength or the vision within the night to hit him so far away, but I put the ball in the air and then turned and continued on my flight.

But I focused my will on the wizard's sight. I caught the heavy stone within my mind and flung it straight and true into the heart of that blazing golden glow. Master Seriphenes gave an undignified grunt far behind me. I heard the rustle and thud as he fell to the stone. I watched in my wizard's sight as he skidded five paces along the earth before at last he fell still.

The fiery dance of his lifeblood barely faltered, but the glow of his magical will faded, faded, and was gone.

I felt a moment's thrill of victory. It evaporated quickly. I placed a foot wrong and fell. I scrambled to my feet again. Ten armed men still chased after me, and they were gaining ground. I was tired. I tried throwing another stone, and I dropped one of the guards behind me, but this time I felt the cost. I felt myself growing slower. Perhaps I could have dropped nine of them, but I'd have collapsed asleep in the tenth one's arms. I turned and ran again instead, but once more I stumbled, and my flailing hand barely caught the ground to stop my fall.

The true reality revealed by wizard's sight was not the same as the reality of man. I couldn't run while looking with that sight; I couldn't see the subtle shape of the terrain, just the weight of it. Facades fell away, but right now I needed them. I couldn't afford to miss a little nuance like the lip of a paving stone or a tiny patch of loose mortar.

So I abandoned the wizard's sight, drank deeply of my fear, and turned all my mind to the desperate sprint for safety. I had one advantage. Six weeks in the town had taught me its twisting streets. I left the main way and darted down the alley between Duncan's and the blacksmith's shop. I led them on a chase through narrow back streets, and at last I stopped in the black-shadowed yard behind Thomas Wheelwright's house. I watched seven men go thundering by, all that remained now of my first pursuers, and I used my wizard's sight to confirm no more were waiting nearby.

I could hear a hue and cry going up in the town behind me, though. I glanced back and saw the distant, angry flicker of torchlight gathering in the town square. They would organize a full search, and I could not hope to escape from that.

I gave myself no more than half a minute to catch my breath, then forced myself up off the wall and stumbling down the alley again. I had led them within a hundred paces of the eastern gate, and I stopped in another shadow just long enough to check that there was no one but the baron's guards watching that escape.

I trusted my life to him. I hit the broad street at a full sprint and saw the flash of recognition in the gate guard's eyes. I saw them widen in confusion even as I came abreast of him. Then he heard the shouts in the town square. He turned his eyes that direction, making the connection, but I was already past him.

He had a crossbow at his station. I didn't slow. I ran on, a hundred paces down the road, but I did not hear the strained *twang* of a crossbow firing. I did not feel the searing heat of a crossbow bolt tearing flesh. There was sufficient other pain to bring me down, but for my life—and for the lives of everyone in Isabelle's house—I had to win free. So I ran on, grateful to the guard who had not done his duty.

A hundred paces down the way the road turned south and I kept on straight. I hopped the split-timber fence of old Bredgeman's fallow fields, and kept straight on until there was no glow of fire or life to light the night behind me.

I kept running as long as I could, and when my burning lungs and aching legs forced me to stop, I collapsed in the dirt by the side of a strangled little stream. I gulped desperate drinks of moss-slick water, and fought to catch my breath. For several minutes I lay panting, but then I forced myself up again, forced myself to trudge on.

I turned south, making my best guess by the light of the stars. I'd meant to head for the ruins, and that would have been quite a long way on foot even sticking to the road. But now I had no choice. I was far enough from the path to avoid detection, but it would not be safe to return to the road for days yet.

So I forged a path through fields of cold-shocked wheat and unharvested corn, and I left Teelevon behind. I didn't think—I was far too tired to think—only kept moving. South and east, I learned when the moon finally rose to trace its arc across the sky. I bent my path more perfectly south and tried to guess how I might find my way to the fortress.

But that would not matter for most of a day. First I needed to find my way to somewhere safe. I needed rest. I needed refuge. For three years now I'd been a fugitive from the king's justice, but that night beneath the stars I felt like one for the first time. That thought drove me on, far beyond all reason. That thought gave me strength long after my legs should have given out.

I moved cross-country in the darkness, climbing up hills and fording streams and pressing on as though drawn by a magnet. When dawn broke I was still walking, still searching for some bolthole where I could be sure the king's hunters would not find me. I ignored the pain in my feet and legs, ignored the weariness that kept trying to drag my eyes shut. I scoured every slope, every visible bit of land, and at last I found some suitable cover.

It was a spill of stones on the edge of an empty field, probably hauled there and piled up by some farmer's overtaxed mule. Some of them were as much as a pace tall, most considerably smaller, but all together they formed a pile six paces long and three paces tall at its highest. Bracken grew thick across it, and tall grass crowded around it.

I fell automatically into the wizard's sight as I approached it. I could carve myself a space within. Not now, of course. I would need rest first. But I could make a shelter none but me might find. I searched out the shape of its structure, making certain it would work, even as I trudged slowly in a circle around it, scanning with my mundane senses. For now, I needed only a shadowy corner to catch some rest. Two hours, perhaps three, and then I could have the strength needed to make a more secure lodging.

I saw darkness where no darkness should have been: in my wizard's sight. It lay long and low in the lee of the piled stones. Mind fuzzy from the long exertion, I mistook it for an ordinary shadow and stepped toward it automatically. I stretched out a hand to brush the tall grass aside, and then the shadow moved. Too late, I understood.

It was a drake, scarcely larger than the one I'd decapitated in the ruins of the fortress. This one was the brown and orange shades of autumn leaves, but my eyes fixed on the teeth, the great fangs as long as my hand, and the three-inch claws on its forelegs that were sharp enough to score stone. Those were white but stained with blood. I thought of the farmer who had piled these stones. I hoped the blood had been the mule's.

And then the thing attacked me. It darted forward, and I thought of summoning a sword. I thought of swinging for it. I thought of conjuring a wall of earth to block its path. I thought of all the things I'd done so easily to dispatch the other drake before, but my weary mind and broken body could not do any of them. Some primal panic gave me enough sense at least to back away, but my legs tangled and I barely kept my feet. I stumbled, my strength all gone, and wavered there while the child dragon snaked toward me.

I watched the fangs. They seemed the most sensible attack. The claws could eviscerate me if the beast got them to me, but the long neck made a bite the easiest move. It darted to my left and I tried to run right, but I made it half a pace before the monster hissed and struck at me from behind. I heard it coming. I tried to dive forward, to roll away, to escape from certain death.

I felt the shock and stab of pain as the beast's blunt nose slammed hard against my skull. Light brighter than a wizard's glow flashed behind my eyes, and my arms and legs went limp. I felt the shock of hitting the ground. I felt the stubble of cut grass harsh against my cheek. I felt the young dragon crunch up right behind me, its talons carving sun-scorched earth, but I could not even turn my head. Pain washed up, turning my vision red, and then it ebbed away, and then it came again, red and green and brown. I might have screamed. But then it turned to black.

I woke to find myself stretched out on my back. The pain was still there. It was everywhere. I saw the drake crouching, almost curious, by my right arm, and another like it down by my left knee. The first snaked its head forward to bump me under the right shoulder, to prop me up, and then I felt at last the beating blasts of winter air driven down against my face.

I looked up and saw the adult dragon hovering there, scales as red as hearthstone coals, and the drake supporting me raised my shoulders higher. I saw the dragon swoop down closer to me, saw its talon reaching, and then I heard a voice like devastation thunder in my mind.

He is awake, it said. It broke my mind and drove me into blackness once again.

The next time I woke, perfect darkness pressed close around me. My muscles ached with exhaustion and a thousand other pains screamed at me, but I could not yet process them all. Whatever rest I'd gotten had done little to clear my head. I found myself sitting up, arms wrapped around my knees, my back and head both leaned against a hard stone wall.

I blinked uselessly, but there was no light here at all. Memory and fear piled up in my mind. I had spent too much time trapped in darkness. I tried to rise, still leaning on the wall for support, but I'd made it less than a pace up the wall before I cracked my head against a ceiling that felt like stone.

Light flashed behind my eyes, and my knees gave out. I fell back into the same position. I stretched an arm out in front of me, but I bruised my fingertips on cold stone just short of my arm's length. Without moving I could trace every edge of my stone prison.

Panic gibbered in the back of my mind, but I was too tired to give it much ground. Instead I fell forward, face down to the cool stone floor, and stretched the aching muscles in my neck and back. Then my shoulders and sides. I curled up on my back and stretched my legs up above me until they touched the ceiling. I put my toes against it and pushed hard to stretch the protesting muscles in the back of my legs.

The ceiling shifted. Without even trying, I pushed it up a quarter inch, and a brief flare of light fell into my cage. The grating sound of stone on stone filled the little space, too, screaming in the stillness. I relaxed again, letting the cover stone fall back over me, and lay for a long time in silent darkness. I strained my ears for any sound of my captors approaching, but all I could hear was my own frantic breathing.

I tried to slow my pounding heart, to work through calming exercises I'd mastered long ago, but my pulse only thundered louder in my ears. Faster. I strained to hear outside my prison, I waited anxiously for the stone to slip aside again and reveal my captors. But nothing happened. There was no sense of time in that place, only the wild tattoo of my heart, and soon I was flinching at every beat. Then at last my fear took hold. I fought against it, but the fear won out.

My breath escaped me in a whimper, and still no one came. It became a sob before I could stop it, and I would have wailed my terror if I'd had the strength to fill my lungs. I curled up on my side, arms wrapped around my legs, and trembled in the darkness. I tried a dozen different times to reach for my wizard's sight, but it required inner calm, and I was a shattered mess.

In time, it passed. Perhaps I faded into sleep, perhaps I simply found my peace. There was little difference within the darkness. I know I lay in utter silence for a great age, and then at last I caught my breath. I flexed my fingers and closed my eyes and worked the exercises I had learned at the Academy. My breath caught as I felt the immensity of the mountain around me. I lay imprisoned beneath the floor of a great cavern, and outside the cavern was earth as far as I could stretch my mind.

I shivered. Buried in the heart of a mountain, I felt incredibly small. But I cut that thought short, measured my breath, and turned my attention back to my surroundings. I looked for my captors, for the pulsing glow of lifeblood. I looked at the black cavity of the cavern above me, searching, but there was only emptiness.

And then a piece of the emptiness moved. Then, for the first time, I recalled the drake that had surprised me on the edge of a farmer's field. I remembered it propping me up for a grown dragon swooping in to strike. I looked on the vast blackness above me, and I saw that it moved.

No. It *roiled*. I could almost see the empty spot of blackness thrown by a dragon in motion, large enough to be the adult I'd seen before, but as I tried to track its flight across the cavern's ceiling, it passed another Chaos shadow flashing the other direction. Everywhere I looked, there was motion. I tried to count, but there was no sense of perspective, no distinction between one living darkness and the next. There might have been a dozen or a thousand there.

A prisoner of dragons. I had never heard of anything like it. I shifted in place so I could crouch on my knees, then turned my attention back to the space above me. Beyond the dragons, behind them, the cavern yawned wide. It was easily a hundred paces in all directions, perhaps more. At one end of it, a sudden, sharp edge dropped off into a terrifyingly deep chasm. At the other end a wide, shallow pool danced with the soft azure sheets of still water.

And in the heart of the cavern was a blazing inferno. Not fire, not real light, but the blazing flash of pure power shaped by the oldest magics of man. Silver, gold, and steel. Coins and gemstones, relics and treasures. I could not see the shape of any given item with the wizard's sight, but I could taste the human purpose that had imbued them with such focused energy.

It was not the treasure store of a king; it was the wealth of a nation. The nearest edge of it was perhaps thirty paces from my prison, but it climbed into a mountain of precious metals. It blazed in the darkness. It called to me. I raised my fingers to the wide, flat stone that sealed my cage and, as carefully as I could, pressed up and to the side.

Stone on stone screamed again in the silence. I moved it perhaps a finger's width, and for all my care it still dragged and scraped. I swallowed a curse, blinked my eyes, and then lifted the stone away with my will. I lowered it to the earth without a sound, but I felt the strain of it in my fingers and wrists. I paid it little mind. My eyes were drawn to the hoard.

Even without the wizard's sight, the gold shone in the darkness. A thin, strangled light reached the cavern's interior through a wide cave mouth set high in one wall, but the treasure gathered the light, focused it, and threw it back bright and clean. The hoard glowed within the darkness.

A handful of it would have been enough to buy me a life of luxury. If I could have filled a pack from it, I might have been as wealthy a man as Isabelle's father. If I could have loaded a farmer's cart, I could have shamed the king. And still I would not have touched a tenth part of the dragons' store.

The thoughts came unbidden and went mostly ignored. I looked upon a sparkling treasure like I had never imagined, but the darkness hanging over it devoured all my attention.

To my wizard's sight it hung like a great cloud of smoke, hovering above the pyre of perfect gold, but fear shattered my concentration and I looked up only with the eyes of a man.

I trembled.

Sprawled atop the hoard was a dragon. Dark and red as midnight embers, as heartblood in a pool. I remembered the adult red that had come for me on the edge of the farmer's field. Long and strong, wider at the shoulders than the beast that had aided me at Teelevon, but as I looked up at this monster, that same red dragon went flashing by above. Larger than a house, with a belly full of fire that could have routed armies, but the adult dragon looked like an insect buzzing around the monster that sat upon the hoard.

One insect in a swarm. There were indeed dozens of them, in all the shades of earth and fire. Greens and blues and browns, reds and blacks and one sleek yellow almost as bright as the gold. There were drakes, too, upon the ground. I only noticed when one bumped me between the shoulder blades with its snout and sent me stumbling three steps forward. Then I looked about frantically and saw them gathered in a wide, loose circle. All around me. All around the hoard. They watched.

In the vast height above—above a neck as tall and thick as the Masters' Tower at the Academy—the monster at the heart of the cavern cocked its head and stared down at me. I wanted to run. Even with an army of drakes behind me, a swarm of adult dragons capable of tearing me to shreds, I wanted to try an escape. I wanted to flee the horror hanging over me. I couldn't. I couldn't move at all.

The yellow flitted lightly to the ground just before me, on my right, and a heartbeat later the red I'd seen before slammed to earth on the left. Both stalked closer, heads low, eyes fixed on me. High above, a sharp *huff* moved the air, like a snort from a fortress-sized warhorse. Even without flame, I could feel the heat of it in the air. I could not even flinch away.

Then a voice spoke into my mind. *At last*, it said, thunder booming out over the terrified turmoil of my thoughts. *You are smaller than I expected.*

If I could have moved, I would have been on my knees, palms pressed hard against my ears, screaming at the pain that voice burned into my mind. But I could only stare, up and up at the monster's face, and then I understood.

"It was you." I meant to speak the words aloud, but my mouth would no more respond than my legs or arms. Still, the words formed in my mind, and the two adults crouching before me bobbed their heads in unmistakable nods.

I have scoured the world for you, the monster said. It was the voice I'd heard from the little drake at the ruined fortress, the voice I'd heard from the adult red on the edge of the farmer's field, but here at last I understood. It was a voice as vast and terrible as the monster that crouched upon the hoard.

"How?" I asked. *"How did you find me? How did you know me?"*

You belong to me, it said. It snorted again, and I felt another blast of hot air. I could feel the monster's anger, too. It folded around me like a blanket wrapped too tight. I tried to see the shape of it within my mind and felt my brows crease.

It was not my fear that paralyzed me, but the monster's anger—emotion strong as steel, crowding me out of my own mind. My lips peeled back as I forced a calming breath. And another. With meticulous care, I pressed back against the monster's presence in my mind.

Then, at last, I fell to my knees. I cried out, and in the same instant the ring of watching drakes shrank away from me. Pain like white-hot lances jabbed inside my head, again and again, stabbing at the walls I'd tried to build. I screamed in agony, and the two adults standing over me reared like frightened horses and beat at the air with half-extended wings.

I nearly fell prostrate, but I drove a fist hard against the stone floor and held myself up. I bloodied my knuckles and bruised the bones, but in the same instant I caught my breath. That pain was real. That pain was mine. I narrowed my eyes and focused on the flash of agony and poured my will into it. I built new walls around that point, built a sanctuary of identity around my injury, and though the monster hammered at it again and again, it could not break me.

I let my eyes close and drew a breath. I pushed against the stone and rose to my feet. I exhaled, long and slow, and straightened my shoulders. I could feel a fury like a thunderstorm pounding against my mind, but I wrapped myself in quiet, perfect darkness and waited. I raised my chin. I smiled.

At last the assault relented. I nodded once and opened my eyes.

The drakes were gone. The adults who had come to stand over me had left as well, though I saw the yellow soaring once more in the slow, chaotic swarm that hung around the monster's head like a nightmare halo. That head was closer now, barely ten paces above me. It hung over me like an avalanche. It snorted, and the furnace blast knocked me back three paces.

You are not my equal, it said. *You are my prisoner. You are my toy.*

"*I can hold your mind at bay,*" I thought. "*I am more than you imagine.*"

A sound like a forest fire's roaring crackle rattled in my head, and I recognized it as the monster's laughter. *Your eyes are far too small,* it said. *You retain some shred of sanity by power stolen from me, and you think that is a victory?*

I barely saw the blur of motion as the monster lazily flicked its tail. Thirty serpentine paces of plated muscle rolled in an easy arc, curling forward around the mountain of gold, around the monster's body, and the tapered end of it whipped toward me. It hit me like a battering ram, crushing my right elbow against my ribs and flinging me across the hard stone floor. I landed hard and scraped across rough stone.

I started to struggle to my feet but a drake leaped from the darkness and landed with all four talons on my back. I slammed hard against the stone again, breath driven from my lungs. I wheezed a cough and clung desperately to the tiny fragment of my mind I still controlled.

The monster laughed again. It brought that terrible head close to me until I could feel the puffing heat of its breath, and it spoke into my agony. *You are a diverting puzzle,* it said. *And you are useful bait. But do not dare imagine you are any more than a plaything. You will be food for my drakes before three moons have set.*

"Why?" I asked. The word sounded shrill in my own head. "Why do you want me at all?"

The head rolled to one side. A flash of curiosity from the monster broke across my mind like a wave off the sea. *You don't know? Because you stole from me. No one steals from me and lives.*

I frowned. I turned my eyes back to the mountain of treasure and shook my head. "I have...I've stolen nothing from you."

The monster reared until it towered above me. Even the vastness of the cavern seemed strained by the dragon's immensity. It roared until the very air grew heavy with the sound. Then it slammed down hard enough I could feel the shock of it through the stone, and with no warning at all it burst the bubble of sanity I'd built within my mind.

But there was no pain. There was no screaming fury. There was just a moment's perfect clarity as it seized my thoughts. My perspective shifted as the monster dragged my awareness up and out of my body. I'd done the same once before, when I was still new to the wizard's sight, and now as then I hung some distance above my body and looked down on me.

I did not burn with the bright red light of other men. I did not glow noonday bright, like the wizards I'd seen. There was a thread of red, a cocoon of pure white light, but the power of my life was tainted, dimmed, by a bed of absolute blackness that suffused me. All three energies washed together, roiled, and left me cloudy and indistinct—but also unique, unlike any power I had ever seen.

And then the vision vanished. I fell into my mind again, into my body, and the monster was barely there at all. Instead I felt the full weight of my fear, the vast inventory of my injuries, starving hunger and burning thirst—all the angry complaints of a body dragged far beyond its limits. And over it all, I felt a devastating understanding.

"Vechernyvetr," I thought. The black dragon that had spared my life and stretched that blackness behind my soul.

He belongs to me, the monster said, sparing my mind by its own restraint. I had no strength left to hold it off. *By whatever trickery you have stolen his power, you have stolen it from me. Better for you if you had stolen more, for I can snuff you out like a pale ember.*

The monster turned away from me, its enormous tail flicking casually through the air above me with force enough to raze a city's walls. It climbed back to the top of its hoard, turned once in place, and settled down almost like a cat. It ended with its head resting on a spill of silver coins just above the stone floor and fixed baleful eyes on me.

But you will make poor bait if you are dead, it said. *So rest. And heal. I have use for you yet.*

I heard a beating of wings, felt the blast of air, and then a nightmare swarm of dragons came to tend to my needs.

5. In the Dragon's Lair

There was no real sense of time in the dragon's lair. I felt hunger and thirst and exhaustion in waves, and none of them was ever satisfied. The dragons brought me meat too charred to recognize, and I devoured it despite the tooth-marks and the dirt. They allowed me to leave my hole to drink from the pool that tasted like sulfur and ash. Apart from that they kept me in my cage and under watch.

At first I tried my best to sleep—too exhausted to fight them by any other means—but I could scarcely rest in the heart of such a den of monsters. They scraped and thumped. They hissed and roared. Fire blasted and gold spilled. From time to time an adult dragon would dive into the pool with a screaming splash that sent heated water spilling all the way to my prison. Then the water would steam and hiss while the dragon rumbled a purr loud enough to shake the stone floor.

It was a place of constant motion, an endless battle of primal forces, and every moment of it a stark reminder how small I was. Even the drakes were larger than me, fast and strong and fierce. The adult dragons could have carried me in one talon, and the huge red monster loomed over it all like a mountain.

That monster was the worst. The rest of the beasts ignored me, even when they served me, but any time I fell beneath the monster's eyes I could feel its attention on me. It washed into my mind from time to time, too, pouring hot and slow like molten iron, pooling behind my thoughts and memories. It tore me from my dreams, it shattered my careful exercises, it always came without warning. Every time I had to fight to keep from screaming. I had to fight to keep my sanity.

It spoke to me too. It taunted me. *Such a pretty girl*, it said, the first time it ripped me from uneasy rest. *I have seen that girl somewhere before.*

I only lay on my side on the cold stone, eyes straining wide and heart hammering, and fought to raise my defenses. While I did, the monster washed among my memories. I saw Isabelle again as I'd seen her in my dream, begging me to come back home. That memory dissolved, replaced with one of her riding with me out to the ruined fortress, telling me about her lands. And then one of her walking with me in her father's garden. Of her listening in fascination as I tried to describe life at the Academy. Of her waiting, bold and beautiful, outside the door to the king's study on the day we first met.

Those memories crashed against my will, bright and clear, more precious to me than all the treasure in the monster's hoard. I wanted to wrap them around me and get lost in them, but I could feel the writhing thread of the monster's malicious curiosity as it dredged them up, one after the other. It was looking for her. It was studying her.

So I fought my favorite memories. I forced them away along with the dragon's presence in my head. It took every last gasp of determination, but in the end I won the battle. I built my corner of careful, empty control and watched the memory fade away like a dream. Then I blinked my eyes clear and rose to stare up at the monster.

It rolled its shoulders, acres of leather wing rustling uneasily, and then it turned its head away. *I can find her when I need her*, it said.

Before I could answer, it lashed out at me. With nothing but its will, striking only in my head, it buried me beneath an agony as bright and hot as forgefire. I screamed and screamed and screamed.

Some time later I felt its attention come pouring over me while I was washing my face in the bitter pool. This time I was better prepared, and I raised my defenses quickly. I knelt there, unmoving, waiting for the attack to begin, but for a long time nothing happened. The monster hung dark and heavy in the back of my mind, but it made no other move.

At last I growled deep in my throat. *"What do you want of me?"*

Only what is mine.

I started to rise, to turn and face the monster, but it hit me with a stab of perfect agony in the back of my left knee, and I fell hard to the stone floor. The first pain began to fade, but another stabbed down just beneath my left shoulder blade, as though someone had pinned me to the earth with a broadhead spear. Behind that came pain in the arch of my right foot, then stabbing sharp across my throat. Blackness hovered before my eyes, but I never passed out.

The pain went on and on while the monster toyed with me, and behind all the agony I felt its interested curiosity. It was amused, and patient, and pleased.

When at last the monster tired of me, I crawled back to my hole. I dragged the stone back over its top and lay broken in the darkness. In time exhaustion overwhelmed the lingering pain, but I held sleep at bay. I pressed myself up into a crouch and carefully erected the walls within my mind.

It was easier without the monster hammering at them. Weariness slowed me, but I could not afford to sleep. I could not maintain my concentration asleep, and after the monster's meticulous torture I dared not let it have complete control. I mastered my fragile emotions. I mastered my body's pain and my mind's exhaustion. I mastered the hunger and the sapping sick warmth of this place. I closed my eyes in the darkness and focused on my breath.

And then it was there again. A whimper escaped me as I felt another presence in my head. I tried to lash out at it, throwing every shred of my will at the intrusion, but all I got for my effort was a flash of amused surprise and condescending pity. Then a voice of stinging authority shouted, *Get up!*

I frowned. Without really meaning to, I slipped into my wizard's sight and flexed invisible muscles. The stone door to my prison drifted aside. I felt a tearing pain in my legs and back, but it was nothing against the agony the monster had thrown at me before.

Get up! the voice commanded again, and I obeyed. I rose and heaved myself up out of the pit. A handful of drakes turned baleful eyes my way and began moving lazily toward me. A few always followed me like old retainers whenever I left my cage. I spotted the gold dragon too, banking out of its high, gliding halo to swoop down closer. That one seemed to keep a careful watch on me.

But this time I had no more idea what I was up to than my watchers did. I moved slowly, my body still protesting at the pain it had recently endured, but I moved unstoppably across the smooth stone toward the wide pool. Out of habit I knelt down at the pool's edge, cupped a hand to the acrid water and raised it to my lips. Then I heaved a great breath, and some force shoved me hard from behind.

No, no force outside. My own legs, my own strength hurled me forward into the water, and I hit its surface like one of the fiery adults. I half expected to feel the heat and hear the angry boiling hiss of the water, but there was only cold darkness. I looked with my wizard's sight and saw the deep, uneven bowl of earth cupping the billowing sheets of water. An impulse drew my eyes toward the outer wall, tracing down and down, deep beneath the surface, searching for some seam, some outlet, some escape I hadn't found before, but there was none.

And then that same force that had flooded my mind took control again. It used my will, reached out through my wizard's sight, and grabbed several threads of air from the cavern above. It wrapped them around me like a cloak. I took a breath of captured air, then that other will pressed out and down against the water, and I sped to the surface like a piece of cork. I just had time to prepare myself before I was thrown out of the water. I landed on the hard stone, stumbled once, then caught myself and turned.

The drakes were there—that handful that had come to watch over me, and dozens more. They gathered around me as they had that first night, and the dragons screamed on the wing above me. The gold adult flashed past just above my head, hissing like an angry snake. The huge red monster, too, had turned to watch, to stare. Its massive head hung low over the pool, barely a pace away from where I stood, eyes fixed hard on the depths. Fire boiled in the back of its throat, and when the monster roared, every beast in the cavern took up its cry.

I could feel their rage, their hatred for me, but not one among them looked my way. They all stared at the water. For a moment I froze, overwhelmed by my own curiosity, but then I heard the voice one more time. *Go! Stupid human. Move now, Daven!*

And once again the thing took control of me. I had a moment's understanding, in the tiny part of my mind still left to me. A moment's recognition. The voice was not the monster's. Not *that* monster's anyway. It was another's. And now it threw me into a reckless sprint, straight at the hard stone wall of the cavern. Fear bubbled up in my chest, but it could not reach me in my cocoon of calm.

A thousand filaments of air still wrapped me head to toe, and that other mind flexed my will to reshape them at every footfall into cushions beneath my feet. I went a dozen paces over hard stone without making a sound, and then as I reached the wall the air unraveled around me. Though I did not guide it, I saw the shape of the plan one heartbeat before I struck the wall. My will stretched out toward the numberless grains of earth energy that combined to make a mountain of solid stone.

I saw how easy it would be to exert authority over them, to make them bend and spread and wash around me just like water. I imagined myself diving through a mountainside as easily as I had dived into the cooling pool, swimming through the earth and out to safety. But in my wizard's sight I could see three hundred paces of earth and stone between the cavern and open air. And I knew what the dragons did not—I knew the physical cost of altering that much reality. I hadn't enough strength to shift one pace of earth around me, let alone a whole mountainside.

But the presence in my mind had full control. I scrabbled frantically to stop it, to extend the barriers of my concentration, to stop my churning feet, to catch a breath. I panicked inside my own head, and it gained me nothing. The dragon threw my body at the stone wall, through the stone wall, *into* the stone wall.

I felt pain like a thunderclap in every inch of my body. It was the weight of a mountain pressing down on me from all directions and my body screamed in agony. Darkness hit my mind like a hammer, and ringing through it I felt a sudden flash of surprise. And then annoyance. And then a fire bubbling up through my stomach and catching in my heart.

I felt heat like a geyser blast upward into my mind, out through my limbs, and suddenly the darkness was gone. Suddenly the pain was gone. Not just the weight of the mountain, but the agony of days of torture, the fatigue and hunger and fear. All of it evaporated beneath that blazing heat, energy and power raging through me, and then I began to move again.

I looked out through the mountain and saw the Chaos blackness waiting for me there. No...not blackness. I'd called it emptiness before, the void in reality that marked a dragon's presence, but now that I had tasted of its power, I understood. I recognized it. The thing was darker than reality, stronger than eternity, the perfect endless authority, and everything else went pale around it.

There were more like it behind me—a great and terrible swarm of them—but this one was mine. I grinned a cruel snarl and sprinted through a mountainside as though it were open air. I planted one foot inside the mountain, and the next on nothing, and ran on over both of them like crossing the village green.

A cliff fell away beneath me, a hundred paces down to a stony dell, and beyond that a sun-seared mountain range stretched out toward the sea. But there in the air before me was the black dragon Vechernyvetr. I could feel him in my mind, could feel the bond we'd made between us, and the night-black flood of power he was pouring into me, through me, as I took another step on empty nothing and flung myself into a leap over the great depth to land right at the base of his neck.

"You came for me!" I screamed in my mind, even as the dragon beat its huge wings and hurtled itself away and down. *"You've saved my life again. That monster—"*

Pazyarev, the dragon said, bitter in the back of my head. *He is powerful. And cruel.*

"Not just one. He has an army." I twisted in place, clinging tightly to the dragon's neck while I tried to orient myself. I found the narrow cave high on the mountainside a moment before a pair of dark green dragons shot through on the wing. They turned opposite directions, moving fast, and it took only a moment before one of them caught sight of us.

Instead of giving chase, it banked away, but a moment later a roar like an earthquake shook the mountain beneath me. Then the cave mouth erupted, spewing dragons like hornets from a hive. The whole great swarm came out, speeding toward us like arrows.

"An army," I thought again, watching in awe as they flew in something resembling a military formation. Vechernyvetr beat his huge wings, neck outstretched and flashing over the earth faster than any racehorse, but the monster's swarm streamed after us. *"They obey it. All of them."*

No, Vechernyvetr said. *They are* him. *Pazyarev is an elder legend, one of the strongest among dragons. He has a swarm of nearly two thousand bodies.*

I barely listened. My attention was on the creatures trailing us. Some of them were larger than Vechernyvetr. Some of them were catching up. I should have been afraid, but I could still feel the fire of the dragon's power blazing through me, and it burned fear for fuel. Instead of worry I felt anger and exhilaration. I focused on the dragon closest on our heels, the smallish green that had first spotted us, trailing maybe a quarter mile behind us and closing fast.

My lips peeled back. I let go of Vechernyvetr's neck with one hand and pointed it toward the green. I remembered a stone I had thrown in the Teelevon. I had no cobblestones here, but I did not need one. The dragon power was raw reality. I narrowed my eyes and looked out through the wizard's sight.

I could not hurt them with a wizard's magic. Magic was man's construct, and it drowned against the depthless infinity of a dragon's nature. But now I had that nature in my hands. I tapped into the rush of power, stretched out my will, and summoned a bolt of pure earth energy in the air between us. I saw the dragon's surprise, saw it swerve in shock, falter mid-flight, but it was coming on fast and it took no more than a thought for me to send my bolt hurling toward it.

I shaped it as it flew. A shapeless ball stretched into a spear-tipped blade that plunged into the beast just left of its breastbone and tore out the back, black with blood. The monster had half a mile to fall, but my attention was already roving, searching for another. I saw the gold beast that had watched me so closely, and I set my jaw.

"Go slower, Vechernyvetr. I will answer for them."

I admire your hunger, he answered. *But you are a fool. You slew one. Pazyarev will throw a thousand against us and suffer us a fate far worse than death.*

"Let him try," I growled. *"He has never seen anything like me before."* My spear trailed along behind us half a mile back. I had trouble controlling it any farther away than that, and the dragons seemed to know it. The fastest of them hung just far enough back that I couldn't touch them.

I grinned. With a thought I broke the paces-long spear into half a dozen splinters. They drifted apart into a loose line at the full extent of my reach. I watched the chasing dragons as they shifted and bobbed, trying to keep wary eyes on Vechernyvetr and on the strange structures hovering so much closer to them.

I raised the spearheads up, all at once, maybe a pace higher than the formation of dragon. I frowned, weighing them in my mind, then went another pace higher still. Then

I gave them a shove back, as far as I could reach, and I released my will.

In an instant, six sorcerous constructs became simply six sharp-edged stones hanging half a mile above the earth. Momentum and affinity flung them like catapult shots into the formation of dragons, and I imagined the sick wet *thud*s as four of the six struck home. Four adult dragons were ripped from the air, flapping and spinning and falling away toward the surf.

I reached for the power again, manifesting earth in bolts like arrows of solid steel. I made a score of them at once and flung them as I had the stones, and though I saw no dragon fall, I heard the roars of anger and pain as my weapons struck home. I threw another volley and another volley, and on the third I saw a red plunge to earth. Another had to break away and curl back toward the lair. I couldn't fell the yellow, though. My eyes fixed hard on that one, and I tried another volley, another, but it always dodged away.

"*Go back!*" I screamed. He tried to object, but I ignored him. "*I am a match for them all. Pazyarev has a debt to pay.*" I forgot the little arrows and instead fashioned myself a blade. I had done something like this before, calling up dusty earth and shaping it by the strength of my will, but now I made it of nothing but power. It was blacker than obsidian, harder than steel and as light as the wind within my fingers. I made another, too, a perfect match, and released the dragon's neck to hold a sword in each hand. "*I will carve them from the sky.*"

You will burn yourself to ash, Vechernyvetr said. *It is good to thirst for blood, but you must know when and where to strike.*

"*Here and now,*" I said. The swords felt hungry in my hands, perfect weapons for this fight, and I could already imagine the taste of the dragons' blood on the air. "*In violence and blood. Take me back to them.*"

For a moment Vechernyvetr said nothing. He did not slow. If anything, he strained harder beneath me. Then he banked right, flashing through a wide, low pass, and broke out over the arid plains of the Southern Ardain. I saw the world of men spread out below me, a swarm of dragons hard on my heels, and I imagined the glory of slaughtering such a force where men might actually see.

I rose up, balancing on my toes, and bent my knees. The cloud of Pazyarev's dragons was still nearly half a mile behind us, but I felt an incredible urge to jump, to throw myself at them, and somehow the whole distance between us seemed trivial. So, too, the hard earth far below. I shifted in place, trying to find the right footing, and Vechernyvetr screamed in my head, *What are you intending?*

"If you will not take me to them, I will go without you."

You do not have the strength. You will fall. One way or another, you will fall.

I laughed into the rushing wind. *"What have I to fear from earth or wind? I am no more concerned with the fall than with the nightmare monsters on our heels. In all the world, I want only to rend their hides and spill their blood."*

Still so small, he said. *And still so stupid. You're weak as a worm.*

I wanted to laugh again, but I felt him reach through my mind again as he'd done before. My fingers opened and I watched the perfect Chaos blades fall away through the empty air. My body twisted in place. My knees bent, and I was distantly aware that they screamed in agony. That they had no strength left.

The dragon drove me forward, back to the base of its neck, and flung my arms up to grip his scales tight. There, too, I noticed the protesting muscles in my shoulders. My head was throbbing. My body ached. I could no more *feel* the pain than I had the weight of the mountain crushing me.

The searing fire of the dragon's power obliterated it, but in that moment I became aware of it. The dragon caused me to hook my knees beneath the joints of his wings, until I was stretched out as securely as I could have been anywhere on his back, and then he said, *You will not like this.*

Even drunk on the dragon's power, I had felt enough in the last few moments to guess what was coming. I had no time to brace myself, though. I could not have braced myself against this. In an instant, between one beat of those great wings and the next, the power went away.

The fire died, and with it went my strength. My pain returned. My weariness and weakness and everything that had been done to me. I still felt the thirst for blood, the animal fury calling me to lash out at the ones that had hurt me, but without the buffeting buffer of the dragon's power, I saw it for the frantic and senseless thing it was.

Pain. I had felt the pain right away, but it took time for my mind to process it. It hit me again, some seconds later, like a wave crashing down and crashing down and crashing down. I kept expecting it to end, and it kept coming harder. It crushed my breastbone to my spine. It twisted at the bones of my arms and legs. It thrummed inside my skull and crackled along my skin. I gasped. I grunted. And then I cried. I screamed myself breathless in the rushing wind, and still the pain grew harder and harder and harder.

And then I slipped. Between one moment and the next, I lost my grip. I slipped down the dragon's back and spun sideways for a moment before slamming my head hard against the long, powerful arm supporting the dragon's left wing. Lights flashed behind my eyes, and I washed up and down and head over heels. I tumbled along the dragon's body as though I were suspended in breakers, churning with the current. I dropped a short distance then cracked my right side hard against a talon. It stopped me for a moment, and then I fell into open air.

I heard the dragon shouting curses in my head. I felt the grinding pain and wrenching stop as its talons closed hard around me. I felt a blast of flame that singed my whole side. Then destruction and darkness and exhaustion buried me, and words I could not quite hear chased me to my grave.

6. What Dragons Know

I woke again on hard, cold stone, the taste of sulfur and
stale water in the air. Darkness, too, stained gray by the spill
of sunlight through a gap in a distant wall. I felt a moment's
crushing despair, remembering the dream of my escape. I
tried to heave myself to my feet, to go for a drink, but my
muscles screamed protest, and I didn't make it off the
ground.

Frail human body, a voice boomed in my mind. I felt its
sneering contempt...and still I breathed a happy sigh of relief.

"Vechernyvetr," I thought. *"You are real."*

More real than you. He landed on the floor before me, resolving like a darker shadow from the gray light. *Two nights
beneath the silver moon and still you groan like a child.*

"Our bodies do not heal like yours," I thought. I tried to sit
up, to meet his eyes, but I could not even do that. I ached
all over.

Blistering red light tinted the darkness as fire began to
roil in the back of the dragon's maw. He made a sound, too,
an avalanche rumble like the growl of an angry dog.

Be still and let your body mend, he snapped. *Day and night you
sear within my mind like an unhealing wound.*

"You feel my pain?" I asked. And then the things he'd said
before struck home. *"Two moons? I've been here days? And all
the dragons hunting us—"*

82

Are gone, he said. I felt his weary calm within my mind, and it eclipsed my sudden fear. *So many fell, they would not chase me past the edge of Pazyarev's territory.*

"Pazyarev," I said, tasting the name. And then I remembered our mad flight, soaring miles over the earth, past trackless mountains and well out over the southern plains. I frowned. *"Just...where is his territory?"*

The dragon knew no names of human cities, nor the roads or river names that defined our borders, but he showed me more clearly than any words would have. He drew an image within my mind, a manufactured memory more detailed than any map.

From high above and far away, I saw the green lands around Tirah in the heart of the fertile Ardain. I saw the hair-thin line of the river Teel and the lands around Isabelle's home. I saw the dusty fields to the south and the impassable mountains to the west, towering over the stormy sea. I saw the sheltered cove beneath the city of Whitefalls that no army could ever take. I saw a third of the continent, hundreds and hundreds of miles square. I waited for him to move the image closer, to define Pazyarev's territory within it.

Instead, he said, *Here. These lands belong to him. We are outside his domain now, in a territory all my own.* The image swam in my mind, spinning dizzily, and showed me the smaller range of worn-down mountains that sprawled along the barren eastern coast. Now he moved in, narrowing the field of view to one mountainside of rough rockfalls and scrawny trees. I saw perhaps two miles square, of little more than dry, cracked stone, and felt the vast imbalance between Vechernyvetr and the massive broodlord.

"He is hunting you," I thought.

I know. He has been calling me back.

"How?"

For a long time, Vechernyvetr gave no answer. I felt a great emptiness from him, something like fear. Something like despair. And in answer to that helplessness, I felt a blind, furious rage. *I once belonged to his brood*, the dragon said.

I thought, *"He told me that. But why? And what does it mean?"*

Again he paused. Then he drew away. *You do not know what dragons know*, he said. *I can scarce explain it*. I felt him bank the emotions burning in the back of my mind, until only the anger remained. *You need food. I will go and fetch some. You should sleep and heal.*

"But—"

In time, he said. *In time. But not while all your agony is buzzing in my head like a summer storm.*

Frustration flared up in my heart, then echoed back much magnified from the dragon. He hit me with his will, poured pressure on my soul, and all my desperation could barely hold him for a heartbeat. Then he washed me away in darkness and left my body resting.

Vechernyvetr's lair was not the fearsome prison I'd found beneath the monstrous Pazyarev's control. It was a large cave, but only just high enough for Vechernyvetr to walk beneath its dark ceiling. It had a cooling pool, too, but his was barely three paces across and perhaps a foot deep at its center. The cave floor opened through a wide fissure onto a broad sun-baked ledge, and the breeze that sometimes rustled in tasted like pine and winter frost.

There was a wide spill of gold and silver treasures against the back wall—easily enough to drape a man in luxury for life—but compared to the great flowing mountain of riches in Pazyarev's lair, it seemed a sad pittance.

And then there was no brood, no army of retainer drakes. There was just Vechernyvetr alone. During the day, most days, Vechernyvetr slept curled atop his gold like a beggar on a threadbare blanket. I could feel his shame long before I understood it.

Most nights he would go hunting. I could lie upon the stone within the lair and feel the wind beneath the dragon's wings, taste the hunger and rage, feel the thrill of every kill. I could feel, too, the itching fear. The resentment. It boiled and burned and ground him down. And it all stemmed from his memory of the broodlord Pazyarev.

It took me three days to overcome the crushing weakness that followed my escape from Pazyarev's lair. For those three days I could barely hold consciousness for more than minutes at a time. I drank acrid water from Vechernvetr's pool and ate the meat he brought me, but mostly I slept.

In time that weakness passed. Far faster than it should have, perhaps, because of the dragon power that drove me. But even when I could retain awareness, I was not much a man. Vechernyvetr's presence was too strong in my mind. I felt his sensations more than my own.

When I tried to move, my limbs felt awkward—clumsy and weak against the memory of the dragon's great power. When I tried to think, my attention always drifted back to whatever held the dragon's interest. A dozen times I tried to put myself through the wizard's exercises to still my mind, and always I was interrupted by the graceful motion of a doe in full flight, or the sudden sharp scent of soot on the air. I never left the lair, but still wherever the dragon went, he carried me with him.

He spoke with me, though, in the border hours between day and night. On the fourth day he found me awake and waiting when he returned. I was sitting just inside the cave mouth, staring west over trees and rugged hills to the distant plains of the Ardain. The dragon landed awkwardly on three legs, holding up the fourth to protect a wild pig speared on a talon as long as my arm. He took three hopping steps,

wings beating wildly, then settled to a trot back toward me.
He dropped the pig like a prize at my feet.

"*Dinner?*" I asked.

For you, he said. *I had my prey with life still in it. Tastier that way.*

I nodded. For a moment I wished I didn't understand.
But I could remember the thrill of the hunt, the pleasure
he'd taken devouring a buck still whole. Mostly whole. I
wanted to shudder at the memory, but the dragon was reliving it too, and his quiet satisfaction overwhelmed any response of mine.

I took a slow breath, gathering my courage. Then I asked
the question that had been nagging at me in whatever
awareness I'd had for days. "*I'm your broodling, aren't I? I'm like the drakes.*"

That massive head swung to me, faster than should have
been possible, and eyes like cauldrons narrowed. *We should
not speak of this.* His displeasure rumbled in my head.

"*I do not know what dragons know,*" I thought. "*But you can
tell me. And perhaps I suspect more than most men could. Pazyarev is
not the master of that swarm of dragons. He is the swarm. The drakes
and winged adults are not...they're not his servants. They're part of
him.*"

That is astute, he said. *For a human mind.* He blew a puff of
flame and charred the pig's hide to a cinder. Then he slithered past me into the depths of the lair. *But there is so much
more than that—*

"*I know,*" I thought. "*There had to be. Because drakes are not
born into that slavery. They're...conquered. Overwhelmed.*"

How can you know this?

"*They don't match,*" I thought. I felt his puzzlement and
rushed to answer it. "*The dragons in his brood don't look like siblings. Their colors, their shapes and sizes...they're all different, as
though he gathered them from everywhere.*"

A feeling of shock washed over me. And then laughter tolling in my head like an immense bell. *They do not match*, he scoffed. *Such is frail human reason.*

I frowned. *"I'm wrong?"*

You're right. I heard his snort in the cavern behind me, and felt his irritation. *You're right, but for all the wrong reasons.*

I grinned, satisfied at that. *"I knew it! And the ones that serve Pazyarev are like his trophies."*

No. My mind rang with the beast's disdain. *Not trophies. They are his power.*

"Power?"

His authority. His dominion. His reach.

I thought of the territory Vechernyvetr had shown me. I thought of the swarm of dragons that had attended upon the monster. I thought of its great hoard of gold. I swallowed. *"Which comes first?"*

I do not understand.

"There are three measures of a dragon's power. No, four." I felt a prickling in the back of my head, discomfort and irritation. He did not want to speak of these things, but my curiosity compelled me. I rose and entered the cave so I could meet his eyes across the still pool. *"Territory,"* I thought. *"And the brood. And the gold hoard."*

His mouth fell open in a hiss, his long, sharp teeth flashing white within the darkness. Shame and vulnerability bubbled up hot in my head, and I found myself hissing, too. I shook my head. I took a slow breath and steeled a corner of my mind until my thoughts cleared, and then I nodded to the gold again.

"That is your power, too."

For a long time he said nothing. He didn't move. His gaze burned hot and his breath rasped, but I did not back down. He pressed at my mind, too, but I refused to relent.

For the first time in days I felt human again, and I would not give up.

At last he backed down. *And the fourth?* he asked. *You said there was a fourth.*

I nodded to him. "*Your size. In men, that one is easy. We grow with time, gradually and steadily, and the larger we are, the stronger.*"

As simple as that? he asked, and there was mockery in his tone.

I nodded instantly, but then felt doubt. The dragon relaxed some, his long tail rolling out and wrapping lazily around him, then he settled to the floor. *Strong men have power*, he said at last. *You take much power from your strength. But women in your world have power, too.*

"*Well, we protect them out of need—*"

He laughed and laughed. Without forming a word he showed me the sense by which he'd meant power, a memory of Isabelle and the feel of her soft skin beneath my fingertips, and a blush began to burn in my cheeks. He went on as though I hadn't interrupted.

And there are wizards. Wizards greater than you who take power from their understanding, from their clarity of vision. And kings who take their power from their blood. And rich men buy their power with their gold.

I nodded understanding. "*Of course. You're right. We are at least as complicated—*"

Not by half, the dragon said. *But nothing is so simple as it seems. A dragon does not grow in time, like man. We grow by spilling royal blood and devouring the strong. We grow by stealing human wealth and by shattering understanding. And the reward for all of this is power. It's control. It's dominion over reality.*

"*Like wizards—*" I began to say, but he cut me off with a snarl that burned in the dark cavern.

Not like wizards at all, he said. *I thought you, among them all, would understand. Wizards exercise dominion over nothing. Over the gossamer shades of illusion men call real. But it is daydream and fancy. Dragons are reality. Power is reality. Chaos is reality. And only we can tame it, control it, command it.*

"We," I thought. "The dragons. And me."

And you, he said in agreement. *I have never known it done before. Men should not know what dragons know. Your kind stains the world enough at six removes.*

"I gained it from you," I thought. "When we bonded on that mountainside. You gave me a power wizards don't even dream of." He said nothing. I could feel his uneasiness again, gnawing at the back of my head. I pushed it away. "You told me you could not kill me. You wanted to, but you could not. I think I understand."

Do not confuse one insight with understanding, he said. He pushed arrogance at me, condescending with all his might, but I could feel his fear behind it. I smiled in sympathy.

"I became your brood," I said. "Not your conquest. Not your prey. Still your enemy, but now a part of you. You could no more easily kill me than I could cut off my own hand."

It can be done, he said. *Easily enough, at that.*

"And you tried your best," I thought. "But would you have, if you had understood? Would you have tried to destroy me, or would you have tried to overwhelm me?"

I braced myself. Three measured breaths and every ounce of concentration while I erected defenses in my mind. It took a heartbeat longer than I'd expected, but then he lashed out at me. He struck at my mind with as much force as I'd ever felt from him, and it was enough to blur my vision and drop me to my knees, but I did not give up.

And then it passed. It ebbed away, leaving me gasping and my head throbbing, but still entirely myself. I could feel the echoes of my own pain from him as well, and I nodded slowly.

"You should have tried back then," I thought. "You could have done it, then. When I was senseless on the rocks outside the cave. I've learned to shield my mind from you, and from Pazyarev's harsh attacks. I could not have held you off back then."

Perhaps, he said. He sounded tired.

"I used to think it was an exchange," I thought. *"I used to think you gave me dragon power, and I gave you man power. Whatever that might be. But I think it was not so much like that at all. I think I just became like a dragon. I became part of that...that...."*

Power, the dragon said. *We are living power.*

"I can't imagine what I gave you in return."

Pain. And fear. And weakness. Loneliness.

"*Humanity,*" I thought, and my mouth twisted in a bitter smile.

He chuckled in my mind. *You gave me more than that,* he said at last. *You gave me light.*

"*What light?*" I asked.

Freedom. Hope. He shifted his great bulk, and turned his head away. *You have forgotten I belonged to Pazyarev.*

"I haven't," I thought in answer. *"I just hadn't gotten to that yet."*

He chuckled again. *He conquered me during another swarm. Some other time now lost to time. But just at the end, as the fires were waning. I'd gained a broodmate and a clutch of my own. I'd gained much wealth and power. And then Pazyarev turned his eyes on me. He snuffed me out, but not before he tore my clutch to shreds.*

I felt a stab of sympathy, hot like ice in the pit of my stomach. "*I'm sorry—*"

It does not matter. Dead or slaves to Pazyarev's will, it makes no difference. He growled and closed his eyes. *And then I fell into darkness. Then I belonged to him, and I know nothing of the years between. I know he must have slept—we must have slept—because this world is new and different and not yet burned.*

He trailed off, and in the corner of my mind I felt an unsettling anticipation of the destruction still to come. I shook my head and tried to catch his attention. *"What happened next? How did you break free?"*

Did I? he asked, repeating me. He snorted. *I know nothing but the nothingness while under his control. And then I woke upon a strange mountainside, in a strange world, with a strange little man all stained with blood and stretched out like a corpse beneath my nose.*

"I set you free?"

Somehow, he said. *I do not know. It never has been done. There's never been a man with power like yours. There's never been a broodling set free from his broodlord. We did not know it could be done.*

"So Pazyarev is hunting you."

And you, he said. *He'll know it now. He thought you were some pet I'd found, some toy. Perhaps a friend.* Vechernyvetr laughed at that. *But he has seen you carve his dragons from the sky. He has seen you thrum with borrowed Chaos like a broodlord on the wing. He won't forget you now.*

"That wasn't me," I thought. *"I...borrowed Chaos? That's what that was?"* I remembered the thrill of it. The white-hot power, the intoxicating control. I remembered too the rabid madness that had seized the reins. And the pain that had come after.

Vechernyvetr hissed his displeasure. *I showed you how,* he said. *But you have much to learn to control it.*

"I can control that?" I thought, disbelieving. *"It made me bloodthirsty. Some kind of monster."*

I felt a flash of confusion. *That is Chaos power,* he said. *That is the point. You'll learn to fear it enough that you do not borrow quite so much. You'll learn to control your own hunger, so you do not pay for days and days. But no, you cannot control the power itself. It is violence and blood. It's destruction and dominion. There's nothing else.*

"But what of wisdom and restraint?" I asked, remembering long hours in crowded lecture halls. *"What of clarity and understanding?"*

They are but ways to live with weakness, Vechernyvetr answered. *They are meaningless when you have access to true power.*

"*Some might say they are all that give the power meaning,*" I suggested. "*They may guide how we use the power—*"

He raised his head so I could see his yawn, then rolled one huge eye to look back at me. *There is no meaning in this conversation,* he said. *There is no choice. Chaos power does not answer your discretion. And no other power will survive the days to come.*

I felt the finality in his words, but I could not let it end there. "*That's not enough,*" I thought. "*That's not enough for me. I'm not a monster. I do not want to be a monster.*"

Then perhaps you should have died the first time you faced me. He yawned again, then tucked his head beneath a wing. *It matters not. You'll have opportunities enough.*

After that, he would not answer me. Moments later I felt the shift in the back of my mind, and shortly after that he began to snore. I left him there and went back to watch the rest of the sunrise over the lands of men.

I was cold. Even this far south, the winter had its grip upon the mountains. But there was a chill deeper than anything the weather could offer. I'd suspected it before, in the broodlord's lair. I'd been considering it for days now, but it chilled me to the bone to know Vechernyvetr could have subsumed me. If he'd acted in the right time, in the right way, I might be nothing more than a vessel for his wrath.

But that was past. That chance was gone from him. The elder legend, though...he'd been able to touch my mind as well. He'd crushed me more than once. Was it my bond with Vechernyvetr that made me vulnerable to Pazyarev, too? Could *he* have subsumed me? Or was I safe from all but Vechernyvetr? I had to hope that was true or pray the elder legend never found me alive.

I shivered in the cold and felt very, very small.

And yet...I'd lived. Pazyarev had held me in his lair, and I'd escaped alive. I thought back on what Vechernyvetr had told me, and I reached out with my will. I'd tried before to work magic with idle air and it had done nothing for me, but now I remembered the gust of wind I'd summoned to cloak me in the broodlord's cooling pool. I remembered bolts of earth wrought from nothing but my will. Vechernyvetr had called it borrowing Chaos.

I focused my attention and took on my wizard's sight. I instinctively scanned the land beneath me, the skies above, but I saw nothing more with my that second sight than I would have expected: the weight of the earth, the play of the wind, the slow, quiet throb of life in the forested hillside.

But beneath it all was a quiet thrum, an ancient, inky darkness that stretched forever. I remembered a time when the intricate lines of reality's energies and power had seemed enormous and complex, but now they looked no more substantial than a gossamer film draped over the Chaos. All the world, all of reality, as thin as a spider's web. And beneath it was the power that had freed me from the broodlord's clutches.

I remembered the madness. I remembered my own objections, just moments ago, and I had no intention to become a part of that Chaos power. But perhaps I could borrow. Just a bit. Just enough to survive. I could see the way of it. I stretched out my will—not to the real world around me, but to that steel-hard spot of darkness deep inside my own heart. I touched it, and I felt the shuddering turbulence of that power.

Another shiver shook me, and the idea sprang clear into my mind. I thought of fire warm on the baron's hearthstone. I thought of the sharp red shape of its underlying energy. I stretched out a hand to the stone ledge outside the dragon's lair, and touched the vivid darkness in my heart.

Fire, perfect fire, came to my call. I half expected another avalanche of maddening power, an explosion of flame to drive me from my feet. Instead I felt only a quiet hum, a nervous thrill of excitement, and a well-tamed hearthfire glowed on barren earth.

And it was real. I felt its warmth. I sank down beside it and extended both hands, and soon the winter's chill fell away. I sat before my fire and remembered the monster that had tortured me and knew I could survive. I had power.

I was two miles away and a quarter of a mile up when Vechernyvetr woke. I felt his awareness more strongly than I had before. Confusion turned to surprise to fear. He poured his attention toward me and I felt that through the bond. I almost laughed at the intense heat of his anxiety.

I could feel the direction of him, too. I had never done that before. I looked down and down through empty air, and watched with my wizard's sight as the midnight blot of his presence stained reality. He launched himself from the ledge and soared out and around. Down. Away from me. I laughed out loud.

Where are you? he screamed, his rage battering at the back of my mind. *I can feel you. I can find you.*

"*Can you?*" I asked. "*Then why are you so afraid?*"

Because Pazyarev can find you, too. Far below he finished a low sweep over the foothills. I felt the first hint of a suspicion from him, and then he was sweeping up. *Any of his dragons might find you,* he said, *and they would find me. You should not have left the lair.*

I frowned at that. "*Am I your prisoner then? As I was his?*"

He bent his trajectory more directly toward me, but it was still off. That surprised me. He was certainly coming upward now, and he should have seen me hanging there....

Is a child a prisoner in its mother's house? he asked. His irritation tasted sour in the back of my mind. *Is your hand the prisoner of your arm? I only mean to protect you. To teach you.*

I forced a sudden tension from my shoulders, from my jaw. I spun slowly in place, keeping him in sight while he spiraled up and up, closer and closer, but never directly toward me.

"I will not be your broodling," I thought. *"You missed the chance for that."*

No. But you will share my lair. You cannot make one of your own. Powerful as you are, you cannot survive without me—

He drifted by close enough that I could have stretched out a hand and touched his wingtip, but he kept on looking. I laughed out loud, and that long neck spun fast as a striking snake. He looked right at me, and yet still the eyes were not quite focused. They did not stop moving.

I touched the borrowed Chaos and the web of air around me and lifted myself lightly up, another four paces. Then I drifted to the left, watching his eyes, but the beast's furious gaze didn't move. I left him staring at empty air.

This is not a game, he raged within my head. He bellowed, and the sound of it split the still air, but I held my construct and waited for the echoes to die away.

"You can't see me," I said, and I felt a flash of feral fury from him. I moved a little farther away. *"Why?"*

Before he replied, understanding blossomed within him. It washed over his anger like cold water, but did nothing to improve his attitude. He snorted a little puff of flame, then banked and fell back away toward the cave.

Ah, he said. *I see. You are toying with your magic.*

"I am practicing, as you advised me. I am doing things you taught me to do."

Foolish to do it where you might be seen. Ordinary human foolishness.

For a moment more I hung in place, suspended three hundred paces above the bare stone peaks and staring out over all the world. I lay within a cocoon of imaginary air softer than a feather bed and wrapped in the quiet euphoria of the utterly extraordinary.

But curiosity won out. I let myself fall after the dragon, guiding my descent with glances, and I called out in my mind, *"Why can't you see me? Is it the air? It blinds you?"*

Not air, he said at last, grudgingly. *Order. Human reality.*

"This is not reality," I thought. *"This is borrowed Chaos. Like you described."*

Not like I described, he said. *Dragons do not spend our power on constructs. We do not play such games.*

"Perhaps you should," I thought. I stepped out of air and onto the ledge as easily as climbing out of bed. I followed the dragon back into the darkness of its lair, and summoned living flame to hover like a torch over my hand. *"There's power in it. A whole new kind of power in shaping reality—"*

He snorted, and condescension stabbed through at me. *The games wizards play. What have you done with your power?*

I thought of my afternoon, playing with fire, scaling impossible cliffs, and soaring in the sky. I felt him sniffing at my memories. *All the power of your vast imagination, and you do nothing more than a dragon does on its own. I do not need your tricks to fly or make a fire. I do not need your fashioned blade when I have teeth and talons.*

For a long moment I said nothing. Then I nodded slowly. *"I do,"* I thought. *"I have no talons. I have no wings. And I will not be a prisoner."*

Ah. So you can fly and grow a fang, and now you think you can conquer Pazyarev?

"No," I thought. *"I do not want to conquer him. I do not want to rule the world or burn it down, Vechernyvetr. I am not a dragon."*

It matters not what you want. Pazyarev wants you dead now. He will come for you.

"And I can hide from him. I know that now."

All your life? You will wrap yourself in air and never let it go? No. Human patience does not stretch so far.

"I would rather try that fate than spend the rest of my life in this cave."

Ah. I cannot blame you for that, he said. *But we will not be long in this cave. Not with the power you have. Not with the power you bring me. There is a green dame two valleys over. We will go and subsume her, and whatever we can capture of her clutch.*

I felt a queasy sickness at the sensations I felt through his bond. I caught flashes of image, of anticipation, and it reeked with the scent of blood and brimstone. Worse still, I recognized the feeling of elation he felt as he imagined it.

We will take her lair and take her hoard, he went on, oblivious to my disgust. *And that will be just the beginning.*

I could imagine. In my mind's eye I saw a flight of dragons a thousand strong, and Vechernyvetr's black shape at its head. I could see myself standing tall on his shoulders, wind and flame draped around me like a robe, and death within my hand. It was the dragon's daydream, destruction all around us, and it tasted like ash in my mouth.

"I do not want a brood," I thought. "I do not want an army. I do not want a lair. I only want a home among my people. I want to go back to them."

He brought his head down close to me and met my eyes. *I am sorry, Daven, but you cannot have what you want. The dragon-swarm is here. Pazyarev is here. I offer you a chance—*

"But I am not a dragon."

You can be, he said. *Or you can die.*

I took a slow step back and held his gaze. "Is that a threat?" I asked.

It is wisdom and understanding. He turned away, looking bored. *Get some rest. Heal. Your mind is overtaxed.*

I heard the words he fed to me, and still I felt his emotions, too. I felt his secret thoughts. I felt the glory of that dragonflight, and the thrill of victory. I felt the hunger for violence and blood. I felt the certain knowledge that all mankind's silly civilizations would crumble, and the burning animal need to gain as much personal power out of that turmoil as my body would allow.

And deep in my heart, in that tiny of core of darkness that had wrapped me in wind and flame, I felt that it was right. There was power to be had. There was victory in fire.

I tried to fight it. I tried to deny it. But I remembered Pazyarev upon his mountain of gold. I remembered a thousand dragons on the wing, chasing me through the sky. I remembered my weakness and my pathetic, toothless fury. Power was the answer. I needed power.

The dragon was in my mind. I could feel it, but I couldn't fight it. I practiced my old exercises and struggled to raise my defenses against Vechernyvetr's assault. But he was not there. He was biding quietly in his corner. The bloodlust screaming in my mind was all my own.

I needed power. I needed power to survive. I needed victory and death.

But first, Vechernyvetr said, *you need some rest.* I moved to his side entirely of my own accord. *And there is still so very much for you to learn.* I curled up upon the stone beside his warmth. *A little while more, and we'll be strong.* I took some comfort in those words and went to sleep.

7. Flight

After that the days and nights passed like running water, and the world went on without us. I learned to forget what the world was like outside, what human company had been like. Most of the time I even forgot that there were those who communicated out loud. When I remembered, it sometimes struck me as terribly lonely how much time I spent in the silence.

But I did not often remember. I lived within the quiet thrum of borrowed Chaos. I wrapped myself in air and summoned bursts of flame. We went to capture the green dame's clutch, but a vicious frenzy fell over me, and I tore three of the seven drakes to shreds before I bound their mother to the floor. Then Vechernyvetr crushed her mind beneath his own. And we grew strong.

We took her lair and added his hoard to hers so that our territory covered two and a half mountainsides. Some time later we found another lair just on the border of Vechernyvetr's new territory and subsumed a blue barely old enough to fly.

That one had no hoard to speak of, but it gave us another pair of wings, and we would send it searching every night for some new fight. It found villages and farms, but nothing rich enough to run the risk of facing men. It found a pair of drakes on different days, but by their markings they seemed to come from the same clutch. Vechernyvetr sent it searching farther and farther along the mountains, but it never found the dame.

The only item of any value from its hoard was a silver mirror set in gold. I'd fixed it in the wall of Vechernyvetr's lair and made myself a razor of Chaos power. The sixth night of the blue's hunt for the missing dame, I stood shaving at the mirror by the moonlight.

I barely recognized the man who looked out at me. I was skinny now, long and lean and hard as steel. My face was pale and sunken. And there was a sharpness to my eyes, an animal ferocity. I had never seen it in a mirror before, but it felt right at home for me. I grinned at my reflection, and all I saw was teeth.

A motion tore my attention to the cavern mouth as the blue came settling in. I turned to Vechernyvetr, sprawled lazily on his hoard. *"Anything tonight?"*

No. There is no sign of her anywhere inside my territory.

I growled low in my throat and stalked toward the blue. A Chaos blade formed in my grip as I went. *"We cannot trust in this one. It is weak and useless."*

It is me, Vechernyvetr snarled. *I use its wings, its eyes, but it is me, and I am not weak.*

"Are you useless, then? Why can't you find us a fight?"

He huffed two furious breaths before he answered. *She does not intrude on my domain. I cannot find her if she doesn't come—*

"She can't be far," I thought. *"Let's go to her."*

We should not leave my territory. Pazyarev has not forgotten us.

I spun the sword's blade in a wide arc, testing the feel of it. *"I have not forgotten Pazyarev either."*

For a moment I felt worry from the dragon's heart, but then he laughed inside my head. *I have never had a man within my brood before. Have patience, little man. There are many nights to come, and much power yet to gain. We will fight Pazyarev in our time.*

"I have no wish to wait. It has been days since we spilled blood."

Shall we strike against the farms, then? Just for fun? His huge eyes fixed on me, intense, while he waited for the answer.

I considered it, and my eyes flicked to the dame, to the tired blue, to the handful of drakes fighting on the floor. At last I shook my head. *"Farmers who live this far from civilization will not be soft men. And what will they offer us? No. We need dragons for now."*

Vechernyvetr's mouth fell open, and I realized after a moment he was trying unconsciously to smile. His delight glowed in the back of my mind.

That is your reason? You don't object to killing men?

I frowned. Something deep inside me shouted, "Yes. Of course I object." But the words never reached my mouth. There was power to be had, and that came first.

"No," I thought at last. *"I don't guess I do. But first, I want to find that dame."*

I'll send the blue again at sunset, he replied.

"That's fine, but I am going now. Perhaps I'll find something you overlooked."

He hesitated, concerned, but he did not stop me. I nodded once, then headed out onto the hillside. I flew on the threads of air and stretched my legs across the steep terrain. I found a huge black bear and speared it through the eye for fun. I tracked all across Vechernyvetr's land, but I found no sign of the dame. At sunset I went back.

Are you satisfied? he asked.

"Not at all. I'll try again tomorrow."

After that, I didn't bother scouring the ground that he already searched. I went out to the border, and just as I approached the boundary he spoke within my mind. *Do not go far.*

I didn't answer, I just left his mountainside and went exploring. The locations of the drakes we'd found offered a general direction, and it should not have been too hard to find her lair. Weeks living with Vechernyvetr's brood had taught me what to look for: boulders carved into a star by dragons sharpening their claws, abandoned corpses of their meals left undisturbed by scavengers, the scaling walls, the airing ledges, the charring vents.

Half a mile out, I caught a glimpse of a sharpening stone and cautiously crept closer. The rock was most of a pace across and scored with a five-pointed star. That represented strength enough to be a full adult. I scanned the shape of the terrain and found a likely-looking ledge. My wizard's sight revealed the opaque shadow of a dragon's lair buried in the hillside.

"I've found her lair," I thought, but I got no reply. I looked over my shoulder, toward Vechernyvetr's lair, but it was miles away. He'd heard my thoughts from the far edge of his domain, but he couldn't hear them here.

I almost went back, but after threatening the blue for returning empty-handed, I wanted to be sure. My disguise would hide me well enough, I knew, and if it came down to a fight I'd probably win one empty-handed. I had powers no dragon had ever seen before. A sneer curled my lip as I started forward. I suspected my disguise alone might be enough to win the day. I wrapped myself in threads of air and called a Chaos blade into my hand.

But no blade came. No thunder pounded in my veins. The threads of air I'd caught danced lightly on the folds of my clothes, then washed away. I stopped, startled, then caught the smell, then saw what lay before me.

There was a dragon on the ledge. The dame I stalked, mottled green and brown, lay cooling on the stones outside her lair. She was breathing, if just barely. Her blood painted the dry stones, and her maw gaped as she wheezed a feeble keen. The belly was torn open, and the talons scrabbled weakly at the air.

For too long I stood paralyzed, stunned and motionless, then I turned on my heel and ran, straight for Vechernyvetr's lair.

I nearly made it there.

Pazyarev's voice came crashing in my head, victorious and smug. *I smelled you from a mile away.*

I stumbled from the weight of it, then shored up my defenses. They were much stronger now. I tried again to spin a cloak of air, but it would not manifest. I scanned the sky above and saw a dragon coming from the west. It was not Pazyarev, but one of his broodlings—perhaps the red that had carried me to his lair. It flew in low and fast, aiming for me like an arrow.

I ran.

I was ready to give up. He laughed. *Ready to forget these worn-down hills. I killed a hundred wretched little worms trying to find your lair. And now you come to me.*

I didn't answer. I sprinted for all I was worth, trying desperately to recognize the spot where I'd last heard from Vechernyvetr. It shouldn't have been far, and I could feel the right direction, but nothing looked familiar now.

Thirty nights I've searched for you. You hide like a champion rabbit. But I've been savoring the kill that was to come. And not just you. He laughed again, and it hammered at my mind.

I missed a step and slipped on loose stone, and the stumble saved my life. The dragon's talons closed on empty air where I had been. I rolled aside and barely dodged the tail strike, then I was on my feet and running again. And there, ahead, I saw a fallen log I recognized.

I dove for it while the dragon doubled back.

A clever hare, he said, still so self-assured. *But I will have you yet. I'm near, you know, or this little red couldn't reach your mind. I've cast my shadow over cities on the plains. I've burned some down. But there's no pleasure while you both still live.* He sighed inside my head. *It won't be long.*

I leaped the fallen log, heart hammering in my chest, and now I felt a counter-tempo beat. Chaos power came flooding in. The dragon passed again, and as it came I made a blade. I spun and dove and slashed, and the monster's blood carved an arc in the air over my head. The dragon roared in pain and rage, but I didn't stay to fight it. I wrapped myself in air and flew away.

I saw the injured red circling down below, searching for me, and in the distance heard Pazyarev's voice, the thunder falling smaller and smaller with distance. *I'll find you yet. Now I know you're here. But not just you. I've tasted your memories. It will be fun to kill your...Isabelle.*

The name was barely more than a whisper, but it nearly ripped me from the sky. My concentration shattered and I lost control of the web of air around me. I barely kept enough focus to hold my camouflage in place. I hit the ground as fast as a galloping horse and rolled a dozen paces over stony, rough terrain.

I skidded to a stop, then lay perfectly still, fighting for my breath and focusing on my thin disguise. I watched the sky, but the commotion of my crash had not drawn the red's attention. Still I waited, Chaos fear and anger pounding in my veins.

But there was something else. An unfamiliar warmth, an empty pain deep in my belly. My chest felt crushed, and I fought to catch a breath. Inside my head, I heard her name again. *Isabelle.* My Isabelle. I could see her blue-gray eyes and taste her scent. The memory of human touch—of her soft fingers on my skin—sank into me like hunger. Loneliness and fear and pain that I had held so long at bay while in the Chaos fever dream all now came crashing down.

I remembered Isabelle when Pazyarev spoke her name. He meant to harm her because he could not harm me. I imagined Teelevon beneath his shadow. They had no walls; they had no guards; they had no chance against a dragon.

Scrapes and bruises could not stop me. I found my feet and wrapped myself in air again and flew toward Vechernyvetr's lair. As I went, I heard him in my mind.

You are alive?

"*I am. Where have you been?*"

Watching him. He spent some time within my territory, searching for you and calling out to me.

"*Now he's gone?*"

For the moment, yes. He was silent for a while, angry and afraid. At last he said, *I told you not to leave our territory.*

"*It would not have mattered. He was close. If any of us had been near that border he'd have seen us.*"

But it was you he saw. You almost died.

"*I got away*," I snapped, my mind on other things.

The Chaos threads of air set me down inside his den, and I went straight to the corner I considered mine. There was the mirror in the wall, a pile of blankets on the floor, and a pathetic little hoard off to one side. No treasures there, but human things—castoffs and scavenged clothes. We hadn't raided villages, but the blue had found abandoned farms as well, and I'd collected boots and cloaks and clothes my size.

But now I had to leave. I had to go to Teelevon. With the power I controlled, I might protect them. It was a better chance than they had on their own, anyway. I tried not to think what had happened near the dame's lair. It didn't matter. I had to go to Isabelle.

I traded out my belt for one slightly less worn and kicked several boots aside but saw none better. I stooped to grab a heavy cloak and swung it around my shoulders, then glanced in the mirror. My face was torn and bruised. A hand scrubbed across my cheek only smeared the mud and blood there, so I shook my head and turned away.

Vechernyvetr stood before me, blocking the cavern's exit. His head was low against the ground, his eyes narrowed. *What is in your heart?* he asked.

"We have to go to Teelevon," I told him. *"You've been there once before. We must protect them again."*

He shook his massive head. *We will not leave this place. Not while he still hunts us.*

"I have to go. There is no choice. Pazyarev means to kill my family. He means to destroy my home."

You have a lair right here, he said, his voice a growl. *You have a brood with me.*

I stretched an imploring hand toward him. *"You are my brood. You're all I have against that monster. But this is something I must do. Take me there."*

No. It would be foolish to go now. I told you that already. We bide our time, we build our strength—

"I can't wait for that. He's hunting Isabelle."

There are other dames. Your kind has quite a few.

I stared at him for a moment, trying to find the words. There was something that felt like reason in his argument. Something inside me wanted to stay here, to cower from the bigger beast and conquer smaller prey. Fear and hunger, survival and power, they'd driven me for days outside my human reason.

But Isabelle had brought me back. Even as I felt the Chaos madness in my soul, I focused on the memory of her touch. It ached to think of her, it made me weak and small and frightened. But when I thought of her, I knew what I had to do.

"It doesn't matter how hard I train, or how much power I gain, it gains me nothing if I can't save the ones I love—"

That's simple human foolishness, he said. *You are better than that now. You are nearly a dragon. Leave that world behind.*

"I do not have a choice in this. You understand? I have to go." I glanced past him, at the harsh terrain outside. I tried to guess how many hundred miles it was to Teelevon. "*It would be far easier with you.*"

Impossible without me. I will not let you go.

I smiled sadly at him. "*You cannot stop me.*"

His head sank lower still, his muscles bunched beneath his scales. *Cannot kill you,* he said.

"*Vechernyvetr, let us at least part as friends.*"

We were never friends, he said. *You were a trinket on my hoard, and that is all.*

I sighed and shook my head, then started past him. His tail lashed forward, and at the last instant turned the deadly tip aside. Still it struck me hard in the chest and flung me back to crash against the wall.

This hurts me near as much as it hurts you, he growled, and I could feel his anger in my soul. *But I will do what I must. You will not go.*

I wrapped myself in threads of air, but he rolled his eyes and swiped the space where I had been with his massive, plated snout. I almost slipped aside, but he caught me on the hip and spilled me into the pile of stolen clothes. He saw the disturbance, and the tail slashed around again. It caught my shoulder as I dodged and threw me to the ground.

And he was not alone. He was a beast with many bodies. The drakes came swarming across the lair, rushing to surround the spot where I had been. But now I did as Vechernyvetr had done through me in Pazyarev's lair. Wrapped up in energy, I ran on pads of air, and unlike then, I raised the steps up higher and higher as I went, so I sprinted soundlessly above the closing ring of drakes, and dove past Vechernyvetr's spine toward the outer ledge.

As I passed above him, I felt the panic in his heart. The huge head swung this way and that, but he could catch no glimpse of me. He was not hateful; he felt fearful and betrayed. Compassion touched my heart as I stepped out onto the ledge. I turned back to him, and thought, *"I'm sorry, Vechernyvetr. I leave you stronger than I met you, but I must leave you."*

Suspicion flared and he turned my way, though he did not focus on me. *No! You are more than a man here! You are strong. You are fearsome. Why would you leave that behind?*

"For love. It is a human thing and nothing to do with Chaos. I have tasted Chaos power and it is sweet." Behind my eyes, I saw Isabelle's smile. I nodded to myself. *"But it is nothing against love."*

He stalked in my direction, but he didn't strike. He only lowered his head like a hurt dog. *Then go as a friend, human. Perhaps something of humanity has touched my heart. I cannot understand your choice, but I would not have you for an enemy. Show yourself to me, and teach me to say goodbye.*

I hesitated only a moment, then let the robe of wind wash off me. I didn't go to meet him but waited there at the cliff's edge. I spread my hands. *"I'm sorry, Vech—"*

There were no words, only an animal snarl as he sprang at me. I felt no shock at his deception. The Chaos power still roared within me. It lashed earth around me—not the delicate elemental coat of air I'd worn before, but half a turret of pace-thick stone. The dragon's talons screamed against it, and the long neck snaked above. Sharp fangs flashed and he snapped down at me, but I was already moving.

I waved a hand, and a doorway opened at the base of the strange stone wall. I stepped through, under the beast's belly, and the power raging beneath the thin veneer of my humanity screamed at me to strike. There was a blade already in my hand, of Chaos more than earth and flame, and I could have carved Vechernyvetr down to bone.

But he had been a friend, and he had saved my life. I darted out from under him and wrapped myself in air and darted down the mountainside as fast as I could run. He roared behind me, bellowing his rage, and threw his will against me.

It was not a blind attack on my consciousness as he and Pazyarev had tried before. Now it was an order to his brood to take me down. Somewhere deep inside I felt it, felt a compulsion to obey even to my own destruction, but the power in me drowned it out.

The others came, though. My brothers and sisters, now. Limbs of my own body. They came to overwhelm me. I drifted down the mountainside, but the broodlings were hard on my heels. I could feel Vechernyvetr's rage like a physical thing in the air around me, feel his animal hatred overwhelming any shred of reason in his head.

He sprang from the ledge above me and spewed flames in a torrent, but they never came within a pace of me. I felt the shape of his compulsion, sensed the drakes slipping soundlessly among the trees beneath me. He rose up high above and sent the dame along behind me.

I shook my head. *"You do not have to do this. We were friends."*

You ache, he said, and it was snarling accusation. *From the very first, you ache. No matter how long you rest, no matter how well you heal, no matter how strong you grow. Your body always aches.*

"And you will fix that by destroying me?"

I cannot destroy you. But yes, I would have fixed you. You are broken. Your power's flawed.

"I am a man." I thought. *"It is not enough to be strong. We will always ache for those we love."*

A roar split the air, high above, and I felt the fury of it clawing at the back of my mind. I shrank away from it.

I gave you all the power of Chaos, he said. *And you have given me this.*

I saw him circling above, and I remembered the day he first came looking for me in the sky above. He couldn't see me, but he could sense my location through his connection to the lair. He'd missed with wild fire, but he had many weapons.

I remembered her just in time. The dame came in fast from my left, and I flung myself forward, out, up away from the hillside. I hurled the Chaos blade toward her and drove it with my will, but Vechernyvetr hit me, striking from inside my head. He battered at my mind and I held him off, but it cost me concentration. The blade only glanced along the dame's ribcage, but worse, the web of air around me tattered. I hit the boughs of winter pines like a catapult shot.

Tree limbs cracked and crashed and tore beneath me, and instead of grabbing for some purchase I turned my attention to the ground below. I plunged straight to the uneven slope, but I grasped the strength of stone and wrapped it around me like a shell. I let myself fall to the earth, into the earth, and it swallowed me like a still pool. I sank down, dragging a great bubble of air with me, and the earth closed over me as though I had never passed.

For a long time I crouched in my strange little sanctuary, catching my breath, and Vechernyvetr searched for me above. I could feel him in my mind prodding, feel all the other broodlings prowling, but I contained him now, and he could not find me. I could feel him in the world above, sweeping out in wider and wider circles as he searched for me, his rage a flame in the depths of my mind.

110

Then he spoke, and his words sounded dull, as though I were hearing them through a long tunnel. *This is a foolish thing you do, Daven. You are only wasting your life. You cannot save them.*

I took a deep breath to steady my nerves, but for the first time in a month I felt sure. I had a purpose. *"I can, and I will. I am the only one alive who can save them."*

You believe that? Man cannot stand up to Pazyarev, Daven, much less the dragonswarm. They will be washed under, and if you go out there, you will be washed under with them.

Cautiously, I looked out with my second sight, searching the world above me for Vechernyvetr, and once again he'd heard my thoughts. He was coming for me, but he was far off. I found the drakes, living shadows among the glowing life of the forest, and they were nowhere near. The dame was injured now, her strength used up, and she was circling back to the lair. I felt the pull of it myself—an urge to return to the comfort of its confines—but my stomach turned at the thought. I shook it off.

Before he could reach me, I began to fold the earth back, slowly rising to the surface. It was harder to do now, more complicated than I'd realized, but I forced my way up. When I broke the surface, he was just a speck on the horizon, but he was coming back as fast as he could fly. I was already moving, though. I wrapped myself in air again, and ran down the mountain, away from the lair. I went in great leaping steps, never quite touching the ground and without making a sound. As he came close, he brought with him an inferno of emotion that bloomed in the back of my mind. I could feel his frustration—his pain, his loss—and it felt devastatingly familiar. I had given him a human heart, or enough of one to ache.

You will not leave, Daven! His voice thundered in my head, but I could hear the desperate fear behind it. *You must not leave! Stay here.* He landed behind me, crashing down where I had been, and I glanced back to see his great head swinging back and forth as he tried to find me. His voice brimmed with desperation. *Please don't leave me. You are the only friend I have ever known.*

I never expected that plea, and it rocked me. I remembered his deception on the ledge above, and dared not give myself away with any answer. But I could feel his true emotion. He would have crippled me to keep me, but he truly wanted me.

A tear stole down my face, but I steadied my thoughts, aware that he must still sense some of my emotions. I gripped the web of air around me, breathed a heavy sigh, and pulled myself quietly, carefully away from where he waited.

I watched him as I went. He circled for a while, searching. He called into my mind. But I gave no answer, and at last he went back to his lair. I hung for a moment near the top of a pine and watched the drakes scurry home as well.

Then I turned away. I looked out over the world of men, gathered a breath, and prepared myself to return home. I flung myself on threads of air as hard as my will would let me and soared out high over the forested hills. I flew like an arrow, arcing up until I could see the black smoke boiling out of a burning city miles and miles away. I could see dragons flying in loose formations, scudding over empty fields like the shadows of clouds.

The mountainside fell away beneath me, replaced with rolling hills and thinner forest. I looked down and saw the fringes of humanity. I saw towns on the horizon and villages just beyond the hills, and even a farmhouse here and there.

While I watched, I felt the thrilling song of the Chaos power fade within my soul. The hammering force of it lessened, and with it went the comforting buffer that protected me from reason. I saw, in a glance, the world that I'd forgotten. I'd abandoned it—I'd nearly agreed to raid against it—and though it wasn't burning yet, the dragons would be coming.

My arc curved down. I began to fall toward the earth, but I had crossed a dozen miles with a thought, and at that rate I could make my way to Teelevon before midday. I reached out with my will and shaped anew the net around me. I flung it with a thought to launch myself out over the plains.

It didn't work. I felt a wrenching jerk that barely slowed my plummet. The fragile fabric of air tore apart around me, and I fell. Panic stabbed at me. I reached down deep to the core of blackness, borrowing Chaos again as I had done before. But it was thin. It was too far away. Even as I reached for it I felt the darkness slipping from my grasp. Down, deeper inside. But at the same time...up and behind me. In the direction of the lair.

I thought of the map Vechernyvetr had shown me before, of the limits of his domain. I thought of the hoard we had acquired, of the broodlings we'd overpowered, and I thought how my power had grown. I reached out desperately now, falling faster and faster, and strained with all my might to summon a thread of air to slow my fall. It shivered and broke beneath my will.

Trees and hills and stones grew huge beneath me. They flashed toward me, and I fought against a panic every bit as black and blinding as the dragon's glamour. I flailed for some plan, remembering the magic I'd known before I ever borrowed Chaos. I touched the air—the natural air, the inconvenient reality so thin compared with Chaos—but it lacked the strength to hold me up.

I looked to the earth instead. I remembered the trick I'd used to escape Vechernyvetr before, falling like a bubble through the earth. But I remembered the price I had to pay for bending the energy of actual reality. It cost in bodily strength. Perhaps I had the will enough to make the earth swallow me up, but I would have to climb back out again by the strength of my own arms.

The trees reached up for me, and I spun in place and touched what wind there was to throw me at a high-branched fir. I caught a limb and bloodied my hands and nearly ripped one arm from its socket, then I was falling again. Another heavy branch caught my hip and spilled me over, and I folded double over a wrist-thick limb. I hooked an elbow and a knee before I could slip off, and spent ten slamming heartbeats trying to catch my breath.

The limb creaked. It started to crack, but I reached out desperately to the threads of earth and water that gave it shape and reinforced them with my will. The branch held. My grasp didn't. Suddenly weak arms gave out, and I flopped upside down. Then loose. It was twenty paces down to the ground, and there were ten limbs along the way. I landed on my back gasping desperately and aching top to toe.

For ages I lay still, breathing slow and thinking fast, and three more times I tried to borrow Chaos. I couldn't reach the inky power. It was there, but it was very far away. I could turn my head toward the distant sensation and stare across the miles at the tiny cavern upon the mountainside. I couldn't see it, but I had no doubt that it was there.

I craved the power. I needed it, to heal, to fly, to fight. I'd fought to gain my freedom, and it had cost me everything I was. I almost headed back. Every pace would make me stronger, and I could meet Vechernyvetr with open eyes this time. What choice was there? I couldn't fight Pazyarev, I couldn't help Teelevon without the dragon's power....

I thought of Isabelle. I thought of the home I'd known before the dragon's lair. I'd been a warrior and wizard-trained. I'd saved the town before. I'd made myself a hero before I ever borrowed Chaos, and if my people needed me at all now, they needed me as a man. Not as another dragon. I dragged myself to my feet, threw one last look toward the distant mountain peaks, then turned and stumbled down the hillside.

8. Forward and Down, into the Darkness

It was the tantalizing song of water that finally stopped me. A mountain stream burbled across my path, crystal water dancing across a shallow bed of stone. I fell into the water, gulping it as quickly as I could. I splashed the icy water on my face, dipped my whole head into it, and then shook out my long, wet hair. Then I leaned my back against a tree and breathed in the air around me, drinking in the odors of the forest and at last beginning to relax.

I was on a moderate slope, somewhere in the foothills near the base of the mountain. Pines and evergreens grew all around me, and I was stretched out on a soft bed of needles and moss. The canopy of limbs and leaves blocked out much of the sun, but a tiny shaft of light fell across my face, a dazzling gold that I had almost forgotten.

"Get up!" A man's voice suddenly shattered the forest silence, full of such command that I found myself instantly on my feet. There was a pause, and then, "Good. Now turn around. Slowly."

I did as he directed, but I fought to keep contempt from my expression. I had faced dragons today; what terror was there in a man?

He stood three paces away. On a bed of dry leaves and dead branches, he had come within three paces, and I never heard. He was a monster of a man, tall and heavily muscled, and his skin was black as night—an Islander. He was dressed in a shepherd's simple clothes, but over them was draped a once-fine tabard, threadbare and faded with age.

The hilt of a great two-handed sword rose over his left shoulder, and lighter broadswords hung on both hips. He had a crossbow in his hands, the iron-shod tip of a bolt trained on my heart.

"Who are you? What are you doing here?" His voice was deep, commanding, and it held only a trace of the Islanders' accent.

"I am Daven."

He waited for more, and when I didn't offer it he growled. "Bad times to be a stranger, Daven. Tell me your business in my mountains, or I'll drop you where you stand."

He did not blink as he waited for my answer.

"I am no threat," I said. The shape of the words felt strange in my mouth. I grimaced. "I am lost and alone, and my only business here is to leave these mountains."

"Bound for where?"

"Tirah,"

"Tirah?" He snorted and jerked a thumb over his shoulder, toward the plains. "Tirah." Then he pointed up the slope. "And you come from that way. There's no man for a thousand miles in that direction. To come here, you must come *from* Tirah."

My mouth fell open to answer, but after a moment I shook my head."I couldn't even begin to explain." I started to turn away, but as soon as I moved he fired. The bolt flashed toward me, but I touched it with my mind, unleashing little threads of water within the wood—last echo of life in a crafted thing. They expanded at my touch, and the bolt shattered to a thousand slivers midair. The heavy iron head fell to the ground at my feet. The soldier showed no sign of surprise. Slowly, eyes locked on me, he reached to his belt for another bolt.

I sighed. "Please don't do that. It's a waste of good craftsmanship." I tried hard to look bored and prayed he didn't reach for any of those swords.

Still watching me warily, he drew the crossbow's heavy cord with a smooth motion and placed the bolt in its cradle. He half raised the weapon, then seemed to change his mind and dropped his arms to hold it casually at waist height. I noticed it was still aimed at my heart.

"Very well," I said. "My name is Daven Carrickson, and I come from Terrailles. I have been prisoner in a dragon's lair, and I wish to return to the world of man." I watched his eyes for some sign of surprise or doubt, but he only nodded.

"Daven Carrickson. I am Caleb—they call me Caleb Drake, now—and I grew up in the Bateiyn Keys." He looked at me for a moment, measuring, and then added, "I am hunting a dragon."

My heart went cold. "In these mountains? How can you know where to look?"

He narrowed his eyes and considered me for a moment, "Dragons are everywhere. I must only look up. But the beast I hunt keeps a lair in these hills."

I fought a desperate urge to glance back and up toward Vechvernyvetr's lair. "Are you sure of that?"

"I know it well. She and her drakes have long haunted our village."

"Your village?"

He jerked his thumb back toward the plains again. "Below the mountains."

I felt a flash of relief. "Please, take me there. Is it far?"

"It is not far."

"Show me the way. It may cost you a few hours in your hunt, but it could well save my life."

118

He ground his teeth tight until the muscles bunched on his jaw, and his nostrils flared with a little huff of anger. "There is nowhere to take you. The village is gone."

"Gone? How?"

"This dragon burned it down. Slaughtered man, woman, and child. I alone survived."

The breath went out of me. I hung my head. "I'm sorry."

"As am I. You must be weary, but these is no refuge while the beast yet lives. Come with me to kill it—"

"I cannot."

"You face a crossbow like a warrior. You turn a bolt to splinters. You have escaped a dragon's den. You will be a powerful ally."

I shook my head. "I cannot help you. I'm sorry for your loss."

He considered me a for a long time. Then he dropped the crossbow to his side. "Today I woke with a home. An hour ago, it was taken from me. I will not sleep again until it has been set right."

"I'm truly sorry," I said again. And then I stopped. I frowned. "An hour ago?"

"If that," he said. "I have come from there—"

"Just now?" Despite myself I turned and glanced toward the dame's lair I'd visited, then quickly back to Caleb. There couldn't have been time. "Where is this lair?"

He pointed just where I had looked, along the slope to the south. "Perhaps a mile up. Among the low hills."

"How many are there?"

"Just the dame," he said, his voice a dirge. "Her seven drakes are dead."

I felt the hunger surge up in my gut, rage and regret that we hadn't made them ours. So much power to be had, so close, but this man had killed her seven drakes. We'd killed two more, and Pazyarev the dame.

It didn't matter. I was not a dragon anymore. I shook my head. "She's gone. The dame is dead this afternoon."

"She isn't dead. I've seen her shadow in the sky above this place. She's on the hunt."

I shook my head. "Dragons don't hunt by day."

His teeth flashed in something like a smile. "This one does. And she led me straight to you."

My jaw fell open. I threw my gaze to the sky, looking out with the wizard's sight, and searched for the Chaos shadow. I saw it, coming low and fast over the trees. Not straight at us—we must have been hidden by the canopy—but it had the right direction. I pointed wordlessly, tracking the shadow with my hand, and Caleb only nodded, still and silent as a stone.

But as the dragon passed overhead, he raised his crossbow in a smooth motion, sighted down my tracking arm, and fired a bolt that struck the beast dead center. It screamed in rage and fell out of the sky, crashing over treetops before it settled into a small dell some way down.

Caleb didn't run. He sprinted straight toward the sound of the downed dragon, but that bolt could not have done serious injury. It had surprised the beast at best. Caleb didn't seem to care. He stopped by a towering tree three paces thick, hiding behind one of its exposed roots. Very slowly he raised his head to peek over, then sank back quickly. He waved me over, and I tried to move as silently as he had while I crossed the little space.

When I dropped down beside him his eyes were closed, his breathing slow and steady. He was preparing himself for battle. The tree stood atop a small cliff, holding together a wall of earth with its ancient roots. Between them, a great hollow in the hillside stood protected from the elements. Pazyarev's red sat upon its haunches in the gully, snapping with its razor teeth at the bloodied fletchings just protruding from its breast.

Caleb raised the crossbow to his shoulder and fired again. I watched in two worlds as the heavy bolt tore the evening sky, missed the dragon's throat by a hand's breadth, and drove home just in front of its hind leg. Blood spilled, dull and gray to my wizard's eyes, and the beast roared in hate and anger. In an instant it was in the air and flying straight toward us.

Caleb was already readying another bolt, and before the dragon reached us the warrior fired again, but this bolt glanced harmlessly off the monster's plated shoulder. In an instant more the beast would be upon us.

Fury clawed at the back of my mind. Even without the Chaos power to draw upon, days of bloodthirsty madness had left their scar on me. The fight called to me, and without thinking I rose in answer. I stepped up onto the heavy root, grabbed the hilt of the sword on Caleb's right hip, and leaped high into the air, all in one fluid motion.

I tore a fistful of earth energy free with my mind, stretched it into a beam perhaps three paces long and as wide across as my heel. It lasted just long enough to hold me. I sprinted to the end of it and sprang.

The beast was coming fast. I saw the flash of recognition in its eyes, felt the sneering contempt that would be words of challenge, but I had no time for banter. I cut a short arc through the sky, bending flimsy threads of air to guide my path, and landed on its head while it was still five paces from Caleb's hiding place. I held his sword reversed, and as soon as I landed I gripped the hilt in both hands and struck. The sharp point came down with all my might, driving through scale and bone and clear through the dragon's head. There was no splash of blood, no cry of pain or anger, only the crack of bone, the sigh of steel, and then a last beat of dragon's wings. I slew it in an instant, but its velocity still carried us forward and I only just leaped clear before the heavy body smashed into the ledge.

The ancient tree trembled, but it did not fall. I landed hard, but in an instant I was up, eyes darting. There was no threat. The beast was dead. I knew it before I even looked. I could feel it. And as I turned my attention to the corpse, I *saw* it. I saw the darkness, the black void of dragon power overlaid on reality. It shimmered like silk and flowed like water. It drained across the uneven earth and poured toward me.

The darkness pooled around my feet, and I felt stronger. I shivered at the sensation.

I didn't notice the silence until Caleb broke it with a cry. His shout was wordless, full of vindication and victory, but fueled by a heartfelt pain. He came scrambling down the slope, hopping onto the jumble of its broken body halfway down and climbing from shoulder to knee to head, then to the earth. When he reached the ground he stopped, and the victory seemed to drain from him as he sank down on one knee beside the mighty head, its sightless eye still open. I waited while he made his peace.

Then he rose gracefully and retrieved his sword with a grunt of effort. He dragged its blade against the edge of his sole to clean it, then let its point rest lightly on the ground between us. He stared at me in awe for several long seconds, then shook his head. "You are...something."

I shrugged one shoulder. "I know some of their secrets."

He shook his head. "I've seen what they do to wizards. I've seen they what they do to soldiers." He took a deep breath, then dropped his eyes as he sighed. "I didn't much expect to walk away."

"I'm glad I could help," I said. "You paid a great price for this little victory."

He towered over me, easily six inches taller and made entirely of muscles and scars. He wore authority like a cloak. And yet, in that moment, he looked small and afraid. He met my eyes and opened massive hands in a helpless gesture. "What do I do now?"

I turned my head vaguely in the direction he'd indicated for his village. "Nothing remains?"

He shook his head.

I looked back to the dragon. I took a deep breath and let it out. "You can come with me."

I said it almost as a question, but I saw a flash of gratitude in his eyes. He dipped his head once in a nod. "Anywhere."

"There is a town south of Tirah," I said. "Teelevon. My people are there, and they are in danger. I must help them."

He nodded once, gravely. "That is many miles. The world is a dangerous place. We will find more than one enemy between here and there."

The feral hunger in my heart nearly grinned at that. Enemies meant things to kill, and killing things meant power. That thought turned my head to the corpse before us. I closed my eyes to focus my attention and felt the cold sear of black Chaos power deep in my heart—the power I had taken from the slain red. It was just a tiny shade of the power I'd held in Vechernyvetr's lair, but it burned in my heart now and filled my mind with visions of vengeance.

"We will teach them fear, Caleb. Mankind will stand."

"How?" There was no doubt in his voice. Only desperate hope. "How can you defy them?"

I felt a fire in my eyes. "I know the ways of the dragons, Caleb. I know their strengths, their weaknesses...their secrets. And I know how they can be defeated."

He raised his chin and stared down at me for a while, considering. "You don't intend to run? To hide? You really mean to fight them halfway across the plains?"

"I mean to kill them all," I said.

"Teelevon, you said? Somewhere near Tirah?"

I nodded.

"I don't recognize the name, but I can tell you this: A month ago Tirah was as well defended as soldiers and steel could make it. A month ago the dragonswarm hadn't come that far into the plains. Perhaps there is yet hope."

"As long as I have breath there is hope, Caleb. I just have to know."

"Then come," he said. "I know this area well enough. I'll show you the way."

We left the dragon's little gulch and quickly found the open, rolling plains of the southeast Ardain. The sky was overcast, full of clouds—fat, gray, and lazy—that drifted slowly from east to west. The sun was an angry orange burn stealing across behind them, but its light never broke through. The air was sharp and chill, and I shivered in my cloak as we pressed across the plains.

This far south the plains were trackless, covered in tall, wild grass that reached up to our chins. Caleb walked ahead of me, forging a path that cut through the grass straight as a blade. Late in the afternoon, as we were coming down out of the hills, we stumbled across a narrow, overgrown trail among the weeds.

Caleb walked right past without noticing, but somehow my eyes fell on the packed ground, marked here and there with a patch of gravel. I looked down at the old road for a moment, and then caught Caleb's shoulder. "We should go this way." I nodded in the direction of the road, more to the north than we had been heading.

He turned to look at me for the first time in hours, a question in his eyes at the interruption. He glanced at the road and then back to me. "Why?"

"There are people that way. We should go get them."

He looked down at the road again, looked off to the northwest where it led, then shrugged and turned back toward the wall of grass, continuing west. Over his shoulder he said, "What can we do? Warn them? Help them bury some of their dead? We can hardly save them."

I opened my mouth to retort...and stopped. I had no answer. He was right, of course. Perhaps I could save this little town, if I dedicated my life to it, but I owed my allegiance to another little town first.

And yet something within me was fighting even then to drag my steps toward that abandoned road. Something within me yearned toward any sign of other men. I couldn't shake it.

Caleb noticed my silence and at last he stopped. He turned back to me. "What?"

"I need...them. I need people, Caleb."

He frowned at me for a moment, then he tossed his head with a derisive snort. "Followers? Soldiers? You've got me. Be glad of that. But a townful of Ardain dirt farmers won't gain you much in a fight."

"No," I said. "No, I didn't mean that—"

He wasn't listening, though. He shook his head. "You don't really know what you're up against, do you? How long were you in their lairs? Have you seen the darkness that has spread across this land?"

As if on cue a shadow rose up against the sky, far off to the south. It soared from east to west, a full wing of dragons in flight. Little flares were visible from here when they breathed their deadly fire. I waved in the direction they had gone. "I know the threat. They come in endless numbers, they fight together or alone, and it takes a hundred men to kill one."

"I can kill one. I could perhaps kill a dozen."

I grinned. "I've seen you fight one, so I believe you could kill a dozen. But you are only one man."

"We are two," he said. "And you could kill a thousand."

I nodded slowly. "And that is not nearly enough. That's why we must find more men." He opened his mouth to argue, but I cut him off. "Not farmers. Soldiers. There are soldiers enough in these lands. But I must go among men to find them."

"For what?" he growled. "Find men—*recruit soldiers*—for what? Are you so anxious to lead good men to their deaths?"

"I am leading you," I said.

He pressed his lips tight for a moment. "I am no good man, and I will welcome death when it comes for me. And even I don't hope for—" He stopped, then shook his head. "Have you ever had that responsibility? Have you ever watched a man die at your command?" His voice burned with an anger I had not caused.

"I cannot sit idly by. I must do something."

"What can you do, by yourself? What could you possibly hope to achieve? The world's already broken, and nowhere will be safe against that. No power can defy them all. Settle for something less—"

A piercing shriek suddenly split the silence of the afternoon, cutting him off. We both turned to look east toward the sound. A flight of dragons—five or six, all of them mature and none of them familiar—came soaring down from the mountains less than a mile away. They came flashing toward us, straight as an arrow over the path Caleb had carved through the tall grass.

Steel hissed on leather as he drew two swords. At the same time, I reached inside and borrowed Chaos. Chaos answered, bleeding that hammering power into my veins. It was not enough to fly, not enough really to face a flight of dragons, but there was enough to summon a sword. I stretched out a hand, and one of the iridescent black Chaos blades sprang fully formed in my grip.

There was enough to wrap myself in a cloak of air, too, but one heartbeat before I dropped it in place to disappear from their eyes, the lead dragon gave its piercing cry once more, and then the whole band of them veered off to the north. They swept around us in a wide, lazy circle. For a long time Caleb only stood and watched them fly, but I turned my attention back to the road and started walking toward the world of men.

When he caught up to me he grabbed my shoulder. "What was that? They *must* have seen us." For a while I walked in silence, thinking, but he caught my shoulder again and demanded, "Tell me."

"They were not Pazyarev's brood. But I think they know me. I think...I think perhaps they fear me. News spreads among them already."

He fell in step beside me, silent, and we walked for some time before he said, "A flight of dragons fears you. They *recognize* you?" He thought for a while, and there was awe in his voice when he spoke again. "You really know how to defeat them?"

"I have some ideas."

The silence returned, broken only by the sound of footsteps on the dry earth. Later, "I would have followed you to my grave, Daven, if it had meant a chance to kill even one of them in vengeance. But this...this is beyond reason."

I shrugged. "Leave, then. I won't keep you."

"No." He sounded thoughtful, serious. "But you're talking about doing the impossible. Postponing the inevitable. Man can do nothing to hold the dragonswarm at bay. It's hopeless."

I laughed, and in my head it sounded like the dragon's cruel laughter. "You've just described the life of man, Caleb. Forward and down, into the darkness, and we hold our heads high like victors."

Sometime later he said, "You are a hero or a madman. But if you will truly bring war against the dragons, I will give my life and count it an honor."

"And what of other men's lives, Caleb?" His earlier words burned hot and troublesome in the back of my head. They itched with an insight I couldn't quite grasp yet, but I could feel something like destiny dragging me down this road, and Caleb had already guessed what lay at its end. "If I need you to lead, will you lead good men to die in that war?"

It took him four paces to answer, and then he only grunted.

"I may ask it of you before this work is done."

"At least tell me what you plan," he said.

I took a deep breath and let it escape me. "I plan to follow this road back to the world of men."

He waited, expectant.

I shook my head. "I plan to find the survivors. And then...I'll see what I can do."

I had nothing more to offer. He thought upon it for a while, then he said quietly, "Whatever you ask. I'm your man."

An hour or two later the grass we walked through had lost a foot of its height, all the way to the horizon, and the road had gained a foot across. We came then across a little beaten path of earth, rutted from the wheels of a narrow cart, that cut back into the field to the east. This time when I tapped him on the shoulder and headed down the track, Caleb gave no objection at all.

A mile from the road sat a sad farm. Huddled among the wilderness grasses were a handful of humble acres of corn and potatoes and a pen of angry chickens that complained loudly at our approach. I watched the single, small house carefully as we went, and while we were still a long way off the door slammed open. A small man with a large crossbow waddled out onto a ten-plank porch. He held the crossbow high and sort of folded his body around it, but he seemed angry and afraid, and those together are always dangerous.

Caleb automatically reached for the crossbow on its hook at his belt, but I placed a calming hand on his arm and after a moment, reluctantly, he let it go. The old farmer watched us warily as we followed the path up to a crude gate. With exaggerated slowness I reached down and un-latched the gate, pushed it open, and stepped through. All the while the farmer watched.

I took another step into his yard, and he stepped down from the porch toward us, but he waved the crossbow threateningly and said, "I've got nothin' for you. Move along. There's nothin' here you'd want anyways."

"I want nothing but news, farmer. I'm not here to take anything—"

He snarled. "Shaddup, you!" He was about twenty paces away now, and if he had any skill at all with the crossbow he could hit a man from that distance. Caleb laid a heavy hand on my shoulder, trying to get my attention, but I shrugged it off and stepped forward.

I watched with my wizard's sight, focusing on the thin shaft of the crossbow bolt. I could destroy it mid-flight us-ing nothing but its own natural energies. I tried to let that confidence sound in my voice. "We're humble travelers—"

The farmer snapped, "Don't you come any closer. I have *nothin'* for you, and I won't have you on my land."

I stopped. I tried to offer him a smile but ended speaking through gritted teeth. "I am no threat to you, good man. I would ask only water and some news. I'm sure you could spare me that much hospitality."

Caleb spoke behind me in a voice that barely reached my ears. "It's no good, Daven. Let's go." I took another step forward, but Caleb caught my elbow and pulled me back. "I mean it. This man will shoot you if we wait much longer. He is just a simple man, and he has no trust for strangers."

I remembered Caleb firing on me for no more reason. I threw him an irritated glare, and that was all the provocation the old man needed. I heard the twang of the string, saw the flash of energy in my wizard's sight, and a sudden hot rage billowed out of my heart. I reduced the bolt to splinters just as I'd done before, but the same casual effort of will blasted the crossbow apart in the farmer's hands.

Hot red blood flowed from a dozen tiny injuries on his hands and arms and face. The farmer fell in a heap, whimpering and covering his head with bloody hands. Caleb shouted something behind me, but I ignored him. I crossed the distance between us without really even willing it, until I stood looming over the farmer. His fear tasted sharp in the air. His humiliation sang in my blood.

I stood over him and asked again with a perfect politeness, "Please, good sir. At least tell us where we can find refuge." He moaned miserably and I prodded him with my foot. "Where does that road lead? Is there a town near?"

He trembled for a moment, then stabbed a hand out toward the north. "Chaaron. An hour's walk. But they won't...won't...."

"Won't what?" I asked. He glanced up at my smiling face and gave a miserable little cry.

I was about to ask again when Caleb's hand closed heavy on my shoulder. I frowned and turned on him, but his dark eyes stopped my cold. "They won't welcome us either," he said. "Still, I suspect we have to go."

I glanced down at the cowering farmer and felt a twinge of confusion and regret. A shiver chased down my spine, and Caleb nodded slowly as he watched it pass. "Go ahead," he said. "I'll catch up."

The farmer drew my attention again, and it was as though I were seeing him for the first time. His hands were caked red and brown with dust and blood, his face streaked and creased with fear. I looked around, saw the slivered remnants of the crossbow I'd destroyed—probably the man's only weapon in a suddenly dangerous world.

My heart began to hammer hard and fast. I licked my lips and shook my head. Caleb nodded slowly and waved toward the road again. "Go. I'll get him bandaged and follow after."

I hesitated for a heartbeat, then nodded my gratitude and turned away. Four paces across the lawn I broke into a run and went all the way back to the road at a desperate sprint. Then I fell to my knees among the tall grasses and pressed my eyes tight shut and fought for breath.

What had I done there? Why had I attacked the man? Even as I wondered the answer came loud and clear. *He was impudent and weak. Barely better than food.* The words felt right and true, even as I hated myself for thinking them. It was the dragon's voice. Not Vechernyvetr crowding into my mind. Not Pazyarev. Me. It was the dragon's voice in me.

It took a long time for the tremors to subside, for my breath to come naturally. I'd suspected it, hadn't I? How long *had* I spent in the dragon's lair? How much had I borrowed of Chaos, and how much did I owe it now?

At last I pushed myself back onto my heels and scrubbed both hands over my face. I climbed to my feet, blinking away the fear and darkness, and turned to find Caleb waiting still as a shadow in the middle of the road.

"Caleb..." I began, but I had no words to explain what I'd become.

He held my gaze and said, "Hero or madman, I'm with you."

I floundered for a moment, then gave up and turned north. We walked in silence, searching the fields of grass and winter wheat for some sign of Chaaron. As I went, I tried to prepare myself, to prevent a recurrence of the events at the sad little farm.

When I closed my eyes I could feel the billowing desires and emotions at war within me, and once again I found myself going through familiar motions, building up walls against a wicked voice in the back of my mind. But this time it was mine. This time it was me. And no matter how carefully I pinned it up, I feared the bindings could come undone in a heartbeat.

It was sunset before we saw another human structure, but there before us a great watermill turned lazily in the evening's crimson light. Less than a mile beyond we saw a sprawling farm complex some distance off the road, but by then the glow of fire and smudge of smoke were clear on the horizon to the north. A town.

When we entered the village of Chaaron, there were few people out in the streets, but those who saw us walk into town watched with open suspicion. Mothers gathered their children close by as we walked slowly along the town's main street, and men glared. Hands strayed to the hilts of swords, and more than one young man watched us pass with an arrow held to the string of a bow.

"They're terrified of us," I said. My voice sounded eerie, too loud within the lonely silence of the villagers watching us pass.

"The dragons are not yet the worst monsters on the plains," Caleb said. I flinched at the words, feeling in them an accusation he perhaps had not intended. He certainly seemed as unaffected by my violence earlier as he was by the silent, hateful stares. I noticed his hands rested on the hilts at his sides, but he moved with a relaxed grace that I envied.

Halfway through the town I spotted an inn. It stood on the main streets, with a simple sign hanging above the door. I pointed it out to Caleb, and he nodded. As we crossed the twenty or thirty feet of space separating us from the inn, the silent spectators began to whisper among themselves, a dark rustling at the idea of us lingering here overnight. When we were still two paces from the inn's door, it clattered open to reveal a red-faced man wearing an apron. We stopped in surprise, but he scowled and waved a bony finger at us.

"Don't you come one step closer, you hear? I want no strangers in my place of business."

I stepped back, looked up at the sign, then looked at the skinny old innkeeper. "It's an *inn*."

"Even...even so," he stammered. "Times are...times are hard. And we've no place for you here. Move along."

Caleb barely shifted, barely adjusted his shoulders, but as he stood with both hands resting on the hilts of his swords, I saw he was ready to do great violence of his own. It was not the animal madness that had driven me before, but quiet, resigned authority. He watched my eyes and waited for the order.

Something in the back corner of my mind howled at me to unleash him and glory in the blood that was spilled. I focused on a calming breath and held it at bay, then turned back to the innkeeper. "Sir, we mean no harm to you or your town. We just need a place to stay the night and a warm meal if you have one."

The muttering around the square became a muted roar as the villagers protested my small request. The innkeeper stood on his toes to look past us and saw for the first time the angry mob building outside his inn. The sight gave him courage. "Ah! Listen here. I have neither a meal nor a room for the likes of you. Now go!" He looked past us again and nodded to himself. "You hear me? You can't stay! Now get out of here. Go home!"

Behind us someone shouted, "Move along!" And another, "Get on, then! Get out!" The innkeeper smiled grimly and slammed the door in our faces.

I reached out to pound a fist, to call him back, but Caleb batted my hand away. "No use," he said. "This is going to get ugly." He jerked his head toward the crowd behind me. His eyes were moving fast over them, calculating, and his hand moved up toward the massive sword on his back.

"It won't come to that," I snapped. "They're just town-folk! We can't—" A fist-sized rock hit my shoulder hard, knocking me back against the inn's door. Another smashed into the wall beside my head. Caleb shrugged.

"They're a mob now." He drew the heavy sword, but the rain of stones continued.

I remembered what I had done to the farmer, but I remembered too that he had been so ready to fire on me before I ever acted. I pressed hard against the walls I'd built in my mind, then looked with my wizard's sight just in time to see the coal-gray streak of stone before it slammed into my left hip. My breath escaped in a hiss, and fire flared up hot behind my eyes.

"Forget the sword," I growled. "Let me handle this." A stone that might've hit Caleb's head skittered off to the left and shattered a window of the inn. I had more time to concentrate on a brick hurtling toward my midsection, and with a snarl I released its energies into a fine puff of red dust.

More were coming, but I tapped the throbbing darkness in my heart and fashioned threads of air into a kind of shield, half a dome, invisible, that I suspended at arm's length before us. Caleb was already moving forward, blade bared, and the men closest to him broke and fled. I had no wish to see him harmed, though. I wrapped him in bonds of air and hauled him back behind me and pinned him there.

No one seemed to have noticed the shield I'd made. They kept throwing stones, and now I saw a brick land on empty air a foot from my head. It hung as though caught in a web, alongside a hundred others. More came, and I felt the furious force of each stone slamming into my will. It made no difference—every stone stuck fast—but the anger behind it fed the fire burning inside me. Stones continued to rain down for some time, and I waited until the last to move. I waited until they were all watching, curious.

Somewhere inside me, part of me watched, too—a curious spectator, wondering what would come next.

A confused, curious hush fell over the crowd. The web of stones hung between us like a perforated wall, and I let my gaze pass over the crowd gathered there. All too easily I could envision the damage I could do. I had felled dragons on the wing with scarcely more munition than this.

Behind me, Caleb said softly, "Hero or madman." I unleashed his bonds.

"I came here to help them," I said. My voice trembled.

"They don't want your help." Caleb's voice rang like an indictment in the silence on the square.

The dragon voice clamored in the back of my head. *Kill them. Kill them and take their power.* My own thoughts, but from a darker part of me. It worked that way for dragons.

Perhaps it did for men as well. At the least I could take food and drink. I could find weapons in this town. Armor, even, with some little luck. They had attacked me first. The proof of it hung heavy in the air between us.

I growled, deep and angry, and poured all that throbbing fury into the web of stones. I threw them. Not at the crowd, but up into the air. I fired the whole mass of them a dozen paces up then blasted them to dust that rained down across the square like ash.

The townsfolk gasped in fear, screamed in terror, then broke and fled in perfect panic. I looked back over my shoulder at the inn's door. I could have reduced it to splinters, could have demanded a feast and no one in this town would have dared defy me. Not now.

But I would not take what I had won by might. Not from helpless villagers. I met Caleb's eyes and jerked my head toward the road. "There will be other towns. We'll find refuge elsewhere."

He nodded solemnly and with a swift motion sheathed the cruel sword. He stepped up beside me, and we followed the road out of town and into the night.

9. Half a Monster

Caleb was worried about the villagers coming after us, and I was worried how I might respond if I had to face them again, so we both moved quickly down the road. It curved gradually back toward the west which suited me well. Teelevon still called to me—Pazyarev would find Isabelle in time—but if I came to her this monster, I might do as much damage as the elder legend.

That thought dragged at my heels. Sometime after midnight I felt too tired to go on, and the night was cold, so I finally urged Caleb to stop. We made a little camp within sight of the road. I borrowed Chaos to make a campfire and bent threads of air around and above us to hide us from men and monsters alike.

I sat beside the fire, warming cold fingers, but Caleb turned his back and sat a small distance away, looking toward the road and keeping watch on the whole vast night. He cocked his head at noises I never heard, and his eyes traced paths in the night that could have been the flight of dragons or the movements of armies, but I saw nothing.

After some time I said, "Are you not cold?"

He shrugged but didn't turn.

"You can come closer to the fire."

He shook his head. "Bad for my night vision."

I laughed softly. I fell into my wizard's sight and looked out on a world glowing with the light of countless little swirling energies. The iridescent shapes of reality danced and blazed beneath the knife-edged beams of moonlight.

There were no armies, and no dragons near enough to threaten.

"I can see for us both," I said. "Enjoy the warmth."

Still he shook his head. "I trust my own hands. I believe my eyes and ears. I take more comfort from the watch than from your fire."

"But you have seen my power," I said. "You saw what I did when they threw stones at Chaaron."

He nodded, never taking his eyes off the black night. "I also saw the one that hit you. And the one that barely missed." He tapped the side of his head. "I will do things my way."

I shivered and moved a little closer to the fire. Silence fell across the world. Then sometime later he said, "Explain it to me."

The words barely reached me. I raised my eyes to the back of his head, and he shrugged. "If you can. If you would. If you ever will, tell me now." He fell silent for a heartbeat, then said, "It makes no difference, but I want to know."

"Know what?"

"What are you? Why...why? I could understand the farmer. I could understand the village. I cannot understand them together."

I closed my eyes against the searing light of the fire. "The farmer was an accident," I said. "A mistake. I lost control."

"Aha," he said, and the sure understanding in his voice twisted in my gut like the blade of a knife.

"It's worse even than you know," I said. "And you should know. You deserve the truth, if you will travel at my side. I'm tainted by the blood of dragons. I lived among them; I think like them. I can borrow power from that part of me, but it makes me reckless as well."

He shrugged one shoulder. "That is the nature of power."

"No." I gave a violent shake of my head. "No, you don't understand. I am half a monster, Caleb."

"As I said." He raised a hand before I could argue. "Every man who deals in death carries that secret knowledge in his heart, Daven. You are not the first, and you won't be the last."

"But that farmer—"

"Is not dead. There are men with far less power than you who would have done far worse to him just for the boots on his feet." He paused, then he rose and turned to me. He met my eyes across the fire. "Why did you not demand a dinner at Chaaron?"

I tried to laugh the question away. "We were not welcome there—"

"You had them subdued. If they brought anything else against you, you could have resolved that as well. And your stomach has been growling since even before the farmer's hut."

"I can survive without stealing—"

"They tried to kill you. Understand that. Those stones were not thrown in jest. They tried to kill you, and you conquered them. You were due some spoils."

I sighed and broke his gaze. "I don't want to conquer men. I want to war with dragons."

"And you mean to raise an army," he said. "And you will need a stronghold. These are the ways to wage a war, and you cannot succeed if you do not follow the rules."

"Conquering the weak, stealing spoils...that's how the dragons gather power, Caleb. I'm afraid of—"

He nodded, solemn. "There," he said. "There is the truth. You are afraid."

"Should I not be?"

He shrugged, just a shadow beyond the flames. "You will wage no war until you are willing to embrace your power." He turned away. "You will wage no war at all if you starve beneath these stars."

I frowned at his back for a moment. Then I closed my eyes and looked out with my wizard's sight. Everywhere among the tall grasses danced the dim red tracery of life-blood, and I soon found the frantic, vibrating glow of a creature of prey. I reached out with my will, wrapped it up in bonds of air, and slung it like it a stone toward our camp.

With no more warning than the sound of the poor animal in flight, Caleb had one sword drawn and the other half from its sheath before the hare crashed to the ground at his feet. Caleb skewered it on his blade and threw me a critical glance, but I just smiled up at him.

"Let's neither of us starve," I said. "And we can both work on embracing my power."

He grunted, disapproving. After a moment he chuckled. Then he drew a skinning knife from a sheath on his boot and bent to dress the hare.

We shared the rabbit's rich meat between us, and before we were done we picked the bones clean. Then Caleb went back to his vigil, and I stretched out on the grass to sleep. I dispelled the fire with a thought, and my shadowy companion nodded his approval.

After some time he said, "But what did you intend?"

"Hmm?"

"At Chaaron," he said. "Why did we go there at all? I thought you meant to recruit them."

"I think I did," I said. I swallowed hard, remembering the feeling that had dragged me down the road. It *was* a dragon's instinct. I had meant to subdue them or destroy them, and either way gain power. But even after his little speech, I couldn't admit that.

"They surprised me," I said instead. "That village reminded me of one I grew up in, a long time ago. I still can't believe the suspicion, the hate. I've *never* seen someone throw a stone at a stranger before."

He grunted. "Welcome to the world of men. How long *were* you in the dragon's den?"

"I wish I knew. At least a month. No more than two, I think. Why—" The starlight dimmed as a shadow passed over us. I looked at Caleb, and he had seen it, too. His eyes followed the path of the shadow's motion, but it was already lost in the darkness.

I waited a moment, but he was still staring off into the night to the west. After a moment he rose and absently gripped the hilt of the sword on his belt. "That one was low," he whispered, tilting his head. "I can almost hear—"

Again the wizard's sight peeled back the night, and I silenced Caleb with a gesture. I could see the dragon's Chaos shadow clear as sunrise, and I could nearly read its power as well. A single adult, and not a strong one at that. And it *was* near enough for us to strike.

I was about to give him the directions when a shout broke the night. A man's voice cried, "Help!" It was distant, almost inaudible, but when I heard it Caleb was already moving. He drew both swords and sprinted off into the night. Cursing, I gathered up the threads of our little shield and ran after him.

We tore through fields of waist-deep wheat at a dead run. I had to drop the wizard's sight to run, but I strained my ears. The first cry for help was not repeated, and I began to fear we would arrive too late. As fast as I was running, Caleb was already three paces ahead, and he was quickly pulling away from me.

Then a burst of light exploded before us, like a lightning strike in arm's reach, and I was blinded. A wash of heat rolled over us as Caleb roared wordless defiance, and I heard the slap of his boots on earth as he charged, but I could see nothing. My second sight confirmed my fears, though—the soul-stealing black of a dragon hid everything else from sight. Caleb was only visible by his motion, a lighter shade against that ancient darkness.

It took only seconds before I could see, but I didn't wait. I threw what threads of air I had around Caleb in a weightless robe, hoping it would give him some advantage. I saw the beast's long neck stab down, away, and while Caleb had the dragon's full attention, I darted around the other side.

Gradually the purple afterimage faded from my sight, and as soon as I could make out shapes I rushed forward and leaped high up on the monster's back. As I flew, the Chaos blade formed in my grip and I stabbed it hilt deep, heaved myself up, and drove a new blade in higher up. I drove at the monster again and again, aiming for the soft skin just in front of the hind legs while I climbed up toward its spine.

The dragon screamed in pain, a shriek that battered against the defenses I'd raised in my mind. But a heartbeat later the sound cut off. The body sagged beneath me, suddenly limp. I jumped clear without looking and landed in the midst of a blaze.

We had fought on packed earth—a wide wagon road that stretched north and south—but the fields of wheat grew right up to the road's edge, and the dragon's flame had caught in the grasses. I cried out in surprise more than pain, but in an instant I caught the threads of half an acre's worth of wildfire, reeled them in, and bound them to the earth at my feet. Between one breath and the next flames flashed out and darkness fell once again, held at bay only by the one bright little blaze at my feet.

Then I looked around. The shadowy mound of the dragon's motionless body was within arm's reach. I reached down and scooped up the tiny wildfire, holding it harmlessly in the palm of my hand. Then I raised it like a torch to look around.

The dragon's corpse wasn't whole. The neck ended about a pace from its shoulders. The rest of the neck and head lay cleanly severed two paces away, at Caleb's feet. I saw the greasy nothing of the dragon's power pooling around him—pouring toward him as it had done me when I killed Pazyarev's red before.

But the power didn't bleed into him. It didn't stain his hearth-hot blood. It bubbled and boiled and burned away around his feet, dissipating into nothing. He stood in the midst of the black vapor, entirely unaware, staring grimly down at the cooling corpse. He held the two-handed sword still extended before him, and as I approached he swung it warily in my direction, squinting against the unnatural light. Then he shook himself and lowered the blade.

"You lived. Good." His breath came heavy, but otherwise he seemed utterly calm as he tore up a handful of grass and scrubbed the dragon's blood from his blade. "That was...rewarding." He crossed to the heavy corpse and bent down, grabbing hold of two scales. Then he grunted and heaved upward on the dragon's bulk and shoved it backward with his shoulder. The whole body rolled back several inches. His broadswords were both buried to the guards in the dragon's breast. He pulled them free and examined the blades critically, then wiped them clean as well and sheathed them.

He nodded at me again. "Good work. Clean kill." He dusted his hands together, then clapped me on the shoulder as he passed, already heading back to our campsite. I let him get three paces before I said quietly to Caleb, "You've forgotten someone." I checked in my second sight, nearly stumbled on the even road, and switched back to the light from the dragon's flame. I needed only another dozen paces before the light revealed an open wagon, and a human form slumped against one wheel. The figure groaned as I walked over.

I left the little flame suspended in the air, just above head height, then bent to examine the man on the ground. He gave another coughing groan as I knelt before him, and while I was still looking for the stain of blood I realized the man was laughing.

"Did you see that?" he croaked. "Wind and rain, I've never in my life...big green bastard nearly had me for dinner, then the Islander came in like a shadow out of midnight."

I heard Caleb's footfall just behind me. "Who's this?" he asked.

"The one who yelled for help."

"Screamed for help!" the figure said. He grunted and pushed with an elbow and lifted himself up onto his knees. "Give me some room and I can probably stand."

"Are you sure?" I asked.

"Thanks to you and the shadow there. Strangest fight I've ever seen. He comes in screaming, and the dragon spins around to attack him. It rears up. It opens its maw and I thought for sure he was a dead man."

"It looked that way," Caleb said, utterly unconcerned.

"But then the monster just froze. It looked confused. Silliest damn thing I've ever seen."

"Haven's name," Caleb grumbled. "Who is this?"

"Jake," the figure said. "Finest turnips west of Whitefalls. And mighty obliged to you both. How did you do it?"

"Three paces of steel, judiciously applied," Caleb said. "It's easy when they don't fight back."

"I confounded it," I said, catching at Caleb's sleeve. "Just give me a moment next time."

"Oh, but thank you for your haste this first time," Jake said. "Otherwise I'd be broiled dry."

"Jake is strange," Caleb said from the other side of the wagon. "And now you should ask him why he called for help."

It seemed a senseless question, but instead of laughing, Jake suddenly went pale. He threw a nervous glance out into the night. He scanned the darkness for a moment, then turned back to me. "I was attacked."

Caleb said, "By men." It was not a question. He came around the wagon carrying a heavy crossbow bolt. He tossed it to me, then turned to Jake. "How many? Did they seem organized?"

Jake shook his head, "I wish I could say, but I didn't see a one of them. All I know is they were over that way." He pointed out over the fields to the west. "One o' them bolts smashed into the seat right next to me, and I screamed and jumped down on the other side o' the wagon. Then I hear a noise right above me, and I look up, and the whole world goes hot and yellow. Then along comes the heroes."

Caleb nodded, but his eyes were distant. After a moment he noticed I was watching him and nodded toward the wagon. "Go look at the other side." I did, and Jake followed one step behind me.

The wall of the wagon was a pincushion of dozens of heavy bolts. The driver's seat was just as heavily hit. There was no sign of the horse, though most of the harness lay in a mangled heap in the middle of the road.

Jake let out a low whistle. "Wind and rain."

Caleb grunted. "Has there been much activity around here?"

"Oh, aye!" Jake nodded vigorously. "They're always out at night, but not this close to town. I didn't expect anything, I can tell you that." He looked out over the fields again, wariness in his eyes. "You think they're still out there?"

Caleb looked to me for an answer, but I was still out of my depth. I glanced sideways at Jake, then gave a little shrug and asked, "Who?"

"Bandits!" Jake said.

"Organized," Caleb said. "The old rebels. They're building a power base along the marginal trade routes."

I thought of the long-ago attack on Tirah, and of Vechernyvetr's words as he offered to help me end the rebel siege around Teelevon. I thought of all the things I'd learned in his lair. "The dragons chafe at our organization," I said. "If there's any kind of power base forming, the dragons will assault it. I suspect that was this one's real goal."

Jake blinked. "It was trying to save me?"

"No," Caleb and I said at the same time. I nodded. "The dragons will kill everyone. They just kill the powerful first."

Jake paled. "Aha." He brushed absently at his shirtfront and looked around. "I uh...I seem to have lost the services of my cart and horse. And the night is full of surprises."

"We are headed to town. Would you like to travel with us?"

"As it happens, yes," Jake said seriously. Then he went to the bed of his wagon and began rustling through it in the dark. "And I'm sure you wouldn't mind shouldering a little load?"

Caleb grumbled something sarcastic, but I shot him a dark look to shut him up. "We would not mind at all," I said.

Jake tossed me a heavy burlap sack stuffed full, and it nearly took me off my feet. After a moment's effort I slung it over my shoulder, in time to see Caleb easily managing a sack in each hand. Jake dragged one in the dirt behind him, too.

I sent the little magic flame drifting down the road ahead of us, lighting our way, and wove another thin fabric of air to hide us from above. Then I glanced over to see Caleb frowning at one of the sacks he carried. "These must be valuable goods you're transporting to have drawn so much attention from the rebels."

"Oh, aye," Jake said. "Precious indeed. I should've known better than to travel at night."

Caleb tested his grip on the sack, prodding it as he tried to guess at the contents. "What is it? Leather armor? Some kind of flask? Heavy for that."

"Not even close," Jake said. "Your friend here knows."

He jerked a thumb at me, and I blinked in surprise. And then I laughed out loud.

"What?" Caleb asked. He started clawing at the knots at the top of one of his bags, but I shook my head and stopped him.

"Turnips," I said. "Jake is famous for them."

"Even a bandit's got to eat," Jake said proudly. "They'd have feasted for a week on these fine beauties."

Caleb frowned at him for three paces, then frowned at me for four. "Why are we bringing him?" he said.

"So I won't have to conquer this town," I said. "And so you can sleep on a feather bed. Is that reason enough?"

"That seems a fair reward!" Jake laughed. "They don't like strangers most of the time. But they'll let you in with me."

"I don't like strangers much either," Caleb grunted.

I glanced at Jake, but he didn't seem to take offense. He shrugged his shoulders and turned down the corners of his mouth good-naturedly, then trudged along. I met Caleb's eye. "He gets us in," I said. "That's what really matters."

Dawn was already touching the sky by the time we hauled Jake's harvest to the rough-cut gates of the next town, but the guards standing duty there nodded a familiar greeting to the old farmer and let us pass without a hint of challenge.

As we moved through the streets, the few townsfolk up and about seemed far more curious about us than concerned. Even the fearsome Caleb would have been a hard man to tremble at as he lumbered down the packed dirt road under two heavy sacks of turnips. By the time we dropped them in the town square, Caleb and I were the talk of the town. Strangers armed and bloodied as we were would always draw attention, but this time it set rumors flying instead of broken bricks.

And Jake was true to his word. He led us straight to the big inn's kitchen door and knocked one time before the innkeeper himself let us in. The common room wasn't yet open, but a big cook fire was already blazing, and the innkeeper put together breakfast for us while Jake rolled out a handsomely embellished version of the night's events. The tale was enough to earn us room and board for a night, and Jake promised to see us on down the road with a pack full of turnips at half the market price.

A serving girl showed us up to a pair of empty rooms just as the rest of the place seemed to be coming awake. I doubt Caleb slept. He never seemed to need it. But after the hearty meal and a full flagon of spiced wine for breakfast, I scrubbed my face and hands and feet, then slept the sleep of the dead. Caleb woke me just at dusk.

When we came down, the common room was set for dinner, and with the winter market on in town the common room was crowded tonight. A dozen sturdy wooden tables stood scattered across the floor, each surrounded by five or six wooden chairs, and the walls were lined with deep booths, all illuminated by glowing candles. A great fire blazed in the hearth at the south end of the room, and the innkeeper bustled out from behind the bar to lead us directly to a long table next to the fireplace.

"Best table in the house, this is, and it's only fitting we offer it to our heroes. Now take a seat, take a seat."

Warm mead and plates piled high with food appeared with surprising speed. I was just slicing into a pork cutlet when Caleb caught my eye across the table. "Watch yourself," he said under his breath. "Everyone else is."

I leaned back and looked around. A soft bed and a few warm drinks had knocked some of the edge off my suspicion, and it had certainly tempered the animal fury I'd felt before. I saw a few curious faces among the inn's patrons, but nothing menacing. I gave Caleb a frown.

"Nobody seems to be paying us much attention."

He grunted. "And they're spending a great a deal of effort doing it."

Before I could answer, a stranger stepped out of nowhere and clapped me on the shoulder. He was short—he would barely have come up to my shoulder if I'd been standing—but he was dressed in finery compared with the other people of the town.

I saw Caleb start, as surprised as I by the short man's sudden appearance, but the newcomer gave no notice to the sudden potential for violence that flashed across my companion's face. Instead, he gripped my shoulder like an old friend and spoke as if in answer to Caleb's last quiet comment.

"Pay no mind. They're just excited. News of last night's adventure is the talk of the town."

Caleb eased himself back into his seat, eyes narrowed to slits. "Who are you?"

The newcomer sank down in a chair next to me and threw Caleb a big grin. "Stephen Dehl! I'm mayor of this town, and the way I hear it I owe you two a great deal of gratitude."

"We saved a farmer," Caleb growled, like it was no more significant than squashing a bug.

"We killed a dragon," I added, anxious to keep the good will we'd earned in this town.

"A dragon. Hah! Yes. So I've heard!" The mayor chuckled and shook his head. "But you certainly saved our Jake from a bandit raid, and he's a well-liked man in this town. You two made friends here."

"Friends we could use," I said. "More than anything else, we need news."

He seemed surprised. "News? How do you mean?"

"Are you familiar with the land west of here? I need to know what has happened to the town of Teelevon."

He looked back and stared theatrically up at the ceiling, silently mouthing the name Teelevon, then shrugged, "I'll beg your pardon, friend, but I don't know the place. Perhaps you could tell me the general vicinity?"

"It's outside Tirah. Five days' ride to the south, along the King's Road—"

The mayor brightened. "Then you have nothing to fear! The monsters won't go anywhere near that area. Tirah they avoid, and they know better than to strike along the road."

"Are you sure?" I asked.

He nodded. Across the table, Caleb raised a finger as though to interject but then sat back again.

I frowned at both of them, then turned all my attention to the mayor. "How do you know so much about them?"

"Ah, they've been a mighty nuisance for months now. We've had chance to learn much of their ways, more's the pity." He held up a hand and ticked off points as he came to them, "They always strike at night, and in large numbers. They take one man at a time when they can, but the smaller villages have been attacked outright. They kill for fun, but their real goal is to plunder anything of value."

"That's...not quite right," I said. "But it's very close."

The mayor frowned at me, but before he could argue Caleb sat forward. "Anything of value?" he asked. "Even turnips?"

"Of course, you'd know that!" the mayor said, his grin returning briefly. Then he shook his head with a sigh. "They're getting more dangerous as they get hungry. Winter's going to be rough."

I looked across at Caleb, utterly confused. He rolled his eyes. "There people aren't afraid of dragons."

"*Dragons?*" The mayor asked, his voice going shrill. "Not *really* dragons? I mean...I'd heard, but I thought they were rumors the bandits spread."

"The dragonswarm is here," I told him, keeping my voice level. "And it is very real."

Caleb nodded into his beer. "They're still not much on the plains, but give it a couple months and they'll burn this town to the ground."

The mayor looked back and forth between us, and at last the showman's color seemed to drain from his face. He shrank in on himself and stared glumly down at the table. "There's not much left to burn," he said after a while. "The brigands have taken everything already. A little gruesome fire might be better than the long, slow starve." He waved to one of the maids.

"These are the same brigands who attacked farmer Jake?" I asked. The mayor and Caleb both nodded, but something Caleb had mentioned the night before only then struck home. "The old rebels?" I asked, shocked.

The mayor frowned at me. Caleb tilted his head, calculating, and said, "You do know about the rebellion, right?"

"It was months, Caleb, not years. But the rebellion was put down."

Caleb shrugged. "It ended, anyway."

"Not even that," the mayor growled. "It only changed its focus. Instead of robbing and warring with the king, they rob and war with the little villages now."

Caleb nodded. "They've been a problem for a long time. On the plains, they're the bigger threat."

"A bigger threat than the *dragonswarm?*"

Caleb sighed. "You do seem to know a little bit about the rebellion." I nodded, and he nodded. "Do you know about the army Brant raised in the process?"

I had spent a day tracking them through rough country, and another day a prisoner in their camp. And I had put a whole army of them to flight with the help of one dragon. I knew them well.

"Ruffians," I said. "They were just rabble, right, and he trained them up to fight for him?"

"Exactly. Thousands of murderous men, and he taught them to live off the land. To hide among the population. They strike at night, unseen, against their opponents' weaknesses. He made a pretty impressive force of them." The mayor huffed at that, but he didn't contradict the soldier.

Caleb went on. "The king sent an army to put down the rebellion, and they should have been sufficient to wipe out Brant's men in spite of their tactics, but it never happened."

"It did," I said. "The king came in person and took Tirah with barely a fight."

Caleb's eyes narrowed again, and he hesitated before he went on. "Without a fight at all, in fact. Because they were not there."

"Well, no. They were...well, they were in Teelevon with the wizard Lareth. Staging for a strike. But they were scattered before they could attack."

"Were they?" he asked, and I realized for the first time that the truth of that night might never have reached outside Teelevon. I had carried word to the king's highest officers, but they had not deigned to listen.

And then I understood what the mayor had been saying, what Caleb had meant about the old rebels building up a power base—not scattered groups of deserters banding together, but an army meant to win a rebellion.

My jaw dropped at the thought. "The army still stands?" I started to my feet. "They never tracked them down? They never *ended* it?"

Caleb shook his head. "When Brant was dealt with, the rebellion hardly mattered anymore. His men returned to the lives of crime from which he had summoned them, and likely the king's officers believed local law would eventually see them all in shackles or nooses."

The mayor slammed a tiny fist down on the solid oak table hard enough to set the dishes rattling. "Oh, yes, they became brigands and highwaymen again. Hah! But with the training and organization that Brant had been giving them for years."

"And the equipment they'd plundered from guards and garrisons," Caleb added.

The mayor nodded solemnly. "They began to terrorize us all, and now we didn't even have the duke to call for help. No one could restrain them."

Caleb said, "The king's army made Tirah secure, but he had not brought enough to track a thousand little bands across the whole of the Ardain. Wherever they heard of a force gathering near a major town, the Guard would ride out and drive them off."

"Aye," the mayor said, "They drove 'em right off into the plains. So instead of fighting king's men they're fighting farmers and shepherds out among the wheat. These days the bastards kill whenever they can just for practice, and they rob anyone they meet of anything worth anything. These are the renegades that you know nothing about."

As they told the story, I could only stare at them, unbelieving. When they finished I felt numb. "All that has happened?" They both nodded, grave. "This is what has become of the world? This is what mankind does when faced with destruction? The dragons don't even have to come. We will destroy ourselves!"

Caleb nodded, grim. "Something should have been done, but now it's too late. They are scattered."

I shook my head. I still felt numb. "Dragons fly to kill us all, and an army of deserters and criminals roams unchallenged to prey on the towns of the Ardain." I thought of Teelevon, strangled by the siege, and a king unwilling to send them any aid. I turned to the mayor. "Has anyone faced them?"

The mayor held his palms up, helpless, "Brant took all our fighting men years ago. We have only shepherds and seamstresses now. What are we going to do against them?"

I rounded on Caleb, but his eyes were on the table. Still he answered my silent question. "The king's army is just a show of force, now. They hold Tirah and grant refuge to anyone who asks it there. The wizards, the Green Eagles, and all the regiments hide behind the city walls while Timmon once again secures his power."

"And we are left to die," the mayor said sadly, as though from a long way off.

Caleb looked up at him, grief in his eyes, but I interrupted. "This *will not* continue. Caleb, let's go."

He looked up at me in astonishment, "What? Where?"

Gone was the gentle warmth of comfort and good nourishment I had felt before. Animal fury burned in my heart again. But now I did little to restrain it. I focused the pounding anger, I shaped it in my mind. I began to design a new reality and looked for ways to make it from my rage.

"I need an army to fight my war. Perhaps I cannot ask good men to die for me," I said. "But I would gladly put these rebels to the task."

I was already at the door, bristling with energy. Caleb covered the floor in two long steps and turned me to face him. "You want to take control of the rebels? Are you mad?"

"It's simple," I said. "We'll find this army—we *know* they're not far off—and I will do what I must to tame them."

The mayor jumped up, his eyes cautious. "But...but...you're going to *join* the rebels?"

"No," Caleb answered him without taking his eyes from mine. "No, he means to conquer them. He means to make a weapon of them."

"And when I'm done...." I was shaking with excitement and fear at the path unfolding in my head. "When I'm done, we'll face whatever chaos threatens this land. I don't care if it's dragons or rebels or mobs of peasants, we're going to make this nation whole again."

Energy seemed to crackle through the room, bouncing out in whispers and rebounding in murmurs, in exclamations, in shouts. But Caleb stood one pace away, his eyes on mine and his expression serious. "Where will you take them?" he asked.

A moment before I hadn't even considered it, but as soon as he asked I smiled a sad smile. I would conquer my brood, and then build my lair. "Palmagnes will stand again."
I did not say it loudly, but the words had weight beyond

their volume. I heard several people in the room gasp. I nodded with a dreadful certainty. It felt right. "The fortress will stand strong, and I will remake a nation from its ruins."

Caleb's eyes were wide too. I waited half a heartbeat before I saw just the hint of a nod from him. Madman or hero, he'd said. I stretched a hand out to the hearthfire and called two hot golden flames to dance in the air above my hand. The noisy audience fell silent at that, hushed in terror, and I remembered another common room I had once cowed with flame.

I had hated myself for that display, but I could not spare such sentiment now. The world would not survive without my fire. Perhaps I had to be the dragon. Perhaps I had to embrace that dark nature. But even as a monster I would bend my power to the good of the world, when wizards and kings could not be bothered to do that much.

I growled low, and the flickering flames pulsed with my hammering heartbeat. I raised them into the night and set them dancing above my head, a beacon that could not be missed. Then I set my feet on the open road and headed out to defeat an army.

10. The Army

"Should we discuss this?" Caleb asked as we passed through the town's rough gates.

"We should speak," I said. "I'm counting on them finding us, after all."

"You could have made a better plan."

"I don't have time for a better plan," I said, and then I stopped. I glared up at Caleb. "I mean this: I cannot *afford* to stop and think, or I will make the same abominable decision the king has made. And this mayor. And every authority from here to the ruins of Palmagnes."

That thought sent me thundering down the road again. Caleb had no trouble keeping pace.

"Your heart does you proud, Daven. The sentiment is noble. But you are too valuable a warrior—"

"Who were you?" I asked. I did not shout, but the words were enough to cut through his speech. He didn't answer me, and I threw him a look from the corner of my eye before I asked again, "Who were you before the dragonswarm? Before the village?"

"A deserter from the king's army," he said. The bitterness in his voice told me to leave it there, but I had already seen deeper.

"You were an officer," I said. "You were a Green Eagle, weren't you?"

He was silent for some time. Then I heard him swallow. "An unlikely guess," he said. "Not many Bateiyns get that close to the king."

"But you were an exception," I said.

"I was an exception." He sighed. "How could you know?"

"You came here to end this rebellion, and you alone were unsatisfied when the king's commanders decided that was done."

"Not alone," he said. "But yes. I was unsatisfied."

"I saw it in your eyes when the mayor was speaking. I saw it in your pain when you failed to save a village from a dragon raid. And I saw it in the sword you wear on your right hip."

He frowned at that. I caught the motion as he looked down. "What?"

I smiled to myself. "I once owned a sword like that," I said. "I tried to use it to kill a dragon, and I did something else altogether. I had won it from the Green Eagle Othin."

"He is a powerful warrior," Caleb said, his tones measured.

"And I was a fortunate child," I said. "And for that he wants me dead. But I am not curious at all why you deserted that post. I want to know how you were made a Green Eagle at all."

He shook his head. "I made a name among my own. I caught the right man's attention on the right day. They said I was born to be a leader...." He trailed off. After a moment he cursed, then said, "They were wrong. I am a proud fighter, a fearsome soldier, but I was not meant to lead."

I turned and faced him. He stopped and only reluctantly looked down to meet my gaze.

"Anyone with a Green Eagle's training would make a fine leader," I said. "An Islander who rose to that rank? A man would be a fool not to follow you."

He smiled down at me. "Just a warrior. An officer, perhaps. But I can't command unless I have men given to me. I can only act by borrowed authority. As soon as he tightened my leash, I was no leader at all."

"Is there any other way?"

He laughed, and I remembered how Vechernyvetr had laughed at the same question. "There's officers, and then there's kings. Kings get to act on will alone. And *you*," he said. "You could be a king."

I shook my head, but he jabbed a finger at me. "For three years I was the king's personal bodyguard," he said. "For three years I was never more than twenty paces from his side, and he was a great man. Greater than most give him credit for, I would say, but not as great as you. You fight like a warrior, think like a wizard, and speak like a king."

"No, Caleb." I spread my hands in total honesty. "I have power, and that is all. I cannot build another relationship on an imagined past. I was born a peasant, and I have been despised by all manner of men. I am a failed wizard, a wanted criminal, and a hated hero. The best I can boast is this: I am a survivor desperate for a home. That is all."

He shrugged. "Believe what you will, but to me you are a lord." He drew the sword that hung on his right hip and fell to his knees, holding it with the tip grounded before him. "I pledge to be your man, Daven of Teelevon, to serve you with my heart, my soul, my mind, and my strength, as long as you have need of me. I bind my honor to your honor. I bind my life to your life. I bind my sword to your sword. I live for you and take you as my lord."

I stood frozen, unable to respond. When he had finished the short pledge he slowly rose, staring into my eyes. I opened my mouth to object, to refuse his oath, but he spoke first. "I told you before that I'm your man. Maybe this will make you understand."

I wanted to answer him. To call him mad. To reject the offer. But I could not speak. I had never meant to take on the wizard's sight, but still I could see the power pooled around him, hard-edged and unbreakable, strong enough to shatter stone. It wasn't the inky black of pure Chaos, it was the vibrant fire of lifeblood, but still some measure of it washed from him to me, as it had when I'd slain the dragon, and I felt the pounding of new power thundering in my veins.

Still Caleb was speaking. "If you are right, the dragon-swarm you describe will break our nations. Perhaps one day Timmon shall be my king again. If you win your war, perhaps he will have a kingdom to rule. But here and now, and in this world, you are the only king I know."

I looked at him, incredulous. I gasped for breath enough to say, "You are mad."

He nodded. "I am. Mad enough to follow you into the night, looking for an army of renegades and thieves. Mad enough to follow you against the whole nightmare swarm of dragons. As I said from the first: I am your man."

The song of Chaos still blazing in my spirit, the wizard's sight bright in my inner vision, I closed my eyes and extended my awareness. In an instant I could see for miles, and I skimmed the world for lifeblood. The lives of men were startlingly bright, deliberate, compared with the lifeblood of other living things, and it was easy to find farms and villages, towns and even the hint of a city far to the west. But those were always surrounded by the careful, manufactured structures of their dwelling places.

Night had fallen, and the times were hard. In all the vast plains I saw few souls outside the safety of their thresholds. Just Caleb and me. A hurrying shape in a distant village. Four men together in the town behind us, and those perhaps the gate guards. And there ahead, gathered in empty fields as though they were a vibrant city, I saw a throng of men without a home among them.

They were not hunting for us. Not now. Perhaps, if the timing had been right, we might have stumbled across that raiding party of seven, but if not for that we would have passed the army by. My breath escaped me as I looked on the blazing fire of so many men gathered together. My anger escaped me, eclipsed by fear, and the vision slipped away.

But still I knew. I knew without a doubt. I turned in place and looked across black night toward their camp, and I could *feel* them waiting for me. "There," I said. I pointed for Caleb. "Perhaps three hundred of them. Perhaps five. Two miles to their outskirts."

"And how do you mean to move among them?" Caleb asked.

I let my breath out slowly, deliberately, and gathered my will as though I were still a new student. I focused my attention, then reached into my core and borrowed Chaos as I had learned to do in Vechernyvetr's lair.

I had not done it so carefully since the power had failed me before. I hadn't dared to try. But now it answered as I had hoped it might. I felt the full, raw power available to me. It was not the vast store the dragon had acquired, but it was more than I'd dared to hope.

Threads of air spun out easily around Caleb and me, and I threw us into the air as I had done above the dragon's mountain. I heard the warrior curse in the darkness, and then he screamed bloodfury at the thrill of flight. We crossed the miles in mere moments, and he fell silent as the fires appeared below us.

Not the lifeblood fires of the wizard's sight, but a hundred campfires, two hundred torches. This was not a casual gathering but a military camp, and I heard a note of caution in Caleb's voice when he said, "Daven."

"I know," I said. I held us high above the camp, suspended and still. There was steel among them. I could feel it. I could almost taste it in the air. Far more than I'd expected. Not just rotting leather armor and hunting bows, but swords and shields and heavy chain.

"Daven," Caleb said again, and I glanced over my shoulder at him.

"They are better appointed than you'd expected," I said, speaking for him.

He nodded. "Yes, but that was not my point." He gestured up above us. "I think you would do well to hide your lights."

The flames I'd borrowed from the common room's hearth still danced above my head. And then, before I could release them, I watched the first wink out. The second followed a moment later.

"Wind and rain," I said. Panic hammered at my ribcage, but the words came out almost thoughtful. Caleb looked to me, and I sighed. "They have another wizard."

Then we began to fall.

It was nothing like the sickening, bottomless drop when I'd lost the power from Vechernyvetr's lair. This time it was a violent tug. We dropped three paces then stopped. I had just time to catch my breath—Caleb had just time to curse—then it happened again. The next time we were hurled sideways instead of downward, but it was just as jarring.

"What's happening?" Caleb shouted.

I tore my eyes from the ground, still forty paces beneath us. "It's just air," I said.

"What?"

"The power that's holding us." I scanned the earth rapidly, but it was tiny figures and flickering flames and far too much shadow. "It's just air. I made it—wizards can't make it—but now that it's there, he's working it around us."

Another tug, and we plummeted ten paces before the threads of air caught us up. Caleb cursed again, but my attention was all on the ground.

"Why don't you fight him?" Caleb growled.

"I never learned how." I fell to my hands and knees within my airy cage and looked closer, but before I could make a plan he was there again.

I saw the effects without knowing the method. My shimmering skein of neat blue threads of air twisted itself into a rope, a blast of air instead of a bed. I did as I'd done before and released the threads from my will. Borrowed Chaos vanished, and whatever magic the wizard had worked vanished with it. But so too vanished the energy that had held us up.

We fell perhaps a pace this time before I could get the new threads in place, and while Caleb was still grumbling I let those go, too, and summoned more another pace down. It bought me a moment, the rebel wizard's will still focused on energies that were already dissolving.

It gave me long enough to breathe, and in that time I looked down through the wizard's sight. Once again I saw the vast sea of lifeblood, but now that I knew to look it was a simple matter to find the glowing sheen of wizardry at work in their midst. A hundred paces off across the face of a hill, just below a massive spreading oak. I stretched out a hand, touched the darkness in my heart, and shaped raw power into a ball of earth twice the size of a slingstone but moving just as fast.

That gave him time enough to work against my web, and this time instead of pulling it away, he sent it gusting down.

I gulped and cried a wordless warning to Caleb as we slammed toward the earth, then summoned just enough of air to stop the fall from killing us. Still I hit the ground hard enough that lights flashed in my head and the breath was knocked out of me.

Caleb landed just as hard, but he nearly seemed to bounce. In an instant he was up, swords in both hands, and not a heartbeat later steel rang on steel as he deflected a powerful blow. I groaned and rolled aside and heaved myself upright, then threw another look.

Surrounded. Warriors for miles, and closing on us fast. I sought briefly for the telltale shine of the wizard's working, but I had no time to find it. A human shadow sprang up before me, both arms raised around the hilt of a reversed dagger and bloodlust burning in his eyes.

I moved by old instinct, left foot sliding back, right foot twitching forward, arm outstretched to meet the lunge. And new instinct tapped the inky Chaos in my heart and built a perfect blade within my grip. Between one heartbeat and the next I gained a sword, and my astonished attacker fell full upon it. He skewered himself up to the guard. Blood washed warm over my hand. His mouth made an O of shock and confusion and then the life went from him.

My stomach twisted in revulsion. A scream bubbled up behind my breastbone but I couldn't find enough breath to let it out. I released the Chaos blade, and the dead man slumped to the earth. Another soldier who had been on his heel turned and fled, but I could feel the wash of men around me. I could hear the thudding footsteps, smell the stink of fear and fury, hear the hiss of arrows in the air.

That snapped me from my stupor. Something animal surged up in answer, unfazed by the guilty horror at what I'd just done. It turned my head and tapped my powers. It narrowed my eyes, spoke a word, and forge-hot fire blos-

164

somed into a ball no more than a foot across—just large enough to swallow the arrow mid-flight.

Just bright enough to reveal the archer, terror in his eyes. And then it was gone.

The next ball of fire blossomed inside the man's midsection and vanished to leave him empty. He fell to the earth with a sick wet sound.

I wanted to shout, "No!" but the word wouldn't come. The horror couldn't either. It cowered in the back of my head, in the tiny corner I reserved for monsters. My humanity hid in the shadows, and the dragon power answered the threat around me.

The power was stronger, too. I'd felt it as the rebel spilled his life across my hand, and I'd felt it again as I burned the heart from the archer. Crackling, sparking *pop*s like a wet log on a blazing fire, as new power flowed into me. I caught motion from the corner of my eye and spun, summoning a new Chaos blade as I went, and it took the head from a man in shining chain.

Pop.

He had two companions with him. One charged me, a pike stretched out before him, but I glanced to the earth at his feet and it swallowed him like water. *Pop.* The other turned to run and I gave him a good head start. Then I snapped a hand and raw air curled out toward him like a whip. It lashed around his throat. I jerked it back. The man's own momentum ripped his feet from under him and slammed his weight against the invisible noose.

Pop.

The monster within me laughed, and the sound rang out eerily loud even in the noisy night. I closed my eyes and looked with my other sight, trying to count the scurrying glows of the rebels, trying to separate them from the wavering threads of fire all around the camp. Then something out of Chaos whispered a suggestion to my rational mind, and my mouth curled in a smile.

Fire. Living fire, raw fire, not borrowed power but still at my command, and it was everywhere. I took a breath, and for a mile around me in all directions, the fire winked out. The threads of flame flew to me like prize falcons, invisible power, and for a moment I stood in the utter darkness and savored the taste of terror in the wails of terrible men.

To that sweet accompaniment I sculpted the fire's power. I shaped a hundred cooking fires and the light of twice as many torches into a single piece, a pillar five paces across and thirty paces tall. Invisible. Unreal. Potential. I built it like a tower around me, grinning all the while. In the darkness someone shouted, "The wizard! Where is the wizard? Get the wizard!"

Then I exhaled, and in the same moment I unleashed the power of the flames. The pillar of fire exploded into reality all around me, blazing hot as a mountain's heart and roaring like an elder dragon. I took one long step forward, and the pillar moved forward with me. I gloried in the screams.

In my wizard's sight I could see them running, tumbling over one another, fighting desperately to get away. And I could see a direction in their flight, a rough shape to it, as everyone before me bent their paths toward a particular hillside. As I looked now I could see the slow pulse of earth and life at the top of it—the spreading oak.

Aha. The wizard. "Get the wizard," they'd said. I followed, unafraid. Grass and earth and stone scorched black where I walked, and men fled like terrified cattle before me, and all the while the thunder in my veins and the roaring of the flames went on and on like some mad harmony. I broke into a run, hungry to obliterate their only hope within this mess, and now the fire's song gained words, pounding along with my leaping stride.

Destroy the world!
We'll burn it down.
Obliterate the bonds that hold!
And tear apart the lives that thrive.

I threw my arms out wide and screamed in primal fury, and around me the pillar of fire unfolded into a shape like a man. I smiled at that and swung an arm as long as a dragon's tail, and three dozen of the rebels were turned to ash. The sudden rush of power dropped me to my knees.

Destroy the world!
We'll burn it down.
Obliterate the bonds that hold!
And tear apart the lives that thrive.

The world. The whole world was within my reach. I could feel it. I could see the shape of it. The Chaos power spoke to me again as it had before, showed me the structure, and I trembled as I pulled down the pillar of fire. I pulled it into me again, energy untold. Darkness fell once more. I heard whimpers and tears and scurrying feet, but in my mind I could see all the bodies. Fighting desperately for escape, but still close enough for me to touch.

I trembled again. I rattled like a reed within a gale, but the black spirit that drove me was resolute. It stretched the threads of fire as thin as gossamer and laid them out like a spider's web. It borrowed the Chaos, too, and twined its inky black among the burning red, laying out a dancing pattern that glowed against the face of the earth.

It shone like timber coals and molten tar, a hair-fine lace that stretched for miles. As far as the army's camp, as far as the very last rebel among them. The monster in my heart strained to push it farther, threading more and more black power into the web, and reached another hundred paces beyond the last of the fleeing rebels. My breath rattled in my throat and my forehead dropped against the cracked, blackened earth as the web's outermost line fell into a perfect circle.

And then it flared. I couldn't see it, more than a mile away among the rolling hills, but in my mind's eye it was clear as day. A wall of Chaos fire taller than a man, blazing roar, and hanging like a curtain in a perfect circle nearly a league across.

In the same instant it appeared, one of the panicked rebels ran into it, unable to stop his momentum. I felt it happen. From a mile away, I felt the little ecstatic tremor in my soul as he died. And then another, another, perhaps two dozen in the space of two heartbeats, all around the circle, and the new power poured into it.

They came back then. I could feel their footsteps along the web of power, I could taste their maddened panic, I could watch them shrink away from the fire and come reluctantly back toward me. The fire and the midnight raged, and that voice whispered in my mind again. It showed me the shape of the thing I'd wrought. It showed me a web stretching to the horizon, but that was just the beginning.

It showed me how I could touch the web here, and here, and here. How I could unfold it with my will, and let it loose upon the world. Let it run across the plains and sear the mountains down to coal. Let it boil in the seas and set fire to the skies. It was power, pure power, absolute destruction in my grasp.

I panted at the memory of the power I'd gained from two dozen deaths, and the darkness whispered to me that I could kill them all. I could kill them all, and have power enough to make whatever world I wanted.

Destroy the world!
We'll burn it down.
Obliterate the bonds that hold!
And tear apart the lives that thrive.

They were coming. The whole vast array of men, not in a panicked rush, not in an angry charge, but like sheep before the shepherd's hound. They'd seen the fiery corral, and they'd seen the pillar at its heart. They came to me now, to be judged and destroyed. The darkness offered them to me like a gift. It showed me how to bend the web, how to flex its threads like breathing in and out, and consume three hundred men with just a thought.

I pushed my hands against the earth and tried to rise. The Chaos rang in my arms and legs until they trembled, but I made them hold. I coughed and fell back on my heels, then with a grunt of effort I heaved myself upright.

Shadows swayed around me, dark but for the soul-bright shadow of Chaos fire beneath their feet, silent but for the weary, wounded sound of their beating hearts. They were not men; they had no faces for me. They were power ready to be tapped. I could consume them all as easily swallowing some tender morsel. Unsummoned fire blazed behind my eyes.

And then the earth crunched beneath a footfall, near at hand. Behind me. I did not turn but looked out through the thread of flames, and they showed me a shadow near as dark as night but bright with power. Living power. *Human* power. And he was mine.

My mouth twisted in a grin. "Caleb," I said, and fire crackled in my voice. "You have survived."

"You've embraced your power," he said. There was a note of admiration. It made me tremble.

"Not...yet," I said, and the darkness whispered once again.

So easy. So very easy. Like catching my breath, and hundreds of lives of power could be mine. And then the world.

"These men are yours," he said.

I trembled again, but I kept my feet. "One way or another," I said.

He nodded. He took another step toward me, then asked with a voice like frightened secrets, "What's in Teelevon?"

My knees buckled, then crashed to the ground. Fire flared around me, shapeless and wild, but I pressed it down with my will, and it bled back into the web. I shook my head. "Not now!"

He cleared his throat, and still at half a whisper asked again, "What's in Teelevon?"

Eyes. Within the darkness in my head, I caught a glimpse of a memory. Eyes of blue and gray like autumn storms, and a scent like summer sunsets. The monster within me growled a warning, and fire erupted around Caleb.

I found my strength and heaved myself to my feet, turning. I stretched a hand and the fire fell away, leaving Caleb singed and slick with sweat, but he never tore his eyes from me. He set his jaw and caught his breath and gave me a sad smile. "What's in Teelevon?"

"Home," I said. It rolled out like a growl, and I could feel the flare of fury from the monster once more, but I was ready for it now. I caught it up, diverted the raw power back down into the earth, then forced that wretched spirit from my will. I walled it off and drove it back. I thought of Isabelle and fought for hope.

It might have taken moments—it felt like days—but I won my spirit back from the Chaos I had used. Not Pazyarev, not Vechernyvetr, but the Chaos in my heart every bit as black and blinding as the beasts I'd had to battle.

I fought until I could breathe again. I fought until I could smell the acrid soot on the winter wind and see the distant sparkle of southern stars. I fought until I felt the horrified weight of the murders I'd just done. Then I hung my head and sighed.

"Every man with power is half a monster," Caleb said. "You must remember what it's for."

I opened my eyes and looked. Beneath the silver stars I stood at the center of the web I had created, and I remembered the nightmare song. It had been so tempting to set them free. It would have taken only a thought, and I could have released all the fires of Chaos on this world. In the fever of a hallucination, I had almost done the dragons' work for them.

Then I heard the voice again, a little louder this time. Insisting, begging, pleading to be released. The web still waited around me, ready to unfold.

Disgusted and afraid, I gathered the threads of my terrible creation and bound them into the ground, contracting and containing them into a single point, right at the heart of the circle. I pulled down the curtains of flame and gathered up the web of oily Chaos.

When all the power was bound I stepped away, backing slowly, and then released the wild fire. It burst into the heavens, a single pillar of flame that seared the sky and lit the night like day. The heat blasted outward, and a burning wind tossed me back like a doll. I crashed against Caleb, but he did not yield at all. He caught me, steadied me, then let me go.

And then the fire was gone. The shadows remained.

I ran my eyes along the line of men, still stunned, still waiting, still afraid. They wilted wherever I turned my gaze, fighting to hide from me but unwilling to try to run. Their clothes were singed and their faces and hands red from the heat, but all their attention was on me. Here was the army I had come hunting, all standing silent and afraid.

I stepped forward slowly, slapping at the oily soot that covered me from head to toe, and when I did the men nearest me drew back. At the heart of the ruined earth I turned slowly, taking in all the men around me, and then I spoke with a solemn voice, loud in the unnatural silence.

"I am Daven of Teelevon, and I have come to take command of this army. Who is your leader?"

For a moment no one spoke, and then a hesitant voice said, "It was the wizard, but he is dead."

I hesitated only a moment, then said, "Will any of you stand against me, then? Is there a man among you who dares challenge me?"

There was no answer, only fear in their eyes, and I nodded. "I am a power greater than any wizard or lord you yet have served. My will is burning flame." I shuddered at the memory and had to catch my breath. "But I have come to burn a fire against the darkness. I would make peace, and I would make it with the swords and arrows that you carry. I have heard about your crimes," I turned again, meeting as many eyes as I could, "and I hold you accountable. Now you will make amends in service to me."

I waited for some argument, some objection, but none came. They only stood, transfixed, watching me like I was a rabid dog. Finally I sighed. "If none dares challenge me, I call you conquered. Come before me, one by one, and I will accept your fealty."

Behind me, Caleb raised his voice. "None leaves until all have sworn."

There was a note in it of authority. Not a high demand, not a heavy threat, but the easy command of an officer, and even these rebels had some amount of soldiers' training. I saw it in their eyes, in the sudden change of stance.

Then Caleb stepped past me and fell to one knee. In a voice that carried to the others, he said as he had before, "I pledge to be your man—to serve you with my heart, my soul, my mind, and my strength, as long as you have need of me. I bind my honor to your honor. I bind my life to your life. I bind my sword to your sword. I live for you, and take you as my lord."

Some among the circle muttered surprise at the depth of the oath, but I did not wait for them to wonder. As Caleb rose and stepped behind me, I raised a hand, manifesting a Chaos blade within the gesture, and pointed it at the man directly across from me. "You! You're next."

His eyes went wide, but he didn't dare refuse. He crossed the circle and fell on both knees before me, haltingly repeating the oath Caleb had sworn. When he finished he rose, meeting my gaze with fear in his eyes.

New power thrummed into me, but it wasn't the angry black *pop* of murder done. It was the strength of a man. It was the honest weight of weary muscle.

I smiled at my new vassal. "You have seen my power. I will punish oath-breakers."

He nodded, mute, then moved to stand next to Caleb. Another came unbidden, and then another. They crossed the circle one by one, and every man swore oath to me. Some were dressed in shoddy leather armor or tattered clothes, but I also saw the suits of chain, the shining plate, the equipment they had won.

Every man among them had the bearing of a soldier, and they wore their weapons with old familiarity. Dawn came before the last of them had knelt, and when he went to take his place among the ranks, I turned and felt my heart leap at the sight. A whole column stood in file, a small army sworn to serve me. And in the first row, victory glowing in his eyes, stood Caleb.

I nodded to him, and he stepped forward. "My lord?"

I looked out over the rest of the men, then back to Caleb. "Can you organize them?" He nodded. "Good. Then I must ask you to be a leader once again." I raised my voice so those near enough could hear, and said, "If you have any trouble with them, I will settle it." Fear paled the faces of those who heard, and I trusted rumor to carry the word.

But Caleb shrugged and answered with a voice for me alone. "I shouldn't have much trouble. They are soldiers—they're accustomed to authority. And you've put the fear of Haven into them." He saluted, then turned to face the men.

"Deal with it, then. I'm exhausted." I turned my back on him and headed uphill toward the spreading oak. It would make as good a place as any to rest. I couldn't sleep. I didn't need to sleep. My mind and body both hummed with the new oaths of fealty. I could have run miles or wrestled a bull to the earth.

But I needed silence and a place to clear my head. I needed a moment to sort through the chaotic maelstrom I'd survived and adjust to the idea of having followers. Of having an army. I was perhaps a hundred paces off, halfway up the hillside, when I cast a glance back over my shoulder and shook my head in awe at the sight. Three hundred men in rank and file, hungry for blood, and Caleb prowled among them like a lion.

From my vantage I could see his towering figure. The one column I had left behind was now broken into a dozen smaller squares, and Caleb walked a grid between them, stopping here and there to speak with someone inside a formation. I watched as he finished one of these conversations and moved on, and the man he had spoken with left his place and moved to stand in front of his square.

Officers. He'd known these men for no more than hours, and started as an enemy, but already he was handing out promotions, creating order among them, making them his own. And I saw no man out of place, no uneven lines among my ragtag warriors. They had their training, and Caleb had his, and the two fit together like pieces of some gruesome puzzle.

He was making me an army. I shook my head, amazed—hundreds of men at my command, and a Green Eagle for my general. Then I turned back toward the hilltop and heaved a weary sigh. There had been more yesterday. The blood was on my hands. They were not good men, but it had been a monster that destroyed them. I would have to answer for that, but I'd answer for it with a pile of dragon corpses.

My next breath came more easily. I could not make myself clean, but I could fight the dragonswarm. With an army, I could do real good.

And there was a mercy in the monstrous things I'd done. I'd left no wounded victims. I'd left no reminders, no messes that needed cleaning up. Only soot on the trampled grasses and a memory dulled by madness.

Except...except just there ahead. Two boots, once fine but tattered now. I frowned as I came closer. A cane lay fallen in the grass, polished mahogany with an ivory handle. The wind had tugged a long cloak's folds out over the fallen figure. Its hem danced and rustled on the breeze, old suede rubbed down to smooth leather.

I understood when I saw his head, caked thick with blood from a blunt injury. The scalp had broken but it didn't look to have been a killing blow. The figure still twitched with shallow, even breath. One shot, one strike before the fight had truly engaged, and I'd knocked him out cold. It was the wizard who had nearly ripped us from the sky, the once-leader of these rebels. I summoned a Chaos blade before I knelt over him, then reached out carefully with its tip to push the blood-caked, dirty blond hair back from a face stretched thin and hollow over its skull.

The whole body was frail, shriveled and bone-thin, but the staring face was worse. His eyes and cheeks were sunken and marred with permanent bruises. His lips were pencil-thin and split with cracks like fissures. The cleft in his jaw poked prominently past the thin stubble of a nomad life.

He was sickly and broken, made all the more nightmarish by the dried and flaking blood. Worse was the char-black scars that covered half his face. One eye was gone, one ear, and what remained of that half of his mouth dragged down at the corner and gapped over black-seared teeth.

The worst was that I knew him. I'd killed him once already.

11. The Wizard

The figure on the earth before me was Lareth Undinane—the rebel wizard who had started every darkness in my life. I rose, and gently lifted back his flapping cloak with the tip of my Chaos blade. He wore a frayed old silken doublet underneath it. I stared at the faded fabric, but I don't dknow what I expected to see: oozing blood, perhaps, or the bulge of thick bandages. I'd stabbed three feet of flawless steel clean through his chest. But that had been a hundred days ago.

He had not recovered well, but he had recovered. My teeth ground together in anger, and my hand ached from its grip on the sword's hilt. I felt the frantic thrashing of the monstrous rage in the back of my head, but I gave it no rein. Not even for this one. I took a slow, calming breath instead and focused on the lingering thrill of my new authority.

Still I could not tear my eyes from him. I shook my head in slow disbelief and breathed his name. "Lareth Undinane." It sounded like a curse in the still morning, and as I spoke the corpse stirred. I growled low in my throat, and his good eye snapped up and fixed on my face. He lay perfectly still, his breath wheezing through the scarred gap at the corner of his mouth. The eye flicked to the sword in my hand, gleaming black and smooth as silk, and then back to my head. His tongue flicked out to wet his lips. Sweat stood on his forehead.

I said, "You lived."

He did not offer me a pithy response. He didn't grovel or beg. He didn't draw a deep breath or fling up his hand dramatically. He just narrowed his eye and spoke a word of power.

It caught me entirely unprepared. Too much had happened too quickly, but more than that he did not look a threat. He looked pathetic. He looked weak and small and helpless, but he had nearly obliterated me and Vechernyvetr together the last time I'd faced him. He lashed out at me, a complicated working entirely of his own design, and I felt the shape of his will settle like a handkerchief over my mind.

I remembered the working. I remembered reaching for my wizard's sight and falling to my knees in agony. I remembered the utter helplessness under his power. Sudden fear spiked hard and hot beneath my heart, and I fought down the desperate panic that screamed for me to reach to the Chaos power. Instead I kept my eyes fixed firmly in reality and raised the tip of my sword until it hung just above his good eye.

"Release this spell," I said, more steadily than I felt. "Or I will do a more thorough job of killing you this time."

Half of his mouth curled toward a smile. "With a sword?" he said. "By strength of arms?" He closed his eye, and unseen chains latched tight around my wrist and jerked it back. More bonds constricted around my legs, slamming my knees together so I crashed to earth before him.

Still he smiled, though he did not open his eyes. "What *have* you been up to?" he asked. "Your colors are all strange."

New bonds caught my arms beneath the shoulders. I opened my mouth to shout for Caleb, but solid air crowded in, thick and smothering like sand. I shook my head, trying senselessly to get free, but a new cord curled around my throat and constricted.

Red flooded my vision, and my pulse rang like a gong inside my skull. I tried to raise a hand, to tear at the cords on my throat, but my arms would not respond. I tried to kick, to scream, but he had me completely bound. And all the while, my instincts screamed at me to reach for power.

At last, in utter desperation, I relented. My eyes fell closed, and the darkness pulsed with the staccato flashes of suffocation. I stilled my mind as best I could and opened my eyes to the wizard's sight.

I saw Lareth there before me, his lifeblood feeble but his willpower shining like a beacon. I saw the shape of his working on my mind, as well, a complex net stretched over me, knotted and cold and blue as gemstones, and I remembered the deadly pain that it could cause.

But there was more to me than there had been before. I was a churning blaze of energies, red and white and midnight black. I caught one glimpse of my own mingled, blinding power, and then the frail net of Lareth's mindtrap began to close around my will.

I felt the knife-edged pain for half a heartbeat, and watched in my second sight as the well of power within me flared up brighter still, and burnt the wizard's cruel working in its fire. The spell cracked, then splintered, then shattered into motes and disappeared. His mindtrap could not have lasted longer than a moment, then the pain was gone.

And he was screaming. He curled into a ball upon the ground, bony fingers scrabbling at his black-scarred face, and he keened like a wounded hare. His bonds were still upon me, but with the wizard's sight I could trace the shape of them plain as day. It was living air and nothing more. I rolled my neck and flexed my will, and his crushing noose unraveled. I spread the fingers of my hand and called the energy of his bonds into my palm. The little threads wavered for an instant, bound in service to his will, but mine was greater. I huffed one irritated breath, and the air flowed into my hand and set me free.

Still he screamed, all unaware of me. Perhaps he'd tried to fight my force of will, as wizards sometimes did. Or perhaps this was a peculiarity of the strange spell he'd worked against me. I couldn't say, but he was caught within the costs of all his pride. I raised my Chaos blade toward him, thinking to silence the aggravating shrieks, but then decided better. Too many men had died today.

Instead I bound his hands and feet with ropes of air and forced a gag into his mouth, though he went on and on and on all unaware. I shook my head and reached out to the patient earth and unfolded it beneath him so he sank through dirt and grass like water. A grave swallowed him whole, and I sent along enough air to last him for a day, then closed the world above him. For some time I stood there, breathing slow and steady, remembering humanity. It was no easy thing.

Some small sound caught my attention and I turned. They were there, my army, their neat formations broken now. The wizard's screaming must have called them, and they had seen what I had done. I hadn't meant it for a public show, but it would serve. I ran one long, slow gaze out over all of them, then turned my back and trudged on up the hill.

Behind me, Caleb barked an order, fierce in his frustration, and a few hundred men all moved at once to do as they were told. I left them to their orders and went to rest beneath the oak.

"Daven." Caleb's voice, pitched low and urgent. "Daven. Rouse your sleeping ass. My lord."

I cracked one eye, scowling up at him, and fought a yawn. Then I noticed the darkness behind him, nearly absolute, and I jerked upright.

"You let me sleep all day?"

He cocked his head, curious, then looked away. "I let you sleep for two. And it was a mistake."

"Caleb!" I lunged to my feet and then had to catch myself against Caleb's arm as something shot out from under my foot. I frowned at the darkness for a moment, then slowed down long enough to really notice my surroundings.

"You brought me to a tent?"

"The men were growing worried," Caleb said. "Rumors were taking root. I brought you here myself."

I conjured living fire to light the tent's interior. It was nearly three paces high at its peak and five paces to the wide tent flaps. The space between held a finely-carved desk and several comfortable chairs, a heavy bound chest and a tall standing mirror chased in silver. A rack against one wall supported a dozen bottles of wine, and the bed I'd been stretched upon was made up with thick fur blankets. I saw the pillow that had slipped from under my foot, its fabric fine black silk, and the tent itself was made of the same.

A low growl rose in the back of my throat. "You brought me to Lareth's tent?"

"To their leader's tent," Caleb said, his voice sharp. "And that is what we must discuss."

"Lareth?" I asked, and then memory stole over me. I felt the blood drain from my face. "What's he done?"

"Done? He's buried in the earth," Caleb said. "I suspect he's scraped his hands to bone is what he's done, but I need you to bring him out."

"He's not escaped?"

"Not that I can tell," he said. "You'd better hope he's not."

I frowned at Caleb. "Why?"

"You need him. Now."

I shook my head. "I have no use for that man. I should have killed him clean."

Still, I closed my eyes and looked through my wizard's sight. It took me several beats to find my bearings, nearly two hundred paces beneath a different hill than the one I'd gone to sleep on. But I found the spreading oak and found the spot beneath it where the wizard waited.

He was still alive. I could see the glow of his life, the brighter sheen of his active will. I frowned, wondering how he had survived, but then I looked closer and it came clear. He had not escaped. Not with me still up here. Not after I had so easily overpowered him. But he was still a wizard. He had undone his bonds, and he had worked the earth above him to provide a narrow chimney, a passage narrow enough that it would be easy to overlook, but enough to give him air to breathe.

"He could have gone," I said, more to myself than to Caleb. "He knows the trick of traveling. I've seen it. But he bides."

"Good." Caleb planted a hand between my shoulder blades and propelled me toward the tent flaps. "Go and dig him up."

I dug in my heels and met the soldier's eyes. "Why?"

"He'll make a powerful ally."

"He's tried to kill me three times now," I said. "He has tortured me more than once. He takes the blame for this rebellion—"

"Which means he made this army," Caleb said. "Your army. They respect him. Make him yours, and—"

"He is my enemy," I said. "Almost as much as the dragons."

"Almost as much as the king?" Caleb asked.

I frowned. "What? No. I have no quarrel with the king." As soon as I said it, I blinked. And then I shrugged. "Very well. But he considers me a criminal, not an enemy of state."

"That was before you left Teelevon," Caleb said.

I frowned up at him. "How did you know about that?"

"The rebels had a prisoner before we arrived. I only learned of it this afternoon, and I have been to speak with him."

"A prisoner?"

He nodded, grim. "A scout from the King's Guard. They've been looking for Lareth's army."

I frowned. "They have? But you said the king had not been willing to hunt the rebels."

"He had not." The words fell down like stones. After a moment he spat. "He had decided the rebels didn't matter. He had left the problem to resolve itself. And then he made a trip to Teelevon in search of a man named Daven."

It felt a lifetime ago. I remembered Othin stalking down the halls of the Eliade house. I remembered dropping from Isabelle's window. I remembered running away from one monster and straight into the clutches of another.

"I only just escaped," I said.

Caleb nodded. "You did. And then rumors began to spread that the rebel army had a new leader. A wizard. Everyone had heard that Lareth was dead—"

"By my hand," I said. "But...not. It took him those months to recover."

"And when Lareth returned, the king believed it was you," Caleb said. "You escaped him, then went to make yourself an army. He has gathered back the force he'd sent against Brant to track you down."

"No. No. He was wrong."

"Yet here you are," Caleb said.

"But *I* didn't build this army!"

"Did you try to assassinate the king in Tirah? I don't be-lieve it, but that's why he came hunting you in Teelevon."

"Well, no, but—"

Caleb nodded, slow and serious. "I know this Timmon well. If he has set his heart against you...if he finds you among these men...."

"Then we must move."

Caleb shook his head. "That is not enough. You need the wizard."

"Why?"

He narrowed his eyes. After a moment he said hesitantly, "You have two options there."

"What?"

"Get his help. If Lareth swears an oath to you, it will bind these men far more than anything else you've done. Without that, we'll need weeks before they're useful, and much longer before I can trust even a handful of them."

I shook my head. "But you would have me trust *Lareth*?"

"Never. I would have you conquer him."

"Even if I knew a way, that isn't reason enough," I be-gan, but he raised a hand.

"It isn't all the reason," he said. "The king's forces are al-ready assembled. They will move against us soon, and they have the numbers to cast a wide net."

"And?"

"Your wizard can outrun them."

I opened my mouth to ask the obvious question, but stopped myself long enough to consider it. I thought for a moment, then asked, "How fast can we move three hun-dred men?"

He nodded slowly. "These men? Ten miles in a day. Give me a few weeks with them and we'll triple that, but give me the wizard—"

"And we can step to the other side of the continent." I had seen his travelings firsthand. I still hated the very thought of it, though. "What is my other choice? Just let them go? You and I alone could travel much faster."

Caleb shook his head. "No. That will not stop the king. He will still hunt you."

I nodded. The truth of it tasted bitter in my mouth. "He will obliterate all the little bands of Lareth's army and have his hounds inspect every last corpse until he's certain I am dead."

"He'll find you. Wherever you go. And then you'll have only me to fight his thousands. I cannot kill them all."

He said the words as level as everything else, but they hit me like the shock of cold water. I searched his eyes for some sign of mocking, but there was none. As he had told me more than once, he was my man.

"So what," I asked at last, "is my other option?"

"Give them back to Lareth. Then we run."

"No," I said. There was no room for discussion in my tone, but Caleb spread his hands.

"It is your only other option," he said. "Give the wizard back his rebels and let the king's army find *him* behind the organization. Perhaps even Timmon will see the truth if it shows up in moth-eaten wizards' robes."

"No," I said again, but more slowly this time. "I cannot turn him loose. Look at what he's wrought. Even with the king on his scent—"

"In that case," Caleb began, and I silenced him with a dark glare.

"I understand," I said. "But how would we even begin? How could I tame a man who has tried so often to murder me?"

"I think," Caleb said slowly, "I think perhaps you already have." I barked a laugh, but Caleb pressed on. "There is no trace of good in him, but his wickedness is at least consistent."

"Consistent?" I said. "He's a madman."

"Some would say the same of you."

I started to shout, "He's a monster!" but the words died on my lips. I could already hear Caleb's answer.

My general nodded. "Lareth is a man who chases power. For all his wild ferocity, he served Duke Brant faithfully until we caught the man."

"Yes, but he never tried to kill the duke," I said. I remembered the length of the Chaos blade pinning the wizard to the earth outside Teelevon, and I shuddered. "And I'm sure the duke never tried to kill him."

"You are wrong on both counts," Caleb said. "That is precisely how Lareth came to join the rebels' cause."

I stared. Eyes wide, mouth open, I tried to comprehend the mind behind the wizard's actions. "He would truly follow me?"

"He is patient, he is careful, and he is clever. All of these make better reasons for him to follow you than to fight you."

"But he lashed out at me—"

"Before he knew. And you can rest assured he threw everything he had at you. That is not a man to hold anything in reserve. He has already done his best, and you buried him beneath the earth."

I had done more than that. I remembered how easily I had shrugged off his mindtrap. I remembered the flare of mingled powers, blindingly bright to my wizard's sight, and the ease with which I'd shattered his workings. If his mind truly worked the way Caleb suggested—

"And there's more," Caleb said. "He will have as much reason to fear the king's response as you do. There are worse than just Guardsmen coming for us."

"A Green Eagle, I'm sure," I said. "It's Othin, yes?"

"Yes," he said, "but I meant the wizards."

"Which wizards?"

"Masters of the Academy," Caleb said. "It is said they came to Tirah to prepare defenses against the dragonswarm, but when they heard the king meant to hunt you down, one among the Masters volunteered—"

"For me? For me in particular?"

Caleb shrugged one shoulder. "We don't have to share that part with Lareth."

But I shook my head, slow horror dawning. "No," I said. "No, Lareth must *not* be told that part."

He frowned, at last sensing my mood. "Why?"

"It has to be Seriphenes."

His frown deepened. "Yes, how—"

"Seriphenes and Lareth are in league," I said. I swallowed hard. "Or they were. A year ago." I caught a deep breath, thinking frantically, and then I let it go in a great sigh. "Very well. You're right. We cannot release him. I have no other choice."

"Good," Caleb said. He nodded once, sharply, then crossed the tent and lifted the outer flap to hold for me. "We should do it quickly."

I sighed again, then went past him out into the night.

The moon and stars were bright tonight, and despite the hour they showed me a camp full of activity. I saw a formation down in the wide valley training with shortbows, and another nearer by apparently packing and sorting the fine steel armor I'd seen before. Every man that I could see was dressed in leather or linen now, lighter clothes for faster travel. I nodded understanding, and in that light I realized even the men gathered around campfires or kneeling next to tents were not at rest. They were breaking camp.

"This afternoon, you said?"

Caleb raised his eyebrows in question. "Hmm?"

"You learned of the prisoner this afternoon?"

He nodded.

"And you immediately gave the order to break camp?"

He shook his head. "No. First I had to leave him time to escape and slip away. That took longer than expected."

We walked two paces in silence. At last I said, "I am glad you're on my side, Caleb." He didn't answer. We moved down into a camp full and bustling as hundreds of men worked to break down and store as many tents. Off to the west a string of mules was being loaded with equipment. Some of the men nearest noticed when we passed close and saluted. Caleb nodded back, and they returned to work.

I stifled the question as long as I could, but the farther we walked, the more it demanded asking. At last I said, "Just...how many men are there in the camp?"

"Three hundred and thirty-five swore oath to you yesterday at dawn, and at least two dozen who had fled before the fire have come back out of curiosity or fear while you were sleeping. I took all of their pledges in your name."

"And none have fled in the daylight?"

"No. As I said, they're still coming in. These kind of men *seek* powerful leaders. Lareth is not alone in that."

"But I am not that kind of leader," I said.

"You are the kind with power," he said. "That is all they really need."

"And they will serve me? You said I will be able to trust them in time."

"In time, yes. As long as you continue to show them your power."

"Very well," I said. I stopped at a spot of empty ground on the hillside beneath the spreading oak. "Call them, then."

He turned his back and bellowed, "Officers!" so loud it left my ears ringing. All the quiet little sounds of serious industry fell still behind me, and Caleb shouted one more word. "Assemble!"

The officers passed on the order, because I heard more distant shouts throughout the camp, and soon the sound of footsteps on the trampled grass. I put them from my mind and turned my attention to the task at hand.

I stretched my hands out before me in a gesture more dramatic than necessary while I gathered and shaped the powers of earth. I reached down through the soil to the wizard's quiet, patient glow, and with delicate care I fashioned a shard of earth as strong as steel and sharp as glass. For one long moment I let it hang in the air before his eyes, then I settled it with a careful precision down until it rested on his collarbone, its pointed tip just pricking at his throat.

Behind me, my army assembled in its ranks, and while they found their places I repeated the same careful process again. Another Chaos shard appeared before his eyes, then sank to rest beside the first. I made a dozen of them, each perhaps the size of a silver coin, and strung them in a necklace 'round his throat.

When that was done, I caught my breath and pulled my hands apart, and the earth rumbled as grass and stone and dirt split along a line, folding back with a roar. Then I raised a hand and a pillar of stone stabbed up within the fissure, lifting Lareth out of his grave until he knelt upon the platform one short step above the ground, his battered head still well below my own.

He stared back at me with eyes more sane than I had expected, and not a trace of defiance in them. Instead I saw hope. And admiration. Not for a superior opponent, I realized, but for a more deadly one. That was his only measure of power. He had understood every nuance of the darkly-gleaming necklace I had hung around his throat, and it had won me his respect.

I did not let my shiver show. I took one long step toward him, with all the army watching behind me, and I said, "Lareth Undinane, I call you conquered. I offer you the chance I gave your men."

Before I could say more, he slid his hands palms down along the floor of his narrow pillar until his forehead nearly touched the earth, and he cried out with a voice surprisingly strong, "Daven Carrickson, I yield my life to you, my only lord. All that I may have, all that I may do, all that I may be I give to you. I am your bonded slave. Spare my life if it pleases you, and it is yours to use."

I had one heartbeat to gape at him, and then the force of his oath crashed into me. I fell back a step, as fever heat seared on my lips and in my ears and at my fingertips. The wizard saw it happen. His eyes narrowed, his lips parted, and then he must have looked with his wizard's sight because he dropped his jaw.

And then he laughed. He laughed and laughed with the sort of boundless glee I had only ever heard from a child. He laughed until it became a roar and then at last subsided into hacking coughs. And still his shoulders shook, still his good eye shone.

I raised a hand, ready to strike with a dozen different kinds of force, but he shook his head and dropped his eyes and wheezed. "You're even more than I had guessed," he said. "I barely began to dream that I could serve a sorcerer, but you are something else altogether. You've nothing left to fear from me at all." He slipped his hands out and kissed the ground before me once again, then met my eyes with a ferocious hunger in his. "I will do anything to follow you."

I had to fight down another shudder of disgust, but I could not doubt his sincerity. He trembled with excitement at the power he had seen. "I do not trust you," I said, pitching my voice for him alone. I could never trust him. But in this moment, I needed him.

"You can," he said, with another little chuckle. "Smoke and shadows, I'd slit my mother's throat if you asked it of me."

I growled at him. "You should think more of your own throat."

It took him a moment, then his eyes widened and a hand drifted up to touch one of the Chaos shards almost reverently. "I remember an orphan boy who only wanted to save the world." He smiled. "My, my, how you have grown."

I opened my mouth to snap at him, but it would have done no good. Instead I gestured to the west and said, "The king is coming. With wizards and warriors enough to wipe us out."

"Not you," he said.

"Perhaps," I said. "But I have use for all these men. I need you to open portals to get us safely away. Can you do that?"

"Of course" He licked his lips, thinking for a moment, then asked, "How many do you want? Just these, or all of them?"

"All of them?" I asked.

"Oh, you don't know!" He shoved himself up until he sat bouncing on his heels and grinning like a child. "My lord, my lord, my lord," he cackled. "You are going to like this."

12. All Across the Ardain

The wizard's last motion had broken even Caleb's calm reserve. He darted up to stand by my side, and I noticed the hand on his hilt, but I sighed and shook my head.

"He's harmless, Caleb." The wizard's one good eyebrow arched at me, and I sighed again. "To me. He is harmless to me."

Caleb only grunted, unconvinced. I turned my attention back to the wizard. "What are you so excited to tell me?"

"Tell you? No. I'll show you." He raised a hand, and that was enough. Caleb's sword flashed from its scabbard, its sharp edge pressing lightly against Lareth's throat without seeming to pass through the space between.

The wizard didn't even blink. He began to chant instead, but his other hand rose almost dreamily to touch one of the shards I'd made, and Caleb noticed them for the first time.

"What in Haven's name?" he breathed, as rattled as I had ever heard him. He pulled his own blade away and stood staring.

"A threat as sharp as yours," I said.

"A gift from my new lord," the wizard said, his chanting done. "I cherish the reminder."

"You're mad," my general said.

"I'm done," Lareth said. When Caleb and I both looked blank, the wizard nodded past us. "Behold."

We turned to find a green flame hanging in the air. I recognized it well, and as I glanced back to Lareth, he shrugged. "I thought you might wish to study the working, or I would have opened the portal directly."

I could find no answer. It was a fine suggestion. I turned back to the eerie green flame and looked with my wizard's sight. The thing I saw was twisted and wrong. Not the flame itself, the hallmark of Lareth's strangely delayed magic, but the working underneath. Energy was there, the glowing threads of ordinary reality, and I could see the soft glow of Lareth's will overlaid upon it.

But his will was not tied to one energy, to one thread of wind or one blast of fire. Instead it lay spread out across the scattered sum of powers that made up this place, this little bit of Ardain, and wherever his will lay the energies themselves were...vague. Distorted. They seemed to shimmer like a heat haze even in the stark reality of the wizard's sight, and after a time I understood.

It was another place. That was the traveling. This place and another place overlaid until they nearly were the same. It was not just a matter of stretching or tearing or opening, it was a matter of matching realities. Not an imaginary scene, not just the shape or earth of the bite in the air, but all of it. All the thousand little energies trapped, contained, coerced. I saw it, and I understood, and I knew with a deep certainty I could never do such a thing.

The realization left me feeling very small. I shifted my attention to reveal the dazzling bonfire of forces that blazed around me, the thunderous power at my disposal, but it comforted me little. I could obliterate Lareth's delicate working with nothing more than a thought, but for all my power I could not begin to replicate it.

The sight faded as quickly as I could blink, but his green flame burned in quiet reminder. I turned my face away and growled to him, "I have seen enough. Show me what you will."

From the corner of my eye I saw the motion as the flame unfolded into a doorway. I heard the distant sound of chatter, laughter, and closer there was the riffle of shuffling cards. A curious glance showed me another camp much like this one, though in the flatter lands out west, and the men in that camp seemed much more comfortable than my own.

Less than a pace from the new gateway was a soldier in cavalry plate that looked almost new. Caleb brought up the sword he'd turned against Lareth, but I stopped it short on unyielding threads of air.

"It's not an ambush," I said quietly, focusing on the soldiers sprawled on the grass around a game of cards.

"Not for *us*," Lareth said with a wicked twist to his mangled lips.

The soldier in question stood no more than three paces from us—though he might have been a hundred miles away—yet he showed no reaction to anything we'd said, nor even to the sword Caleb still held on a hard cut toward his neck.

The soldier only snapped a smart salute. "Master Lareth!"

Lareth nodded at him, then waved me over to stand beside him. "Well met, Garrett Dain. Your men are ready?"

The soldier nodded, "Always, Master. You have news?"

Lareth smiled, "Very good news indeed. We have a new protector greater by far than the failed duke."

Garrett Dain's eyes snapped to Caleb for two slow beats, then flicked to me and away. "Fine, sir."

Lareth cackled for a moment then cut it off abruptly. "Inform your men. We'll likely come to gather you by dawn."

"We stand ready."

"They all do," Lareth said, as an aside, then he held a hand toward me. "This is Lord Daven. Your oath is now to him."

The soldier looked confused for a only a moment, but then he turned to me. "It will be an honor to serve you, Lord Daven. Direct me, and my men will follow."

And just like that, I felt the force of new power. As much again and more as I had gained from all the oaths of the men in this camp, delivered at once with a word from the other army's leader—and that at Lareth's direction.

I swayed in place as the power washed over me, and behind me the wizard made a sound that was very nearly a purr. Caleb dropped a heavy hand on my shoulder to steady me.

"What's going on?" he asked.

"Power," Lareth crooned. "I've never seen it manifest. It's beautiful."

"Daven?" Caleb sounded unsettled. "What happened there?"

"I gained another army," I said, fighting for my breath. "Halfway across Ardain, I just gained another army. Like this one."

"Not an army," Lareth said. "A detachment, I liked to call them. Large enough to raid a good-sized town, small enough that we could afford to lose one to the King's Guard without ending all our goals."

Garrett Dain nodded calmly, and Lareth chuckled. "Although we'd certainly miss Mister Dain. Yes?"

"Another like this?" Caleb asked, turning between Lareth and me. He finally lowered his sword and stood looking thunderstruck. "*This* is one of your detachments?" He waved beyond the portal to the neat formations he had brought, still waiting, still watching.

"Of course," Lareth said.

Caleb shook his head. To me, he said, "They've been talking about detachments all day. All across the Ardain, they say. I pictured raiding parties of ten to twenty."

"Oh! Ha hah!" Lareth barked. "No, no, no, no. This is one of the smaller detachments. I was only here to speak with the prisoner." He frowned. "You do still have my prisoner?"

"We sent him back to his masters," I said sternly.

"I'm sure that you know best. Of course. But yes. But no. Mister Dain's detachment is nearly six hundred strong."

"Battalions," Caleb said, almost under his breath. "We would call them battalions in the Guard."

"Is that...is that bad?" I asked, trying to read his expression.

He met my eyes, as much afraid of power as Lareth seemed to lust for it. "It gives Lareth something close to two thousand men."

"Not Lareth," the wizard said, his voice cracking with glee. "You. This is your army now. Two thousand, eight hundred, and fifty-seven at last count, but more coming every day. The poor little Guards do *not* enjoy a fight on our terms."

"Cut-throats and deserters," Caleb said, but without a touch of contempt. I met his eyes, and he nodded toward Lareth, "Can he get them all?"

"To a man," Lareth said. "Ohhhh, yes. We can have you on the throne in Tirah before another sunset."

I shook my head. "Close the portal, Lareth."

"But—"

"Close it. Now. We'll see you shortly, Mister Dain." I'd barely said his name before the portal folded back into the sickly flame, then I turned my attention to Lareth. "We will not march on Tirah."

"Oh, but we can take them."

Caleb scoffed. "I interviewed the prisoner, wizard. They have seven men for every one of yours, and the fortified position."

"And still we would defeat them," Lareth said. "We have the advantage in tactics."

"In the open, perhaps—"

"Enough," I said.

"Oh! Of course." The wizard nodded to me as though ceding a point in some debate. "It's moot now, isn't it? Daven alone could burn the city to the ground."

Caleb frowned over at me. "Could you really?"

I opened my mouth to deny it, then stopped. I thought of the bonfire blaze of my collected powers. I thought of the Chaos energy I'd nearly unleashed from within a web of flame, and that had been before six hundred men and a ruthless battle wizard tied their lives to mine. "With two thousand more drakes beneath my wing?" I asked after a moment, and gave a slow nod. "I think perhaps I could."

"Drakes?" Caleb asked.

Behind me, Lareth laughed and laughed.

Caleb had been right about the wizard's usefulness. The men had watched me already with a quiet, obedient fear, but now that I had the support of this madman, they one and all looked at me with adoration and excitement. I saw that same malevolent hunger, dimly reflected in every man's expression. They were here to wage a war. They were here for blood and glory.

They *were* like little drakes, prowling across the floor while dragons on the wing soared overhead, and all of them alike just waiting for another shot at violence and blood. Dominion.

We walked among them now while they scurried to finish packing up the camp. Where we went they stopped to watch us, awestruck, until Caleb snapped them back to work. Lareth only shook his head.

"These are not your soft-sided noblemen's sons, ground to obedience beneath the king's heel. These are another breed of warrior."

"Undisciplined is not a breed," Caleb said. "It is a liability. I will correct it."

Lareth turned his argument to me. "We won't defeat the soldiers at Tirah if we agree to meet them on their terms."

"We won't," I said. "But that is not my goal."

"It's not Tirah?" Lareth asked, surprised. Then he hung his head. "I'm shamed to say I cannot take us farther than the coast. It would be a fine thing indeed to put the City to the sword—"

"We won't," I said more sharply still, "because we do not go to war with men."

Lareth frowned. "Then whom?"

"The dragonswarm," I said. "As many there as all the king's forces in Tirah, and every one is worth an army in itself. How is that for a challenge?"

Lareth threw his hands up in the air, "I do not want a challenge," he whined. "I want more *power*."

It was my turn to laugh, if darkly. "You have seen some part of it," I said. "Somehow you understand what even I don't. But there are other ways to grow my power."

"Greater ways than killing a king?" he asked. "Greater rewards than all the power in Tirah?"

I thought silently of Pazyarev, the elder legend who had bent a thousand dragons of his own against me. I recalled the time I'd spent within his lair and saw it with different eyes now, with different understanding. I recognized the markers of his power—his brood, his lair, his hoard, and all the things that he had killed.

And then I gave the frail wizard a grin as twisted as his soul. "Far greater things to kill than kings," I said, imagining the power that would come from cutting that one down. "Far greater power than all the riches in Tirah."

"Among the dragons?" Lareth asked, doubtful, but he seemed to take some assurance from my expression.

"In just one lair," I said. "Kingdoms rise and fall, and dragons barely notice."

"And you would fight them?" Lareth asked. He looked to Caleb. "And *you*? You're just a man."

Caleb raised two fingers, "I got a brace of them already, not even counting the little worms. I hope to get a dozen before I die."

"I'll give you a thousand," I said. It was more than I had ever promised when Caleb and I had spoken before, but everything had changed. Everything. Two thousand men? A wizard hungry to kill anything I would let him, and an officer like Caleb to make an army of this rabble? I could do more than protect Teelevon with power like that. I could storm Pazyarev's lair and pull the dragonswarm from the sky. I took a deep breath and felt the maelstrom of power surging forever all around me. It billowed and whorled and blazed with living powers ready to serve me.

"We'll kill them all," I promised Caleb. "And we will be so much more than kings," I promised Lareth. I could feel their satisfaction as they pondered it. Everything they wanted, and I had no doubt I could make it real. With power like this? I could have faced a hundred dragonswarms.

But even as my two lieutenants played bloody daydreams in their heads, I felt my gaze dragged west. Teelevon. I had not forgotten it since Caleb asked me two days before. With this army at my back, I could give Caleb and Lareth precisely what they wanted.

And, in a sense, me too. I had to keep Isabelle safe. To protect Teelevon from Pazyarev. And after that, a thousand other little towns from a thousand other broodlords. For home. Not just for the home I'd briefly had, but for all the wretched lives that would never know a safe and happy hearth at all if the dragons were not stopped.

I could give them that. I could not go back to Isabelle, not with these for my allies. Not at the head of the army that had once laid siege to her father's land. But I could hardly make a different choice. Caleb had told me precisely why I *had* to ally with Lareth, and for reasons just as strong I *had* to have this army. It would cost me what I wanted most, but it would allow me to do exactly what I had to do.

I shook myself and scrubbed both hands across my face, then turned back to Caleb and Lareth. They were chatting now like old colleagues, talking strategy and plans. They were united, so quickly, by the promise of blood.

"I hate to interrupt," I said softly, "but there are first concerns before we can begin our pleasant work."

Caleb nodded. "The king's forces."

"Ah, yes," Lareth said. "But killing them should not take—"

"We kill no men at all," I said. "My word is law. Our only war is with the dragonswarm."

Lareth showed his teeth in a teasing smile. "But...will...do you really expect the king to bide that law?"

Caleb grunted. "He has a point."

"It is not an easy task, but that's the price of killing dragons," I said. "I will not give you one without the other. Find some way to keep us out of war, gather your battalions quickly, and get us to the tower. I will do the rest."

"The tower?" Lareth asked.

Caleb barked a laugh. "Oh, you don't know!"

"He'll find out soon enough," I said. "Come. We have two thousand men to snatch before the King's Guard finds them. We should probably move swiftly."

We did, and even with Lareth's portals and Caleb's efficient authority, we worked all night to fetch just two. They were ready, one and all, prepared to strike against Tirah at no more than a moment's notice. But I did not intend a rapid strike. I meant to take them away, and for that we needed their rations and resources. It took time to break such extensive camps.

Three days, in fact, we moved from camp to camp all across the wide Ardain. We gathered news and spread the word and organized the move, and then we went back, one by one, and helped them as we could. The second night, as we left one camp behind and returned to the first, three of Pazyarev's greens came swooping in.

They killed thirty of my men in the first pass, but then I went to meet them. The elder legend had barely begun his taunts before I dragged all three beasts out of the air. My soldiers watched in awe. Then Caleb barked an order, and without any special training, without much in the way of tactics, my first battalion fell upon the stricken beasts and tore them to shreds. That silenced Pazyarev's voice in my head, and flooded my heart with more black power. It did not boil and drift away as it had when Caleb struck the killing blow before. Because these men were mine. Oathbound. They fed me power, and I trembled with it.

My soldiers buried what remained of their dead, then drank themselves to stupor in celebration of the victory. Caleb grumbled; Lareth joined right in. They celebrated late into the night. Then at dawn Caleb roused them anyway, and Lareth opened a portal wide enough for a dozen men abreast. While the soldiers from the first camp filed through, Lareth jumped to the next, and the next, and the next, lingering only long enough to set them moving.

They left no sign of their camps at all, but I left three huge, stinking dragon corpses where the king's scout would lead his men. At dawn on the third day I stepped through the final portal to find all Lareth's men gathered into a single massive force upon an empty plain far from prying eyes. Seven battalions in all, and Caleb ordered them into seven columns. I stood for a long time staring out over the huge sea of men. They had been the scourge of the Ardain, and already I had ended that by bringing them away, but I would do so much more good with them.

"Tell me, then," Lareth said, stepping up beside me. "Three days you've kept it from me, and I have done as I was bid. But now I've seen the enemy, now I've seen your power expressed, I have to know what place could ever hold you. Where do we take your men?"

"I told you already. South, to the end of the continent." I pointed to the distant jagged shadows of the cruel mountains that skirted both coasts this far south, pinching in from east and west. "Another sixty miles at least. Perhaps a hundred."

He shook his head. "You're fortunate I could bring you this far," he said. "I cannot work a traveling to a place I've never been, and no one alive has cause to go so far from the world of men. There is nothing south of here."

"There will be," I said. I saw it already in my mind's eye. "But if this is the best you can offer, we should sound the march. Get them moving."

"Where?"

"South," I said. "South until there is nowhere else to go. Beneath the shadows of impassable mountains we'll make our stand."

He frowned, mouthing something silently to himself, then shook his head. He shrugged. "They have their orders already. But before they go, there's something we must do."

"That is?"

"We must swear our fealty."

"You've done it already," I said. "They all have, directly or indirectly."

"Indirectly, for the most," Lareth said, licking his lips.

Caleb came to join us then, returning from some task among the columns, and frowned down at the wizard. "Is he ready?"

"For what?" I asked.

"The ceremony," Caleb said.

"I thought," Lareth said, licking his lips once more. "Ah. I thought we should make a ceremony of it."

Without meaning to, I took a step away from him. "You want to see the power," I said. "There is a sickness in your soul."

Lareth grinned as though I'd made a clever joke. "We'll make you shine, my lord."

Caleb looked back and forth between us, then settled his gaze on mine. "Do it. There is much to gain."

Lareth nodded. "Give the men a show—a single point in time they can remember and look back on, saying, 'This is when my lord became my lord.'"

I ignored him, all my attention on Caleb. "Is this really necessary?"

"It could well be." He shrugged one shoulder. "It cannot hurt. But we should hurry. The messenger should arrive in Tirah by noon today."

I sighed and relented, and we went together to stand before the great assembled mass of my army. Lareth made a speech that hung in the air and boomed even over the farthest formations. He introduced Caleb and me and drew our faces in the sky so every last man among them could look up at me with awe. And then he turned and led them, all as one man, in an abject oath of total obedience that nearly lifted me from my feet with the flood of sudden power.

I could not speak, could barely think for half an hour after that. The whole world buzzed. Lareth, too, sat to one side and giggled, but Caleb never wavered from his duties. He moved among them, and when finally I went to join him the army was already on the move. The stamp of their feet rang like thunder as they marched south toward the mountain.

For a moment, still light-headed from the oaths, it looked like all humanity arrayed before me, drawn up in lines and ready to fight the Chaos tooth and nail. We left them marching and took just a handful from the first battalion north. Lareth dropped us nearly a mile from the outskirts of Tirah, and as the sun reached toward noon, we crept close enough to see the gates.

We left even our handful of escort some distance back, huddling close to the ground beneath a shield of invisibility that Lareth and I concocted. Only my two lieutenants came with me, and we prowled like hunting cats through the tall grass until we found a place close enough that we could see the great eastern gates standing open on the road.

We'd come in time to watch the escaped prisoner ride a stolen horse into the town, and now we waited while he gave his news. Now we watched to see what it would bring. With any luck at all, they'd close and bar the gates and settle in. According to our best reports, the city had three Masters of the Academy and half a dozen full wizards in its walls, as well as all the force of fighting men and still the king himself.

The wizards had come down to shield the town against a dragon raid, and with all their focus combined even I might not have been able to break in. Their wisest course by far was just to hold, and if they sealed the gates and raised their wards, we could lead our army right from the world of men and turn our only focus to the dragons.

On my left, Lareth hissed, "I don't care what their man tells them, there is no way the Eagles will leave our renegades alone. The men caused too much chaos in the outlying villages before I could get control of them."

From my other side Caleb shot a black look at the wizard. "Your strikes against the Guard forces will matter more," he said. "They did far more damage under your authority than they ever did on their own."

"It doesn't matter," I said, and both men looked at me. We'd had this argument from start to end twice already, but I reminded them once again where it had ended every time. "It all comes down to me. The prisoner saw what I am capable of—"

"What you *were* capable of," Lareth said, his breath rasping. "You are so much stronger now."

I had to suppress a shudder. "I am," I said. "But even that display of fire should be enough to keep this army hiding safe within its walls."

"Only if reason is in charge," Caleb said.

I nodded and carried on. "And if it's not, the prisoner's news will just confirm that I am there." A drum began to pound within the distant city, and I caught the sound of a trumpet, too, blaring out some call to arms.

I whispered desperate prayers and watched the open gates. We were not high enough to have any vantage beyond the city walls, but we could hear the sounds of commotion, the movements of great hordes of men. I held my breath as a rider darted through the gate and went to speak with the soldiers in the guardhouse to one side. Then he wheeled and crossed to report to the other guards. And then at last he turned and disappeared inside the walls again. I had some hope.

"They'll close the gates," I said.

"They won't," from Lareth and from Caleb both at once.

And then the drums beat louder and a wild fanfare rang within the city, and I heard the shouts or distant cheering from a great assembly. Then horses' hooves on cobblestones. It was distant, faint, but the number swelled the sound to a distant rumble. I finally saw motion as a single horseman came riding slowly, gracefully through the arch of the city gates.

Even at that distance I did not need to strain my eyes to recognize the haughty figure. He wore his stately armor, plates in green and gold, and as he rode clear of the gates' long shadow I recognized the cruel form of Othin.

Caleb gasped at the same time I did. "An Eagle!" He said it like a curse. "There will be an army behind him, then. We must run."

Before I could answer him, Lareth hissed, "We have been spotted."

I spun to stare back down the slope and found Othin standing in his stirrups, gazing straight toward us, shading his eyes with a gauntleted hand. Behind him I could already see the vanguard of a long column of cavalrymen. As I watched, Othin threw out his arm and pointed directly at us, shouting something over his shoulder. I didn't wait to see the charge, "Run! Run!" I shouted, and suited action to words by leaping to my feet and sprinting for the top of the hill.

In a moment Caleb was by my side, easily matching my stride, and even frail Lareth came puffing up on the other side. "They will shoot us down, Lord Daven! Turn and fight!"

I stabbed a hand toward the portal as my only answer, then spun a desperate shield of air behind us. I dared not try anything more. If I gave Lareth half a hint that he could fight, he would rain fire down across the Royal Guard. We had no need for that.

Still, as we dashed over the crest of the low, rolling hill, I felt a dozen arrows slam home in the airy shield behind us.

"Rise!" I cried out, sprinting down the hill toward my men. "Rise and through the portal!" And as we flew down the hill, I felt the flash and pulse of power when Lareth reached out and unfolded his green flame. The men of my honor guard were still climbing to their feet, shaking off the magical illusion, when Lareth's portal settled into place. It showed an empty field nearly a hundred miles to the south, and on the far horizon the dusty stain of a large body of men on the move.

"Through! Get through!" I shouted, running past them with Caleb and Lareth right behind me. The others followed quickly, and just as a wave of cavalry crested the hill and filled the whole horizon where we'd been, I lashed out—half in panic—and tore Lareth's complicated working into shreds.

His mouth and eye gaped wide in sudden, silent pain, but the portal disappeared. I had to catch my breath, but then I went to the wizard and steadied him with a hand. "I didn't think," I said. "I only meant to cut them off."

He waved a feeble hand dismissively, but still he strained to catch his breath. "Such power," he said. "Such power. Ohh, such power." A tremor shook him, then he hissed a breath through clenched teeth and met my eyes. "We have our answer, I believe."

Caleb grunted. "Looks like war."

I silenced him with a dark look. "Perhaps that's their intent. It isn't mine." I waited until both men nodded before I went on. "We must join the rest of the men and press south quickly. We'll be hunted, and they will waste no time."

Lareth chuckled, "They'll waste a little. I spread a hundred false travelings across the plains for their old wizards to chase down."

"Let's not waste our advantage, then. Let's go."

We were once again upon the spot where the army had sworn its oaths. The field was empty now, tall grass trampled down to dirt, but in the midst of it all stood a single picket line, a dozen fine horses saddled and waiting. We mounted up, glanced once back toward Tirah and the army now setting out to hunt us down. Then we turned south and rode hard to catch up an army meant to hunt more fearsome prey.

We found them late in the afternoon, and cheers and rumors rippled along the lines like waves on the sea while we rode to the head of the columns. We made good time throughout the day, and as the sun set in the western sky, I led a legion past an unmarked border post and into the lands of the Baron Eliade. My eyes dragged west again, toward the town, and I hoped against hope that he would forgive me for what I meant to do.

I tried to keep us moving after sunset, but Caleb overruled me. We already moved on trackless land, and even with the cooperation Lareth had gained us, these men were not well trained for forced marches. Certainly not as a body of this size. Pressing hard at night would only cost us men and mules and gain us paces more than miles.

So we made camp in a field of soybeans, destroying some good farmer's crops. I sat upon my horse, arms crossed and brows drawn down, and watched an army settle down to rest.

"It's not so bad," Caleb said, appearing suddenly at my right hand. "I know how Eagles think. They'll let the wizards try to follow our trail. Perhaps they'll chase down one false path or two, but after that, they'll return to what they know."

"And what's that?"

"One of their own saw you at the head of a battalion a hundred miles east of Tirah. They should have other scouts as well, other reports on the positions of the battalions. They'll go there first. You saw them leaving Tirah out of the eastern gates."

"How long does that buy us?"

Caleb thought for a moment, then grunted and shrugged. "They're done with the wizards by now. I'll swear to it. And they will have to rest as well. They'll send fast riders to check on all the battalions' locations, but they will march toward the one where you were seen."

"Out east."

He nodded. "Seven days, depending on their pace, to get them there. But within five the riders will start returning. Everyone will say the camps are empty."

"And then?"

He took a long breath, thinking for a while, then blew it out. "And then they will go back to the wizards for help," he said. "Unless some rumors have reached them. Unless they have some spies who saw our passage. Unless they know to find us here, they will not wander blindly."

"The wizards will find us," I said. I didn't know exactly what powers the Academy Masters might have, but by the way my powers blazed, they would have to find me. They would barely have to look. "And then how long?"

He shrugged. "There are too many questions. Will they use travelings, or will they march? How far south have any of them traveled? It all depends. Perhaps a week from now, perhaps two months, but they will find us even here."

I nodded. "Two months would serve me well."

"We'll make do with what we have," he said. "But you should not fret too much at stopping for one night. We've made good time, and we will beat them to Palmagnes."

I looked away and sighed. "It's not the time that bothers me. It's the devastation."

Caleb looked out over the field of stringy vines, the dusty farmhouse, and shrugged. "It's only beans."

"You see that barn?" I asked, pointing to a humble open-side structure just beyond the farmhouse. "I helped build that barn. I know these people."

"And without your help, they'd all be dead," Caleb said, clapping me on the shoulder. "There is a price for protection from the darker powers. There is always a price, and it's always the farmers who pay it first."

"It shouldn't be that way," I said.

"It is. Even here. Even without the dragons. These men pay with their lives, with their sad little beans, for the local lord to protect them from hard times, from thieves and highwaymen and...."

"Rebel armies?" I supplied. I sighed. "This place was my home once. Not for long, but it was the happiest time in my life."

"We could leave. The fortress has appeal, but we could take this war elsewhere. Lareth wants to, anyway."

"No, Caleb. No. This is where I need to be. The dragon-swarm is coming, and if I'm going to save anyone, these are the people I most want to save."

"I understand, but that only raises another question. Why the fortress? Why go so far? You fear the baron would raise soldiers against you if he saw you coming?"

I scoffed at the suggestion, and that was answer enough for him.

"Then let us move toward the town. Beds and food and craftsmen ready to support us. If you only want the tower's walls, we can build some walls."

"No," I said. "I have considered it, and I believe the baron would welcome me." I faltered at that. I *thought* he would welcome me, but I could not know for sure. Not with this army behind me. But I shook my head, because it made no difference. "I cannot set the king against that town."

"Daven, if you have half the power Lareth suggests, we could hold the town—"

"We could hold it," I said. "We could win the war. But at what price? No. I chose these men because they owe a price in blood that I will gladly spend. I cannot say the same for the people of Teelevon. And you know as well as I the king's quick temper. I will not give him reason to turn against this town."

"Very well," he said. "Nothing changes, then."

"We march for the fort and hope for time to settle in before they come to drag us out."

"We should be safe," he said. "Now get some sleep. We'll move again at dawn."

I hadn't budged when Lareth found me, still staring glumly at the distant farmhouse. I couldn't quite recall the face of the farmer who lived there. Odds were good he was old and poor and desperate. Most of them had seemed that way.

"You're looking glum," the wizard said, and I could hear the warmth of wine on his voice. "Have you at last realized you're rushing *away* from all the soft comforts of a world you could command?"

"I have no interest in soft comforts," I said. "I only wish we could rush a little more."

"Aha. Well as to that, you're on your own. I could move us all a good deal closer to a pretty little town out west—"

"No!" I growled, but he didn't seem to hear the animal anger in my voice.

"Oh, don't get me wrong. It's small, but it is fine. Good wine, good beer, and lovely little women I recall."

I didn't turn but struck him backhand hard enough knock him from his horse. "You will not speak of Teelevon."

"Of course I won't," he said, still just as merry, but there was a brittle edge to it now. "And yet, ha hah, it's as I said before. All these rolling miles of dirt mean naught to me. I couldn't even move you to that barn."

"I've been to that barn."

He shrugged and tried unsuccessfully to scramble back into his saddle. At last he gave up and just stood leaning heavily against the horse's bridle. "There you and I depart. And as I've said before, if you will only make the portals—"

I looked away, and he cut himself short. I heard him catch his breath, and after a moment he spoke with a clarity that belied his drunkenness if not his madness. "I have offered more than once to teach my lord."

"And I have tried," I said. I shuddered at the memory. Lareth had learned at the feet of Seriphenes, and Seriphenes had been the worst of all my teachers in my brief stay at the Academy. Twice now Lareth had tried to teach me, and it had taken every shred of self-restraint to stop myself destroying him before the lesson was done.

"My power is my own," I said. "Academy magic serves me little."

"But as I've said before, it shapes your purpose, lord. I cannot imagine what you might do with all your powers, if you employed the focus I could teach to you."

"And perhaps in time I will," I said. "For now, I cannot spare the energy, and you should count yourself lucky for that. It gives me reason to keep you alive."

He grinned and laughed. "You have me there. But if you want to move more swiftly than this march—"

"What about..." I began, already knowing his answer. Still, I had to ask. "What about my way?"

He shuddered, top to toe. "No! No, my lord. No. Don't you *ever* try it that way. Better far to walk."

"But it is only power," I said. "All of it is power. I can move power around. Why not move the lifeblood?"

"What is a life?" Lareth asked, with a lecturing-hall tone. "Is it your will? Is it your awareness? Is it your brain? Is it your body? Who knows what you would move?"

"But—"

"No," Lareth said, lips peeled back to show his teeth. "*Never* try it that way. Unless...."

"Yes?"

He brightened and met my eyes. "You could try it with one of the soldiers! You should have done that at Tirah. Just send them all away."

"And see what happens then?"

He nodded, eyes gleaming.

"But you still expect it would be horrible?"

"Not horrible, then. Not with *soldiers*. No, then it's merely wasteful. But interesting at least. It should be interesting to see."

I heaved a sigh. "Go away, Lareth. Go get some sleep. I order it. No more wine, no clever ideas; just get some sleep."

It took us two more days and most of a third to cross the barony, stopping only once a day and then again at sunset. I kept the men close by and directed us through rougher terrain wherever I could spare a farmer's field. Lareth and Caleb both called me foolish for it, but I wanted to impact the farmers as little as possible. I *knew* these men. I'd helped them work some of these fields. I hated the price they paid for every step along our way.

By the third day, though, the fields fell away, leaving only sun-scorched earth and broken stone and scrubby, twisted trees with cruel thorns. I pressed harder then, standing in my stirrups and begging the army for speed and straining my eyes south. But sunset came too soon, and once again we had to camp.

When the last of the daylight failed, when Caleb and Lareth both were busy with the work of rest, I slipped away. The terrain was untrustworthy here, pitching and rolling and falling away in the treacherous foothills beneath the cruel coastal mountains. I followed a little path barely recognizable across the barren land. I found it more by instinct than by sight, but the sense of familiarity dragged me on.

I rode for miles on my own, far past sunset, and finally stopped when the looming shadows before me resolved into a mountain of rubble separate from the distant range. It crouched upon the earth, just as I remembered, a pile of memories and legends and broken stone. The FirstKing's fortress. Palmagnes.

And here, where the long-forgotten road meandered near a twisted black tree, I saw the spike of earth that I had made. I stared in awe, and memory came crashing back. We had come here with plans for a future. I was supposed to hide in these ruins for a day or two, and if it took longer than that, Isabelle would come and join me. She'd wanted so much to be with me.

The sight before me dragged me from my saddle. I slipped down, moving as if in a dream, and drifted forward. We'd brought some rations, some resources for me while I camped here. I'd buried them beneath the earth and raised this spire to show me where.

But now, beneath the spire, there was a pit. Someone had dug down into the earth. Two paces deep would have made a hard day's work even in friendly soil, and this was rocks and gnarled roots. But someone had recovered the saddlebags. Not a treasure, but enough to keep a man alive while he waited for better days.

214

Now that I knew to look, I could see the remains of the campsite too: a circle of fist-sized stones, a bit of charcoaled wood, a broken bottle, a tattered blanket. I instantly took on the wizard's sight and stretched my gaze as far as it would go, but there was not a sign of life between this place and the wildfire light of my army miles to the north.

But I should not have worried at all. The campsite was clearly old, abandoned for months. As I looked more closely at the fire ring, I saw another stone precisely in its center. Underneath the stone, a bit of parchment. I caught it up and summoned a brilliant flame above my shoulder so I could read.

It said, "I know you can't be dead. I don't know where you are. I waited as long as I could. Come back to me. I love you. Come back to me." She hadn't signed, but I knew Isabelle's careful hand. I read it again, and my tears stained the weathered parchment.

"Come back to me," she'd said. I turned to the north and sank down in the place where she had waited for me. I wept for what I could not have. I loved her too, and that was why I would not go. But I would wage war with death itself to keep that woman safe.

13. The Stronghold

It was well past midnight when I finally came in sight of the camp again. The night was still and dark, and even my horse's steps barely broke the deep silence as I rode toward the sleeping army. I felt bone weary, and my heart felt raw. I only looked ahead to one blanket on the hard, cold ground and perhaps four hours of sleep before we moved again.

A shadow stepped out of the darkness of the night, barely three paces ahead of me, and resolved into the shape of Caleb. Thunder crashed behind his eyes, and his voice was a growl. "Are you a fool, my lord?"

"I'm either a madman or a hero," I said, with acid to match his annoyance. "So I've heard. Right now I am tired."

"You have responsibilities," he barked. "You're not some brave and lonely child anymore, free to run wild in the night."

"Say your piece tomorrow," I said, and heeled my horse ahead despite him. "Right now, I need a bed."

"No. You need to think!" He grabbed my horse's halter as it passed and hauled down hard. Nothing I could do would urge the beast forward after that. The dark warrior glared up at me, anger in his eyes.

"I am your lord," I said through gritted teeth. "Is this how you'll behave?"

"Toward a lord, no. Toward a reckless child—"

"Enough," I snapped. "If you call me child again, I will be hard-pressed to ignore it."

"I've no desire to be ignored. I am your man. I have sworn my life to you and that comes with a price as well. You chafed at the price the farmers pay, but lords pay prices, too. You owe me, Daven."

"I owe you dragons' blood," I snapped. "That was the deal we made. I'll give you chance enough—"

"No. Everything has changed. This is not the arrangement we made upon the ashes of that village."

My eyes narrowed. "You would be released from your oath?"

He held my gaze for a long moment. Then he released my horse's bridle and took a long step back. "No. I won't. But everything is changed. You made yourself a king and made me a general. You lay plans for war. The path you're walking now...you cannot act alone. Two thousand lives are tied into a knot around you now. Understand? When you risk yourself, you risk us all."

"There is nothing safe in what I do, Caleb."

"And that's why we should not make it worse."

My answer died on my tongue. After a moment I looked away. "I'm sorry."

"A lord is never sorry," Caleb said. "You may chastise me for challenging you. It is within your right."

I shook my head. "You pledged your strength in my service. Among your strengths is knowledge. Training I don't have. It would be a grave betrayal then to hold your tongue."

He considered me for a moment, calculating. Then he said, "You are a mystery."

I laughed in surprise. "Why?"

"You have two faces I've learned to know well. I've seen the cruel master who brought Lareth's madness to heel. I've seen the affronted wizard prepared to strike down a farmer who would not offer a stranger some water."

I scrubbed my hands over my face at the memory. "That is not me, Caleb."

He nodded slowly. "I begin to understand that. For there are times when you are this...this kind young boy."

My jaw dropped at the comment, and he shrugged an apology. "I mean no disrespect. I swore an oath to the monster when he offered me the chance to kill some dragons. I am no different from Lareth in that. I responded to your power."

"But not like him," I objected.

"Perhaps," he said. "Perhaps not. But I would make that oath again. I would serve that monster as long as he could get me what I want."

"I'll get you what you want," I said. "I mean to fight the dragonswarm."

"And there's the boy," he said. "There's the noble hero. At times I thought it was a ploy. A clever show to win the hearts of men. But that is you."

I looked away into the night. I heaved a sigh, and Caleb took a noisy step closer. "Daven. I will serve that boy with all my life. I do not care what you offer me. If that is who you are, then that is cause enough for loyalty."

"That is who I want to be," I said. "It seems a thousand years ago, but you and I sat beside a fire beneath the stars and I told you I was afraid of becoming a monster."

"Ah," he said.

"You told me every man is half a monster."

"It is usually not so stark a distinction."

I smiled sadly at that. "Caleb, I have access to powers man was never meant to wield. I can shape reality as well as any wizard, if in different ways, but I have other options too. I can create reality. I can summon pure power to serve my will."

"Fire?" he asked, and I could see the memory in his eyes.

"Yes. Anything, really, but yes. That fire was Chaos power."

"It was strong."

"Stronger than me," I said. "I have never borrowed Chaos without losing hold of...well, of that kind young boy you mentioned. Me."

"But here you are."

I shrugged. "Perhaps. But I am not as kind as I once was. I do not see the world as bright as I once did."

"The world is not as bright as it once was," Caleb said. "And you have looked deep into the darkness. But you are not a monster."

"It's much easier when I don't borrow Chaos. And it's been days."

"Then take more days. You said you do have other powers?"

I laughed. "Caleb, I glow with power I don't even understand. But yes. I can shape whatever exists at no more cost than physical exhaustion."

He frowned at that. "That is not a minor cost."

"No, it's not," I said. Then I frowned. "But even that has not cost me much for weeks." I tried to recall the last time I'd felt weakness in my arms for crafting a blade of earth or flinging fire across a room. I remembered the staggering price I'd paid to bury those saddlebags, but I had done the same to Lareth days ago and never even blinked.

Caleb watched the confusion cloud my expression, and when I offered no answer to it he shrugged. "This sounds a question for the wizard, not for me."

"I do not trust him that far."

"You should," Caleb said. "I am not a trusting soul, but that man will do anything for you. He loves you like a puppy loves its master."

"He is dangerous and more clever than his madness makes apparent, and he need only find a more powerful master before that love will turn to hate again."

"*Is there* a more powerful master?"

I shook my head. "It matters not. I cannot trust that form of loyalty. I much prefer the kind that will challenge me when I'm a child."

He nodded back past me, toward the south. "And what did you find?"

"It's not six miles to the tower from here," I said. "We'll have our lunch tomorrow inside the walls, such as they are."

Caleb nodded. He turned back toward our camp and jerked his head. I fell to a walk beside him. After a moment I asked, "How much do the men know?"

"By my order, they know we are moving into a vulnerable but defensible position. They know it will take work to prepare the defenses, and the king will come to test those defenses within days or weeks."

"That's all?"

He shrugged. "By my order, that's all they've been told. But I'm sure every man knows it's Palmagnes, the way rumors spread. Most of them know you plan to rebuild it, that you want to be king of the mountains, that you're a total madman, and that you are the FirstKing's ghost." He threw a glance up at me. "Some among them have even suggested you intend to fight dragons, but outside the first battalion, most consider that a baseless lie."

"Excellent," I said darkly.

He barked a laugh. "It's the nature of rumor in a body such as this. It's not worth troubling over. They should be ready for the work ahead. That's what matters."

"We've pressed them hard," I said. "And rebuilding those walls will be no small task. Pass the word that they can have tomorrow afternoon to rest, and we'll begin at dawn the day after."

"No, my lord."

I looked down at him, surprised. "No?"

He looked back with a gaze like stone. "You bid me challenge you when you were wrong. And you are wrong in this."

I crushed a harsh response before it could even resolve to words, and let it go with a long, slow breath. Then I asked him quietly, "What should we do instead?"

"Put them to work tomorrow. The moment we arrive. You do have a kind heart at times, but these are the wrong kind of men for that. *You* may rest tomorrow, but these men respond better to orders than to leisure time."

"That seems reasonable," I said.

He frowned as though I'd argued with him. "*And* we have an army bearing down on us that would tax the defenses of Whitefalls, let alone this pile of rubble you've described. We cannot spare the day."

"I understand," I said.

"The easy answer is this: Do not tell me how to run the army. Tell me where to point it, what to teach it, and when to let it loose, but *don't* tell me how to run it."

I nodded, thoroughly chastised, and managed a meek, "Yes, Caleb."

He grunted. "You are most gracious, my lord." My horse approached the first row of tents then, and Caleb caught my bridle almost absently and began to lead me through the camp. As we went, he continued, "We'll start out at dawn, and I'll wait until we're well and truly moving before I pass the arrival orders. We'll need an honor guard, too. How many men do you think will fit inside the walls?"

"All of them."

He threw a measuring glance back at me, as though to see if I were mocking, then shrugged and turned forward again. "That is better than I had hoped, but I think you misunderstood. I'm planning for tomorrow, and right now it's just rubble. Before we start rebuilding, how many can this fortress house?"

"Twice our numbers," I said. "Have you never seen Palmagnes?"

"No man alive has," he said. He looked north, beyond the sprawling camp to the baron's lands. "Not even these farmers, I would guess. It's miles to the nearest house."

"True." I chuckled to myself. "Does Lareth know it yet?"

"I think he half suspects. But then, like all grown men, he knows it's just a legend."

"Well, we will make it real," I said.

He stopped, then offered me a hand down from the horse. "At dawn," he said. He'd led me to a bed I hadn't bothered to prepare, an unlit fire built within a shallow pit, a water skin and a wax paper bundle of rations. "For now, you need to rest. You push yourself too hard."

"And you?" I asked. "Do you *ever* sleep?"

"Not while I have enemies awake," he said. "But I am made of stronger stock than you."

"I think perhaps I have encouraged you to speak too freely."

"Perhaps," he said, every line of his face perfectly serious. "Only time will tell."

"Good night, Caleb."

"My lord." He led my horse away, and I watched until he disappeared into the darkness. Then I fell gratefully among the thin blankets, and lay there long awake anticipating what the next day would bring. I barely thought of Isabelle at all.

Dawn found me already alert and mounted, waiting anxiously. Caleb had apparently anticipated that, because he had the men ready to strike camp before the sun was even up. Still, I chafed to wait in quiet review of my troops. Instead, I inched along the line, closer and closer to the head of the column, and when the order to march was given, I rode ten paces ahead of the front line.

I saw no sign of Caleb himself, but I recognized his handiwork when three mounted warriors came galloping past the column to fall in just behind me. My bodyguard. I glanced back over my shoulder and discovered I'd crept another forty paces ahead of the line. The tower called to me. The chance to act called to me. I shook my head and set my eyes to the south and fought to rein against my own impatience.

Over the course of the next two miles, nine other soldiers came forward to join my guard, and as the last of them drew close I finally gave up my efforts at restraint. I cast one quick glance among them, nodded to the south, and kicked my horse to a run. We covered the barren miles quickly, then slowed to a reverent walk as we approached the tower.

We passed within a pace of Isabelle's abandoned campsite, but no sign of it remained. I'd destroyed the tiny obelisk and refilled the shallow grave and buried the circle of stones. The note she'd left I carried near my heart, but nothing else remained.

I led a dozen of our best men over the rough slope of the crumbled archway and into the courtyard of the ruined fortress. The morning was strangely quiet as we all dismounted and stood in the awesome immensity of the rubble-strewn courtyard. I closed my eyes and looked with the wizard's sight, searching every shadow in the place for any sign of a lurking drake, but there were none this time.

Too far from men, too far from wealth, too far from any power except the memory of man. The drake I'd met before had been a hunting scout of Pazyarev's. But he had seen me all across the south Ardain. With any luck at all he was still scouring the mountains or the plains where I had slain his greens. I would face him. With this army, I could face him. But first I needed time, and a stronghold worthy of my power.

I stretched out a hand and brushed aside a pile of rubble paces tall as though it were just dust. I remembered the staggering toll it once had taken for me to raise a wall of earth, but here with far less effort I did much more work, and none of it with borrowed Chaos. The men behind me hushed with awe, and a smile touched my lips as I pressed forward, clearing off a hundred square paces of courtyard floored with the chipped and crumbling paving stones that the FirstKing had placed more than a thousand years ago.

When Caleb and Lareth arrived at the head of the column, my bodyguard was already busy scouting the vast premises of the fortress, trying to define its exact dimensions among all the ruin. I sat waiting at the foot of the broken stronghold. A quiet satisfaction stole over me as I watched the trotting column slow without an order to a reverent walk, just as we had done, every neck craning as the tired men filed through the gateway gap.

They looked on rubble and ruin barely distinguishable from wild nature, but every eye carried a far-off look as they mentally reconstructed the old glory of these crumbled stones. They could see the reality that wasn't yet real, and they thrilled at the chance to play a part. They knew what I meant to do—or at least some part of it—and I saw the faces of men I had forced into service suddenly glowing at the thought of the future.

Perhaps I had a chance.

Caleb had little time for me, then, as he began the process of securing the perimeter as well as setting up an orderly camp for so many men. I didn't envy him the task, but he had found a competent staff of officers among them, and he seemed to have a plan.

I needed to speak with Lareth, though. He'd entered the walls a step ahead of Caleb, at the very front of the column, but he seemed as overwhelmed at the power of the place as I had been. He stood transfixed just inside the gateway while the soldiers came flowing in around him. They parted to avoid him, hundreds of men walking past, but Lareth ignored them all.

When he finally moved, it was with a slow and measured step that carried him directly toward the tower. I watched him come, his eyes searching the sky above for the fabled floors that no longer stood. His eyes were on the reality of the past, not the shadow of the present. I understood.

When he reached me, he stopped. He said, "It's real."

"Yes. And it is mine by right."

His eyes met mine, and I shrugged. "It was, at least. And I will make it mine again." I waved a hand at the empty sky, where a tower should have stood. "And I mean the tower to stand."

He nodded, his eyes far off again, but then he looked at me sharply. "All of it?"

"All of it. I mean to rebuild the whole fortress."

"And they say I am mad."

"Lareth, I mean to fight the dragonswarm. Brant's rebellion, the king's petty vendetta, all the politics of men cannot compare with the horror that is rushing on the world."

"It has arrived," the wizard said. "Perhaps you know. But these last days the men have shared their rumors. They think it odd that such similar stories reached such distant parts of the plains, but every camp has heard it now."

"They're to the plains?" I said, not really asking. "That is not the beginning, Lareth, that is the end. They started in the mountains, in the depths, in the high dark passes. I shudder to think what has transpired in the Northlands, or high along the western coasts."

"There have always been dragons," Lareth said.

"One or two, perhaps. But now they all awake. Across the world. In their thousands. Whole broods that strike with one mind and unimaginable power. And *they* do not look to capture thrones. Their only goal is to set the world on fire."

Lareth looked past the rubble of the tower, the ruins of the walls, to the huge black mountains that clawed at the horizon to east and west. "And you brought us into their midst?"

I nodded slowly. "I brought us out of the world of men. When we strike, they will strike back."

He turned his eye to me. And then I saw the subtle change in his expression as he looked on me with his wizard's sight, and the tiny, hungry tremor that shook him. "For that you've gathered all these men?"

"And men are just the start," I said. "They are a tool, but I need more. I need—"

"You need a fortress of legend. You need an army unafraid of any power. You need a man like living death to be your shadow."

I smirked at that. "You mean Caleb?"

"He terrifies me," Lareth said, his voice far away. And then he snapped right back to reality, and his gaze dropped shyly away from mine. "And you will need as well a...a wizard?"

"I need a wizard, Lareth. I do not need a madman drunk on the ecstasy of power." He blinked at me, and I took a heavy step closer to him. "I do not need a conniving rat scrabbling for every scrap he can get. I do not need a traitor or a monster. I need a man who is willing to fight against the darkness."

I raised a hand and touched one of the sleek black shards still pricking at his throat. The skin beneath its point had raised a jagged, star-shaped scar. Lareth's eye followed its every subtle motion as I lifted away the shard, thin as paper, and considered it for a long moment. Then I let it dissolve into dust.

"Can you be a man, Lareth?"

His eye snapped to mine. He swallowed hard, and a handful of the shards I'd left pressed dents into the scars they'd raised. Then he dipped his head once, and a wheeze touched his voice. "For power like you have—"

"No," I said, firm, and he cut off sharp. I held his gaze. "I do not believe that you are mad. I have seen too much of you. It serves you well to play the part, but I demand sanity. As your master, as your lord, I demand you give me reason."

His mouth fell open. After a long moment, he gave a tiny shake of his head. He looked away. "You ask too much."

"Find it in you," I said. "I have been a monster. I have tortured men and I have killed with glee. I've been a puppet in the power of mighty things, and I have tasted Chaos on my tongue." I bent a thread of air to turn his head until he faced me again. "I know every shade of your madness, Lareth, and I will not allow it in my tower."

I raised a hand, and another of the shards lifted away from his throat and floated to me. I called them one by one until they rested in a pile in my palm. Then I turned my hand, gripping just one between thumb and forefinger, and let the others melt to ash. He flinched as though I'd struck him.

I held the one remaining shard out to him. "I should have done this days ago. Keep this as a talisman or drop it down a well, but I tell you this: I will not keep a man like a dog upon the leash. I will not keep you here if I must do it under threats and promises of power."

He took the shard and turned it over and over in his hands. He tested the edge of it with the pad of his thumb and drew a tiny line of blood. He shrugged pathetically. "But that is just the nature of a man. Every kind of king—"

"I am not a king," I told him. "I am a protector, and I cannot do that if I let the dark abide. If you can be a man by your own will, you will have a place here. If you can only be a monster, mad with power and hungry to burn the world, then I must destroy you as I will the rest of them."

He shook his head, and his words came out in a whisper. "It can't be tamed."

"It can," I said. "It can be crushed. Humanity is stronger than the darkness."

"In you, perhaps—"

"Then look to me!" I said, throwing my hands up in frustration. "I'm using all the strength I have to make humanity stronger. Perhaps I save some farmers' lives. Perhaps I save a kingdom. Perhaps I save your soul. It's all the same. It all comes down to fighting off the madness and standing up for hope."

For a long time he only stared down at the black shard between his fingers, while blood pooled in his palm. At last he met my eyes again and licked his lips and said with a dry, thin voice. "I will try my best."

"Good." I nodded, and shook myself as if waking from a dream. I looked around and saw my army in the courtyard, busy at whatever tasks Caleb had given them, but every man in earshot watched us with surreptitious glances. I frowned and met the wizard's gaze.

"I did not mean to call you down in front of them," I said, my voice cast low.

"But it is good," he said. He swallowed hard, then raised a hand to touch the star-shaped scars on his throat. His eye snapped up to mine. "You have powers in your head that I have never even glanced, don't you?"

I shrugged and looked away, and the wizard gave a sigh. "I would have a moment."

"You can have a morning," I said. "Meet me after lunch. There will be work to do."

I felt him slip away. A moment later Caleb's shadow came to stand by mine, and I felt a bitter smile twist my mouth.

"None of that was planned," I said.

He nodded. "It was well done, and better today than tomorrow."

"But all the men heard—"

"Just a handful," Caleb said. "But with any luck they'll spread the story far and wide. And now they're firmly yours. His portals brought us clear of the king's forces, and you've secured the loyalty of his men." He clapped me on the back. "You've taken all you needed from him, in only days. Well done."

"It was not a ruse," I said. "It came of what you and I discussed last night, but I meant it for him. He can save himself if he will try."

"And if he won't?"

I closed my eyes. "I cannot keep a man on fear of execution. It would be a nobler thing by far to kill him clean and be done with it."

Caleb nodded again. "Good. I do agree. And now, I know we'd planned a council, but there is more to do than I had guessed. I'd be more use to you working with the men, if we're to have a reliable defense ready before nightfall."

"Tonight?"

"You'll be amazed what two thousand men can do, Daven. Even with this."

"Very well," I said, "but use your reason. They'll be useless to me if they don't get *some* rest."

His eyes glittered in a dark reminder, but he didn't say a word.

"I know, I should leave you to run the army. But we will need our strength in the days we have ahead."

"Of course, my lord." He clamped his teeth so tight the muscles on his jaw bulged out, but he dipped his chin in a shallow nod and slipped away to oversee the work.

And then, surrounded by nearly three thousand men, I found myself alone. The soldiers all had jobs to do, and my lieutenants both were hard at work trying to find some hope for a future in the rubble of long, slow devastation. I glanced in the direction Lareth had gone, and back across where Caleb stood in quiet conversation with a handful of his men. Then I turned to the soaring mound of stone at the heart of it all. The ruined tower.

I looked with my wizard's sight, tracing the shape of worked stone beneath a thousand years of detritus. Even after so much time and buried under layer after layer of accumulated nature, the shape of the artificial construct revealed itself.

A human will had exerted its authority upon the environment—not by sorcery or arcane force, perhaps, but by the strength of two hands and the vision in a desperate heart. Palmagnes had been built as a bulwark against a different tide of destruction, but the shape of it still burned beneath the dirt and creeping vines.

I waved a hand again as I had done before, as one might brush the dust and cobwebs from some relic long in storage, and soil and stone rolled back across the courtyard into two great heaps. More paving stones were revealed, but then a solid line, a crumbled step that stretched ten paces left and right, and then another step, and above the third a wide platform half a pace above the courtyard floor and thirty paces end to end.

Around me, soldiers hard at work stopped their tasks to watch, but I could barely notice them. My focus followed the clean, straight lines of human will beneath the jumbled piles of time and nature. I cleared the whole platform, and two or three paces of paving stones all around it on three sides to define the shape. The fourth side, the south, was a soaring spear of broken stone. The tower itself.

But there, too, I could see the shapes that were meant to be. What looked like solid stone as heavy as a mountain concealed its own tunnels, its own caves and caverns deep. I stood in silence for some time, measuring, exploring the weight of earth and the traces of structure, and then I pressed two hands together before me, caught my breath, and pulled the hands apart.

Stone creaked and groaned and set up a rumble like thunder, and then it flowed apart. I could not brush this stone aside, but I forced it back, folding its energy up and out into the great arched doorway that should have been.

After every gesture I waited, head cocked, and curiously tested the muscles of my back and legs, my arms and shoulders. I felt nothing. No twinge of pain, no sapping weakness. I pressed ahead.

There was clutter sprawled for paces and paces between the base of the fallen tower and what had once been the door in its wall. I stretched my will in a line straight ahead of me and forced the clutter aside or propped it up on its own energies, so that instead of a pace-thick doorway to the interior of a tower, I created a long, irregular tunnel into darkness. I kept it up, reaching past the remade doorway into what should have been a wide open chamber, forcing rubble back by strength of mind until at last I breached the inner darkness.

I felt it happen. One long sigh of life-warm, musty air rolled over me, and then it was done. I opened my eyes and looked deep into the darkness, and a smile touched my lips. I stepped forward into my lair.

Or, at least, I tried. Behind me, Lareth shouted, "Smoke and shadows, man! What are you doing?" Lareth had climbed the steps to the tower's wide porch and now he came to join trotting toward me, terror in his eyes. "Don't dare set foot in there!"

"It's safe," I said. "I made it safe."

"*That?*" Lareth asked. "It's not a building. It's not a manufactured thing. It's a pile of rocks."

"Can you see its energies?" I asked, genuinely curious. He frowned at me. He frowned at the fallen tower.

After a while he shook his head. "No. And that is odd enough. I can't see anything near here. It's blank right to—"

"Right to the walls that don't exist," I said. The thought turned up the corners of my mouth. "Come with me. I'll make it all make sense."

He caught my sleeve, nervous fear in his voice. "Can *you* see through the stone?"

I nodded and let my gaze drift up the ruined tower once again. I could see the remains of the fabled Tower of Days in the skeleton of this mound of rock. I could see the broken gaps of six floors at least, see where the pillars had been, and interior walls, and the great wide stairways climbing up the outer walls, the narrow spiral at its center like a spine.

I couldn't turn away. The heart of the tower pulled me like affinity. Deep down inside I felt a need to see this through. The dark vastness of the tower's interior cried out to me, and to my shame I knew precisely why.

A shudder shook me as I realized that *this* was what had dragged me ahead of my men, had filled my heart with hope. Not the journey's end, not the promise of some refuge, not the fortress or even the dream of rebuilding a tower out of legend. It was that vast and midnight cavern under stone.

I needed to go inside and take possession of my lair. It felt like home, and I had been too long away. Something like homesickness twisted behind my breastbone, a quiet ache that had lived there for so long I didn't even notice anymore. But now I was so close, it burned like ice.

Lareth must have seen it in my eyes, because he gave a weary sigh. "You're going to go in," he said. "No matter how I plead. But I could fetch your scary shadow—"

I threw a sidelong glance and half a smile. "Caleb couldn't stop me either."

"It's dangerous, you know?" Lareth asked, but there wasn't much hope in his voice.

I met his eye, shook my head, and left him standing there. The darkness swallowed me up and closed around me and pulled me to its heart. I'd gone ten full paces before Lareth cursed and came stumbling along behind me, nervous fear wheezing in his breath. He summoned a ball of green flame to light his way, but the vastness of the cavern overwhelmed its feeble light.

I needed no light at all. The cavern felt as comfortable, as familiar as my own skin. Lareth came close upon my heel, but I felt almost alone within the quiet chamber as I moved straight into its depth. My footsteps echoed, and the dead, still air washed around me like water. And there, at the center of what once had been a great hall eighty paces end-to-end, I found a dais six inches off the ground.

It held a throne.

The thing was made of gold and marble and silver. Not carved, not inlaid or chased or cast, but made all in one piece. It was like my Chaos blade, one artifact of perfect craftsmanship untouched by age. Lareth bumped against my back, then leaned aside, and then he gasped.

"Is that the FirstKing's throne?" he asked, incredulous.

I shook my head. I turned, and there before my worst retainer—a madman who had tried to kill me more than once—I took my throne. I closed my eyes and sighed, and felt the huge darkness around me gasp and sigh as though the tower itself were a great living thing. And on the exhale, it settled all around me, into me, and in the next moment my senses extended to the great hall's farthest corners.

With a little concentration I could feel the courtyard, too, feel the thousand little lives scurrying over sand and stone, setting tents and scavenging firewood and wondering if any of this was real. I found Caleb standing on the porch just outside the tower's entrance, peering down the tunnel I had made. Worry wrinkled his brow.

My eyes snapped open, and I met Lareth's startled gaze. "It's mine," I said. "This place is mine. Now let us make it strong."

14. Behind Strong Walls

After a moment, Lareth's voice quavered in the darkness. "Could we just give it light?"

Still drunk on the feeling of home, I nearly borrowed Chaos to make a flame. I stopped myself just short and forced the stain of offered power back into the depths of my awareness, then turned my eyes to Lareth.

"You trained under Seriphenes," I said.

He frowned above his green flame, but after a heartbeat he nodded.

"He had a test," I said. "He asked me to make light."

The wizard's jaw dropped. "Well...well, yes...."

"Show me," I said.

He shook his head. "That relies on the memory of shape," he said. "It needs a lingering power, an occasional flare of torchlight or sunlight to recall. This place...."

"This place has you scared?"

"It doesn't you?" He trembled and craned his neck, staring into the empty darkness. "Can't you feel the weight of it? It's like a blindfold, like manacles, like...." He shuddered again, top to toe. "It is like being buried alive."

I didn't meet his gaze. Instead I looked around, because I did not understand at all. "Can you still not see the shapes of energy?" I asked. "I...I feel at home here. I cannot say it more clearly, but even apart from that I need only look at the lines of power—"

"I see no lines of power," he said. "That is what I mean. This place is blind to me. It's black and empty; it drags at my eyes and leaves me feeling hollowed out and helpless." He dropped his head. "Please, my lord. Let us go from here."

"Would it help to know *why*, at least?"

He met my eyes for a fraction of a heartbeat, then looked away. "I think I know," he said. "That is how a dragon looks."

"Calm your heart. There are no dragons here."

His eye flicked up to mine again, and he held it this time. He released a heavy breath. "Are there not, my lord?"

I smiled. It tasted sad and bitter, but it was a smile. "I am not a dragon, Lareth. Not exactly."

"Not exactly," he said wryly. "But it was not so hard to face you when you let me hide from reason."

"You'll grow used to it in time," I said. "I'm not a dragon, but there are similarities. This place will be my lair. That army is my brood. And you. And Caleb."

He straightened his shoulders and focused on something far off. His voice took on the lecturing-hall tone. "And yet...you're *not* a dragon. I have seen your power. There is eerie Chaos there—"

"But lifeblood, too," I said. "And some small amount of wizardry. And everything I've taken from the men who call me lord."

He nodded at that, a new curiosity in his eyes. "You can blaze like a bonfire," he said. "But how do you use it?"

I opened my mouth to answer him honestly, but then I hesitated. He had shown no sign of madness, not since he had met at the tower's mouth, but this man was not my friend. This, though...this was something I needed to discuss, and no one else I had could help me here.

At last I shrugged and told him openly, "I don't know. I don't know how to use it. I grow less tired, I think. I do not thirst, perhaps? But what is that? The power around my soul seems so much stronger than that."

"It is," he said. "And I have seen you use it. On the steps outside the tower. I watched you waved aside these tons of earth—"

"No," I cut him off. "No, that's a power I received from the dragon blood. I can reshape the raw reality with will."

"But there's a cost," the wizard said. "There always is a cost. In mind or in body, in power or in precious stones. There always is a cost."

"It used to make me tired," I said, as I had told Caleb the night before. "But that has changed."

He nodded in sudden understanding. "I see. I see. And now I understand. You pay the price of power with the strength of all those lives."

"I what?"

"You burn it up, you *spend* the blazing lifeblood so you don't have to spend your own."

"I do not like the sound of that."

He shrugged. "It is a power. Like all powers, it has a purpose. But yes, I saw it happen. I saw your glow diminish when you pushed the stone aside."

"It did?" I felt a sudden panic, fought it down so I could see, and looked on myself with the wizard's sight. And then...perhaps? Perhaps I did not burn as bright as I had done before. I couldn't say. The fire wasn't gone as I had feared, guttering like the stub end of a candle. I breathed a little easier at that.

"But you could see me? You could see my power?"

He snorted. "You burn brighter than the sun. I could see you from half a world away."

"You should be able to work magic in my lair," I said, worried. "You are my brood."

"Perhaps in time," he said. "Perhaps I have to feel at home, and right now I only want to leave. But you have far greater concerns. You must learn the limits of your power."

"You've barely finished telling me I blaze like the sun—"

"Yet still you need to know. There always is a price." He was lecturing again. "I do not understand the shape of all the powers you now wield, but every student who has ever passed through the Academy's halls learned this: Before you work your will, you pay the price. It can't be dodged, it cannot be put off. Learn your limits, every nuance of your power, or one day you will burn yourself to ash to light a candle."

I looked away, the heat of my shame burning in my face. The Academy had taught me that. I'd heard the words, at least. But these last days had been so wild, my power so unnatural, I'd never stopped to think. I'd never tried to apply the neat and ordered rules the Masters had tried to teach me.

But I had once summoned light. I'd done the spell that Lareth had described, when first Vechernyvetr had me cornered in a narrow cave. It had been months since I had even tried to work the wizards' forms, but now I closed my eyes and felt my way through once-familiar patterns. I quieted my mind and focused my attention and shaped my will.

Where Lareth saw only darkness, I saw every thread of power in this place, every stain of human of will, every memory of light. I saw the ghosts of candles and torches and great hearthfires. I saw the sunlight and the moonlight that once had graced the unworked earth. All around me hung a light that was, a light that had been, a light that could be. By will alone, by strength of my desire, I called it forth.

And there was light. Not by my will alone, but by the ready answer of my lair. The earth itself, the tower, seemed eager to comply. I saw the flare of power behind my eyes, and then I blinked and looked for the first time with ordinary eyes on my domain.

"Smoke and shadows," Lareth breathed. "It's beautiful."

I could not even catch my breath to swear. The ruins around the tower were so aged and crumbled they could easily have been mistaken for natural rock formations, and I had expected to find the same in the tower. But now, beneath the clear white light of my wizard's working, the floor of the FirstKing's tower seemed almost untouched by the ravages of time.

The floor was of cut stone, polished smooth, and the ceiling hung fifteen feet above, supported every ten paces by a heavy stone pillar. Even with the unnatural light, the far walls were all lost in the distance. There was not a wall to break the sprawling hall, only here and there a fine-carved pillar. And just behind my throne, a staircase hewn of stone and chased with silver twisted up into the mountain overhead.

I heard Lareth suddenly catch his breath, and when I looked at him he seemed more afraid, not less, to have the light to see. I asked, "What's wrong?"

"Look at the size of it," he breathed, as though a word too loud might bring it crashing down. "Did you not see the *mountain* overhead? There are no walls. There's only little pillars, and they look like sticks beneath that weight."

I hid my smile and left my throne to stand before him. "You must trust what you can't see," I said. "And trust that I can. I can see every single stone above and underneath. And all of it is wonderfully made. Do you understand? More than a thousand years it's stood like this, with all that weight above, and never changed."

That stopped me, even as I said it. I turned to stare hard at the eerie throne, and then down at the flagstones underfoot. They looked like hand-carved blocks, but to my wizard's sight I saw the cracks were carved right in. The mortar was of one piece with the stone, a texture carved to look like binding clay.

The man who made this tower had worked with powers like my own. The FirstKing, our great and holy hero, had built this place with no magic made for man. My jaw fell open, I gaped at nothing, and behind me Lareth whispered, "What? What is it you see?"

"We're safe," I said. "That's all." I set aside the sudden understanding to consider more closely later, then turned to Lareth.

"Can you see the magic in the air? Can you see the working of the light?"

He focused for a moment, then gave a nod. "I can. That's odd—"

'That's your domain," I said. "Nothing else is in this place, but that is wizard's work. Can you bind it for me? Can you keep it there?"

He grinned. "I can do more than that," he said. "You've seen my sigil fire."

"The green flame?"

"Indeed. It is a working all my own, and it will let you bind this light to burn forever. To turn it on or off at just a word. To light this room, but not the one above. Not one among all the Masters of the Academy could give you that. It's mine alone, and I will teach you how."

He burned with pride—not at the power to break a crown, not for lives or fortunes stolen, but for a spell to light the dark. I smiled across at him. "You will," I said. "But not right now. Just bind this spell for me."

I was already past him, breaking to a run toward the door. He took some scurrying steps after me and called, "Wait! Where are you going?"

"To fetch my deathly shadow," I yelled back. "I've left him worrying too long."

I made my way out into the courtyard, then, and caught my breath at the sight before me. Men were hard at work, some stripped to the waist in spite of the winter chill. The boundaries of a stone wall were beginning to appear within the rubble spilled all around the tower. And as they cleared out the foundations, they revealed a shape as much a part of legend as the Tower of Days. The storied walls of Palmagnes had made a triangle with a peak pointing south and the tower at its center. Legend named them five paces thick and ten paces high, and the structure my men were uncovering could easily match those dimensions.

The courtyard itself was already stripped bare—stones of all sizes were needed for the walls, and the thick brush and vegetation that had grown in the rocky crags for the last thousand years had burned in an hour to give my soldiers lunch. The low mound that had filled the gateway gap was gone now, too—larger stones stacked in neat piles on the cleared courtyard, smaller rubble gathered in a pile near the eastern wall.

I'd cleared the tower's porch and a path across the courtyard perhaps thirty paces wide, but the guards had already done much more. The north wall stretched more than a mile east to west, and when it was done the north courtyard would be large enough to house a small village. That nearly seemed accomplished, with the neatly-ordered picket lines for horses and mules just west of the now-clear gateway. Beyond them the supply wagons stood in even rows, set out like the blocks of a little town.

And to the east the camp was setting up, clearing ground to pitch two thousand tents and lay the fires and station guards. Wagons trundled toward the eastern wall, their beds filled up with gathered stone. Here and there a soldier passing on some errand would stoop to snatch an errant rock and toss it in.

Caleb stood upon the wide stone platform and watched the men at work. I came without a sound to stand beside him, and he never turned his head. But as I stopped half a pace behind him, he grunted. "You're right. There'll be room enough for all of them. But not tonight. Not unless they want to sleep on heaps of stone."

"They could make beds inside the tower."

He scoffed. "They're not as mad as you. It wasn't wise to go in there. My lord."

I smiled. "It's safe enough." Before he could argue the point, I turned on my heel and headed back toward the tower. I snapped, "Come! That's an order, General." A moment later I heard his footsteps following after.

He followed me through darkness and into the light, and as he stepped beneath the ancient arch of the outer doors, he stopped to stare around the sprawling room. He showed no signs of awe, no gasp of surprise. He took three long steps into the room, and then I saw his eyes narrow as they picked out the distant shape of the throne. "That gold?"

"Some gold," I said. "Some silver. Marble, too."

He nodded once. He turned to his right and traced the gentle curve of the wide, arched stairs climbing into shadows up above. He looked up, considering the high ceilings with his eyes for a moment, and then he met my gaze. "Not bad."

"We'll make kitchens and a barracks on the floor above," I said. "There are the shapes of walls and rooms up there. But we can spread our beds down here for now."

"How large is it?"

"Eighty paces, end to end. Pillars here and there, but mostly clear."

"That's massive," Caleb said. "You could house an army in this place."

"I intend to."

He met my eyes. "Very well. I'll spread the word." Some motion caught his eye and he turned to watch Lareth moving among the distant pillars, muttering to himself as he bound the light in place. Wherever he went the pure white light took on a very slightly green glow.

The old warrior met my eyes again. "How much of this is his work? How much is yours?"

"He's only working on the light," I said. "The rest is...call it mine."

"I'm thinking of the work you did outside. The way you waved and cleared the rubble from the courtyard. It took a hundred men with carts and mules more than an hour to do what you did with a word."

"I have my tricks."

"I'm thinking of the walls," he said. "We have two choices. You said you meant to rebuild Palmagnes. Those walls are more than a mile long. We have the stone—Haven knows we have the stone—but it's rocks and mud as much as quarried blocks. And we have many hands, but it will take us weeks to build those walls higher than your head."

"Unless I help," I said, guessing at his purpose.

He shrugged. "Or we could scale back. We don't need a full square mile inside the walls, especially if you mean to house the men in this tower."

"It's true," I said, but I let my reluctance shade my voice. I wanted no half-measures for my home.

"But either way, we'll need your help," Caleb said. "These men are not building walls I'd be proud of otherwise. Two thousand men can work *fast*, but they aren't masons."

"I see."

"And I'm no architect, come to that. We'll need your help—"

I glanced back over my shoulder to the distant shape of Lareth, thinking again of prices. But what worth was there in power if it went unused? The FirstKing had bent reality to make this place, and now I would spend my strength to spare my men. It could not cost too much. Not for my lair.

"Come with me," I said. "You'll have your walls."

I led him at a trot back down the tunnel and out into the early afternoon. Once more I met the noisy dance of so many men hard at work, five thousands hands all bent to make my stronghold more secure. I drank it in like hot spiced wine and shared a grin with Caleb.

"Watch," I said. Then I closed my eyes and slowed my breath. I looked out with my wizard's sight, but it was easier now. It was magnified. New senses I had felt upon my throne revealed to me the crumbled stone, the strong foundations, and every life sworn to my service. My reason reeled at the enormity of it, but without strain at all I could hold the whole of the fortress in my mind in exquisite clarity.

And there within the heart of it I stood. I looked down upon myself, upon the huge bonfire blaze of human strength. It echoed now out through the stronghold's grounds, but still the heart of flame was me. Lareth said that fire had diminished when I worked raw reality, but it looked no smaller now. I felt no weaker. Still, I would use care. I'd watch. I wouldn't use too much.

But even as I promised caution to myself, a grin curled at my lips. It was not the monster's cruel glee, not the vicious dragon spirit that had seized me more than once before. This was my very human curiosity sharp with the thrill of imagined glory.

"You'll have your walls," I said again, no more than a whisper, and then without releasing the wizard's sight, I opened my eyes and looked out with human sight as well. North of the tower, to the walls. I stretched my arms out at my sides, palms up, and my grin grew. I grasped the threads of earth.

I didn't even have to try. They were already there, within my power. The same new senses that showed me my domain placed every stone within my grasp. I raised my hands, and thunder rolled across the fortress grounds as stones groaned and stretched and moved.

All around the tower, in all directions, the walls rose with my gesture. A tiny motion of my hands, but as I went I melted the myriad imperfect powers of rock and mud and fashioned bricks into a solid piece, perfect living stone, five paces thick and now a pace above the earth.

Men who had been working on the rubble dove aside, crashing to the ground. Gravel and dirt rained off the top, and shouts of fear rang out within the noise. Three thousand men at once stopped what they were doing and looked toward walls where none had been. And then they looked to me.

I felt their attention wash over me, and I threw back my head and laughed. Just look what I had done! I'd watched, as well, and Lareth had been right: I'd dimmed in power. But just a fraction. I was still a living blaze, and consider what I'd wrought! No mason in the world could have made a foundation so strong, not with perfect materials, and I had made it from weathered stone and sludge.

And now they were watching me. My men. Caleb, too, with more emotion than I'd ever seen him show. Astonishment and hope and admiration. I laughed louder and jerked my hands above my shoulders, and four miles' worth of wall stabbed up two paces into the sky, all seamless, shining stone.

I felt it then. A shock rushed back to me, an echo of weary weakness, and I saw it in my wizard's sight. My fire was much dimmed. Perhaps by half or more. And yet another part of me was stronger. I felt far more aware of all the stronghold. I felt the wild emotions flaring among my men. Without strain, without even trying I could see the curiosity and surprise on Lareth's face as he tried to understand the distant echo of two thousand men crying out in wonder.

My lair. My perfect lair. I thought of Pazyarev, an elder legend with a thousand dragons under his will, and he could only claim a cave. I thought of Tirah, with walls perhaps this tall and half as thick, and nothing like my Tower. I thought of the king's palace atop the hill in Sariano, and even that would look small and plain when I was done here.

I released the southern walls for now and turned my attention to the main wall before me. I used my arms again to focus my will, twisting both hands and carved a soaring arch out of the center of the wall to be our gateway.

More power burned away at that, but I did not yet feel weak. I turned both palms up, stretched toward the east and western ends of the wall, and as I lifted them two rounded towers sprang out of the earth and climbed up the angle of the walls. It took no effort at all to spin a stairway up the middle of them, carving perfect steps by nothing more than thought from nearly a mile away.

I marveled at what I could do. Three thousand strong and fearsome men marveled at me, too, and I could feel their awe. It sang in my soul. I watched my fire dim, determined not to let it burn too low, but while there was power yet to use....

I topped the towers with platforms fit for archers. Then I grabbed the walls themselves again and raised them up. It was delicate work now, a careful balance against the power I had left, but I wanted every inch of height that I could get. We had enough to stop a charge, but not to stop a volley of arrows. Not enough to thwart some simple earthworks or ordinary ladders. The king would come in force, and he would come prepared for siege. But I would give him a stronghold no siege could break, no engine could destroy. I raised my hands another inch and gained another pace in height along the walls.

And then among the wild, adoring crowd I felt a new sensation. Not my own, but from one of the men I felt the sudden stab of nausea, the fever flush of sickness. It came on fast, and by my heightened senses I could have pointed to the spot three hundred yards off to my left where he collapsed.

Sweat stood on my forehead now as well, and as I watched my powers burn, they now burned low. Another pace, perhaps, but not much more. I set my jaw and raised my hands.

And heard the groan come from three hundred throats at once. I felt them fall, staccato rapping on my soul as they collapsed, and more men staggered. More men swayed. I felt exhaustion hit them all at once. Then their confusion rang within my head. The awed elation melted into fear as all across the courtyard men collapsed, and I alone among them understood.

They had paid my price. I still burned. I still burned with the lifeblood of three thousand fires, but it was those fires that guttered now. Another ounce of strain, perhaps, and I could snuff them out. I dropped my hands in horror, feeling all too clearly the agony and fear that raged within my camp.

I had strong walls, and I had made three thousand men weak to get them.

They never learned just what had come to pass. Lareth would not let me take the blame. Caleb said that few among them could have understood anyway. Even he had trouble grasping it, no matter how I tried to put the price in words.

Seventeen men died. That was a mercy, though I took it as a blow. Only seventeen among them died, and those who lived recovered within days. So did my fire. Lareth watched with tempered interest, and as my men grew strong again, so too did I.

"It doesn't help," I said, early on the eighth day when the three of us sat together to breakfast. "It doesn't help the ones who died."

"They're soldiers," Caleb said.

"They're here to die," Lareth said. "That's what they're for."

He fell silent when I met his eye. He'd not shown much of madness these past days, but he fell back to ruthless cruelty as easily as breathing. He shrugged and said, "It's true."

"It doesn't matter," I said. "I cannot use a power that does this to my men."

"It didn't...at first," Caleb said.

"You agree with him?" I asked, eyes straining wide. "For a week now you've cursed at having all these men down lame, and now you think it's not so bad?"

Caleb spread his hands. "But now they all improve. I have nearly a thousand on their feet, but by this afternoon they will be back upon the walls."

"And there's no way they would have done this in that time," Lareth said. "One week? Two, even? No. Ten thousand men could not have built that wall so fast."

"There's no number of men could build a wall like that," Caleb said. He had spent hours in the archway, looking for some seam within the stone, some crack, some tiny flaw.

"Their exhaustion is a minor price to pay," the wizard said. "They do recover, given time."

"Not all of them," I said.

Lareth rolled his eyes. "Again, I must agree, you went too far. But now you've learned. Now you know more. Just...just keep more of that power in reserve. Don't use so much at once, spread it out, give it time to build back up. You gained four paces off the ground before the first among them fell. So spread it out. Do half a pace a day, and even if that keeps them in their beds, it will give us ten before another week is out."

"But that is just a number. It's just a legend. This place is not the point! That's what I forgot. The stronghold's just one weapon; I need men to fight my war."

"If you would do it as I say," the wizard sighed, "two weeks from now you'd have your men, *and* you'd have your fortress out of legend. What is wrong with that?"

"What's wrong?" I asked, incredulous. "Even if you're right. Even if they live. Even if two weeks from now they're all as strong as they were before, that's weeks I've stolen from their lives. Do you understand? That fire you see burning all around me is the *lives of men*. I cannot spend it like a currency."

"Then you are not much of a king," the wizard said.

My lips peeled back in rage, but Caleb interjected before I could call the wizard down. "You both have points," he said. "I don't pretend to understand the rules, but Lareth's right. You spread the burden out, and did in an afternoon— or in a week—what should have taken months. That is your strength. That is your special power."

"I cannot risk their lives—"

"You can. You will. And it is well and good that you are so hesitant, but you cannot ignore a power like that and accomplish the things you mean to do."

I glared at him, but I could find no answer. He gave me four heartbeats, then nodded satisfied. "And yet you're right. This place is not the point. Our walls are tall enough to stop a charge. They're tall enough to thwart most any straight assault, and in a day or two we'll have some men hard at work making them taller still. You needn't risk them all at once just for the walls."

Lareth snorted his objection, but he gave it no words. Caleb gave him several seconds, too, then nodded. Then he met my eyes.

"You gave us walls," he said. "You learned the limits of your power. You have grown wiser, stronger, and more cautious. And only seventeen men are dead. Call yourself a fool if you must, but you have to let it go. The day you lead these men to war, you lead them to their deaths. They're soldiers. That's what they are for."

"It will be easier when I can blame a dragon for their deaths," I said, grumbling like a child.

He nodded. "Then blame the king. He brings you war for petty vendetta and drives you to build these walls. You'll need them against the dragons, too. Blame the dragons now. Many more will die before this is done."

"But now," the wizard said, "at least we'll have a chance to start. You bought us time."

"They are impressive walls," the warrior said.

"And what is next?" I asked.

"Training," Caleb said. "You'd asked for soldiers you could teach to hunt the dragons. I'd meant to hand pick some, but we'll just use the strongest for a start."

"Good," I said. The plan had slipped my mind, but now that he reminded me I was anxious to get started. "We'll start today. That's now my top priority."

"Very well." He hesitated for half a heartbeat, then shrugged. "When you're ready—when more of the men are ready—we do need more from you."

I sighed. "What do you have in mind?"

"Wells," he said. "Inside the walls. The nearest miserable creek is more than a mile off. I keep forty men on water duty just to get us by, and when a siege is set...."

"I understand," I said, but a memory nagged at me. The baron had mentioned a clear well. I closed my eyes and reached out to the tower.

I hadn't done that much the last eight days. It was easy enough to push the awareness away, but when I touched it, I got all of it. I felt the convalescing soldiers. I felt the weariness sapping at even the strength of the men well enough to work. The price of my recklessness burned like a coal in the back of my mind.

But I could feel the earth as well. I could feel the ground around the tower, feel the shape of the stones, and there outside the tower's western wall....

"There are wells," I said. "They're buried under rubble, but otherwise they're sound. I'll show you where, and you can set the men to work at digging."

He opened his mouth to argue, then shrugged. "Very well, my lord."

"I'll use my power when I must," I assured him. "I will use every weapon at my disposal when it comes to fighting the dragonswarm. Trust in that. But this work can be done by men."

"Very well, my lord."

I searched his eyes for some objection, some remaining concern, but he met me with a level gaze and I gave up. "I still have much to learn," I said. "And no one to learn from but my own mistakes. Give me time."

"I'd give you years," Caleb said, "but the king will give you weeks at best."

"The dragons give you days," the wizard said. "If you truly mean to protect the farmers near the tower."

Startled, I looked to him. He shrugged. "I've gone up to the town to buy some wine. They've been attacked, you know."

"The town? Teelevon?"

He shrugged. "Outside the town. Some miller's house, and fields out in the west. Not many dead. Not yet. But every night for days now, there've been raids."

I growled low in my throat. "I gave orders no one should go near the town."

Lareth gaped. "You meant *me*? I thought you meant the soldiers."

"I mean you far more than most. If they had recognized your face—"

He scowled across at me. "I do not wear this face when I go into towns."

"You will not go back to Teelevon." I frowned. "Is that where you have been? I told you to go riding in the hills so you can summon portals for our hunters."

He tore his gaze away. "But...there are dragons."

I only glared, then turned to Caleb. "Find us someone else, someone I can trust, and send him to Teelevon. We need more news."

I frowned down at my hands and thought about the miller's house. I thought about the fields out west. "And send me these promising hunters. It's past time we should begin."

15. Unusual Approaches

I had not touched the tower since the day I raised the walls. I hadn't dared to work any energies at all. But still, as Caleb said, I'd gained in power. I'd gained awareness of the fortress, and there were places on the second floor accessible and strong. The outer stairs were blocked both ways, but from the spiral staircase in the center of the tower we could reach the middle of the second floor where four crossing corridors stabbed out toward the walls, north and south, east and west. And there upon the intersection were four vast rooms.

Two of them we'd made into barracks, where men could sleep beneath a roof and in the gentle warmth that Lareth's magic could maintain. Another, at Caleb's suggestion, became an officer's quarters where officers enjoyed a bit more space. Three large rooms off the back wall might have been meant for storage or private studies, but I reserved them to me and my two lieutenants. They had no doors in the empty frames, no windows, no furnishings at all. But after weeks living in military camps or on cavern floors, the bare little rooms felt like royal accommodations.

The fourth great room we made our conference hall, and there we used a broken oxcart's bed as a makeshift table. A dozen camp stools clustered around it, and I'd used memory and ink to sketch the rough terrain around the tower.

I was at the makeshift table that afternoon, reviewing a scrap of parchment crowded with Lareth's narrow script, when a shadow fell across me. I looked up to find a soldier standing in the door. He saw me look and threw a nervous glance over his shoulder. Then he turned back, but he fixed his eyes on the ceiling.

I said, "Dain, isn't it? Garrett Dain?" His eyes snapped down to mine.

"Y-y-es, Lord Daven. The General sent me. You intend to teach us?"

"I intend to start. Please, take a seat." I waved to the crude stools and looked past him to the hall. "We'll wait for the others."

The others weren't long in coming. Caleb had chosen thirty men for this chore, and he'd promised me the brightest he'd found in his short time commanding the men. The felling at the walls had changed his selection somewhat, but as the afternoon progressed, I was impressed with the quality he'd managed to find.

Twelve of them came from the first battalion. They'd been there when Pazyarev's greens attacked. Four more had witnessed dragon raids firsthand. But every man among them seemed attentive, not only fit but smart as well. And they all knew how to sit, silent, and listen. That was the most important trait for any kind of hunter.

I'd set aside the whole afternoon to work with them. First I explained my plan—for the first time I laid out in detail my intentions for this army. "I mean to carry the fight to the dragons," I told them. "There are dragon lairs all through these mountains, and when night falls they fly. More and more, with every day we wait."

"But you will kill them for us?" Dain asked. His eyes flicked to one of the soldiers from the first battalion. He'd heard stories.

I shook my head firmly. "No. *You* will kill them for everyone else."

That got their attention.

"I will make you into hunting packs. Thirty men to a pack, I think, but it depends on what we find when we go out there."

"Go out?" Dain asked, his voice quavering.

"Yes. You will hunt them in their lairs. You will kill them while they sleep."

"But how?" another soldier asked, an ugly-faced young redhead at the end of the table. "We can't fight monsters."

"You can, with sharpened steel. With ruthless tactics. Sneaking and dodging and wearing them down. Strike when they are unprepared and bleed them out, and even a far stronger enemy will start to crumble."

I'd borrowed words from Lareth, from the speeches he had used to give, and now they worked like magic. Another kind of magic. Lareth had spent months convincing these men they were strong enough to fight the king's great host.

"We'll strike and then we'll run," I said. "And when the next day dawns, it will dawn on an enemy dazed and weakened by our cunning."

"But how?" the redhead asked. "Don't dragons fly?"

"They do, but we won't fight them in the open. We will choose our turn to strike, and we will keep them from the sky."

He tried to repeat his question again but I raised a hand to stop him. "It's not easy," I said. "But it can be done. That's why we're here. I know the way. I know their secrets, and we'll develop tactics you can use."

"Us," he said. "You keep talking of us, as though you don't intend to come along."

I glanced toward the door, then on an instinct down and to the left, and realized I was looking through a hundred feet of solid stone toward the northern gate where Caleb stood in conversation.

I shook my head. "We have three thousand men against ten thousand dragons," I said. "We can't afford to lean on me alone. I'll help you as I can—and there is much that I can do—but in the end I'll need a dozen hunting parties out at once. I can't go with them all."

Garrett Dain nodded reluctant understanding, and I saw others among them take his cue. "You're right," he said. "But if that's what you want, what are we doing here? Why Palmagnes, if we're fighting the dragons? Why have us work so hard to build those walls?"

"They're clever, Dain. Word travels among them quickly, and their vengeance is a terrible thing. Once we begin, they will come for us. You can count on it. And we *must* have a reliable stronghold if we're to survive that strike."

The redhead raised his chin. "Where does the king's force fit into this?" Every eye turned to me at that, even Dain demanding an answer.

I sighed. "Nowhere. The king's force is no concern of ours. We'll make a fortress strong enough to stand against dragons, and the king's army can break their teeth on it all day long if they want. They are of no interest to us."

They had their doubts, but soon enough I turned the talk from what and why to how. And then I showed them. I started out sitting, but as I began describing how to force a dragon out of the air I found myself on my feet, going through the motions.

I explained as best I could how to bring one down, and how to fight him once he was grounded. When even Dain seemed uncertain what I meant by some description, I gathered dust into a cloud and spun it out into a faerie dragon, insubstantial on the air. I raised it up and walked beneath its wings to show them where to look for vulnerable spots, where to attack and when. Then Dain jumped up and drew his sword to try some practice swings, testing maneuvers based on what I'd said.

Then the others were standing beside him, offering suggestions, and as I watched they found a routine. Then they were circling the illusion, talking out a strategy. I made it lash its heavy tail, and one of the men barely ducked short of losing his head. They laughed, then listened gravely as I explained a dragon's many methods of attack.

In the end, as I tried to teach them humility, I slowly came to realize their numbers were their real advantage. One blast of fire might kill thirty, but not if they spread out. And apart from that, a dragon might have six different lethal assaults, but it could not really use them to kill six men at once. It could not split its focus so many ways.

The redhead remembered stories he had heard about some region in the Northlands where men fought fearsome bulls, relying on taunts and distractions to wear them down. He and Garret Dain designed a plan from there: One man could draw the dragon's ire while the rest nipped at its heels. We practiced that 'til they were sore, 'til I ran out of clever tricks, and every man among them took a turn as the distraction.

Late in the afternoon, we were interrupted by the sharp clack of Caleb's boots in the stone corridor. He stopped in the doorway and considered us for a moment. His eyes barely touched the dragon form. He nodded once. "It's late. The men are called to supper, and then, if you are ready for it, their first lesson is scheduled for tonight."

The redhead spoke up beside me. "Our first lesson? What was all this then?"

His general's dark eyes fell upon him, and the young man bowed his head. "Sir, I mean."

"He means the lesson you will teach," I told them all. "I will train you, and you will train your teams."

"Our teams?" Dain asked, worried understanding already in his eyes.

I nodded. "Your hunting parties. I mean you each to lead one."

"Are they ready?" Caleb asked. "Or do they need another day?"

"We do not have another day. But they are ready. They can at least begin."

I heard some uncertain murmuring among them, but Dain stepped forward with a question in his eyes. I waited while he found his courage. The others tended to follow his lead, so if I could just convince him, I had it won.

At last he cleared his throat. "Could you...." He jerked a thumb over his shoulder to the empty floor where we had fought an airy dragon. "Could you make more dragon forms like that? For us to use?"

"Easily. Lareth and I together could probably even make a clever one. I'll try to have it by tomorrow."

He nodded. "Then yes. With that, I can teach my men. Do I get to choose my own?"

He looked to me. I looked to Caleb. Caleb shrugged.

"Find volunteers if you can," I said. "It's dangerous work. For all of you. But we are fighting for the world."

They nodded, then they left, the allure of a warm supper dragging them away. I watched them through the stone as they went down the central stairs and to the crude kitchens we'd made of one end of the great hall. Caleb stood beside me, waiting, 'til I shook off that strange awareness and turned to meet his eyes.

"Will they do?"

"They'll do," I said. "They understand the task, and already they make plans. I have some hope at last."

He nodded, silent for a moment, then glanced at me from the corner of his eye. "How long will it take to train them, do you think?"

"This group? They will be ready in a week. Fifteen days at most. But they're handpicked. I don't know after that. Two months, perhaps, for them to pass on what they know?"

"You're still thinking ten-man teams?"

"Thirty, I think, 'til we get started."

"That's a third of our force," he said. "That's quite a lot to set aside."

"To set aside? This is our mission, Caleb. The dragons will not wait forever."

"I understand," he said. "But neither will the king. Your walls are good, but there is much more we should do. For one, the wizard never bothered to teach them how to hold a strong location."

"So what would you advise?"

"Start small. Make this crew your only hunting party. Send them out *together* in a week or two and see how many survive."

I frowned at him. "I'm heartened by your confidence."

He shrugged. "We will not know until we've tried. If anyone survives, they'll come back veterans of war. Captains of the hunt. You'll be amazed what that status will mean to the men. By then, I should be ready to release the rest for full-time training."

"What's our time frame, then?"

"Two weeks from now you take the first group hunting, if we're not up to our armpits in Eagles and Guards. All things go well, you'll have your thirty hunting parties by spring. In the meantime, don't tie up more than an hour or two a day."

"I can live with that—"

"Of course," he interrupted, "that assumes we can get to the dragons. Have you learned Lareth's portal magic yet?"

"I've told you, it's not a simple thing."

"How long?" he asked.

"I cannot say."

He frowned. He seemed to know I hadn't tried. "Three thousand men inside these walls, Daven, and only two of them are capable of magic. Remember that. If the king's army lays a siege, all the training in the world won't help if we're stuck inside these walls."

"I'll *handle it*, Caleb."

"And speaking of the siege, have you considered food?"

I shook my head. "Lareth claims they always kept enough in store to last two weeks. You'd know better than I how much we have."

"That sounds right."

I nodded. "Lareth wants me to release them to forage, but I won't have my men ruining these farmers. I'm still trying to figure something out."

Caleb only nodded. "You'll have a week, then. If you don't figure something out, they'll forage. Your word is law, but these men will do what it takes to get fed."

"I understand."

"Good." He considered me for a moment, then nodded to himself. "You're doing well. There are a thousand challenges ahead, but you are doing well."

"Thank you, Caleb."

"Come, my lord. Let's eat. And then we'll speak of options."

By the tenth day nearly all my men were on their feet, and as they recovered Caleb put them right to work. For seven days after that they learned how to protect the fortress even as they shored up its defenses. As morning burned toward noon on the eighth—our eighteenth day inside the walls—it was amazing how much Caleb had accomplished.

We'd cleared the rubble up to the tower's third floor, as well, and Lareth itched to start work on the fourth. I helped, but never as I'd done on that first day. In little doses, and only when my fires raged, I'd clear a corridor of rubble or strengthen a buckling wall. Workers built the outer walls, as well, above the marble-smooth and perfect foundation I had made, they built it up with mud and brick and when I had a chance I made it whole.

By then only a third of the men were working construction at any time. The rest worked in shifts, hunting and gathering food wherever I would let them, though the return was paltry as long as I restricted them from settled lands.

Others scouted or stood sentry, but the most important work was the training. Caleb and I both helped at times, but the majority of the work fell to our thirty hand-picked hunters, and they shone. Even in the few hours Caleb would give me, the rest of the men learned much from my Captains of the Hunt. The soldiers listened to them and practiced what they learned. And whenever the Captains were not teaching, they were studying with me.

I taught them how to spot a dragon's den in the wild, how to recognize and read the marks of a dragon's passage. I told them how and when to pin a dragon in its cave, and how to use its size against it. In the practice area I built the shadow dragon forms and watched my handful teach nine hundred men how to recognize a dragon's soft spots, how to avoid the massive claws, and what to expect of the powerful tail.

Every day they learned, and every day they grew more confident. The walls and tower grew higher. And somewhere, far off or close at hand, the dragonswarm grew more terrible. Every day I expected grave reports, but they didn't come. Rumors. Hints at casualties, letters gone unanswered, messengers lost. But in Teelevon, at least, the dragons hadn't yet attacked.

At noon on the eighteenth day, Caleb tracked me down and dragged me to the north wall. One great cloud of dust stained the whole horizon. We watched it carefully throughout the day, and though it drew nearer we couldn't yet discern the party that stirred it up.

The men grew anxious. All throughout the fortress, eyes strayed often to the northern wall, wherever they worked. Whispers ran among the men. Things had been too easy, they seemed to say, and now at last the trials were upon us. When the sun set I lost sight of the cloud, but the distant glow of campfires lit the night, miles off to the north. I watched until my eyes burned, straining to see something in the dark, but nothing moved.

And when I could keep my feet no longer, I retired to my place inside the tower. The men without were restless, and their anxiety echoed noisily inside my head. We had strong walls, and very able men, but still I feared. For long hours I lay awake, staring at the stone ceiling, until finally a fitful sleep claimed me.

As I drifted off at last, the knowledge was bitter in my mind: When morning came, it would bring us war.

We were not only warriors by now. The first farmer had come on our ninth day in the fortress, while most of my brave soldiers were still lying sick in bed. An alarm had risen when someone working the north wall spotted him approaching, but I ran out ahead and met the man halfway. His name was Robertson. He had a farm eight miles northwest of the tower, and he had lost a son in the siege.

His eyes lit up when he saw me, and he said, "Daven of Teelevon. The rumors are true. You've come to rebuild Palmagnes and face the dragons."

I only looked at him, astonished, as he knelt before me. "Take my pledge, Sir Daven. I'd like to join your lot." And humble though he was, he too added to my fires.

He bid me send my men to bring in the grain from his barns—scarcely three meals for such a large force, but it was what he had to give. Farmer Robertson had nothing more to offer, but I gave him sanctuary within the walls of my fortress, and he watched the construction with interest.

The next day had brought a handful more, farmers and ranchers from south Teelevon, and every one of them recognized me on sight. Some brought families. They shook my hand or bowed awkwardly or fell to their knees before me, and by the end of the eighteenth day I had a civilian population within my walls. I was worried about them when dawn came on the nineteenth day.

I was worried about my warriors, too. They were not really trained to defend fortifications. Caleb had done his best, but all their experience had been earned attacking from behind, in the dark, not waiting in strongholds. I was worried about the king's soldiers coming to the attack, too. I thought of all the brave young men in the front lines, faithfully charging against my waiting archers.

I thought dark thoughts indeed of Othin ordering them to advance.

At dawn I watched with Caleb as the dust cloud appeared again. They were on the move.

Around the third hour, I heard him say, "Now that is odd...."

I was thinking the same thing. "At least your defenders can stand down," I said. "Put them back to work."

But he and I just watched the horse advance. Around noon on the nineteenth day, an army of peasants invaded Palmagnes. They were farmers and merchants, carpenters and blacksmiths and riverboat men—there were shepherds aplenty, but not a soldier among them.

They came on foot, or leading donkeys on a tether, or some in long trains of wagons. They came in a great caravan, packing hard the ancient soil of the forgotten South Road, and my men watched with open mouths as the crowd poured through the gaping gateway and stood milling in the sprawling courtyard, eyes wide.

It took the rest of the day to sort them out. That afternoon we didn't lay a single stone, we were so busy helping lay out and construct and organize a place for the myriad civilians within our military encampment. Caleb and Lareth and I were harried, moving in and out among the newcomers until well after sunset, first trying to understand and then trying to explain and, at the last, only to organize.

They had come from across the plains. I saw many of the people of the Eliade barony, and they were small surprise after the steady stream of farmers coming to join us in the last week. But I also met men from as far away as Cara to the west, and a hundred villages out east and even north of Tirah. Just at sunset I stumbled across the innkeeper of Chaaron, who bowed and scraped and swore an oath of fealty without once recognizing me. Caleb said later that he'd spotted Farmer Jake as well.

The word had spread from there. I heard my own intentions from a hundred different mouths, and every face shone with hope that I could face the dragonswarm. When I had left that inn, and then the rebels disappeared, the people talked.

I heard heartbreaking tales, too, of the monsters finally come down from the mountains. A man who had told me dragons couldn't compare with the threat of the rebels accepted a bowl of thin barley soup from one of those very soldiers and told me what a flight of dragons had done to his home.

Wherever I saw faces from the baron's lands, I urged them to go home. This place had never been meant to protect civilians, but they cried or begged or stubbornly refused. I had chosen the location for the power of its name, and the name had spread too far. Every man and woman among them *believed* that Palmagnes could stand; some had traveled hundreds of miles to seek its refuge.

So we made them as comfortable as we could, organized them as well as we could, and late into the night we met back in the tower and wondered what to do. Caleb met with his officers for half an hour, then sent them out into the night with further orders. Lareth sat with crossed legs and brooded.

I waited.

Finally Caleb came over to me, "Daven, this is not all trouble."

"It is. They cannot fight. What can we really do for them?"

"You're thinking about it the wrong way 'round. How many of the people you met were from this province?"

I shrugged, "A little more than half, I'd say."

He nodded. "Me too. And every one of them a farmer or cattleman. Daven, these people can support *us*. In fact...we need them."

"No, Caleb!" I shook my head, "We will *not* take advantage of these people—"

Lareth rose. "It's hardly taking advantage. If you believe any part of what you say, these people face destruction. You can offer them some refuge. Use the resources they're willing to give you, and grant the safety only you can. It's why we tolerate our lords at all."

Caleb nodded. "They're willing, too. The ones from around here, especially. They were trying to join the army, Daven. They haven't forgotten you're their knight."

"But I'm not. Not anymore."

Lareth's head snapped around in surprise. "You were made a Knight of the People around here?"

"For killing you, in fact."

He didn't grin this time, but still a smile touched his lips. "You should have said. I would have sent you out campaigning days ago. That title's gold."

"I'm sure it's been revoked," I said. "The king would have his say."

"Not much in this. A Knight is 'of the people,' after all. Unless they turn against you, royal mandate won't do much. And you seem to have respect throughout this land."

"Not just respect," Caleb said. "They adore him. And those who came from farther off adore the rumors."

"So I should welcome them to die because they love me?" Even as I said it, I knew I was wrong.

Lareth scowled openly. "Of course you won't. You'll save their lives. Isn't that what this whole charade is for? You've built a bulwark strong enough to stand the storm, why not welcome every ally come inside? Extend your protection, and triple your fighting power."

I shook my head. "Well, not my fighting power. These aren't soldiers, not even as much as the brigands I've got."

Caleb shook his head. "That's not what he means. He's talking about food again. Get the grain and the cattle. Without it, you won't have any soldiers a week from now."

"Oh, I'm not even talking food," the wizard said. "I'm talking power. Strong hands, strong backs, more fire for you to burn. *Your* fighting power."

"There's that," Caleb said, thoughtful. "There's craftsmen out there, too. You almost have a town. Put them to work. Build us some tables, some chairs. Make the men a barracks and let them sleep on beds for the first time in a year. That will help your soldiers, too."

Lareth's eye lit up. "I would murder for a feather bed."

Caleb almost smiled. He saw the doubt in my eyes, and said, "No, Daven. There's nothing left to argue about. The mage is right. You have a chance like this, you take it."

"And all I have to give them is my protection?"

Caleb shrugged, "It's more than they'd get from anyone else, once the dragons come. For that matter, it's more than they got from the good baron last time these cutthroats were around. There's no justification for turning them back."

And they were right, of course. I couldn't argue much, but I had spent two days dreading the doom that hung over my people, and now I'd only added to the fold. But we'd have beds and blacksmiths, we'd have cooks and carts piled high with food. The siege would come, and all these unarmed men could represent our victory. We talked on, late into the night, ironing out details and beginning the long process of planning out the village that would be. Twice Caleb left to wake one officer or another and start the orders passing.

The second time he left I barely noticed, so caught up in my discussion with Lareth. "Of *course* they're still capable—given the tools—but where will we get the resources?"

The wizard shrugged, "A blacksmith's got iron. A carpenter's got wood. Wood wouldn't be a problem anyway, with the number of men we've got—"

"Yes, but they wouldn't bring iron *with* them! Many barely brought the clothes on their backs."

He shook his head. "It doesn't matter. We'll just go get it."

I blinked.

He laughed. "As long as they live outside this dusty nowhere, I can make portals anywhere to north or east, and we have plenty of hands to bring it back."

I closed my eyes, and saw it all unfold. It seemed too easy. "Just like that? Just slip out the back and bring home their supplies?"

"And food, of course. And anything we need."

Caleb's shadow blocked the door, and when we turned he didn't move. He seemed distracted, worried. "And what about the wizards with the king?"

"What about them?" Lareth asked.

"How much will they interfere with this plan?"

Lareth shook his head. "Not at all. If they were close, of course, they'd see the changing power. That...that we could not afford. They could follow it and step right through our walls. But until they arrive, we're free to come and go."

"Then that's two days," Caleb said.

We didn't ask the question. Caleb answered anyway. "They're outside Teelevon now. They're stopping anyone they find heading here and confiscating goods. We've got two days before they're camped outside our door."

"That isn't time enough," the wizard said. "Not to get everything we need. The feathers alone might take me hours."

"Forget your bed," Caleb growled. "We're talking about war."

Lareth sighed. "My point still stands. The crowd we had today could well supply our needs, but they are scattered all across the south Ardain. We'll need more time to send out gathering parties."

"Perhaps we can arrange that," I said. "Delay the king's men a little bit."

Caleb stepped closer. "I know of ways, but they all break your rules."

"No. No killing. But we could offer them a truce, request parlay."

Lareth tasted the words. "Request parlay? Yes, that could work."

Caleb shook his head. "It won't. Not with an Eagle in command. The way they're trained, a rebel gets none of the rights or honors reasonably afforded foreign foes. They wouldn't hesitate to cut you down under the flag of peace."

"The king's men? They would do that?" I asked.

He nodded.

I shook my head. "I'd expect that kind of thing from Brant, but not the king's elite guard."

Caleb only shrugged.

"It doesn't matter anyway," I said. "I never meant to meet with them; I just wanted to buy time. It might take, what, a day or two sending messages back and forth to arrange the meeting?"

Caleb raised his eyebrows. "I do suspect it would."

Lareth grinned his twisted grin. "Ooh, and if they planned some treachery they'd want to stay as close as possible to form. Might even ask another day to plan the strike."

"And by the time they realize I'm not coming to the meeting," I said, "we'll have the resources we need."

Caleb stood staring down at me for a long time. Then he shook his head. "That plan is cunning and twisted, and predicated on the treachery of other men."

"But will it work?" I asked.

"It should. I'm just surprised it came from you."

I hesitated, then smiled. "I have some fine examples to learn from." Lareth barked a laugh.

Caleb nodded somberly. "That you do, my lord. That you do, indeed."

I stayed up late that night, unable to ignore the rising threat. Caleb had found another risk I hadn't even entertained: spies among my flood of new retainers. It would be easy enough, he had said, to slip some in and let them wait, then open up the gates the day the king arrived.

We had no gates. Not yet. We had our plans, but while the enemy was still far off, we'd stationed guards beneath the arch and spent our attention on other things. I worried about the gates. I didn't worry much about the spies.

I waited 'til the dark of night, when most of the tower had fallen silent, then I sat within my room and closed my eyes. I reached out through the stones and spread my senses until I could feel every living thing in my domain.

Not many were asleep. Most among them burned with quiet worry. Some sat up and whispered rumors. Some played cards. And some were hard at work despite the hours. I looked in on my sentries, sharp and alert beneath the gateway arch, and for the first time they were feeling very small and vulnerable there. There were others on the walls, walking their patrols.

I found the civilians in their camp. Caleb had set them in the courtyard south of the tower, and something like a town had already sprung up. In tents and little lean-to sheds and under heavy-laden wagons, the workers slept. They had some fear—more brittle and jittery than that old familiar worry in the guards—but mostly they had trust that we could keep them safe.

My awareness drifted like a fog among the sleeping forms, and I felt their hearts until I saw betrayal. I found a carter with a dozen barrels full of alcohol and plans for arson in his heart. I opened the ground beneath him where he slept, swallowed him up in its warm embrace, and left him air enough to sleep 'til dawn. I'd go with guards to dig him up tomorrow morning.

And there were more. Nearly a dozen men in all, and three of them among my own battalions, long embedded with the wizard's rebels. I might have found the black betrayal in the hearts if I had looked before, but I had never thought to look. Now I bound them like the rest, beneath the floor where they were sleeping.

I was nearly done, exhausted from the search and thinking maybe I might even get some sleep, but then I noticed someone slinking through the halls. It was a girl, wrapped up in black to hide her in the night. There'd been no women in the camps that Lareth brought, but some had come in with the farmers from the fields and quite a few among the caravan of tradesmen. She had been one of them. She had hidden among them, and I had never seen her face.

I didn't need to now. I knew her instantly. I almost called Caleb to go and deal with her. Perhaps I should have. I watched her sneak along the outer stairs up to the second floor, then turn my way. We had no lights within that passage yet, but there were guards. A patrol headed her way even then, another coming down the stairs would block her in. She would be caught, and we had not yet well prepared my men for harboring civilians. They might not treat her kindly when they caught her stalking.

The first patrol spun around, alarmed, when they heard me coming at a run, but I sprinted past. I took the corner, caught her in my arms, then pulled us both together through the wall into a room that hadn't yet been cleared. It was little larger than the closet where I slept, and mostly full of dirt and fallen stone, but high upon the outer wall a fissure wider than my hand let in some light. I used the trick

Seriphenes had taught me, bound the moonlight in the air and magnified it until we could see, and then at last I let her go.

She didn't step away. She knotted her fingers in the fabric of my shirt and pushed up on her toes to kiss me. She tasted sweet and warm. Like hope. Like home. She made me ache. She made me smile. She made me be the one to break the kiss.

I stepped away and met her eyes. "You should not have come here."

"I thought that was our plan."

I laughed, shocked at the absurdity of it. "That was before. Everything has changed."

"No," she said, stepping slowly closer. Her eyes were bright, her voice was steady. "Nothing's changed. You've always been a hero. You've always been about to die. And I have always wanted to be with you."

"It isn't safe," I said. "They're coming. The king, and all his men. Twenty thousand men. And wizards."

"I know," she said. "They're camped around my town. They are supposed to be our friends, and yet they do as much to hurt us as the rebels ever did."

I swallowed hard and looked away. "I'm sorry, Isabelle. I didn't mean to bring them here."

She touched my face. "You didn't bring them here. Timmon did. One way or another, this is on him. I hear you've saved a lot of lives by gathering these men."

"I will save many more than that before I'm done. But I have enemies much worse than that sad king, and they will come here, too."

"Then let them come," she said. "I'll fight them at the gates, or I will cower in this room. Whatever you ask of me. But let me stay."

"I can't."

"Daven...." She trailed off, then turned her face. The moonlight shone upon her cheek. "I slipped away that night. I waited for you here. Themm came to suggest that I go home. Father came to demand it of me. I didn't leave until the food was gone. The water was gone. And even then I waited, hoping every minute you'd arrive."

"I'm sorry, Isabelle. I couldn't come. I was...a prisoner."

"They say you lived with dragons," she said, measuring me with her eyes. "Some people say you are one, wearing human skin as a disguise. They say a lot of things about you."

"I wish...I could have come to you," I said, fighting for stern authority and falling short. "I wish I could let you stay—"

She shook head. "You can. Please, let me stay."

"They know your name. You're not some peasant farmer seeking refuge. If word should reach the king that you are here—"

"He'll what? Come through those walls to get me?"

"He could bring great harm to your father."

"He won't. The man's as stubborn in his loyalty as in his rage. But even if he did...we all make sacrifices."

"But it's your family," I said. "You have a home. Don't throw that all away to be with me."

She smiled, soft and sad.

I shook my head. "No. You'd make an enemy of the king if he found out."

"Already true," she said. "How do you think these people found your tower? It's hardly on the maps, and Timmon's men have held the northern roads for days."

"You led them here?"

"I spread the word. I knew you had many men with swords, and you would forget you needed men with hammers and needles and thread." She smiled at me. "And they were already flocking to your name. I helped them find a way around the Guard."

I stared at her. "How...how long have you known? How could you arrange that all so fast?"

"Daven, I've been listening. Don't you remember how I fell in love with you? I get rumors of you the way other girls receive love letters."

"I can't believe these rumors. How can word have spread so fast?"

She didn't answer right away. She shook her head with a mysterious little smile. Then she shrugged. "Troubled times set men speaking. As I said, most of the rumors are nonsense. But I knew enough of you to find the truth. Father wouldn't believe it until one of his farmers said he'd seen you in the soybeans."

She took a short step back and pointed an accusing finger. "But speaking of love letters, I passed the campsite coming here. It's gone. I think you found my note. I think you could have come to me."

I looked away. "I wanted to. I wanted to see you so much. But even more than that, I wanted to keep you safe."

"And now you can do both," she said.

I set my jaw. I took a breath to speak my word as law. She just watched, her eyes so bright, and in the end I reached out and took her hand.

"You are amazing, Isabelle."

She grinned and turned her head. "I know. And I will make a wondrous queen."

I held her there, and for a while we talked beneath the moonlight. Then at last she looked around and shook with a little shiver in the cold night air. I took her hand and caught her eye.

"We should find you somewhere to stay."

She glanced uncertainly at the wall I'd dragged her through before and shrank away. "Is there another way?"

I could have folded back the earth to make a way. I could have cleared the rubble from the room to find the door that once had been. Instead I licked my lips and dropped my eyes. "There is a way, if you will let me. If you can trust me."

"Of course I can," she said. She poured herself against me, and I wrapped an arm tight around her waist. Then I closed my eyes and scanned around my tower. We'd cleared the third floor now, and places on the fourth nearest the outer stairs. But I preferred the tower's heart. I looked along the central spiral.

The third floor held a suite of rooms connected by inner doorways, lit with Lareth's spells and clean and empty. I caught my breath and wrapped my will around the glow of her lifeblood so close to mine. Then I...reached. I stretched and tugged, and pulled our lives along the threads of earth until we stood within that room instead.

I opened my eyes and found her staring at me, lips parted, eyes wide. A word from me was enough to raise the lights, and Isabelle stepped away. She turned in place, looking out over a room at least as large as hers within the Eliade manor.

"It wants for furnishings," I said, "but we have craftsmen now, so we'll be able—"

"Did you just move us with your mind?"

I nodded. "We're near the center of the tower now. Maybe thirty paces down the hall, and one floor up."

"I didn't feel a thing," she said. "That's remarkable!"

I smiled at her. "It's something fairly new."

"It's wonderful. Let's go to Teelevon! Now. You can use it on the army there, and send them all away."

My smile faded as I shook my head. "I can't. I cannot force a will that isn't mine. If you hadn't wanted to come with me, if you hadn't trusted me, you'd still be down there in that room."

"Oh." She blinked, disappointed, then forced a smile. "But still, it's good."

I laughed at that. "It's good. It gives us hope. It's something even the Masters of the Academy have never seen. No one even knows it can be done."

Her smile rallied at that, then she came close to me again. She looked up in my eyes and bit her lip and cocked her head. "Is there somewhere you could go to fetch me blankets? The night is cold."

"It will not take a heartbeat."

"Good," she said. "And will you stay with me tonight? To keep me safe?"

"I don't recall you trembling at the dark."

She smiled, and it lit a fire in my veins. "You've been too long away."

"Then not a heartbeat more," I said. I took her with me to the little closet where I'd stayed. We took the blankets and the pillow and the scrap of tear-stained parchment from the floor, and those were all my lordly possessions. Then we went back upstairs, and I hung fire in the empty doorways so she might feel safe. Nothing disturbed us all night long.

At dawn I raised the traitors from their graves and sent them back to Timmon with notes pinned to their shirts. I begged his army for a truce, and the moment they were gone I let Lareth send my men throughout the land to bring in stores against a siege.

I presented Isabelle to Caleb and the wizard, and perhaps Caleb frowned. Perhaps the wizard leered. But neither spoke a word against her, and before breakfast was done she'd won their respect. She knew this land. She told Caleb where and how the king would come, and told Lareth where to go to find abandoned stores of wood and grains.

She knew the locals who had come to seek protection, too, and she told us whom to ask for beds and whom for clothes, which smith among them made the finest locks, and which we shouldn't trust to make our blades. I led her out to the south courtyard where our craftsmen gathered, and she drew curtsies of respect and polite greetings. In the end I left her plotting with the tailors and a promise we would meet again for lunch.

But I had work to do 'til then. My men who weren't with Lareth worked the walls, laying stones and building stairs. My civilians pitched in, too, if they were strong enough and free. By mid-morning we had over two hundred extra men and women helping carry stones.

There were those who had come out of fear of the dragons, and there were locals simply loyal to my name. There were steadfast Ardain landholders displeased with the long stay of the king's forces here. There were those who'd come from little more than curiosity. But as they watched the soldiers work, as they listened to the stories in the camp, they all pitched in. They should have run, the more they learned about what we expected here. Instead they offered more and more, of sweat and blood and goods they'd left behind.

Lareth went off with them, opening portals all across the plains as he had promised, and he brought back loads of food and steel and furniture and anything else that struck him as useful. Including men. Families that hadn't braved the long journey to join the caravan came darting through an easy portal and sometimes left behind a sky flecked with the distant shapes of dragons. In one day Lareth was able to fill our stores to bursting and swell the numbers of civilians in our camp to match the size of the army. I only shook my head, unbelieving, and bent back to the task at hand.

The rest at night was short and swift, and dawn came far too early to herald another day of heavy labor. More portals brought back more resources and more men, but I could not spare Lareth even to gather all that had been offered. As the workers placed stone on stone, I walked back and forth along the line, binding the stones together more perfectly than any mortar could have done. But the king would bring his wizards, and no matter how I burned up the energy of lives sworn to me, I only worked reality. I made more perfect stone, but it was only stone. I needed wizardry to thwart the Masters' power.

So by the second day I turned my wizard to that task, and he walked back and forth along the walls, binding them until the silk-smooth stone shimmered slightly with his strange green fire. He promised it would hold. It would defy the wizards' workings long enough, at least, for me to crush their summoned power.

They sent no messenger that day to take our offer. Perhaps they'd guessed our plan, or perhaps they didn't think they'd need the treachery. Still, the army didn't come. My civilians built a gate from planks of wood. They built it on the ground, laid out flat, and stacked up planks in layers eighteen inches thick. I came at sunset, still aglow with unspent fire, and bound the heavy door as I had done the walls. I raised it into place, one solid piece no battering ram could shake.

Then Lareth bound the living energy and cast a working on the door so it would lower only at my command or Caleb's but rise at a word from any of my soldiers. It was as good as any drawbridge, and I toyed with the idea of carving a moat as well, but I had burned too much already. I didn't dare exhaust my men with war so close.

But in the morning there was still no sign of soldiers. I sent out messengers while I still could, civilian riders to invite back everyone within a half day's walk to come take refuge in our walls. A siege was coming, and I had seen what that could do to the lands for miles around. The farmers remembered, too, and the few still out in the countryside came flocking to join us.

As the afternoon wore on and we grew tired of waiting, I let the wizard go back out gathering again. I sat with Caleb, planning, until Isabelle brought news from the south courtyard. She'd found us cooks to keep the soldiers fed and chosen weaponsmiths and armorers. She'd found an architect to plan the craftsmen's stalls and set a dozen carpenters to work.

In no more than a week, we'd raised a legend out of ruin. We had an army and a town. There were wells, and there would be beds. We had everything needed to get by. We sat at a proper table in the great hall and shared a quiet dinner with Caleb, then went to watch my hunters at their training until dusk. We went to bed with no more work to do.

And then the other wizard came.

16. Enemies Engaged

I awoke to a terrified cry within the night. Fear hung as heavy as the darkness in the air, and I could feel it in my bones as I sat up and rubbed a hand against my eyes. Then I heard the screams, terror piercing the night outside. I sprinted to the chamber door then stopped and closed my eyes and stretched my senses. There was chaos in the courtyard.

Fire rained in great streamers across the paving stones—not the searing lance of a dragon's breath, but hailstones of flame that trailed fire through the air. In the distance, lit in flashes by the deadly shower, I saw the giant form of a man towering above the walls we'd built.

As I stepped straight from my room into the night, a voice thundered through the air, drowning out the screams of soldiers and civilians in a terrible boom. "Fools and traitors! Arrogant children! You spurn the mercy of your king! You taunt the combined might of the Guard and the Academy. You *dare* to stand against us?" The litany rolled on, a crashing sound that rained down with the fire, but I stopped listening at once. I could recognize a wizard's empty work.

I looked with second sight and the web was a simple one, great arcing threads of fire twisted tight that rained illusions on my camp. I stepped out into the flashy rain and severed the threads with a wave of my hand. I spread my senses to the frightened crowd, searching for injured, but the only damage in my camp had been caused by panic. Nothing burned.

This time, nothing burned. Next time, it could be real fire. Next time it could be burning pitch from the king's catapults or spears of dragons' flame. We had done so much to build the walls, but we were open from above. My gaze shifted up, and I felt the memory of frightened villagers throwing stones. I raised my hands and caught the wild breezes high above and stretched them into a shield like I'd done then.

But this one was huge. I drew it out into a band, one long, curved circle hanging in the sky above the walls. I made several, overlapping belts of air that all combined to form a dome above the courtyard, but with gaps between the high wind could blow through. It would have blinded us to a dragon's eyes as well, but I suspected the power of my lair already did that. I left the constructs hanging in the sky, then turned my attention to the gates.

A ragged cheer had gone up when the fires flashed out, as those who recognized me called out their relief. I barely heard. I fixed my thoughts outside the camp, reaching with my will to find the wizard who'd attacked me. But my senses ended at the walls. I called to my hand a sword of earth and anger as I strode to meet him.

That voice still boomed, an artificial thing of air that dared to infiltrate my fortress. I snapped it like a strand of spiderweb. When I reached the drawbridge I waved a hand and called out, and it fell crashing to the earth outside, landing with a thud in the sudden silence. I waved and the towering figure of the wizard melted, the illusion dispelled to leave only a man, alone, on the plains before the fortress.

I crossed the open gate, my steps resounding in the wood and echoing back in the dark night. Hatred burned in my eyes.

When he recognized me, his lips peeled back. "It really is you?"

I said, "Seriphenes."

"What is this game you play?" He took a step forward. "Whatever magic you have learned, it won't save you. The Guard comes to crush you—"

"Let them come!" I said. "I have walls no catapult can break. I have an army ready to defend. I have a power you cannot imagine. Let the king's men come if they must. I cannot be bothered by your threats."

He shouted, "Impudent fool!" and raised a hand suddenly crackling with energy. He hurled it toward me, but I slapped it down with a casual gesture.

"Leave this place, Seriphenes. You cannot imagine what I have become. I have no time for this war. Have Othin take his men back to Tirah."

The wizard sneered. "The Eagle is no longer your concern. The king himself has come to lead his force against you."

I shook my head, disappointed. "He wastes his time. There is a greater trouble coming. Send him back to the City to prepare. Take those soldiers to some kind of safety."

"You really are so arrogant?" He sounded surprised. "I didn't quite believe. But now...I'll strike you down to end this here!"

He lashed out again, calling up another rain of flaming stones and this one too was just illusion. I just had time to recognize his real intent before it could resolve. He sought to make a gateway. I saw the energies around me start to waver as he tried to banish me away. I didn't try to guess where it might lead—a prison in the capitol, a cell at the Academy, or perhaps just miles and miles out to sea.

I didn't care. I stamped my foot and crushed both workings in my will. They wavered longer than Lareth's had, perhaps, writhing and struggling to survive, but it was no more than a heartbeat. Maybe two. The powers broke beneath my will, and my enemy fell back a step. I followed after, stepped down off my gate to bring us on a level, and raised my brows. His face twisted in rage.

"You wretched filth!" he snarled, and I watched the working roll toward me. The earth erupted all around me, but I caught all the energy and tore it loose. His exploding wave of earth became a puff of smoke that hung for a moment in the still air. I waved a hand before my face and shook my head. Then with a nod, I made the earth roll like a bucking horse beneath his feet, and the proud Seriphenes spilled into the dirt.

"Take a message to the king for me, mage. I have no quarrel with him. I take no joy in trading barbs. I only seek to protect his people from a threat that he ignores."

Seriphenes threw himself to his feet, shouting with fury, "I carry no messages. I shall destroy you!"

I did not let him strike this time. Instead I smashed him to the ground with fists of air. He began to thrash in panicked fear as I tried to sink him through the earth the way I'd done to Lareth and the spies. But when he saw that he was caught he only looked into my eyes, his lips peeled back to show his teeth, and shouted some dark curse into the night.

There was a flash of light and darkness, and he was gone. Earth like water sloshed back over empty air. I sighed and turned my back on the night to make my way across the open gate. I'd gone a step or two before I heard Caleb cry out from the battlements. I couldn't understand the words, but I could feel the warning in his heart. I looked his way, confused, and watched a crossbow bolt flash an inch above my nose. Another clattered across the rock-hard wood beneath my feet and ricocheted off into the courtyard.

I didn't wait to understand. I caught myself up in a hundred threads of air and snapped them, flinging me deep into the courtyard. Behind me a hundred different voices called out the command they had been taught, and the great door banged shut. Even as I fell, I spun toward the gates and looked, not with the senses of my stronghold but with a wizard's sight, and saw a host of men outside my walls.

The siege had reached my fortress.

I picked myself up off the ground and brushed irritably at the dirt on my clothes. While I was still grumbling, Caleb came sprinting up, concern in his eyes. "Are you hit?"

"No. Just bruised by my own hand." I felt my wizard ally's presence through the stones and turned to meet his eye as he approached.

"What did he do, Lareth?" I asked. "How could he have brought so many men so quickly to this place?"

"He can't. No wizard could make a portal such as that."

Caleb grunted. "He didn't, then. He brought them slowly, under cover."

I groaned and rubbed my eyes. "Of course. Concealed beneath illusion. I only had to look, and I'd have seen—"

"But why give you any chance to run at all? Why let us see? They could have walked right up and cut you down unseen."

I stared up at my gate, shut fast against the night. I looked beyond it, to the army settling in. "That could have been the plan," I said. "They couldn't come too close, or I'd have seen. If I had even bothered with a glance...." I shook my head. "I doubt he thought I'd come so fast. I know he didn't think I'd break his spells. I made him run. He likely lost control of the illusion when he went."

Lareth nodded absently.

"And where were you?" I asked. "You could have seen it at a glance as well. You could have fought his spells."

He didn't meet my eyes. "I was asleep."

"Seriphenes was your master." I had to force the words through clenched teeth. "You two were friends. And when I needed your support—"

"I was in bed," the wizard said, his voice small and scared. "I crossed a thousand miles today to fetch you food. I never guessed that I'd be needed in the night."

I still held my summoned sword. It rolled beneath my fingers, flashing silver by the moonlight. "It's hard to trust a man who sleeps through storms like that."

Caleb laid a hand on my shoulder. "He was asleep," he said. "I was as well. I'd only barely reached the walls when it was done. How did you come so fast?"

I glanced aside to him, but turned my anger back to Lareth. "You can go to him," I said. "That was the point of his theatrics. They hope the weak will lose their nerve and bleed away. Seriphenes would take you back." My eyes lingered on the wizard's throat, on the scars I'd left there, and I felt the weight of the blade in my hand. "If you gave the king a chance to kill me, even he might forget what you've done. The man is mad."

"He isn't mad," Caleb said. "Petty, yes. But he is sane enough. And even Lareth isn't fool enough to risk your wrath."

The wizard nodded, swallowed hard, and backed a pace away. My lips peeled back from my teeth, but I did not raise the blade.

Caleb squeezed my shoulder. "You struck him down with power. You set that fire in the sky." He waved up at the bands I'd woven overhead. They glowed in faint aurora high above. "How much of the monster are you now?"

His meaning hit me like a blow. I'd borrowed Chaos. It wasn't much, but it had come as easily as breathing when the vicious Master challenged me. I felt it now, throbbing hot and dark behind my eyes, and forced it back. I let my sword dissolve and dropped my gaze.

"I'm sorry, Lareth. You have served me well."

He stepped back toward me and spread his hands. "And I have earned all that distrust. I know it well. I only hope next time I'll have the chance to prove myself. I wish I'd done it here."

"You'll have your chance, now that we have our siege. I suspect you'll have your hundreds." I turned to Caleb. "Have they attacked us, beyond that one volley?"

"They brought in a line of archers, but our men answered back, and now they're keeping out of range. The other lines are setting camp."

I nodded. "Then everything is much as we expected at this point." I took a deep breath, still fighting to calm the anger in my soul. "Just...just the encounter with Seriphenes was a surprise. But now we're back on track."

"I have men patrolling the walls already, and they've had their rotations for a week now. The defenses should be routine, as long as we face no magical attacks."

Lareth pointed up to the layered belts of air that capped the keep like a lid. "Between that and the sorcerous walls, we should have nothing to fear. When did you come up with that, anyway?"

"As I went to face Seriphenes. Can you bind it?"

"I can with ease. And that should help against the dragons, too."

"Then do," I said. "And Caleb...I suspect you'll want to speak with your officers?" He nodded. I nodded back. "See to our defense. If you need me, call. I will explain to Isabelle, then get some rest."

Both men looked surprised. Lareth spoke. "You hope to sleep at all? With this?" He waved toward the wall, but I didn't even look.

"I must," I said. "I'll need my rest. I mean to kill some dragons come the dawn."

We met in council the next morning, and both men seemed surprised to learn I'd meant it. "I should be gone about an hour, maybe two," I said. "I don't intend to take much more than that. Just keep the fort secure 'til I get back."

"You can't intend to leave," Lareth said, trying for a laugh. "Not now! The king is here."

"That's why I must," I said.

"It seems unwise," Caleb said.

"Do you expect them to attack?" I asked.

"No. I've been watching them all night, and it's all good news. They have trebuchets already. That was a surprise. But they rained down rocks and burning tar, and it all slid right off the shields you made."

"It's good you thought of that," the wizard said. "Or it would have been dead cows and rains of stones until they filled the northern courtyard."

I shrugged. "They couldn't touch the tower. There's room enough, and I can make more with a little effort."

Caleb grunted. "This is better for morale. It's good to see them try and fail. And now they're settling in for a siege, just as we hoped. They can't possibly suspect we'd have those wells, and they have some idea how many mouths we have to feed. They'll expect a month at most before we break."

"Excellent," I said, clapping my hands together. "Then there's no reason not to go out on a hunt."

Caleb frowned. "There's not a way, is there? I thought he said the wizards will be watching for our portals now?"

"I did," Lareth said. "And if they find one going out, they might just follow it back in."

Caleb nodded. "But they can't make one on their own?"

"I think not," he said. "Even if one of them had been here before, we've changed far too much of the structure for them to portal in. And that is *why* we do not dare to portal out. If there are Masters in the camp out there, they'd catch us when we moved and trace the continuity back through the walls."

Caleb turned to me. "So. We have established our position. We're secure. Now we have to wait them out."

I shook my hand. "We won't. We can't afford to."

"Well, we could drive them," Lareth said. I immediately opened my mouth to call him down, but he held up his hands and spoke quickly, "I *know* you've no desire to war with men, but they know how to lay a siege. They will sit outside our walls and wait while dragons burn the world of men to ash. *You* are the one who says we need to join that fight. Perhaps we'll have to pay this price before we start."

Caleb nodded. "They'll strip the land, too. All those fields you protected from our men will be pillaged by the king's forces in a week. It might be wisest to attack."

"Gentlemen...." I sighed. They were so ready for a civil war. "My answer's no. It always will be no. I won't send two thousand of my men against twenty thousand of the king's and get them all slaughtered. Please stop advising it." They both only looked at me.

"So you'll just wait them out?" the wizard asked.

"No. I'll go out by another way."

I waited. Lareth comprehended sooner than I'd expected, and instantly said, "No! My lord, I told you no! It is absurd."

"It works."

"It *wouldn't* work. You'd only end up dead, or perhaps obliterated, and then we'd be—"

I spoke softly. "It works, Lareth."

He hesitated, then his eyes went wide.

I nodded confirmation. "I knew it days ago. I can travel the threads of reality."

Caleb rose to his feet, "You *tried* it? Without consulting us, you risked this thing—"

"Sit down, Caleb." He didn't budge, and I said more sharply, "Take your seat. Good. Now, I know how my magic works—I am the only man alive who knows as much. That made consulting with you unprofitable."

"We've spoken of your recklessness," Caleb began, but Lareth shook his head.

"No. This was his caution. What good would it have done to speak with you?"

"I don't mean me," Caleb said. "In this. It should be you. And you've told him all along—"

Lareth narrowed his eyes. He turned something over and over in his fingers. The Chaos shard I'd left him. He nodded. "It's caution, as I said. Daven couldn't trust me. If it worked—he's told us that it works—if it had worked, he couldn't risk letting me know. He couldn't trust me when I told him not to try. Not if he suspected I'd betray him to another lord."

I didn't meet his eyes. He spoke the truth. And for his part, he didn't seem the least offended. He did turn back to me to say, "I wasn't lying, though. I genuinely thought you'd be destroyed. I can't conceive that kind of travel being safe."

I shrugged. "Mine's not a delicate control like yours. It's a simple thing—a blunt thing. I knew that it would work. The only question was whether the mind made the body, or the body made the mind."

Caleb let out a long, low sigh. He shook his head, still unbelieving.

Lareth said, "That's *no* small question, there. I cannot even find some hope that you took my good advice and tried it on another?"

I met his gaze and shook my head. "I'm not that kind of man. And it would not have worked on any but my own. You'll ask that next."

Lareth's eye went wide. "But it will work on others? On your men?"

"If they are willing. If they trust me. I've tried with Garret Dain, and Isabelle as well."

"Then it's safe," Caleb said, breathing out at last. The worry left his face. "If he risked Isabelle at all, he knows it's safe."

"Safer than Lareth's magic, now," I said. "It creates no similarities, it bends none of the superstructure, and it should leave no trails for the wizards."

"So it's a perfect way," Caleb said.

"As close as we could hope to find. And that is good, because as I said before, I mean to start the hunt today."

"But why?" the wizard asked. "Why so much haste?"

"To clear their heads. The king himself laid siege around the stronghold late last night, and that could be a powerful distraction. I want to guarantee we all remember who we're fighting. The king is not our enemy. That's not our war."

Lareth leaned back, considering. "How many will you sacrifice to send that message? They cannot possibly be ready to go out."

"They're ready," Caleb said. "They have learned fast. They've skipped their meals and skimped on sleep to learn whenever I'd allow it."

"And you?" the wizard asked the warrior. "I thought you thirsted for their blood. Why don't you clamor for a chance to go along?"

I turned to my general, curious what he'd say. It had surprised me that he never even brought it up.

He only shrugged. "I am the leader of these men. I take my pride in their accomplishments. I could swing one sword at the beasts, or I could train up thirty swords to swing themselves."

Lareth grinned. He looked from Caleb to me and shook his head. "You choose them well."

"No," I told the wizard. "He chose me. And I am grateful every day."

Caleb grunted and climbed to his feet. "I'll send your men. You'd better bring them back."

"I'll bring them back," I said. "If any of them falls, I'll die inside."

Caleb only shook his head, resignation in his eyes. Beside me, Lareth asked, "And if you fall?"

"If I fall, there's no reason to keep up any of this. If I do not come back today, surrender to the king."

Caleb snorted and went out. Lareth stayed a moment longer, his eyes searching my face. "You really mean to do this?"

"This is why we're here."

"Do you even know where to begin?"

"The hunters spent an afternoon interviewing refugees. I know at least twelve locations in the hills out west of here, and I could probably find a den in any given mile if I went a little closer to the sea."

He licked his lips. "Then I suppose you're as prepared as you can be." He started to turn away, then said, "Just...please be sure you come back home tonight. If you should fall, I won't surrender to that king. Even Seriphenes could not protect me now."

"Then I'll be back. You can count on it. Even if it's just to keep you from gaining that army again."

He didn't laugh. He didn't grin. He nodded, satisfied, then turned and left. I watched him go, then went to find my dame. Isabelle did not fight me half as much as my lieutenants had. She nodded understanding, said she'd miss me, then sent me off dizzy from her kiss.

My Captains of the Hunt met me in the warm light of early morning, just below the shadow of the tower. Every one of them showed up, the thirty who had trained from that first day. They stood in a loose half-circle waiting, shuffling their feet and talking nervously among themselves. I was the last one to arrive, and I wasted no time.

"Gentlemen," I said, "this army was made with one purpose in mind, and you have been trained for a week now to serve that purpose. I count on those of you assembled here as the point of my blade. I have prepared you as best I can, honed you to a fighting edge, but tonight I'll have to test you in combat. I will not always be able to go out with you, but I will do everything within my power to make you successful. Understood?"

They nodded. No one spoke.

I hesitated, then, but there was no more need for speeches. "To the battle, then." I closed my mind and looked with the wizard's sight, stretching my focus as far out as I could. I stared out over the vast array of the king's encampment, still mostly sprawled across the roads up north. They'd stretched to fill the plains, but Caleb promised that in time they'd creep around to east and west until they had surrounded the whole tower.

That could become a challenge, but I had hopes for this night beyond the murder of one monster. I had high hopes. But first we had to get away.

I found a place out in the unforgiving highlands to the west, more than a mile from the fortress and well beyond the farthest edge of Timmon's camp. Then I reached out to the glowing power of my hunters, wildfires I could not begin to tame or bend but that I could embrace, and sent my will along the vast network of earth energies to that point that I had chosen. I tugged and leaped at the same time, and the world washed away around us.

Then we were standing on a high ridge in the early light of day. Far away beneath us we could see the king's soldiers, and that drew nervous exclamations from my men. My mind was already scouting on ahead, tracing the flow of earth and wind to find the spot the farmers spoke of. I found it: a rocky ledge beneath a wild pass where trees grew thin and tall. I grabbed and tugged, and two more miles flew by.

It only took a glance to see the signs of dragon activity—clear in the way they marked their territory, clear in the lack of animal life among the hills, and most obvious in the remains of their meals. Here and there in the night, swarms of flies buzzed around bloody, mangled carcasses of sheep or cows, left out in the open but untouched by the scavengers that no longer roamed the night.

As we stalked the empty mountainside, making our way by the silvery light of the full moon, the men whispered among themselves as they noticed the same signs. I smiled to myself each time they pointed out a charred tree in the center of a stand or a boulder cloven with the five-pointed star.

I could sense excitement among them at knowledge made real, and for a moment it overwhelmed their nervousness. As we moved up the slope I recognized more and more telling signs, and I finally took over the lead, moving more slowly, more cautiously, as they whispered behind me. None of them seemed surprised when I suddenly held up a hand to halt and pointed at the small, dark crack of a cave on a hillside some twenty yards above us.

From there I didn't need the refugees' reports, the hunters' carefully constructed details. From there, I only had to close my eyes and look to see the heavy, sucking shadow hanging underneath the earth. A dragon's lair. I traced its shape within my mind, and I could feel the quiet, hostile power of the place. I'd meant us to sneak in—we'd dressed for stealth—but now that I looked upon the lair, I thought of my own.

Even now, even miles away, I felt the sentiment of the place. I could pick Caleb from the crowd, hard at work and venting anger to mask his fear. Lareth was atop the eastern tower, staring north and drinking. Isabelle alone was not afraid, but she was thinking of me. I could feel her slippered footsteps on the spiral stairs.

Stealth would do no good. If we meant to raid a dragon's lair, we had to go in force. I nearly took us home to reevaluate the plan. To make new tactics for the new approach. Instead I caught their attention with a wave of my hand. I weighed them in my eyes. Then I told them gravely as I could, "Our plans have changed. We charge the beast and kill before it comprehends."

I met each gaze, and no one looked away. They knew too much to play like they were brave, but none among them looked away. That was enough for me. I caught the quiet breeze and draped it around them all in threads, and as I worked I spoke.

"The moment we attack, he will lash out. After that, if we score any strikes at all, he'll try to escape, or at least to rise out of range of our weapons. Do *not* allow him to get off of the ground, or he will overcome us all. Remember his weaknesses, remember his strengths, and be prepared for anything."

There was fear in their eyes, which was good, but it was tempered with excitement. These were men of action. "Remember, you have been trained to deal with him, and he is only one against thirty. And I am fighting with you. Remember your training, work together, and we will win the day." There were nods all around the circle, and I took a deep breath.

"We will not bother to sneak in, but I've still hidden you from his sight, so once the fight's engaged remain as silent as the shadows. Four-fifths of his awareness of you will be sound. Attack where he is weakest, and always anticipate his next move. I will draw his head, you move for his flanks." They all nodded once again, impatient to begin, and I'd done as much as I could.

I made two Chaos blades, drawing nervous grins from the hunters, then caught their eyes and caught their fires and threw us in.

We landed in a cavern ten paces tall and thirty long, and all along one side a fetid pool. The dragon at its edge was fully-grown, but all alone, and it was sleeping when we appeared paces away. I took one step toward it, swords already raised, but behind me the redhead whispered, "Haven's name."

I shouted, "Down!" as one cauldron eye snapped open and hit the stone floor hard just as the monster struck. A body larger than a house uncoiled and sprang into the air as fast as I could blink. It soared above my head and blasted the air with searing flame.

The men were quick, though, and I was quicker, reaching out and dragging the very essence of the dragon's flame from his mouth and tying it in place around the room so that glowing pillars of pure fire raged in place and provided light for my men to fight by. The dragon coughed, a painful sound that shook his whole frame, and landed with surprise clear in his eyes. My men were already on their feet again, and as the dragon swung its head back and forth angrily, they began to form a loose circle around it.

The fight began.

The dragon's rich green scales would have concealed him well within the forest, but in the harsh light between the gray stone walls, he was easy enough to see. Anxious to keep his attention away from my men, I dropped the threads of shield around me and lashed out with them like a whip. He threw back his head and roared at the assault, but then his eyes were on me. He came waddling forward, mouth opening and closing as he approached. I watched him warily, gauging his pace, and at the last minute I snapped the threads around his eyes like a blindfold and swung my sword.

He jerked instinctively away, bellowing again in anger and frustration, but I could see the airy energy melting against his own power. The flash of my steel was a signal, though, and even as his tongue flicked and he stumbled a blind step forward, my men darted in, soft leather boots whispering across the cool stone floor.

I struck a blade against the floor, a noisy *clang*, and watched his head snap back at the sound, then I lunged and stabbed the other blade high, just as the monster struck down toward the sound. My blade bit deep behind his jaw, but too far back for a kill. At the same time my hunters fell upon him from both flanks, darting past his flashing talons to strike at exposed ribs or underbelly.

He tried to roar when their blades began to sink home, but it came out a wet howl, pitiful and weak, and the men laughed. The great head turned then, the beast's eyes straining to pierce the wash of energy around the men, and I took advantage of its distraction. I moved in and struck fast, opening a long gash under its left eye. The dragon snapped his head at me like a whip, the tip of its long fang missing my head by an inch.

My men fought on, and slowly the beast weakened from the blood lost. Twice more the dragon tried to turn its rage against the men on its flanks, but each time I hurt it sorely, and it turned back again. I fought unshielded, without any energy to hide me from it eyes, but it was all I could do to keep the beast's attention on me as they hacked it down.

The long neck pulled back a fourth time, eyes rolling toward the hunters, and I thought at last I had lost its attention, but then the snakelike tail shot forward, and only my reflexes saved me from the attack. I dove to the side, rolling, and came up in a full sprint, but the dragon was already striking with its head, deadly teeth flashing down to bite me.

I waited until the last second, running hard, then caught myself short on a sudden wall of air as the scaled head smashed into the stone floor a pace ahead of me. I held the air for only a heartbeat, and when it dissolved I fell forward, dove forward, and grabbed one of the short horns above the eyes that protected its skull. It was a desperate bid, but I held on tight as it reared up and flung its head back.

A moment later I found myself hanging in the air a dozen feet above the ground, staring the dragon in the eye. I felt the thudding Chaos raging distantly inside and let a laugh escape at what I saw in the expression.

"You recognize me," I said. The dragon tried to throw me off, shaking its head wildly, but I tied myself in place with bonds of air and dropped one blade to hold the other in both hands. I dipped my head in mock salute. "Tell the others I am coming."

And then I drove the sword hilt-deep into the dragon's eye.

17. The Changing Tide

The dragon's black blood sprayed, burning my arm and face, and the beast screamed a liquid gurgle as it twitched. All along its body, my hunters struck as well, sinking swords into its plated hide, and the furious attacks were too much even for the ancient creature. It cried out once and then again as the great head came crashing to the ground. I let myself fall free and landed on a clattering pile of coins and treasure.

When that din settled, silence reigned in the cavern. No one else moved as I lifted myself up and crossed to the dragon. Though dim, a light still shone in its eyes, so I took up my sword from where it had fallen in the fight and drove it down into the skull behind the horns. The body stiffened, then collapsed with a sigh.

And then the hunters breathed. Perhaps they laughed, perhaps they cheered. I don't recall. I felt the shock of new-found power from the monster I had killed, and fought against the raging tide of Chaos.

I turned and made my way to the cooling pool. I bent and carefully washed the burning blood from my arm, dipped my face in the icy water. I noticed two or three others doing the same, silent amid the celebration. I nodded encouragement to them, then rose and turned my back on the dragon. I looked where I had fallen.

The dragon's hoard was piled high against the wall. I had known all along there would be one—I'd rather counted on it—and I had expected something to compare with Vechernyvetr's ransom, but this was more. The whole cavern wall was one long pile built at least as tall as a man, of gold and silver coins, of gems and polished jewels. Garrett Dain stepped up behind me, and I heard others gathering around. I reached out to the light, doused the handful of glowing pillars, and spread the fire in a single thin line along the whole length of the hoard.

Dain whispered, "Lareth thought too small. I could buy a kingdom with a third of that."

I nodded. It was true. And in this moment I would learn how much they'd learned. I could imagine one man rushing for the gold, I could imagine bloody fights among these men. There was wealth enough here to merit such treachery.

But no one moved. I counted seconds under my breath, but there was no rush. Only a gradual hush, the sound of men overwhelmed. Then Dain said, "I guess there's more."

The redhead answered him. "There'll be more dragons, too. Did you see the way it moved? Did you see the *hate*?"

Someone else said, "Did you see it recognize Lord Daven?"

I trembled at the words. Perhaps Dain saw it. He said roughly, "I saw it die. And that's a sight I'd love to see again."

"A thousand times," the redhead echoed. And then I know they cheered.

I stepped away, across the line of fire to stand among the spoils and turned to face them. I counted thirty men, upright and alive. I breathed more easily again and raised my voice. "This battleground is yours. You've won the day. We've killed a dragon and despoiled its lair."

I kicked out almost casually to spill a fortune in coins to the floor and nodded down at it. "This is part of their power. It will be ours. It's quite a handsome reward, but it's the smallest one we'll take away from this. We've seen the enemy. We know these methods work, and you've seen firsthand that my information is correct. We know that we can win."

One of the hunters stepped forward, "Sir?"

"Yes, Captain?"

"The day is young. Let's kill another."

I grinned. "Patch your wounds if you have any, and clean your swords of the dragon's blood, then we move. We have three hours before midday, and I have promised to return by then. How many dragons do you think we'll get to kill?"

Some said three. Some said a dozen. In the end we had little trouble finding fights. Not every battle was as spectacular as the first—once that first shock wore off the men did better at first strikes, and when we caught a dragon sleeping it rarely had even time to slash its claws before it fell. We killed five adult dragons in that first morning and would have done more but the last lair surprised us with a little brood. Three drakes and a dame, and she scored one lucky strike with her tail that pierced my thigh down to the bone.

Dain bandaged me. I fought hard to hide the pain and told the men to gather as much gold as they could carry. We'd brought empty leather packs just to that end, every man among us, and between them we packed up the brood dame's hoard.

Then with clenched teeth, I wrapped us all in threads of will, reached out to the sentiment of home, and took us back in just one leap. We landed in the courtyard of Palmagnes, triumphant heroes, and I felt the cold, whispered breath of gold wash over the stones.

I'd known I would. I'd known it in my bones. The treasure we brought home enriched my lair, and my senses stretched beyond the walls. I couldn't taste emotions in the enemy's camp, but I could feel their footsteps on the soil. I could see the sneaking scouts Othin had sent to search my southern walls, but they would find no gaps in my defense.

I could see into the mountains, too. One little hoard had bought me most of a mile in all directions. Even as my leg screamed out in pain, I sat and grinned to think what we could do. We'd won five lairs, and though none matched the wealth we'd seen within the first, every one of them would grow my reach. We would step right past the siege with just a thought.

And better still, I would find them now. I wouldn't have to search, to jump and hope. I'd sit within my tower and *feel* the lairs that dotted my domain. Caleb came, concern in his eyes, and Isabelle gasped when she arrived to find him pulling bloodied bandages away. But I could only smile and say, "We've won. We've won. We're going to win the war."

The fever came on strong and burned as bright and hot as all the oathsworn fires in my soul. I'd meant to get patched up and take some gatherers back out to bring in treasure or at the very least to send them out and bring them back. I didn't get the chance. Delirium washed over me, shivers and sweats, and for the rest of the day I lay wretched in my bed.

Worry washed like troubled waters all throughout the fortress. It rolled behind my scattered thoughts, a distant fog, and right up close I saw the anxious faces of my lieutenants as they came and went. The hunters came as well, in ones and twos to ask with quiet whispers if they could see me. They had nothing to say. They'd linger over my bed for a moment, looking chewed on, then shake their heads regretfully and go.

Isabelle sat with me through it all. She piled sheets on me when my teeth rattled and ripped them all away when I began to burn. She held my hand, and hers felt cold as ice and that seemed wonderful. She touched my forehead, stroked my hair, and brushed her fingers lightly on my burning neck.

Later I recalled it all, but through a smoky haze. But in the grips of the fever, I only tossed and turned and moaned. I made no plans, and I spoke no words of comfort to the many worried faces. I watched them come and go and wondered idly if I would survive. The only thing I felt at all was fire.

And then there came relief. I felt it like a summer shower, starting gently and drifting lightly down. A coolness poured across my mind, if not my body, and it awoke a part of me that had shut down. I blinked up at Isabelle and saw her eyes go wide. She began to smile. "Have you come back?"

I couldn't speak to answer. I couldn't quite focus on her. My body ached, but somewhere in my senses was the promise of relief. I closed my eyes again and retreated to the place of gentle cool. It came from my awareness of the stronghold. I looked closer, cast about, and found it came from outside my tower. From the courtyard, from the outer walls, from the tower's high, unfinished floors.

It shone like silver in my soul. Moonlight. My breath escaped me at the thought, but I remembered what Vechernyvetr had told me long before: A dragon heals by moonlight. Any damage short of death can be healed between dusk and dawn. I'd never experienced that before, but I could feel it now. I could feel the moonlight like a salve against my soul.

I found the strength to whisper, "The window." She frowned, and I flapped a hand in an ineffectual gesture. "Help me to the window." She called for Caleb instead, and gave me water while I waited, but the distant feel of moonlight on the stone was maddening. I had to fight the urge to drag my broken body across the stone.

At last he came, and he carried me more than supported me across the wide floor of my chosen chambers. There was a window in the outer wall, tall enough to stand in and a full pace deep, like all the tower's walls. I nodded to it, and at last he set me on the empty window's sill.

My breath caught at the sharp, sweet sting of moonlight sleeting down. It drove at me like a waterfall, it tugged against my skin and poured over me. I closed my eyes and sighed, and felt the fever's fires slowly die.

When the fever broke, I felt it go. The wild, cold wash of moonlight dredged it away, but still my leg screamed with pain. Still my body trembled, weak and worn. I waited, but the moon did nothing more for me. I was only half a monster after all. The human had to heal the best it could. I thought of everything I had hoped to do today. I thought of all my brave dragon hunters and how much they needed me.

Frustration flared and I bruised my fist against the solid stone, but there was nothing in my power to heal the injured leg. I heaved a sigh and pushed myself weakly up to meet their eyes.

"I am alive," I said, and my voice sounded strong. "The worst is past. We should let them know."

Isabelle came to me and pressed her fingers to my forehead, then my neck. "The fever's gone," she said. "I wasn't sure—"

"I know," I said. "It helped to have you there."

She smiled with tired eyes. I squeezed her hand. "Can you spread the word? Everyone expects the worst. They're losing sleep."

She glanced to Caleb, back to me, then dipped her head. "I'll go. But when I'm back you need to rest."

I waited until she was gone before I met Caleb's eyes. "I will not walk again for weeks."

He grunted. "Call it days. It's deep but mostly clean. I've seen ordinary men heal worse than that."

"I don't have days. We need to press the attack. We need to gather what we've won."

He shook his head.

I frowned. "What?"

"They told us of the gold," he said.

"It's more than gold, Caleb. It's power. It gives me...reach. I can't explain, but we have to get those hoards."

He shook his head again, and I fell silent. I could see it in his eyes. "What?" I asked.

"They told us of the gold, and the wizard seemed to understand whatever it is you can't explain. He couldn't, either, but he had seen when you came back with those bags."

An ominous premonition settled over me, and I searched my senses, but I found Lareth waiting in his room. He hadn't run.

"What happened?"

"He took them out. When you fell ill. Everyone wanted to find some way to help. He found his."

"Took them? How?"

Caleb frowned. "They dumped the bags they'd brought, then Lareth made a portal past the walls."

"No. No." I swallowed hard. "He wouldn't take that risk."

Caleb shrugged one shoulder. "He traveled south. And then from there he went out east, and then came back. He doesn't think the king's wizards will find the trail."

I nodded slowly, pushing down my panic. Caleb didn't seem afraid, and Lareth knew more of the wizards' tricks than I could guess at. "Perhaps it was worth the risk," I said. "To get that much wealth...."

Even as I said it, I wrinkled my nose. I couldn't feel the wealth, couldn't feel new power from my hoard. I met Caleb's gaze.

For a moment he said nothing. Then he sighed. "We are not alone."

I thought of the sensation of that hoard, the bright, distracting glimmer of the gold, and thought of all the many dragons in these hills. I said, "Oh. It was already gone."

He shook his head, almost imperceptibly. "It was there. Lareth took two hundred men to bring it back, based on the hunters' tales. They were attacked."

My jaw dropped at that. And then my heart. "How many lived?"

"Most of them had never trained. Many were not even soldiers. He only had ten of your hunters in all."

"How many lived?"

"Just nine."

I flinched as though he'd hit me, then scrubbed my hands over my face. "We lost two hundred men today? And one of them a dragon hunter?"

"Eight of them were Captains of the Hunt. They fought it so the rest could get away."

I shook my head. "Nothing to hide them from its eyes. No one to distract it. They didn't stand a chance."

"They died heroes," Caleb said. "And Lareth brought the rest away. I had to drag him through the portal by his sleeve, or he'd have gone back, too, to fight the beast."

"Haven's name," I breathed. "I thought we'd won a victory today."

"We have," he said. "Nine monsters are dead. The bags your hunters brought back could ransom all our lives. And every man inside these walls now knows bone-deep why we're here."

"And they're afraid," I said, but Caleb shook his head.

"They *were* afraid. They thought we'd lost you, too. By dawn, they'll know better, then they will cry for blood. You'll have your war against the dragons. There's not a man among them still thinking of the king."

I leaned my head against the wall and sighed. He spoke the truth. I could feel it through the stone. Word was spreading now that I'd survive, and it replaced their nervous fear with thirst for vengeance—among the soldiers and civilians alike. I shivered at the huge, diffuse echo of that deep and animal malice. I knew it well.

"For violence and blood," I said. "Very well. But first I must get some sleep."

At dawn we met in council around my sickbed and made plans for the real war. Without the promise of that vast, unguarded hoard, Lareth lacked the confidence to open portals from within our walls, but we found an answer to that. I sat aching in my room within the tower and shoved him with my will to the edge of my domain, high in the rugged mountains west of the fortress and well beyond the sight of the king's men.

There we built an outpost. I sent carpenters and masons up to make a meager shelter, and Lareth hung his strange green fire in the air. Then I brought my workmen back and sent up hunters. Twenty-two of those I'd led were still alive, and every man among them volunteered to go back out. They'd brought recruits, as well—another forty soldiers they'd hand-picked and a crowd of other anxious volunteers.

In the end I sent my veterans, and Caleb chose thirty more from among their best selection. We'd trained for thirty hunters to a pack, and there was not yet enough experience to make up more than two. I sent them to Lareth, and from his high place he opened portals to the north. Then the hunters scoured the hills to find their prey.

Two parties went out on their own, and when sunset called them back to the places they'd arranged, one group claimed four dragons dead and the other six. Then Lareth opened portals to the outpost, and I brought them home. Thirty-nine hunters made it back. One of the new recruits was torn apart in the final den, gored and swallowed as he kept the beast from killing his brother.

The rest had watched in horror then swarmed the dragon, pulling it out of the air with powerful thrusts and dragging it down in their fury. They tore the thing apart until its scales glossed black with blood. Then they returned with heavy hearts, but they brought back eight teeth as well. They took the fangs from every one they killed, and wore them around their necks like talismans. That night a thousand mugs were raised in honor of the one who fell, and at dawn we had another hundred volunteers.

There was something about the dragonhunt that could not compare with any other sensation in the world. Every blow they struck fell with the full weight of humanity behind it, and every time my men fell back, it seemed as though all mankind lost ground with them. That duty burned like fire within the heart of every hunter, and echoes of it hung throughout the tower. Those who stayed behind began to gather every night, so sixty tired hunters came back to find five thousand men and women anxious for the day's report.

Because they fought for all mankind, they struck without mercy and marched without fear, and they used every trick they knew to pull the serpents down. They hunted in the daylight, then stayed up hours more to train, then grabbed some sleep, and left again before the dawn.

It was only with a deep regret that I'd sent them out without me, and when they came home with casualties I'd nearly called it off. I'd nearly decided we should wait until I could train them more. Lareth gave no arguments, and Caleb conceded it might be for the best, but Garrett Dain raised a fierce objection. One man had fallen, a new recruit, while their two teams combined had killed ten dragons. They were learning. They were getting better, and now that the walls were done they spent time training others, too. Before my leg was healed, he said, they could have ten parties hunting. Maybe more. And every day we waited meant more dragons to destroy.

So the next day we sent three hunting parties and kept six of my Captains home to train up more. When the rest returned at sunset, they once again brought back the long, curved fangs from every dragon killed, and when the teeth were counted we had thirty-eight dragons in one night. It was a glorious victory, but it carried with it the sad total of twelve men killed in combat, twelve soldiers lost to the dragons. We had a ceremony in the courtyard to honor them, and at the dawn we had more men than ever before volunteering for the fight.

Caleb made the arrangements after that, and the hunters came to me only to send them out and bring them home. By that time there were eighteen of the original thirty, and each of them a legend throughout the camp. The soldiers guarding the walls and working in the tower vied for the honor of accompanying the Captains on the hunt, even though many never came back.

As we carried the fight to the dragons, brought in more and more trophies, we lost more men as well. But the volunteers kept pouring in until even the civilians begged to help in the fight. Then Caleb named another thirty men Captains of the Hunt and gave them men as well. Every morning with the dawn I sent them scouring the hills.

Soon we didn't need the outpost thanks to all the spoils they'd taken. My territory swelled until I could cast a man at will as far as Teelevon, or anywhere among the coastal ranges for miles north and south. The treasure rolled in, concealed in a magical vault beneath the floor of the tower. Metalsmiths worked with iron and steel to fashion specialized weapons for the hunt, and Lareth and I together spent hours every day binding energies into their armor to protect and conceal them. When iron ran out, I gave them the gold and silver that came from the dragons' hoards in such abundance.

I laughed the first time I saw a child eating barley soup with a spoon of solid gold, but we had more of gold than steel in those days, and soon the sight became commonplace within the walls of Palmagnes. Outside the walls, the king and all his army shivered in their tents and waited for us to starve. They brought up ladders in the dark of night to lean against my walls, and they were massive, heavy things meant to survive the desperate efforts of my defenders. But I felt them coming from a mile away. I waited 'til they set the ladders in place, then opened up the earth and swallowed them.

The king sent sappers digging underground. They tried to make a secret tunnel beneath my walls, but every swing of the pickaxe nudged at the back of my mind. I let them waste a week, and they got right up to the walls, then I opened the earth above them, raised them up as I'd done Lareth long before, and left them standing dazed in sudden sunlight. The defenders on my walls jeered down at them, and I sent another round of hunters out to fight the dragons.

That is how the days progressed, filled constantly with the thrill of little victories, the grief of men lost, the tension of battle and the anguish of preparation. Whenever the hunt went out, I met the Captains afterward and demanded of them every detail. We became a council, striving to learn everything we could of the enemy, working to put any knowledge to our advantage. We refined the training, refined techniques, and the men came daily to learn what we had to teach. The training became more intense as we learned more clearly how to fight this new battle and as the soldiers faced daily the dangers we were preparing them for.

Sometimes we would go three or four days without a casualty, and then we would lose a whole party in one night. The dragons learned quickly, and information spread among them like a disease. As our techniques changed so did their behavior. But we won many more than we lost. By the end of the month we were sending out twenty parties a day, and bringing down sometimes twenty dragons, sometimes two hundred.

Of course there were days when my Captains came in to report a staggering loss, but they were always somehow balanced by the constant flow of volunteers from within my forces. And then one afternoon Garrett Dain led his thirty men over a hill and found a band of untrained villagers dressed out in arms. When he approached, they asked if he'd come from Palmagnes. He told them he had, and they cheered, because they'd been looking for him for days. Somehow rumors had spread of what we did, and now throughout the whole Ardain brave bands of men were searching for my hunting parties in the hopes of joining us. Dain brought that first group back to the meeting place at dusk, and when he told me who they were, I brought them in.

Once we knew about them, we found more. Three weeks after the first came in, I couldn't send two parties out without one of them bringing back volunteers. I began to look for them, stretching my awareness out across the plains, and Caleb gave me recruiters to send out and invite them back. I'd pluck them from the rolling hills, or from their village squares. Soon I could reach almost to Tirah, and anyone who wanted to could join in the fight. The more men died, the more flocked to my side.

For more than a month it went on like this, and the Royal Guard sat camped outside the walls of my fortress and wondered how long the siege would last. Lareth loved to laugh at them waiting patiently in their tight formations while we traveled free as thought right through their trap. Then one morning I was standing in the courtyard and staring up at the tower, now almost finished with the seventh floor, when I was drawn from my thoughts by excited shouts from the men in the archers' towers.

Anxious for some change in the dark monotony that had settled over the place, I flung myself to the top of the wall, stepping out of empty air a moment before Caleb appeared sprinting up the stairs. For a moment the guard only looked at me in astonishment, but Caleb barked a command and he proceeded with his report.

"General. Lord Daven. A man approaches from the king's forces."

Caleb scowled. "Shoot him!"

I rounded on Caleb, rebuke on my tongue, but the crossbowman was already nodding. "Yes sir. I know sir. We did fire. All of us. It did no good."

Eyes narrowed, Caleb looked the soldier up and down. "How long have you been with us?"

I stopped Caleb with a hand on his arm. "Your men know what they're about."

The stronghold showed my wizard's sense the man approaching our great gates. I stared at him and wondered. For the first time since Seriphenes's disappearance, another wizard had come forward.

They had tried for weeks to find some gap in our defenses, to twist their spells against the manifest power of my fortress, but their tricks were no more effective than Othin's. I could feel the wizards' attention the moment they began to focus on my lair. It buzzed like a gnat around my ear, and I could swat it with significantly less effort. Every time I did, I thought of the time I'd crushed Lareth's traveling outside Tirah, and how he'd flinched. It must have hurt, because in time they'd stopped.

But now a wizard came to try diplomacy again. I couldn't sense his true intentions; no matter how much treasure the hunters had brought to my tower, that part of my stronghold's senses would not extend beyond my sworn followers. I couldn't feel the emotions of the men in the king's camp, though I could see their lifeblood fires plain as day. And even here upon my threshold, I could feel nothing more from this wizard than his power.

Still, it impressed me much that he came quietly. And looking on his power—no doubt the mighty glow of a full Master of the Academy—I had no fear of him. Here, in the heart of my stronghold, I could obliterate his will. So I acted on a whim. I wrapped myself in power, all of it ready to lash out, then nodded once to Caleb and stepped outside my walls.

And then I blinked in stunned surprise. The king's envoy was Claighan, who had found me as a shepherd. Who had recruited me to fight the dragonswarm. Who had led me to the ambush that set the king against me. The last time I'd set eyes on him, he'd been nearly dead, but years and wars and whole lifetimes had passed since then.

He must have noticed my arrival, but for some time he did not turn to meet my eyes. Instead he stood in silent contemplation, examining the magical construction of my gates with a slow nod of grudging admiration. I watched his eyes carefully as he took in my mighty stronghold—the build of the gate and the seamless walls; the void beyond that even his wizard's sight could not penetrate; the long, high bands of air that shielded us from above.

I watched, waiting for a smile, as his gaze at last fell on me. I waited for a greeting, for some praise, perhaps even for a hug from the sentimental old man. But when his eyes met mine, they burned with rage.

"I meant to make you a hero, boy. What have you become?"

18. Reunions

"I guess the stories are all true," he said, distaste bitter in his voice, "and you're a wizard king. This is quite an impressive show, Daven Carrickson." He said it harsh as a backhand to the face. "Quite a show."

I took a slow step back, then forced careful respect into my voice. "I've never called myself a king. And this is far more than a show."

"You're right in that," he said. "This is more than a mere nuisance, too. You place the whole nation at risk."

Anger, hot and sharp, flared up in my heart. I pushed it down and met the wizard's eyes. "Ah. You haven't come for a reunion, then?"

"No, Daven, this is no reunion. I am here as envoy of the king. I've come to ask that you desist."

I shook my head, incredulous. "He has you, now? Even you will serve that rabid dog?"

"He is the king," Claighan said. He sounded tired. "And even so...no. I do not serve him, and he wastes no favor on me. But I serve this land. I serve mankind."

I smiled, lips pressed tight. "As do I, Master Claighan. As do I."

He frowned past his eyebrows at me, as though I'd made a joke in poor taste. "I can't imagine what has become of you, boy, but whatever it is, I recognize I must bear some portion of the blame. I have come here out of that sense of responsibility to ask you to set aside this mad rebellion."

I scrubbed my hands over my eyes and took a deep breath. "Rebellion. No. You have it wrong."

"You have how many rebels in those walls?" the wizard asked. "Some rumors have your numbers at a thousand, but the Green Eagle says it can't be more than half that number."

"Are they so blind?" I asked. "I have them *all*, and more. Two thousand under arms, and twice again in loyal followers."

"Six thousand men beneath your banner, in a walled city and in defiance of the king," Claighan said, his eyes fixed on mine. "Hardly a rebellion at all."

"I never claimed a thing—"

He paid my words no heed, nodding past me at the walls. "I see the glow of the traitor Lareth's strange green fire. And we have found the traces of his travelings. Has he served you well?"

My jaw dropped open. "He tried to kill me," I said. "He tried to kill *you*. He plotted with Seriphenes over your sickbed, and Seriphenes had Archus take me to the dragon fight to die."

"You are strange allies here indeed," he said. "Yet here you are."

"Yet here I am," I growled. "Persecuted by the king for a murder you arranged. Hated under the same insane pride that drove you from the court in disgrace. And you come bid me surrender myself to him? You have allies as strange as mine."

He jabbed a bony finger at my chest. "I would ally with the Prince of the Burning Lands himself if it would save us from the nightmare that is coming. This is no time for political maneuvers, boy. The world hangs by a thread, and mankind cannot afford to waste its time in petty squabbles."

A bitter laugh escaped me in a bark. "I've made the same complaint myself. Do you know what I'm about? Have you heard no rumors?"

"All I know is this," he said. "There are dragons waking in the world while you play soldiers. This nation needs a king upon its throne, and it needs wizards in every town just to save some shred of civilization. We need those soldiers to defend, not sitting at the darkest corner of the land spread out like a snack."

"Then bid him take them home!" I shouted. "Do not bring this to me. It's his madness has him here, harrying me with nonsense while I fight the very war you called me to."

His eyes narrowed to slits and his breath came out a hiss. "Do not *dare* pretend I put you up to this. I asked you to stand against the Chaos, not to aid it."

"If you would still your cursed tongue," I snapped at him, and my hand flashed up in threat. I stopped myself just short of striking him. Frustrated anger and wild Chaos power sizzled in my veins and thundered in my ears. I fought them back and forced the hand down to my side.

He watched me, eyes wide in shock, and I realized with a start that he'd lashed out. He'd wrapped me head to toe in solid will, and it had melted like a snowflake on a blazing hearth. I stepped forward now and he fell back, cowering in fear.

"You led me into Chaos," I said. "You fed me to Chaos. All of you. You by negligence. The king by arrogance. Seriphenes and Lareth by wickedness. It doesn't matter why. You led me into Chaos, but I *refuse* to serve its ends. I have bound it, Master Claighan. I have snatched it up and tied it down and turned it back against itself."

I held a hand out to him, and fire bloomed above my palm. Black and red, searing hot, and crackling with a sulfur stink that stained the air. I saw him look, saw him examine it with the wizard's sight, and saw his eyes go wide in shock. This was pure power.

He shook his head in slow horror. "That can't be done."

"No. Nor can this," I said, and stretched my will. With barely-conscious thought I found Garrett Dain and all his hunters training in the tower. I found Caleb and Lareth, and with the slightest tug I brought them all to stand behind me.

Caleb stepped up past me, swords appearing in his hands, and one heartbeat later Lareth stepped up on the other side. I felt his reluctance to face the wizard, but he stood by my side and began to gather his will.

Dain's men were dressed out for the dragon hunt. They always trained in their full gear, and after one shocked moment of disorientation, they gathered into ranks arrayed behind me and waited for my command. They would have cut the wizard down without objection. These men went out to battle dragons in their lairs, what fear could one old man offer them?

Claighan saw it, too. He fell back another step, sharp eyes moving carefully among the men I had called forth. I stalked after him, stretching my empty hand back to jab an accusing finger at my hunters.

"You see these men?" I snarled. "And Lareth here. You see the damage I did to his face when he asked me to fight the king?" I felt the acid stab of Lareth's shame at the words, but in the fire of my anger I could feel no guilt. My eyes were fixed on the wizard's as I drove him back.

"This is your rebellion. These men pillaged and killed across the south Ardain, and your king did *nothing* to stop them. I put them on a leash. I gave them purpose. Not to steal some battered crown." I hung the Chaos fire like a coronet around my brow and sneered. "I mean to win a war."

I turned my back on him and stretched a hand toward the stronghold's impervious gates. My word brought it crashing down, and there beyond the empty gateway was my army. They had gathered, silent and anxious behind the walls, straining to hear what was going on. Now six thousand voices cried out, but I could spare no thought for them.

Without bothering to look I knotted a fist in the collar of Claighan's robes and hauled him forward. Past my silent, patient hunters and up onto the gate. The courtyard thronged with my anxious followers, but they were cautious enough not to have pressed too close to the gateway. That left the courtyard clear enough to see the pile of teeth ten paces in.

"Haven's name," the wizard breathed.

"This is what I've become," I said. I stretched my will and brought one of the fangs flashing through the air. It was long as a man's arm and sharp as a rapier's point and white as snow. I hurled it tip-down and let it stab into the gate between Claighan's feet. It stood for a moment quivering, and the wizard could say nothing.

"I've fought the war you called me to," I said. "With nothing you had promised me. I made my own power. I made my own army. I made my own stronghold. And when all the forces of the king came to stand against me, wizard, I made a way to get around them. Do not blame me for whatever senseless treacheries your king commits. It is none of my doing."

"Daven," he said, breathless, shaking his head. Stunned regret clouded his eyes so he didn't really focus when he looked on me. "Daven, I could not have known—"

"And yet you came in judgment and in rage." I saw his flinch, saw the wretched apology building deep inside his breast, but I had fury yet to vent. "You came here in

318

atonement for your sins. You thought you had to fix your old mistakes."

Unbidden, two huge, ornate Chaos blades began to form within my grip, uncurling through the air like deadly vines. The wizard's betrayal seared like a glowing coal in the pit of my belly, and righteous anger hammered in my head. I swung a blade toward him, and Claighan sprang away. He stumbled on his robes and fell, and scrambled backward past my hunters. I stomped after him with Chaos boiling in my soul.

"You'll have your chance," I said, my own voice sounding strangely cold and distant in my ears. "I'll let you pay for your mistakes. You'll take a message to the king—"

"Daven," Lareth said, his voice a warning, but I silenced him with a look.

"You all did this to me," I snarled at Claighan. "And now you'll all pay the price." I laughed, though there was no mirth in it. "Mankind cannot afford to waste its time in petty squabbles. I serve this land. I serve mankind."

Claighan was pale as ancient bone, his eyes mad with fear. "Those are my words. We serve the same—"

"Then here's your chance." I glanced up to the sky. "Tell the king to go. Today. If he's still in that camp at sunset, I will burn it down to ash."

"Daven," Caleb said, and I could feel his quiet fear. I blinked and looked his way. I'd expected him to love this plan.

But Claighan moved and tore my gaze back to him. Still on his backside, still scrambling on his hands, he tried to get away. I hurled one of the Chaos blades and sent it stabbing half its length into the earth just above his shoulder.

He shook his head frantically. "Don't, Daven. Go back inside the walls and fight your war. Forget the king."

"No. I'll forget his sins no more. If he won't leave—"

"He won't," Claighan said. "You know he won't. It doesn't matter what I say."

"Perhaps in words," I mused, and brought the summoned sword drifting slowly back to my hand as I advanced. "But I could make a message of your corpse."

As I passed within a pace of Lareth, I tried to share a grin with him. He grimaced and turned his face away. Then Caleb stopped me with a hand flat on my chest. He stepped up close and leaned down to my ear to rumble, "This is not what you want."

I wrenched his hand away with threads of air and heard him grunt in astonished pain, but he leaned against the bonds to catch my shoulder with his other hand. "This isn't you," he said. "The monster's in control."

He should have trembled at the anger in the gaze I turned on him, but he met my eyes unflinching. "Think of Isabelle," he said. "She brings you back."

She did. She always did. As soon as he said her name, I reached instinctively with my senses to find her in the tower. But she wasn't in her study; she wasn't among the craftsmen organizing some new scheme. She was on the archers' tower, staring down at me with worry in her heart.

Afraid as I had never known her, even when I went to lead the hunt. Even when I lay consumed within a vicious, killing fever, she had held out hope. But now she watched me from afar and saw the weapons in my hands, and she trembled because she couldn't recognize the monster that controlled me.

I dropped the blades. I stepped away from Claighan, but even as he scrambled to his feet something flared up hot and angry in my heart and flung a blast of Chaos fire at his back. Lareth caught it with his will and bent its path so the spear of flame plunged into the earth, turning dirt and stone to hissing sludge.

I spun on him, arm already outstretched, but Caleb caught my hand and dragged it down. Something frenzied scrabbled in my soul, too mad with rage to choose among its targets. Claighan spoke a word of power, and I felt the nervous itch of worked reality within my realm. I stretched my will toward his working, but Lareth lashed out at the airy shackle I'd bound tight on Caleb's wrist. I looked that way. I swung back to my wizard, power flaring in my grasp. Then a flash of motion made me spin back the other way.

Claighan disappeared, his portal ripping shut behind him. But Caleb was there, his hands free, and he hit me at a sprint. He flung both arms around me, crushing my elbows to my sides, and bore me to the earth. Lareth stepped up beside him, his power at the ready though his heart was quailing with fear.

Far above, Isabelle shouted her concern. I felt it in her, begging me to win this fight against myself. Caleb held none of her hope. He held none of the wizard's fear. He was nothing but determination, ready with nothing but the strength of his arms to face any power on earth in service to his lord.

They brought me back from madness, those three souls. Between one heartbeat and the next I felt their fear, and I bent it back against the monster raging in my head. I forced the Chaos down, forced my pounding pulse to slow, and took control over all my power.

Caleb released his crushing grip and pulled away. Behind him Lareth shrieked, "Don't let him go!" Caleb turned to meet his eyes. My attention was on Isabelle, her heart wracked with grief and frantic frustration as she tried to fight her way down the crowded stairs of the guard tower to come to me. I reached out to her with my will, caught her up, and pulled her to me.

She gasped when she arrived, then crashed to her knees and gathered me into her arms. "Daven, what happened? What happened? You didn't bring me out with them, so I didn't try to come, but from the walls—"

"I know," I said. "I'm sorry." My voice sounded strange. It was normal. It was calm. It was mine. After the madness that had ruled me, it seemed strange to speak so easily. I squared my shoulders and looked up to catch Lareth's gaze, then Caleb's.

"All of you. I'm sorry. I let it take control."

"Why now?" Caleb asked.

Lareth frowned, calculating, then he nodded. "You haven't borrowed much that I have seen."

"The king," Isabelle said, her voice an angry snarl. "He sent another wizard—"

I squeezed her hand, then pulled away. "No. It isn't that." I climbed to my feet and closed my eyes. "It's something else." I stretched my senses north and felt a frenzied tumult in the camp as men rushed here and there. But there was something else. There was a fury somewhere in my lands, a heart attached to mine and full of rage.

I looked across the miles, searching, and found it half a day's ride north. In Teelevon. Not the fire of a man, not the wild little spark of human anger, but a bottomless pit, an empty nothingness I knew too well. I licked my lips with sudden, dreadful understanding.

"I have to go," I said.

Lareth said, "Where?"

Isabelle said, "Why?"

Caleb said, "Who will you take?"

I met their eyes, one by one, and then I shook my head. "I'm sorry. This one's mine. Go back inside the walls and close the gate."

Caleb tried to call me down. Isabelle caught my hand, and her fingers were cool and strong on mine. I squeezed again, without meeting her eyes, then stretched my will and tugged. I stepped across the miles to Teelevon, to the Eliade manor, and into the garden where Isabelle and I had loved to talk. Smoke and ash hung in the air, sharp and bitter, black as night.

The flowering trees were charcoal stumps, the lovely marble bench cracked in two, and walls torn down behind it, but I could not see much beyond arm's reach. I looked out with other senses and saw no sign of life in the wreckage, but all about me I could see the stain of death. Here and there my eyes saw scorched and blackened bodies, and the houses and shops of the village were little more than burned-out husks.

A dragon's battle cry tore tatters in the air above me and stabbed against my ears. I felt his presence, too, like the weight of mountains on my shoulders. His anger scrabbled at the edges of my mind, but I held him off.

"Vechernyvetr."

You were a fool to come to me, he sneered. I knew you would.

"No," I told him. *"You should not have come. This is my territory now. You cannot hope to fight me."*

And it was true. Truer even than I'd expected. I remembered when I'd met him, when he had towered like a cloud of empty nothing before my newfound wizard's sight. He had seemed so vast, so powerful, but then I'd met the elder legend. Then I'd learned the secrets of a dragon's power. Then I'd helped Vechernyvetr grow his brood and capture a better lair with a stronger hoard.

The shadow here was nothing like the one I'd left behind. He dropped down through the heavy, choking ash, his beating wings raising cooler whorls within the smoke, then settled just before me. Still he towered. Still he dwarfed me with his size, but he looked like just a shadow to my other sight. He was alone, and small, and weak.

The massive maw snapped down, striking like a snake, but stopped just short of harming me. It huffed a blast of broiling air and rolled its head to watch me. *I wish you'd brought your hunters with you*, he said. *I thought you'd bring them all to deal with me.*

"And why would I do that?"

To save your wretched dame. This is her home.

I looked around, straining through the smoke to see the stricken manor. I wondered what had become of the baron. What of Themmichus? What of the helpful stable boy and the steward? What of the Kind Father and Thomas Wheelwright who had stood as witnesses to my knighthood?

I met the dragon's gaze and swallowed hard. *"You killed them all just to get me here. You were trying to kill her."*

Oh, not alone, he said, almost resentful. *I only played a little part. But they left me to wait.*

Behind his words I felt a dreadful satisfaction. Not joy. There was no thrill of joy within that heart. But I could feel anticipation hot as a furnace. I didn't fully grasp the meaning in his words, but I didn't need to. There was threat enough in "they left me to wait."

I turned back toward my stronghold, still unafraid of the monster bonded to me, and stretched my will toward the safety of my lair. But there was something in between, something waiting on the threads of earth, something dense enough to bend reality around it.

Dragons. Even as I looked I saw them settling all around me. Thousands of them, black as ink, spilled across the world. And from the west I felt Pazyarev coming. He washed over the earth like the sunset's shadow, the vastness of his power blacking out reality for miles.

I reached for home. I pulled, and the world shifted around me. But I didn't make it back to the tower—the ring of dragon black welled up before me, and my will slammed against it hard as a wall of stone. I stumbled, stunned, and looked up to find myself upon the road less than a mile south of Teelevon.

A piercing shriek clawed at my mind, but I walled the pain away and called two blades into my hands. I didn't even have to look; I felt the monster's presence through the land. I dove aside and twisted as I flew and lashed out at the dragon's form as it swooped low. I felt the sword bite through the brown and orange scales, tasted the stink of its blood in the air, and grinned as the beast roared.

Its head snapped around toward me, teeth flashing in the night, but I stepped lightly to the side and slashed upward, carving a long gash up the dragon's plated shoulder. It screamed in pain and leaped away, hanging in the air above me. I saw it draw a breath to hurl fire.

But I did not pursue. I turned on my heel and sprinted south, away from the thing, and cast ahead already with my will. But there was no way clear. I saw the wide ring of dragons that had circled Teelvon now washing past me to the south.

And more. For miles to the south, there was a raging flood of dragon shadows touching down. The whole of the plains seemed to be filled with them. My tower. The walls. The king's encampment. Distantly, I felt the clamoring panic of my stronghold under direct assault.

Too many hearts, too many fears, but I could see shades in them: the careful, measured worry of the hunters who'd been trained; the cold, pathetic helplessness of soldiers ready to fight an army but useless against a swarm of dragons; the heavy weight of responsibility among the officers, Caleb and Lareth chief among them. And Isabelle. I could feel her like a balm. Concerned for me and waiting full of hope for my return. I reached for her, but there was no clear path. I tugged anyway and found myself face-to-face with another brown dragon.

I'd barely gained a hundred paces, and the beast I'd injured came up hard upon my heels. I hit a sprint straight toward the newer one, wrapped myself in threads of air, and fashioned steps of earth no larger than my feet that hung in empty air.

I sprinted up the steps and sprang with all my might. I twisted in the air, both arms slashing down, across, and with one swipe of rage I took the creature's head off. I hit the ground and rolled, and as I found my feet, the wash of viscous Chaos power flooded into me.

The first dragon had lost sight of me, but now it crouched, blocking any escape to the north. It shook its great head in impatient rage, scattering heavy black drops of blood. I stood motionless and silent for a moment, catching my breath, and as I did I saw a new shadow drift in from the north. The mottled orange turned its head and hissed a threat, but then looked back to me.

My thoughts were far away. I felt the battle raging in my stronghold. There was worse than fear within the walls now. I felt my soldiers' pain. I felt them fall. A dozen men at once turned into cinders. A Captain of the Hunt disemboweled by a dragon's tail. A carpenter who tried to stand and fight was torn to pieces by half a dozen hungry drakes. I sought desperately for some way through, but the world swarmed with dragons now.

And still Pazyarev came, rolling like a storm down from the north. He was miles off yet, still not visible on the horizon, but he was coming.

I turned back to the dragons right before me. The mottled one was stalking forward now, head held low and tasting at the air with its long forked tongue. I flung one of my Chaos blades almost casually toward it, too high, soaring in an arc above the beast. Just as it passed overhead, I caught it with my will and slammed it down, point-first, driving through the dragon's skull to pin it to the earth. Then I took a step toward the other, black as night.

"Vechernyvetr. Help me. They're slaughtering my brood."

He laughed within my mind, dark and cruel. *Your family? Your friends? You may use the words. I've learned their treacherous meanings.*

Pain like heartache, pain like human loss welled up in the back of my head. I felt it from him, the same emotion he had shared when I'd left, but that was just the first of it. I felt the crushing weight of grief, as well, the devastating helplessness of love.

I hit my knees. This was raw emotion—his emotion— but nothing native to the dragons' animal desires. *"What happened to you?"* I gasped. Even through the walls of my defenses there was pain enough to overwhelm me. *"How? How could you feel...."*

My brood, he answered, bitter. *My dame. Were torn to shreds.* He showed me. The same lair I'd helped him win, and some of the same drakes. But there were more. There was a dame the shade of moonlight and a dozen drakes that looked newborn.

Dead. The cooling pool was thick with blood, the modest hoard stained black and red. And as I looked on the devastation, I could feel an echoing grief within my soul. I saw Vechernyvetr's lair despoiled even as mine was under attack.

"Help me," I begged again. *"They're doing that to mine. You brought me away just in time—"*

I know, he said. *That was the plan.*

"But why? I didn't do this thing to you. I've never let my hunters near your lair."

It wasn't you. It was Pazyarev's brood. They found me in my lair.

"And now they're raiding mine!" I screamed, frantic. "Take me to the fight! For violence and blood."

He shook his huge head slowly back and forth, a very human gesture. *There is nothing left of me to love the taste of blood. There is nothing but this pain in all my soul.*

"For vengeance, then," I tried, stomping toward him. I reached inside myself, for the wild ferocious hunger of the Chaos heart, and pressed its thunder at his mind. "That is your language. Destroy the ones that did this thing to you."

You did this thing to me. And dreadful though the words were, there was no sense of rage. *Only weary resignation. You poisoned me with your human heart. My kind should not feel pain like this. The moonlight only makes it worse.*

"Then blood," I tried again, but once again he shook his head. *Why would you help them? Why would you give me up to them after what they've done? Why won't you fight?*

Instead of answering, he bent his neck to look back lazily toward the north. *Pazyarev comes. He hates what you have made here.*

"I hate him too," I growled. I turned south and began to run. I cast ahead, but still the shadows boiled around my tower. I caught myself in threads of air and flung myself like a shot. It wasn't enough, but it was faster than I could run. Lashes of air hurled me south across the miles while my people died.

Vechernyvetr came up on the wing. He made no move to strike at me. He only drifted idly along. "Carry me," I said. "If you will come with me, at least carry me."

No. No, I can't do that. It would cost me my reward.

"Reward?" I asked. And then a moment later, "Ah. Yes. For bringing me away."

He has been waiting weeks. For weeks he has not raided, he has not hunted, he has only watched and waited for a chance to strike at you. Two thousand bodies in his brood and every one committed to this assault.

"How can you know this?"

I have been with him. All this time. Begging my reward.

"What can that monster possibly give you? Power? Wealth? I'll give you both if you but get me to my tower."

No. None of that. He will take away what you have given me. He will take my human heart.

It took a moment before I understood, then I spun to stare at him. "You will allow him to subsume you? To destroy your will?"

I have begged it of him. He has refused. But for this night's work—

"That will destroy you! Why not fight him? Why not die, if that's all you desire?"

He will not kill me. He can see my torment. He enjoys my torment.

"No. Do not give yourself to that. Fight him."

There is nothing to be gained.

"There is victory to be gained. Just look at me. Just look at what I've done. Look at the power I have gathered."

I see how easily it gutters—

"But it need not go out. Stand with me. Help me fight."

He gave no response to that. After some time I stopped my desperate flight. The pain and fear still seared throughout my tower, clawing at my mind, and it wrenched my heart to abandon them. But it would take most of an hour still to fly myself that far, and then what would I do?

I could kill them easily enough, even on the wild wing, but I could not save my brood. Two thousand dragons in the sky? I could not kill them all. And even as I tried, that terrible shadow would be constantly approaching from the north.

I turned in place. Vechernyvetr registered surprise, then curiosity. I showed him my resolve and felt his astonishment. "*I will fight him instead,*" I said.

You will die.

"*And what if I win?*" I asked, my heart beginning to hammer in my chest. I watched the storm of Chaos power roll across the earth toward me. "*What becomes of his vast brood if I kill him?*"

You are a fool to even hope. For all that you have grown, your power does not match his.

"*I am nothing like him,*" I thought. "*He is just a monster. I am a man.*" I gathered up my will, caught the threads of air, and sent myself skimming back north. "*He may destroy me. Or I may win. What would happen then?*"

If you killed him? He would die. Every part of him would die.

I looked south, where every part of him swarmed against my fortress. I breathed a silent prayer.

You have no cause for hope, Vechernyvetr said. *You will die this night.*

"*Or I will save my brood and end Pazyarev forever. Either way, you should be at my side.*"

I am not one of your broodlings, little dragon prince of men. You do not control my will.

"*That is not the way of men,*" I said. "*Every soldier in my brood fights by his own will.*"

Against the dragonswarm? That is impossible.

"*That is the human heart,*" I told him. "*It is not entirely a wretched thing.*"

And then, despite myself, I forgot about him. I forgot about my people in the tower. I forgot everything except the shadow in the sky, crimson stain against the sunset, and large as a mountain.

Pazyarev came for me, and he did not come alone.

19. Vengeance

I hung suspended in the air, a hundred paces above the earth, while the northern sky filled with the terrible bulk of an elder legend. Around him buzzed a handful of retainers, perhaps a dozen winged adults, and among them the sleek gold dame that had watched me so closely in his lair. I watched with narrowed eyes as they approached.

But through my territory sense I felt the others come. Across the land to east and west, whatever broodlings he had set to pin me in now rose up and flew toward me. Another dozen? Two? I cast one last, desperate glance south, but there was no way to my tower. Those did not break off their attack.

It mattered little anyway. I would have to kill this one to win. Even if I tore his every broodling from the sky, I'd have to fight him when he came for me. Far wiser, then, to fight him here.

But I would not idly wait. I summoned stone as I had done fleeing his lair, shaped it into javelins, and flung them with my will. I focused on the reinforcements coming from the ground and tore one dragon's wing to shreds, then speared another through the eye. Seventeen in all approached, and I accounted for six of them with that first volley.

Then Pazyarev was close enough to strike, and he struck with many limbs. The gold dame hung back, but all the others rushed toward me. Not in a perfect circle. Not all at once. A dragon on the wing is too versatile a foe to crowd them all together. Instead one came forward faster, mottled green and brown, and belched a lance of fire at my position. The beast could not have seen me clearly, wrapped in elemental air, but I disturbed the world around me enough that it could make a guess.

A good guess, it turned out. I had to fling myself downward and barely dropped a pace below the searing flame. But I carried the motion on, swinging up and under toward the creature's jaw. I wrenched my shoulder as I passed beneath it, stabbing up behind its fangs. My sword parted scales and flesh and cut deep into the dragon's head. Yet even as I struck I saw the forward talons reaching for me. I left the blade inside its skull and whipped the bands of air around me, darting off to safety.

But straight into another dragon's strike. It snapped at me. I tried to stop, to swing myself away, but still its razor fang bit into my left shoulder. It traced a painful line down and over to my spine before I could pull myself away. I spun around in time to see the spike-tipped tail coming around toward me.

I speared my remaining Chaos blade bone-deep in the monster's passing shoulder and let my weight hang on it for a moment. That left me free to whip the threads of air out with my will, wrapping them around the dragon's eyes. They should have left the dragon blind, should have drawn a scream of rage and sent it tumbling from the sky. But this beast was Pazyarev. It was just one little part of a mind that watched me through dozens of eyes. And now it saw me clearly.

The tail struck, shearing with expert precision above the dragon's scales, straight at me. I planted feet on the shoulder and kicked desperately away. A heartbeat later, the tail tore the abandoned Chaos blade out of its flesh.

Then a roar of triumph shook the night around me. I was revealed. A dozen blasts of fire shot toward me. I wrapped myself in air and again dove away.

But I could not survive this fight. There wasn't time enough to look ahead, to stop and think. It took my whole attention to face one dragon, and here two dozen hung around me. My blood-soaked shirt clung cold against my back, and the injury put pain in every motion.

I'd felled the first, I thought, with that jab up through the jaw. The second I had barely hurt. I glanced back now and saw it dropping from the fight, but night was coming soon. In half an hour it would be made whole.

I snapped my eyes back ahead in time to see sharp talons stretching toward me. I jerked myself upward, planted a foot on the top of one plated knee, and sprang higher still. From above, I made a rain of fist-sized stones and sent them slamming hard into the creature's skull.

It fell away, another beast already flapping up behind it. I summoned just one stone for that one. It was a paving stone four paces wide, four paces long, manifested half a pace above the dragon's shoulders. The long, strong bones that held its wings snapped like twigs, and that one, too, went down.

More waited. A pair this time, coming fast from opposite directions. I sprang away and dodged a bite and sprang again. I crashed against a scaled hide hard enough to drive the breath from my lungs. I skidded, tried to catch a grip, and then began to fall. Talons long as sickle blades snapped around me, but they did not pierce. They didn't crush. They held me almost tenderly.

The scales were black. I made two Chaos blades again, but before I struck, I looked up. Then I reached out with my mind. "*Vechernyvetr? What do you intend?*"

The great wings slammed against the air as he climbed up through the fray, toward the waiting elder legend. His nervous indecision rattled in the back of my mind.

They should call you dragonbane, he said. *I've never seen a man do anything like that.*

"I could do more," I thought. "I mean to kill them all."

But that's impossible, he said, without any real emotion. *Even you know it. I can see it in your heart. You fight, and you grow tired. You cannot kill them all.*

"If I could get to Pazyarev—"

Be still, he said with force enough to shut me up. He flew up through the crowd of dragons, and I saw them washing around him, following in his wake, until we all went as one before the massive elder legend. He scudded through the air like some solid thunderhead. As we grew closer, I could feel his hatred like a fire beneath my skin.

You've brought the boy to me, Pazyarev crowed. I heard the words, but with them came the monster's bloody satisfaction, his overwhelming rage, so vast, so strong they threatened to wash away my own emotions. I gasped for air, fought to hold some shred of my defiance, and walled Pazyarev away.

I'd had much practice. I forced the elder legend's thoughts out of my head, but still I felt the hammer of his rage.

Vechernyvetr's thoughts yet rang out clearly. *We had an understanding.*

I felt the pressure of the elder legend's answer, but not the words. Whatever he had to say, it calmed the indecision in Vechernyvetr's head. I felt his heart grow hard, felt his intentions narrow to a point. He was decided.

I shifted awkwardly within the talon's grip and hefted the two sleek blades within my hand. I wouldn't go without a fight.

Then Vechernyvetr spoke to me. *I remember when we met,* he said. *I remember what you did to me. You were just a tiny man, and I was a monster, but still you brought me low. In spite of all my power, you broke me.*

Vechernyvetr couldn't kill me on his own. But now he brought me up before Pazyarev's massive maw. The golden dame came drifting over, shining like sunlight on a pool, but I saw murder in her eyes. For one terrifying moment we both flew in place ahead of Pazyarev.

The talons opened. I was ready with threads of air. I caught myself and snapped them to get away. I had one astonished moment to see Vechernyvetr turn mid-air and strike the golden dame. He tangled his body around her, fangs and talons tearing. The taste of blood seared bright within his mind, and the dame screamed as she fell away.

And then my world was darkness. Hot and rank and crushing. I'd had the barest hint of warning, the bright white flash of teeth as thick as tree trunks, then the monster's maw had slammed shut around me. It was so fast. Nothing as large as that should be so fast. But it had struck even as I tried to fly away, and it had caught me, severing the threads of air.

Now I was left in darkness, the cavern of his mouth nearly as large as my chambers in the tower. He ground those massive teeth and tried to crush me with his tongue, but I slashed desperately up and carved a narrow gash in the roof of his mouth with my Chaos blade.

He roared, a deafening bellow that tore at my flesh. I turned and dove toward the narrow gap between his teeth, but they snapped shut. I barely caught myself before I lost an arm. The tongue stabbed at me again and I slashed back. Where I cut it, ugly, acid blood poured out.

Pazyarev gulped air, not to roar this time. I already felt the fire broiling in his belly. He would burn me down to ash. His jaw was open now again, almost room enough to jump, to get away. I stared at the fangs' sharp points. If I tried to dive through, if that double-row of razor teeth snapped shut.....

I could too easily imagine the pain of tearing flesh. I had felt it before. When I met Vechernyvetr.

Only minutes ago, he'd told me he remembered. Now I remembered. I remembered when we met, what I did to him. Had this been his intention all along? I saw the distant dance of firelight deep in the monster's gullet and had less than a heartbeat to decide.

I dove. Not out past the razor fangs, but back toward the monster's tongue. I stretched a hand out as I went and let it tear against a tooth. Blood gushed across my palm. I twisted, grabbed Pazyarev's tongue, and slammed my injured hand against the bleeding gash I'd given him.

Blistering pain shot up my arm and throbbed into my veins. It was twice familiar. I'd experienced this once before, when I first bonded with Vechernyvetr. I'd expected the pain itself. What surprised me was the shape of it, the feel of it. I knew that as well.

It was the Chaos power, the same hammering, blood-thirsty thrum that burned inside like madness. But now I felt it magnified, a hundred thousand times magnified, until it tore my mind apart and buried me beneath its writhing blackness.

This time, though, there was a light. It was a glow far off, gold and red, the shade of friendly hearthfires. There was a hint of perfect white as well, thin, restrained, and cool. A rich and earthy brown, barely seen against the blackness, but it seemed to stretch for miles around me. And even in the darkness itself there was texture.

I had no body there. I could not feel my human frame. But in that other place, I felt like a living part of the endless night. I could flex my will and watch the midnight shadows wash and roll. There was a *me* within the blackness, and it was something far more powerful, far more vast than I might ever have imagined. Even my territory sense could not compare to this.

There were other shapes within the dark, other living wills, and I could feel them vague and distant and hostile. But most of my sensation came from the mingled points of light. I felt human fear and desperate need and perfect, sweet devotion. I felt anger, too. A wild thirst for vengeance and blood.

And I felt words. I tasted the shape of them before they could resolve within my mind, but they were sharp and hot and heavy. They cut at me and made me struggle within the darkness. I strained to pull my will together, to manifest a man from depthless nothing. If I'd had a voice, I would have screamed in primal need, and all around me the fires flared, gold and red and blue and brown. They burned against the night.

Then I heard the words. *Wake up. Pathetic little human. Wake up. Please.*

I opened my eyes.

I was caught within the monster's mouth, soaked in blood that burned the skin. I was awake, and Vechernyvetr shouted frantic noise within the corner of my mind, but I still felt numb. My head still seemed stuffed with that heavy, untamed night. But then a new sensation broke the veil, brought my attention to a sharply focused point.

I was falling. We were falling. Fast.

Reality came crashing back to me, but still the other sense remained. I understood it now, of course. The life-blood of my brood burned gold and red. The wizard's will was white. I'd seen the colors of my might within the darkness, but the dark itself had been pure Chaos. *All* of Chaos. And I had been a point within it.

That sense began to slip away now, suppressed by my sanity, but while it yet remained I felt the ocean of ink-black power in all directions around me. I felt myself a bubble on its surface. I felt Vechernyvetr near to hand, a smaller spot. And I felt Pazyarev as well. I saw the shape of him, the scope of him, and it was not as large as I'd expected.

Within my will, inside my head, I reached toward that spot. I felt the body around me spasm, and the huge maw rolled. At the same time I saw that point of darkness roil within my head as the elder legend regained its consciousness.

Before he could act, before he could move, I reached out with a dreamlike lethargy and touched my will against his power. I felt him then, a presence in my head made up of raw emotion and animal intent. It was the presence I had often felt from Vechernyvetr, and even Pazyarev before, but those had always started from outside. When I had walled them off, when I had forced them back, it was always to an outer edge.

Now Pazyarev was a spot within. I was as well, and not a larger spot, but for a moment in my mind I saw the whole vast plains of Chaos. My thoughts stretched far and wide, and I could do more than wall him off. I could do more than push him away. I reached with my will, wrapped it around that small black bubble, and squeezed.

I felt one flash of haughty disbelief, one flash of timeless terror, and then I felt a *pop*. And he was gone.

No. Not gone. He was everywhere. He was all around me. He was part of me. He *was* me. I looked out through his eyes and saw the world spread out below us, rushing up to meet us. I spread his wings and banked against the wind without a thought. I soared above the earth and felt the human in my mouth. I crouched within his maw and felt the rough, wet flesh beneath my hand.

This was the Chaos bond, the one the dragons knew. It was not the limited connection Vechernyvetr and I shared. There was no Pazyarev left. There was no will to fight me off, no words and no emotion from the beast. There was only power, physical and raw, at my command.

I screamed my victory into the night with two voices, and one of them shook mountains.

Vechernyvetr answered back with just one word. *Help.*

My territory sense still boiled with the cold, black stain of dragons. Pazyarev's eyes showed me a sky dancing with their fire. Vechernyvetr struggled among them, and I could feel his pain. He was exhausted, torn, and surrounded on all sides by flying death. Talons slashed and fangs ripped. I stretched my will to call them down, but they were not mine.

They were not unified, either. They fought without apparent purpose. I saw Vechernyvetr catch a cruel blow, but I saw as well one of Pazyarev's reds disembowel one of his greens. I saw pairs of them locked in battle. I watched in disbelief for several seconds before Vechernyvetr cried again.

Aid me, Daven. If you let me die at this late hour, I'll make certain you regret it.

I laughed, then wrapped myself in air and dove headfirst from the elder legend's maw. I left my little human body hanging there, safely outside the fray, then turned the mighty monster to the fight. He swallowed a pair of fighting blues, then crushed a victorious red within one talon and swept two more from the sky with his great tail. A blast of fire rose up on its own, and my human body roared at the thrill of it, as forge-hot flame consumed my enemies. The taste was salty bliss.

Vechernyvetr left the fight, fleeing low over the earth, and even when the rest were dealt with, I saw the golden dame skimming after him. I shouted a warning in my mind and rolled the massive body of the elder legend, striking with his heavy tail toward the dame.

But Vechernyvetr intervened. The dame darted easily aside, and at the same instant Vechernyvetr turned and threw his body toward the striking tail. I tried to turn the blow, and slowed it enough to spare the dragon's life, but I felt the shock of angry pain through that distant bond before he crashed to earth.

The gold settled down beside him. She didn't strike. She only waited, patient, until Vechernyvetr heaved himself up. He bled from many wounds and shared with me the pain of his broken bones, but there was victory as well. I felt his wild exhilaration. I felt his joy and quiet pride.

"You conquered her?" I asked.

I have long admired this one, Vechernyvetr said. *I consider her a fair reward, and a fine start to my new brood.*

"She is indeed," I thought. *"But she was his. They all were his. Shouldn't they be mine?"*

No more than I am, the dragon said. *Your Order breaks the Chaos bond. That's how you set me free before. I remember how it felt. Disorienting. Unreal. This time I was ready.*

"I am pleased for you," I thought, but my attention was already far away. I shook my head. *"Heal your wounds, Vechernyvetr. Enjoy this victory. But I must go."*

Then go, he said. *We'll settle debts some other time.*

I laughed and left him there. I took Pazyarev. I wrapped the blinding darkness of his power up with the bonfire light of mine, and reached south to my lair, and tugged.

We landed on the earth outside the walls, virtually the same place from which I'd left. Nothing remained but char and blood where the distant siege had been, and now the massive gate was raised, its wood scorched and scarred with talon marks, but still unbroken.

Beyond that gate, Palmagnes still stood. Its dancing bands of air were cracked and broken, sizzling here and there with living fire, but what remained still spun in lazy circles around the massive central tower. The outer walls, though damaged, still stood high over the cracked earth, and through the stone I felt them swarming with the hot life-blood of men. Defenders ranged along its lines, all in motion, all at war.

Fires burned inside the walls and out, and dragons raged against the keep's defenders, but the men fought back, and the ground was littered with the corpses of the fallen beasts. There had to be three hundred dragons dead, felled outside the walls or in the broken courtyards. There might have been a thousand yet in the empty air, but they fought without control, without direction, and fought each other as much now as they fought my defenders.

They were unprepared for me. I sent Pazyarev on the wing, and he tore a hundred dragons from the sky in just one pass. But while he struck, I stretched my will and stepped past gate and walls into the throne room of my tower.

Isabelle was there, at the back wall, moving frantically among the lines of the fallen. Caleb was at the front, shouting orders to a crew led by Garrett Dain just before Dain led them out into the fray. Soldiers in shining armor filled the hall, frenzied as they tried to prepare a desperate defense.

I sank into my throne while Pazyarev snapped his jaws around a dragon on the wing. I gathered all the raging fires outside the tower and piled them together into a pyre. I opened up the earth and swallowed dragon corpses whole. Then I caught Pazyarev in my will. I unleashed one final column of flame, then pushed him miles away into the mountains. I set him on the hill outside our outpost and left him there.

Perhaps by then there were still a thousand dragons in the sky. There must have been half of that at least. I closed my eyes and tapped the boundless power in my soul, then with it carved a moat outside my walls. I raised the earth straight up, and for a moment it hung in a ring outside my walls. Then I flexed and flung it high into the sky.

Six hundred paces up, the tons of earth split, tore apart, and fashioned into javelins. I stabbed them down, a rain of lancing spears, and pinned every last dragon to the earth. They fell like heavy hailstones, inside the walls and out, and their power washed like blood across the stones and seeped through to me. Pazyarev's brood was all destroyed.

On the walls outside, a thousand frightened men suddenly cried out in unexpected victory.

We could not hear them in the tower. Too many voices raised in their distress. But from across the room, I heard one joyous shout above the noise. "Daven? Daven's back!"

The great hall was thronged with people—dirty, bruised and bleeding, but alive. I climbed to my feet and watched them part as Isabelle sprinted across the floor. She threw herself against me and held on tight, her face pressed hard against my chest. After a moment I realized she was shaking. Her whole body shook beneath the tremors, but I could feel her heart's relief.

Caleb's, too. I looked up to meet his eyes, and from across the room he nodded once. He didn't even smile. Then he caught an idle soldier by the tabard and shouted orders until the Guard threw a desperate salute and fled at a run.

It was a Guard. I recognized the uniform. And there were Green Eagles as well. I could feel them, now that I

spared the attention. Most of the men within the tower—
the uninjured, anyway—were the king's men. They'd
crowded up into my barracks, up into the civilians' sleeping
quarters above. My men were outside on the walls. My men
were stretched out dying in the back of the hall, or quietly
cooling on the paving stones outside. But here, inside the
tower, the king had brought his army.

There were wizards, too. More than a dozen. Claighan
knelt among the wounded, his face a ghastly sheet of drying
blood from a split high on his scalp, but he was tending to
the others. I spotted Themmichus, his black cloaks clinging
wet with blood, but he wore a stunned grin when I met his
eyes. I saw the Chancellor of the Academy and a handful of
wizards who might have been just students when I was
there. And Seriphenes as well, a narrow shadow just behind
the king.

There was the king. In my great hall. He sat behind a
long, heavy table spread with papers, and his thief-taker
Othin stood half a step behind the other shoulder. All three
of them watched me, and I felt the flare of Chaos rage within my soul.

I stepped down off my dais, eyes never leaving the king,
and a quiet hush fell on the crowd. Isabelle followed close
behind, whispering urgently, but I ignored them all. Ten
slow paces carried me to loom above the king. He leaned
back in his chair, and I saw fear in his eyes.

He was right to fear. I felt the song of Chaos in my soul.
I felt the call to burn down the world, and who in all the
world deserved it more than this man? My gaze drifted to
Master Seriphenes. It touched on loyal Othin, fearless and
heartless. But always it returned to that wretched little king.

"You brought your men within my walls?" I asked.

He raised his chin. "It is my right anywhere in this land."

Seriphenes closed his eyes and pressed his lips together. Othin slowly drew his blade. I ignored them both.

"You brought your men within my walls?" I asked again.

The king scowled. "You saw the dragons, boy. Your people let us in."

"And you sought refuge," I growled. "You didn't fight against the dragons. You left my men to die while yours cowered beneath my roof." My voice rose in an outraged roar. "You brought your men within my walls?"

Isabelle caught my hand and pressed close against my back. "We invited them inside," she said. "You would have wanted it." She tilted her cool forehead against the back of my neck, and said almost in a whisper, "You would have wanted it."

The king held my gaze and shrugged. "My wizards helped in the defense. Were it not for us—"

"Were it not for you, we might have killed the dragons while they slept. Were it not for you, we might have trained many more men. Were it not for you—" The fury shook my voice until I could not give it words.

But something else, some treacherous little voice, whispered in my head that, were it not for him and all his petty, childish pride, I never would have gained this power. Were it not for him, I never could have rallied these wicked men. Were it not for him, we'd all have burned.

I closed my eyes. Power hot as hatred roared around my veins, the thrill of recent battle inebriating. And I could still almost sense the Chaos sea that flooded around us all. It buried all reality beneath its waves. Nothing mattered, compared to that.

Still...in the midst of all that darkness, I could recall a tiny, distant light. No other eye could see it; it was mine. Yet it was mine. It was me. I smiled a cold smile, looked down on three men who had wronged me so greatly, and for one exquisite heartbeat I considered all the many ways I could wreak my vengeance.

"Timmon, High King of the Sarianne and Lord of the Isle." My voice echoed in the cavernous room. It sounded like a doom.

Isabelle squeezed my hand and let it go. I raised it before me and built a Chaos blade that drew a gasp from many in the watching crowd. Othin shifted, ready to parry if I swung, but nothing in his power could stop my strike. Seriphenes watched me, glowing with the gathered force of his will, but he had seen what I could do against his spells.

I focused on the king. I shook my head. "This isn't right," I breathed, my voice quiet. I couldn't hear the words over the pounding Chaos song. "This is not how it should be. But if I'm to fight this war...if man is going to shine a light within that sea of destruction..."

The king scowled up at me, confused, but I wasn't speaking to him. I was speaking to myself. The monster and the man in full communion. I felt the wild thrill of all the Chaos I had used this night. I felt the thrilling power of all the mighty lives I'd ended by my hand. I felt Pazyarev's power, boundless and mine. I thought of what I'd do with all that strength.

"Timmon, High King of the Sarianne and Lord of the Isle," I cried again. I raised the sword before me, gripped within both hands, and reversed. I took a slow, deep breath, then drove the point down to the floor.

I sank to my knees behind it. "I swear my oath of fealty to you. Before these witnesses, and in the eyes of God, I pledge to be your man. I bind my life to your life. I bind my sword to your sword. I live for you, and take you as my lord."

Isabelle's relief washed over me like a cool rain. She rested her hands lightly on my shoulders. From across the room

I felt Caleb's disapproving doubt. He fought the crowd to cross the floor, and I reached out and brought him to me. I found Lareth, hurrying across the courtyard strewn with the dragons I'd destroyed, and brought him too.

Othin leveled his sword as they arrived, menacing us all across the narrow width of the table. "The rebel wizard Lareth," he said. He pitched his voice low, for the king, but we all heard. "And one of your Eagles who deserted, now disgraced. And the baron's daughter who led the traitors past our lines." He met my eyes where I still knelt. "You surround yourself with greatness."

"Enough," the king barked, his eyes still fixed on mine. He nodded at me. "That's some romantic show, swearing an oath that was already owed. But you have no right to gather these men. You have no right to raise these walls. This is an insurrection."

"Humanity's an insurrection," I said. I started to say more, then shook my head and climbed back to my feet. I would kneel to him no more. "All of civilization is just willful rebellion against the reigning night. But I have no desire to be a king. I want to fight the dragonswarm. That's all."

He shook his head. "Have you not seen the dragons in the sky? You can't fight that."

"Have you not heard the cheers outside?" I asked. "I've killed them all." I drummed my fingers lightly on the Chaos blade's grip. "And I'll kill many more. I will not let you stand between me and that."

He narrowed his eyes. "Then why swear oath?"

"For you. For your petty pride." I glanced over my shoulder to the crowd, then back to him. "For politics. I will have none of it. I have a war to wage."

The king measured me for some time. Then he dipped his head in a fraction of a nod. He rose and raised his voice.

"I find it well with you, Daven, Son of Carrick. I grant my grace for all you've done in defense of this kingdom."

"So kind of him," Lareth mumbled, but Isabelle silenced him with a glare.

The king pretended not to have heard. "I ratify you Sir Daven of Teelevon, and name you Chief Defender against the Dragonswarm. I grant you the land, the men, and the resources necessary to wage that war. Serve us well."

A cheer went up at that. His men knew when to cheer their king. I didn't smile.

The king spoke beneath the roar of their applause. "That was done well," he said with grudging admiration. "Now you should offer me a feast within your halls. To show that we are friends. Three days would be best, but a banquet will do. My steward can assist you—"

I raised the blade still in my hand, and he fell silent. "I have no more time to spend on you. I fight a war to save mankind. Now take your men and leave this place forever." Chaos thrummed in my ears. "Quickly, sire, while I still believe the dragons are the greater threat."

THE END

About the Author

Aaron Pogue is a husband and a father of two who lives in Oklahoma City, OK. He started writing the high fantasy world of the FirstKing at the age of ten and has written novels, short stories, and videogame storylines set there. He's also explored mainstream thrillers, urban fantasy, and several kinds of science fiction, including the popular science fiction crime series Ghost Targets which focuses on an elite FBI task force in a world of total universal surveillance.

Aaron is also a Technical Writer with the Federal Aviation Administration. He has a degree in Writing and has been working as a Technical Writer since 2002. He's been a writing professor at the university level, and is currently pursuing a Master of Professional Writing degree at the University of Oklahoma. He also runs a writing advice blog at UnstressedSyllables.com and is a founding artist at ConsortiumOKC.com.

About the Publisher

Consortium Books is an innovative publisher with a unique mindset. All proceeds from Consortium Books sales are donated to an organization dedicated to injecting money into artists' pockets and art into the culture.

To learn more about the unshackled, free-thinking publishing world that is Consortium Books, please take a step through the looking glass:

http://www.consortiumokc.com/books/

Printed in Great Britain
by Amazon.co.uk, Ltd.,
Marston Gate.